# Metal Slinger

# CONTENTS

# CHAPTER 1

"If there's a way," I say, confirming the plan.

Kai dips his head in a nod. "Yes, but no one goes alone." He ties his blonde hair atop his head in a knot and looks at Messer. "Agreed?"

Looking at the reflection in the tiny mirror hanging over the wash bowl, Messer smiles at Kai as he rubs a hand across his freshly shaven chin. "Afraid we'll have fun without you?"

"I need you to be serious for ten minutes," Kai admonishes.

The ship pitches to the side and we brace ourselves on the nearest post. My hand lands against one of the latrines, and I make a sound of disgust as I hurry to stand when the vessel rights itself. I shoulder Messer out of the way to stick my hands into his leftover suds.    The closer we get to land, the bigger the swell has become. It's why the majority of our classmates are congregated on deck, eager to see the coastline for the first time in their lives.

Messer places a reassuring hand on his best friend's shoulder. "It's all or none," he says. "We all go, or none of us go.

The rare glimpse of self-control in Messer's eyes works to loosen the worry between Kai's brows as he hands me a towel to dry my hands. They still don't feel clean, but I push the thought from my mind. There's nothing to be done about it.

"Remember, our first priority is to scope things out," Kai says. "Assess the situation. We only attempt to get on land if we're absolutely sure there's a way without getting caught."

"That's not a problem for me," Messer says, hand to his chest. "You two, on the other hand, have a terrible track record."

I roll my eyes at him in the mirror. "You're going to run out of luck one day."

I attempt to tame the strands of hair that have escaped my braid, but it's futile. My hair hasn't obeyed a day in its life, not even when I was born, coming out a copper hue unlike the blonde common for our people.

Voices grow in volume from above, an overlapping sound of excitement coming through the ceiling of the wooden hull along with a thunder of footsteps.

Kai spins me toward him by the shoulders. "Our first objective is to assess the situation," he says, releasing me. "So don't do anything hasty. There'll be other chances."

I can't tell if he's trying to convince me or himself. The Market only happens once a year. There are two groups of Alaha who get the privilege of attending: guards who facilitate the trades and moving of goods, and the future graduating class of trainees. For some of us, it could be decades before ever seeing dry land again, if ever at all.

Today could very well be our only hope.

"We should go up before anyone notices we're missing." Messer pastes his signature smile back in place. "Oh, and I may have told Aurora she could tag along with us."

Kai and I both look at each other, annoyed. We voice our displeasure, but he's already well ahead of us, crossing the interior barracks and moving up the stairs to the deck before we can catch up. Any and all arguments fall from our lips at the sight before us.

Land.

Nothing could have prepared me for the stark differences of the rocky shoreline in comparison to our home in Alaha. All the illustrations and paintings I've seen pale in comparison.

As if everyone is in a trance, the excited voices dim to a silence as we creep closer.

I've never felt so insignificant, never felt as small as I do as I crane my neck to take in its magnitude. Then I see it. The split in the stone cliff, breaking it into two, like a giant used an ax to cleave the land right down the middle.

"Insane," Messer murmurs.

The Market sits between the crevices. From rock face to rock face and as far inland as the eye can see, the dock stretches across the expanse as a neutral meeting ground between us, the Alaha, and the people of Kenta.

It takes a few more hours before we're able to moor. The sea laps between the ship and the dock, spraying water under the feet of the men offloading the dredge of fish we gathered on the voyage here. One of the commanders barks orders as the nets are lifted from the water and heaved into the awaiting wagons for the people of Kenta.

I've spent my entire life waiting for this day, half convinced the land dwellers were a myth. As evidenced by the bustling pier, they most definitely are not.

Dressed in rich colors and strange cuts of fabrics,

3

the Kenta are possibly the most beautiful living beings I've ever seen. Judging by the murmuring of my fellow classmates gathered on the ship's deck as we wait for our turn to disembark, they're as awed as I am.

"Don't let their pretty clothes and jewelry fool you," says our instructor, Gramble, hands clasped behind his back as he paces back and forth on the deck of the ship. "They're as ruthless as the giant squids."

I keep my eye roll to myself. Nothing is feared more than the giant squids rumored to be found in the most remote parts of the oceans. They have no known home, no known origin. The only evidence of their existence are the abandoned boats they leave behind, left wandering aimless without a soul on board. The bodies of the crews are theorized to have been pulled underneath the water never to be seen again. That's if there's a boat left at all.

It's nothing more than a scary bedtime story to keep the Alaha children in line. The image of a snaking black tentacle coming through a bedroom window works wonders as a deterrent for unruly kids. But unlike a giant squid capable of dragging an entire ship to the bottom of the ocean, the Kenta people seem...

Like regular people. I don't know what I was expecting, but they're not at all like the battle-worn Kenta from our history lessons, the people who won the war and banished the Alaha to live over the ocean with little more than the clothes on our backs and a few ships to our name. The host of Kenta soldiers lining the dock and stationed throughout the market do, however, look very much like people who won't allow our people to step foot on soil.

Squinting against the sun, I find Kai on the

4

promenade. He disembarked early to debrief with the guards in his rank. His golden hair has darkened around his temples, damp with sweat. His eyes flit over the Kenta and the boats then up toward me for a brief moment.

Kai would have come last year with his own graduating class of Alaha guards, but he waited for me and Messer to join him on the off chance we could make our way to land.

Gramble continues prepping us. "When we reach the dock, stay with your group. Never more than four, never less than two. Be friendly, but not too friendly. We're here to continue the mutual benefits of Kenta, not to make enemies, understand?"

We all nod in answer.

Gramble deposits four coppers into each person's hand from his pouch of coins. "Don't spend it all in one place." There's a rare and wry smile on his face when he stands back to dismiss us. "To be Alaha," he announces with a fist against his chest.

*In hellos and goodbyes, to condolences and congratulations. We are one.*

We repeat the saying back in unison—*to be Alaha* —and break formation, following Gramble down the gangway and onto the dock. My heart is pounding inside my chest. I glance at Kai, at my classmates who reveal nothing, expressions trained to remain calm and unreadable, at odds with the mixture of panic and excitement in my veins.

The wooden boards of the promenade feel like solid rock beneath my feet after the weeks spent traveling over open ocean to get here. My hollow stomach cramps at the smell of foods and spices wafting in from the

Market.

Kai gathers Messer, Aurora, and me on the deck. He must see my thundering emotions because he gives my wrist a quick squeeze in reassurance. I take a moment to block out the bustle of activity going on around us, focusing on his familiar gray eyes that mirror my own— the only common trait I share with our people. They're safe and comforting, the eyes of my friend.

"I don't know about you," he says, drumming up the smile he's best known for and easing the tension of our entire group with it. "But I'm finding the nearest food stall that doesn't sell fish and eating myself into a stupor."

His cheerful demeanor ripples through our class and garners a few murmurs of agreement. A natural-born leader as future captain of the Alaha people, everyone looks to Kai as an example.

It's the only reason I'm able to be here. Very few females are chosen to be guards, and considering my parentage—or lack thereof—I would have never been given a passing chance to compete, let alone accepted.

Messer slaps a hand down on Kai's shoulder, a broad smile stretching from ear to ear. "What are we waiting for?"

We turn toward the promenade and take in the vendors lining each side of the dock. Every stall has a banner attached, representing the families who've come a long way for this one day of trading. My curiosity jumps from booth to booth, noting the food and clothes and jewelry and different wares on display.

Kenta soldiers patrol, dressed in different variations of leathers and armor, knives and swords sheathed in armor lining their bodies. Some wear helmets made of metal, concealing their entire face except for a thin slit for their eyes to peer through. These soldiers in particular feel unworldly, like anything or anyone could be underneath.

One passes by, eyes sharp on Kai through the small gap, looking up and down his body. Kai maintains a relaxed posture, but I can see the itch of the Kenta soldier's stare crawling beneath the surface of his calm exterior, over his lack of finery and jewels for being the son of the captain.

Aurora's voice is tainted with disdain. "Seems a little overkill considering we're not allowed to have a single mildly sharp object with us." She glares at a nearby soldier with an upraised brow.

With an unflinching stare like hers, I don't blame the guard for breaking contact first.

"Aurora," Kai admonishes. "I'm the first descendant of Wren's to attend the Market. They're smart to be prepared."

She rolls her eyes. "We're the ones on enemy territory."

"We have half a day before we're herded back into that prison of a ship, and I sure as hell am not going to waste it gawking," Messer says, pinching Aurora in the side. "Besides, we know you don't need stabby things to scare people away."

She attempts to slap him in the shoulder, but he's able to dodge the hit, laughing. Kai nudges me with a ghostly touch of fingertips against my spine, guiding me past the line of soldiers, dipping his head in a nod of respect.

It goes unreturned. The Kenta may be people just like us, but they're sure as hell rude.

"Fix your face, Brynn."

Forcing myself to relax, I paste on a timid smile. "It'd be less offensive if they just spit in our faces."

"We're here in peace," Kai reminds me, but the weapons and cold stares say otherwise.

We're obligated to make ourselves yield to them—the very people who've outcasted us—and we're supposed to appear grateful for their generosity, supposed to thank them for allowing trade between our people like we're not constantly on the brink of starvation at their hand in the first place.

Messer leads us to a nearby stall with a variety of pastries displayed, fruit tarts and pies and breads twisted in plaits with sugary toppings. A lot of time and attention went into every cake, and my mouth waters at the sight.

Messer slaps all four of his coppers onto the wood top, drawing the attention of the clerk behind the counter. "Whatever this affords me, give it to me."

Any fear I have over Messer's overzealous behavior disappears as soon as the young woman softens at his infectious smile. She tucks her dark hair behind her ear and asks if he likes prunes, her accent thick around the vowels of her words.

Unconcerned with any of the cultural sensitivity training we've been given, Messer widens his smile in flirtation. "I eat anything if it's covered in enough sugar, sweetheart."

If I'm not mistaken, a blush tints her freckled cheeks. Silver and gold rings adorn her ears and brow and nearly every finger as she spreads out wax paper and packs up one of everything into a carrying pouch, a pouch Messer ruins by unwrapping it and shoving the first pastry into his mouth—whole. Moaning as sugar falls from his chin as he chews, he dips his head in thanks, hands steepled before him as he speaks with his mouth full.

"You're a goddess."

Color further deepening on her pale cheeks, she returns the gesture. It seems all women are enamored by Messer, Kenta and Alaha alike.

The girl looks to me, her next customer, and I inspect my choices. I'm tempted to do like Messer and spend every last bit of my coin on the cakes. The lavender one looks delicious, but there's also a chocolate square that looks downright divine.

Kai's breath sends chills across my neck when he dips his head over my shoulder and speaks into my ear. "I may or may not have a few extra coins in my possession."

I pretend to be unfazed by his proximity, keeping my gaze steady on the goods in front of me. "Wouldn't expect anything less from the spoiled son of the captain."

If Kai's father is anything, it's indulgent of his only heir.

He chuckles. "Spoiled I may be, but I'm also very giving," he says, voice deepening. *Conspiratorial.* "Get whatever you like."

In that case, I pick out four of the chocolate squares, one for each of us. We hold them in the air in a toast.

"To be Alaha," Messer says.

"To be off that godsdamned ship," I amend.

Aurora makes a face. "You got that right."

We all take a chunk out of the dessert and moan in unison. I miss my mouth on the next bite, half of the soft chocolate crashing to the ground.

"Dang rabbits," I mutter.

Messer scrunches his nose at me. "You're so weird every time you say that."

Aurora hurries to shove her own portion into her mouth when it begins to fall apart. "It doesn't make any sense."

I dust off my hands and shrug. "That's why I like it."

We find a vendor serving blackberry teas and munch on our sweets as we peruse the Market. The Kenta people don't seem as wary of us as their soldier counterparts. If anything, they treat us like we're invisible unless confronted with our company, then they seem to tolerate us well enough.

I'm captivated by the skirts and dresses of some of the women. At various lengths and colors, they swish around their legs as they work and venture between booths, some adorned in beads and jewels.

I've never put much thought into what I wear, but I can't help but find my simple trousers and blouse lacking. Even my single braid of sun-kissed auburn hair falling down the center of my back pales in comparison to the ornate plaiting and styled hair of the Kenta women.

Kai shoves me with his shoulder. "You're a member of the Alaha guard—dressing in finery isn't conducive to fighting."

"Not unless you want to look ridiculous," Messer says, adding in his two cents. Always the nosy bastard.

I feel like fighting in a dress would look less ridiculous than the soldiers with giant metal buckets on their heads in this sweltering heat.

We continue strolling down the promenade, heads swiveling left and right. Backdropped by the stark cliffs, the soldiers stationed along their perimeter are a frivolous show of defense. The stone of the land is smooth and free of any blemishes. There's not a single foothold or crack for anyone to use as leverage to scale the walls.

"They have to haul everything here somehow."

Kai doesn't reply to Messer's observation. Doesn't need to. We're all coming to the same dismal conclusion that there might not be a way.

Ever.

We continue further into the Market until a crowd begins to form around a makeshift dance floor in the center of the dock, and we squeeze our way to the front of the circle. A band is set up on a small stage, fiddles and harmonicas and stretched drums. The skirts of the women's dresses flare around them as they dance.

It's stunning to watch. The dancers flit in and out of formation, finding the next partner with their hands before ever laying eyes on them. Laughter and smiles light up their faces, happiness radiating from them as the song continues to increase in tempo. Faster and faster and faster until it's a challenge for them to keep up, and only then do I see mistakes. A missed step, unclaimed hands, stumbling of feet.

Then the music comes to an abrupt stop along with the dancers. The crowd erupts in cheers, and we join in, clapping as the dancers laugh and share smiles, bowing to one another before departing. One of the women passes near me, and I stretch a hand out to run my fingers over the material of her skirt. It's the briefest of touches, but it feels like water flowing between my fingertips.

The lone fiddler begins a softer melody, and a few of

the remaining couples stay on the dance floor, swaying with their partners.

Kai takes my hand in his. "Dance with me."

I lift my brows in surprise. "Here?"

It would be a blatant breach of the Rule of Boundaries, a list of covenants each person of Alaha agrees to abide by once they come of age. There's to be no intimate contact of any kind between the opposite sex until the Matching Ceremony.

More often than not, it's a marriage of convenience, often negotiations between families rather than actual love matches. It was originally put in place to monitor breeding between too close of bloodlines, but now it's to slow the tide of overpopulation.

Kai gives me a look. "Who's going to report us? My own soldiers?"

I look around and spot many of our own people observing the band from the crowd. Looking at Messer, I pass my drink to him. As per usual, I let Kai lead me onto the dance floor. The couples smile politely at us as we settle between them on the decking smoothed by years of feet moving across its surface.

"Hey," Kai says, drawing my chin up with a finger. "Just you and me."

His eyes are unwavering as he coaxes me into a steady rhythm. Our movements are less whimsical without the flowing fabrics, but I close my eyes and force my body to move with Kai's, willing my mind to slow. I focus on his hand on my hip and the smell of home that still lingers on his skin and—gods, the walls are just so tall.

"Brynn, look at me," Kai demands.

So I do, eyes snapping open.

"I'll always protect you."

He thinks I'm scared of being reprimanded—as I should be, considering the harsh consequences of breaking one of the covenants of the Alaha—but I don't fear grunt work or the brigs.

"It wouldn't be the first time we've spent time in the brig," I say, giving off an air of indifference. "Or the second."

I must do a terrible job of pretending because Kai doesn't crack a smile at the subtle mention of the last time we were sentenced to a night in the stone cells. We had stolen the underwear from clotheslines and fastened them to the Alaha flag in the center of the Main. Wasn't worth the punishment whatsoever, but we pretended it was to make ourselves feel better for being stupid kids.

What I'm not expecting are the words that leave his mouth next. "I asked my parents for permission to choose you at the Matching Ceremony."

My heart goes still. "Why would you do that?" I say, voice wavering.

"Come on, Bry," he says, eyes drilling hard into mine. "You had to expect this was coming."

I shake my head.

I've never allowed myself to entertain the idea of ever getting a match. I've disciplined myself to push those thoughts away, to lock them somewhere inside myself so deep even I'm not sure where they're kept.

Kai has his pick of girls and their families vying for his hand in marriage, and true love matches are few and far between. I have no family. No dowry. No incentives for a marriage. I'm at the bottom of the list.

Why would he ever choose me?

"The future leader of Alaha doesn't choose an *urchin* as a wife."

He grits his teeth but doesn't break stride. "You know how much I hate when you call yourself that."

"That's what I am, Kai."

"No, it's not."

His hold on me tightens, but he doesn't push. I inspect him, looking for a hint of what Kai has up his sleeve, but I can't find anything other than anticipation staring back at me.

"You are smart and hardworking and so godsdamn beautiful," he says, punctuating each word to ensure I'm convinced of their authenticity. "Your name has been whispered by my own men behind my back, because they would never dare to speak their interest in courting you to my face."

His statements create a vise around my chest as I stare into his eyes. Kai's been my best friend for as long as I can remember. He's had to defend me to everyone in his life, probably more than he's ever let on, but he's never so much as hinted at any possible interest in me. Not romantically. Not like this.

I shake my head in a daze. "Is this real?"

His gaze is deadly serious as he looks down at me. "Do you want it to be?"

Our movements come to a halt. I've spent what has felt like my entire life waiting for this day, waiting for the chance to come to the annual Market, and he's dropping this on me now?

Gritting my teeth, I shove him in the chest with my palms. When he doesn't budge, I do it again, but harder. He stumbles into the couple behind him, but he doesn't break eye contact as I take a step back.

His eyes narrow. "Brynn—"

I stop him with an upturned hand. He opens his mouth again, but I don't hear whatever it is he says because I turn away, hurrying through the crowd in my bid to escape, to outrun the weight of all the eyes on me.

# CHAPTER 2

I'm deep inside the market.

The stone walls loom closer on either side of the dock, blocking out a large portion of the sun and casting the booths in shadow. The air is different here, rich and earthy. It reminds me of the scent that comes before it rains. It's my favorite.

The vendors this far in are nestled closer together. It's less crowded, filled with more locals than Alaha. There are candles and honey and stoneware fit for royalty, gold and embossed. It'd be downright blasphemy to put the fish stew we've been eating anywhere near them.

The merchant behind the booth doesn't approach. It's obvious I'm not his normal clientele, but he smiles at me as I admire the hand-painted saucers. Deer and rabbits and foxes, animals you'd find on land.

They put my charcoal sketches to shame.

A woman in a knee-length dress approaches the booth, and I move out of the way to not interfere. That's when I notice him. *Again.*

The first time was a quarter mile back. Our eyes connected for a moment when I passed, but I registered a lot in the brief flash of time: the way he stood with his arms folded over his chest, how his smile dimmed when he saw me, and how the conversation he was having with his fellow Kenta soldier stopped.

Dark hair, dark eyes, a gold ring in one nostril. Lips

I somehow know often say crude things—or maybe it's his entire demeanor that tells me that, but there's something inherently vulgar in his beauty.

I'm positive he's been following me ever since. I maintain my gait, not wanting to let on that I know I'm being followed, but I cross the dock to put distance between us. It's far enough to create a buffer but not too far to be suspicious.

*What's your next move?*

Sure enough, he crosses too, staying a few paces behind me. A strap of daggers adorns his chest, the leather embroidered with the emblem of Kenta, signifying his wealth and high rank. I do a quick inventory of my surroundings and can't find one Alaha in sight. There are only Kenta in every direction.

I glance over my shoulder.

He doesn't bother hiding his interest this time, dark eyes focused on me as he weaves through the crowd, towering over the heads of people.

Maybe he's keeping an eye on me because I'm alone. Gramble's reminder to stay in a group rings in my head, but my gut tells me otherwise. My gut tells me I'm being hunted.

I pick up my pace, skipping the next row of vendors before daring another glance over my shoulder. This time I don't look away, letting him know I'm aware of him and I'm not afraid.

He has the nerve to smile. It's unsettling, his grin that's as wicked as it is beautiful. Maybe he just gets a kick out of intimidating Alaha girls.

I stop at a random vendor, hoping if I ignore his existence, he'll just lose interest.

"Any color you're looking for in particular?" asks the

lady behind the counter.

I don't even look to see what she's selling as I shake my head in answer before moving down. I pretend to peruse the stalls, skipping every few in an effort to get closer to the front of the promenade.

The tension in my muscles dissipates when I spot two Alaha soldiers within yelling distance. I see Messer's glossy hair through the crowd, then Kai as they weave between people, heads swiveling as they search for me. Aurora follows, swigging from a cup without a care in the world.

Once again, I look over my shoulder and am further relieved when I don't find the soldier. I wave at Messer, who slaps Kai in the shoulder and points to me. As I wait for them to come to me so we don't lose each other in the crowd, I notice the booth nearest to me has gems on display. Light refracts from cut hanging gems and throws rainbows onto the dock and stone wall behind it. I walk near and run my fingertips across a small stone that looks like sea glass.

"Beautiful, isn't it?" the vendor says, a genuine smile behind his full beard.

Remembering the four coppers still in my pocket, I inquire, "How much?"

"These are very valuable stones," he says, picking up one of the smaller cuttings. "They're hard to find deep within the mines of the earth. One gold coin for this one."

Dreams of hanging one from the window in my room float away. "They're very beautiful," I say with disappointment.

He nods, a dip of his chin in understanding. Before I can move away, a hand slaps down over mine. I suck in a breath as the soldier looms over me, dark eyes rimmed with anger and locking me into place.

"Thief," he says, voice echoing off the canyon's walls.

I shake my head, half in an attempt to defend myself, half in disbelief. I yank my hand from where he has me pinned to the table, but his hold is unmoving. "I didn't take anything."

"Yeah?" He pushes the sleeve of my tunic up my forearm and turns my hand over in his, exposing the stone of light green glass underneath. "Then what's this?"

I gasp. "You put that there."

His dark eyes drill holes into mine. "Are you calling me a liar?"

"Yes," I answer, refusing to back down from his domineering stare.

His hand tightens around my wrist between us. "I heard the Alaha remove the limbs of people who break any of their precious covenants. What is it? A finger or a hand for a thief?"

I speak through clenched teeth. "I didn't take anything."

He regards me for a moment, eyes bouncing between mine. Looking for what, I'm unsure, considering we both know he concocted this entire scheme.

The neighboring vendors and shoppers stop to watch the spectacle.

He breaks first, clearing his throat and signaling to someone behind me. "A hand it is."

I'm wrestled away from the table by another soldier.

"This is absurd!" I flail to dislodge the strong arm around my waist, but the soldier lifts me so I'm unable to leverage myself against the ground. "I'm not a thief!"

My accuser leads us around the booth and behind the row of vendors. The soldier holding me places me before the stone wall, which is like a sleeping giant before us. Warmth radiates from its surface, not more than a foot away. It's the closest I've ever come to touching land.

The dark eyes of the accusing soldier drill into the side of my face. "Place your hand on the wall," he commands.

I don't move or so much as blink as I assess my options. The decade of training should kick in at any moment now, but it's hard to think with the attention of half the promenade on my back. The bustle of the market has dulled to a low buzz behind me.

Everything stills as I take a calming breath, then I stomp as hard as I can onto the soldier's foot holding me, ripping my arm away at the same time. It weakens his stronghold enough to free myself, but the momentum throws me off balance and I fall into the grasp of the dark-eyed soldier.

He's quick to spin me in place, wrapping a forearm around my neck with a blade at the base of my throat. If I wasn't on the sharp end of the knife at my skin, I'd be more impressed by his speed and ability, but panic countermands any rational thought besides calculating a way out of this mess.

I look for Kai, my focus jumping between faces in the crowd, but I come up empty. Only strangers stare back at me.

He orders the command into my ear for only me to hear, sending a shiver down my spine. "Place your hand against the stone." He's not simply playing games with me like I had suspected.

I shake my head despite the sting of the blade. "Why

are you doing this?"

He's done waiting for me to comply. Instead, he uses his free hand to grab mine and places my trembling palm against the warm stone, his hand covering mine.

Pain unlike anything I've ever felt before lances through my body. Heat sears my arm and my chest, down my body and into my legs. It's like a live current, similar to the electric eels found in the coral outside Alaha, but times a thousand.

I scream.

Then, in the span of a blink, it's over.

My eyes fly open and my breath rushes out in an abrupt halt, the scream dying in my throat. I'm on my knees, the wood of the dock cutting into my shins. My senses flood back into focus. The sounds of murmuring and shocked voices filter in through my haze. I lift my hands to my face and am relieved to see I still have both of them attached to my body.

But the pain...

I look up, up, up and into the soldier's face. He looks as stunned as I feel, eyes wide as he stares down at me, breath frozen in his chest.

Kai's voice shouts over the gathered voices. "Let her go!"

But the soldier doesn't break eye contact with me, something between awe and fear staring back at me.

"I said," Kai demands, the voice he rarely uses silencing the crowd. "Let her go."

The soldier is slow to turn, head swiveling in Kai's direction before his gaze slides away from me, face transforming from awestruck to cold as he looks at Kai. "That won't work on me," he says, voice low and undeterred. "You have no power here."

I struggle to get to my feet, legs giving way when I try to put my weight on them. I can't look behind me to see Kai's expression, but the unflinching gaze of the soldier tells me this isn't going to end without collateral damage. He flips the blade in his hand, a visual reminder that Kai and I are defenseless against him and his men.

"Let her go," Kai repeats, more placating than before.

The soldier tips a brow. "She's not yours."

There's a beat of calm before a loud crash comes from our left. Messer leaps over the now overturned booth, glass jars of jellies and jams shattering across the dock. Chaos ensues as he tackles my second captor from behind.

Using the distraction to my advantage, I reach for the blade strapped to the soldier's thigh and make a clean swipe through his heel. He barks in pain, knee hitting the dock beside me. He reaches to grab me, but I swing the blade in a wide arc, forcing him to dodge the blow that comes within centimeters of his face. It gives me just enough time to get my legs underneath me, careful to avoid the surface of the stone wall as I wobble into a stance.

He levels his gaze up at me. "Don't," he says, an air of desperation coating the single word.

Something in the distressed way he's holding my eyes as he struggles to pull himself up on one leg gives me pause, but not enough to actually stop me.

Sensing my intentions to run, he yells to his fellow soldiers. "Don't let her off this dock!"

I stumble toward Messer, who is grappling with the other soldier. Seeing me coming, he gets on top of the man and slams a fist into his face, knocking him out cold. He rushes toward me, wrapping an arm around my waist to help me stay upright.

Kai sees us and begins clearing a path through the people. Alaha has joined the fray, and it's an all-out battle to get all our people back to the boats.

"Are you okay?" Kai asks, taking up my other side.

I don't waste energy replying, concentrating on my steps as my faculties slowly come back into full working order. We sprint for the end of the dock, to the Alaha flags overhead. It's a mass exodus as the Kenta people move out of our way.

"What the hell happened?" Gramble shouts as he runs toward us, eyes flicking over our heads at the angry mob of Kenta soldiers hot on our heels.

He doesn't wait for an explanation, taking the helm to usher the students onto the nearest gangway. Alaha soldiers take position along the dock, a last line of defense as our people rush onto the boats.

Kai halts at the makeshift line. "Where's Aurora?"

Messer slams into my back at the abrupt stop, his chest heaving as he searches for her. "I thought she was right behind us."

An explosion rocks the deck, sending everyone to the ground. Silence rings for a long moment before I'm able to get my bearings. Debris and wood rain down, and I cover my head until it slows to a stop. Messer helps me up, and I shove my hair out of my face as Kai grips me by my upper arms.

"I'm okay," I tell them, voice muffled in my ears. "Are you?"

There's no time to take inventory as Gramble continues to shout for us to embark. The Kenta soldiers behind us begin to rise. Half of them shake off their disorientation as they take in the plume of smoke billowing into the sky from deep within the market. The other half are now filled with vengeance.

Messer pushes me toward the ship. "I'm going to find Aurora."

He stops mid-step as she appears from the fold, unhurried and unconcerned as she stalks toward us, holding the same cup I saw her carrying earlier.

"Figured we could use a head start," she says, winking at Messer's stunned expression as she passes by.

All heads turn to watch as she stalks up the gangway.

Kai shakes his head and urges me forward. "We need to go."

The crew works in a fury to pull up the gangway and push off from the dock, setting off in just enough time to watch the Market collapse in on itself. Seawater swallows an entire portion of the promenade in one gulp, people included.

Hurrying to the mast, I use the last of my strength to climb. Kai yells my name, but I don't stop, wanting a better view of the damage. Nothing could have prepared me for the scale of the destruction. Aurora managed to take out a hole the size of two ships right in the middle of the Market. Hundreds and hundreds of people tread water, clinging to whatever they can find and to each other.

A century of trade and peace...*demolished*. There's no coming back from this. Retribution *will* be coming.

I realize my fist is still clenched and look down to find the soldier's blade clasped tightly in my shaking hands.

# CHAPTER 3

The whispers stop as soon as I enter the hull of the ship.

The consequences of the events at the Market hang in the air like a damp blanket, smothering. The journey home has been nothing but hushed voices and melancholy, in complete juxtaposition to the boisterous and animated atmosphere of the crew on the way there. Everyone is on edge, angry about our time at the Market being cut short, nervous about relations with Kenta moving forward.

And they blame me.

There have always been murmurings about my deviance, rumors about how terrible an influence I am, always getting Kai and Messer in trouble of some kind. Widespread confusion as to why Kai's parents allowed such a friendship, speculations that are now in the eyes of my peers as well even though they damn well know who the real troublemaker is.

Messer looks up from the game of chess he's playing against Lawson, one of the few boys in our training class I can tolerate. He smiles, but it's weak. He hates that I'm always the scapegoat. I've been avoiding him to spare him the grief that comes with being saddled with me as a friend.

I edge around the congregation of card players, pretending the stares of my classmates aren't drilling holes into my back as I weave through the hanging hammocks, mine the very last in the deepest recess of the ship. Well, mine and Messers and Kai's, because they refused to let me be sequestered alone.

I strike a match and light the lantern hanging between our posts, locking the door to the oiled wick quickly, shaking the miniature flame out. The very first part of our safety training before the voyage was fire safety. One wrong lick of flame and the entire ship will catch, sending us all to our doom.

I open the folded canvas of my bed and yelp, jumping away from the furry creature scurrying in the opposite direction.

Laughter erupts from behind me. The rat was obviously planted, the kernels of corn used as bait. I don't bother looking for the offender, knowing it's Paul and his pack of henchmen. They've been the most vocal regarding my social status since I joined the guard with them at twelve, and the betrayal of my crimson cheeks would give away my humiliation.

Instead, I flip the bed over and turn it inside out before climbing in. I suppose it's better than my boots being tied to the mast in the middle of the night or having my dinner dumped on my lap so I smell like fish stew for days on end. Both stunts went unpunished by Gramble.

I wait until the anger dims to a simmer before daring a look over at Messer, but he's not looking at me. He's staring daggers at Paul. As if he feels my eyes on him, I shake my head when Messer looks my way. It's not worth it, whatever it is he's thinking. We're already awaiting our fates when we arrive back in Alaha; no need to add to our list of transgressions.

Thievery.

Inciting a rebellion.

Treason.

All the accusations Gramble threw at me, Messer, and Aurora. Kai was spared his wrath, as is to be expected. He's our beacon of hope to avoid exile upon our return. Captain Wren will have to take into account Kai's recounting of events before doling out our punishments.

I make sure everyone's focus has returned to conversing amongst themselves, the prank long forgotten before I turn down the flame on the lantern so there's just enough light to see by.

I slide the dagger from my waistband. Running my fingers over the wooden hilt, I follow the strip of metal down its seam, then to the initial inscribed at the base.

*J*

Perhaps a family name, considering how old the weapon is. There's a good chance the object carries more sentimental value than actual functionality considering the hairline crack along the handle's spine indicating it was repaired at one point in time. Even so, the blade is surprisingly sharp, and it worked just fine to cut through tendons.

I retrieve my sketchbook from my pack and open to the page I last bookmarked with a charcoal pencil, replacing it with the dagger in the open hinge. I've drawn the weapon over and over. Sharp edge made from a black material, unlike the metal of typical swords and daggers.

Unhappy with any of my unfinished drawings, I flip to a fresh page and start anew. I'm on my fifth rendition when I spot Kai entering the hull from above deck.

He skirts the requests to join in on a game. Messer intervenes before Kai's able to reach his bunk, and I hurry to hide my contraband in my sketchbook, sliding it under my pillow. Their heads are tipped close as they speak, and I don't need to be privy to the conversation to know Messer is informing Kai of the rat in my hammock, Messer's head tilting toward Paul with Kai's gaze following.

I hate it when he does this, notifying Kai of all the terrible things that happen between my classmates and me. It's like he expects him to do something about it when, in reality, it only makes it worse when Kai confronts the situation. The taunts become meaner. Uglier. More backhanded.

Kai claps Messer on the shoulder and takes the shortest route to our posts. I haven't had to work as hard to avoid Kai. He's been doing a perfect job avoiding me all by himself. That's why I'm especially annoyed with Messer when Kai's laden stare locks on mine.

He unbuckles his belt and hangs it on the hook beside his hammock. "Why didn't you tell me about the harassment?"

How do I explain to a man who's never faced true opposition from his superiors, let alone his peers, that anything he does to try to remedy the situation will only do the opposite?

"If you refuse to come to me for help, you've got to at least learn to stick up for yourself," he says, climbing into his bed.

I glare at him. "So that I'll be the one to be punished for it? Gramble invariably believes Paul or literally anyone else over me." I return my gaze to the dark underbelly of the hull. "No thanks. I'd rather not be put on head duty."

Cleaning the toilets is not for the weak on this vessel.
I hear Kai's heavy sigh over the creaking of the
wooden ship. He knows I'm right, even if he can't admit
it. He hates being powerless when it comes to my
position in the guard. Or hell, in Alaha and in life. His
rank as my friend only goes so far.

"It'll pass," I tell him, wanting to ease his worry.
"Many of them will never see land again as long as they
live, and I'm the reason their time at the Market was cut
short."

We're in a floating prison of sorts, confined to live
and breathe the same air without any reprieve from one
another. The entire voyage from home was littered with
squabbles and melodrama. At least the passage back has
been quiet, even if it's because there's a united front of
anger against me.

"Their blame is unfair," he says.

It's nice to hear that he doesn't fault me for the
disastrous turn of events at the Market or the peace
treaty that's hanging by a thread, but the truth is I
do hold some of the blame. If I hadn't run from Kai,
I wouldn't have been by myself, and the Kenta soldier
with dark eyes wouldn't have had the opportunity to
cite me as a thief. I still don't understand his motives.
I don't know if he planned on infringing on the
treaty with the intention to frame our people as the
instigators well before entering the Market, but I made
myself an easy target either way.

Kai and I haven't spoken of any of the day's events
outside the initial questioning from Gramble's wrath
after departing. He said he didn't see the soldier trailing
me or when he pinned me to the table, only the

moments thereafter, except he skipped over the detail of my hand being forced to the stone wall.

I was relieved to not have to explain the strange pain I felt at the moment my palm made contact with it, so I followed his lead and omitted that part. Messer did the same. But the glaring and more complicated subject of his marriage proposal remains like an anchor around my neck. Any time I think I've garnered enough courage to address it, nothing comes out.

"Kai."

He opens his eyes, head turning in my direction.

For the first time, I reiterate the truth to him and him alone. "I didn't steal anything from that vendor. I wouldn't lie about this. Not to you."

Regardless of everything that remains unsaid, his eyes soften in the swinging glow of the lamplight. "I know that, Brynn." He stretches an arm across the space between our hammocks, and I do the same, grasping his hand in mine. "I told you: I'll always protect you."

We fall asleep that way, holding hands.

When I awake to the sound of a boy screaming, my hand hangs limp off the side of my hammock. Kai's is in the same position, and he flips to look toward the cause of commotion.

There's only one lamp left alight in the hull so it's hard to see, but the string of curses give away the source. Paul jerks in his hammock, shaking the bed underneath as well as he kicks and swings his arms and legs.

"Get them off! Get them off!"

Someone has the common sense to light a lamp and swing it in Paul's direction. Black insects run across his extremities as he tries and fails to knock them off.

Cockroaches, I register as he panics and teeters too far to the side, causing him to fall to the floor with a loud thunk.

A smattering of laughter rings out as people come to realize Paul is deathly afraid of the inch-long bugs. He yells, stripping off his shirt altogether, his pants following quickly after, and it only serves to make everyone laugh harder, which in turns makes him angrier.

"Who did this?" He stands, breathing uneven as he stares everyone down. Larger than most in our class, he's not to be messed with, and it effectively shuts everyone up. "Who did this?" he repeats, emboldened by his ability to intimidate.

No one speaks, and his gaze swings over the now quiet hull. He stops when he reaches me, eyes pausing on mine before they flit to Kai at my side then look away.

Kai and I share a knowing look, checking Messer's empty bed and feeling certain who the culprit is. Suppressing a smile, Kai drapes an arm over his eyes in a bid to fall back asleep. I, on the other hand, wait until the hull quiets back down to only snores and the sounds of the ever-creaking ship before crawling out of my hammock.

The deck is haunting in the dead of night. A small crew mans the sails and the helm with nothing but inky blackness in every direction. Aurora leans against the railing as she chats with two of the others on night shift with her. She sees me and tips her head in the direction of the bow. I nod my thanks in return.

We've never been close despite being the only two girls in our class. It's difficult to form a friendship when we've always been pitted against each other because of it. Our formative years of training were spent at odds, trying to become better, faster, stronger than the other. It wasn't until about a year ago that Messer forced us to be civil. Ever the peacemaker of our group.

It's difficult to not fall into the same trap again, however, with everyone blaming me in spite of Aurora's actions of blowing up the Market. She's considered a hero by some for allowing us a chance of escape.

I can't say for certain we would have made it back to the boats in time to escape the onslaught of Kenta chasing us, but I can't say for certain we wouldn't have either. Aurora lighting the booth of kerosene and oils might have saved us temporarily, but it might damn us over time. Some of my peers seem to understand the gravity of the situation and have shunned us both. At least that I can understand.

I march up the stairs to the top of the bow, around the railing, and cuss Aurora under my breath. The girl and Messer break apart when they see me. The girl tries to hide her face as she adjusts her blouse, but it's a futile effort. There's only a handful of female crew, and her blue dress gives her away: Masie, the scriber, and Gramble's daughter.

She scurries off, and I avert my eyes as Messer adjusts the opening of his pants. I brace my forearms on the front of the ship's bow. After a moment, Messer takes the spot next to me, and I dare a look at him.

"Are you trying to get exiled?"

He smirks, all suave masculinity and mussed hair. "Some things are worth the risk, B."

I can't help but smile at his ridiculous statement. "You're so dumb."

He meets my stare, not in the least bit repentant. "I

know."

I shake my head, unsurprised by his blasé attitude. "Well, you can blame Aurora for the interruption. She's the one who gave you away."

"Go figure," he says. "She's still mad at me."

"You?" I say, confused. "For what?"

He looks out at the expanse of nothing ahead of us. "You could say we have a differing opinion."

I raise a brow at his vague answer. "On?"

He loses a little of the brightness behind his smile. "She believes it's time to make a stand against Kenta. To challenge the current agreement."

I'm somehow surprised and not at the same time. "You don't?"

He cocks his head to the side as he looks at me. "I think she's already made the decision for us."

I let out a deep breath. "What do you think the punishment will be?"

He shakes his head. "There's no telling with Wren. Could be a year in the brig for all we know."

It's the most anyone's been sentenced to. Anyone requiring longer punishment is simply exiled, sent out on a tiny rowboat and ordered to never return. There have only been three in my lifetime that I can remember, and all were for far more minor crimes than breaking a century-old peace treaty.

"I'm just ready to get it over with," I tell him.

He makes a face that's hard to decipher. "This ship is hell enough."

That's more than true.

"How'd you know Paul is scared of roaches?" I say, changing the subject. "And how'd you catch so many?"

His smile returns in full force. "I have my ways."

I hold his stare for a long moment before letting my head rest on his shoulder. He tenses for a moment before wrapping an arm around me in a side embrace. It's the most we've ever touched outside of training, and it's a tad awkward.

I pull away first. "Don't do it again."

He knows what I mean, but he smirks. "No promises."

# CHAPTER 4

We've been standing on the deck since daybreak, waiting and watching our home slowly morph into view.

The boat cuts through the trees that sprout off from the Grove like giants from beneath the ocean's surface. Some are as wide as entire ships, others nothing more than the width of a person, their canopies intertwining into a thick copse. They make up the bones of our home, an island with no land.

Sails tucked in, the crew rows the ship into the fisherman's dock. Our welcome party cheers and waves down from above, lots of familiar faces and smiles shining from a spiderweb-like network of bridges stretched between the trees. Kids run along with the ship's creep into port, flags bearing Alaha's emblem held high over their heads, the material rippling with the wind as they run.

I remember this as a child, the excitement to greet the sailors and guards home after having been gone for six weeks, sometimes more depending on weather, and carrying my own flag down the length of the parade. It's the beginning of festivities that will run well into the night. I remember the tired lines etched into the faces of the sailors, thinking they must be so relieved to be home and away from the people of Kenta. How silly. My perspective was so naive and simple back then.

Spending weeks on end in a boat sucks the life out of you. Limited space, no privacy, and never-ending views of the same thing every day. Then there's this one day bursting with excitement at the Market, experiencing people and food and things unlike anything we have in Alaha, before being tasked with the arduous and monotonous journey back.

Six weeks feels like a different lifetime long ago. Everything seems fuzzy around the edges, like I'm no longer looking through clear eyes anymore, and it doesn't matter how many times I blink; the world is colored differently. *Less*, somehow.

The music and cheering grow louder as we anchor behind the boat that arrived not long before us, the crew now off-loading cattle and other livestock. A man has an entire pig tied over his shoulders, and it squeals in protest.

"It's a nice reminder that things could always be worse," Kai says, nose scrunching from the smell of farm animals.

I manage a small smile. "I heard Uche got sentenced to a week of mucking stalls after complaining the pick was rigged."

Kai snorts, spotting the scowl on Uche's face as he swats a calf on the rear, trying and failing to get the animal willingly down the gangway. "Someone has to draw the short straw."

Quite literally. His commander didn't take well to being accused of treachery, despite the rumors that he does in fact lick the longer straws so his favored crew gets their pick.

"Make sure you're not leaving anything behind," Gramble shouts, standing beside the gangway and making sure everyone departs the deck in a civilized manner. "Clean up and rest. You've got a party to attend tonight."

He means everyone but Kai, Messer, Aurora, and myself. He came to us first thing this morning and instructed us to go straight to Captain Wren's after disembarking.

"There's not going to be any water left by the time we're done being put through the wringer," Messer says.

The one and only luxury of living on Urchin Row by myself is I don't have to share a water reserve with anyone. I just hope I'm allowed a shower before being thrown in the brig.

Kai sniffs Messer's shoulder. "You do stink."

Messer feigns indignation, giving Kai a playful shove. "Speak for yourself. You've been smelling like sardines for days, but I didn't want to tell you because I'm *nice*."

I roll my eyes. "You're only nice to people with breasts."

Kai and Messer's heads both whip to me, astonished that those words came out of my mouth.

"What?" I say, defensive. "Are we pretending Messer isn't a total rake?"

After a beat, Kai breaks out into laughter, then Messer lets out his own burst before yanking on the end of my braid.

"Then you should be grateful I never used my wiles on you," he says with his most charming one-sided smirk on display.

"I'd like to see you try," I smart back.

With Messer looking as if he's genuinely interested in testing me, Kai clamps a hand down on his shoulder. "Let's not," Kai says. "I've seen her knock you on your ass on more than one occasion."

"It was twice," Messer says, holding up two fingers. "And it was because Gramble made us train blindfolded that week."

He's not wrong. I'm convinced he went easy on me as well, but I still milk the two takedowns any chance I can get. Kai, too.

Aurora joins us, sardonic smile on full display. "Whatever you need to tell yourself."

Last to disembark, we make our way off the ship and up the stairs to the first story. News mustn't have spread to the people yet, because everyone seems as excited to see us as they were for any past trips returning from the Market.

The three of us get to the Main and wait for Kai to finish making his way down the line of people vying for his attention. The center bridge is the widest and busiest of the city, spanning from one side of the grove to the other. It's a middle ground of sorts to travel any place in the grove and is usually filled with foot traffic as people venture in and out of the shops carved within the massive trunks of the oldest trees.

Everything is decked out with ribbons and tables for concessions for the party tonight, and games are being set up further down for the kids. The group of wives who form the event committee for Alaha are sitting around one of the tables as they stuff satchels of chopped and dyed leaves to be used for confetti, celebrating another successful year of trade.

Kai meets us, taking the lead for us to continue to the second story. We take one of the many flights of stairs, bypassing the shiels of lesser ranking commanders on the way to Kai's family's living quarters. Kai looks at us, and we all prepare ourselves for whatever is to come next.

The first person we see when walking through the door is Dupre, the commander of the guard and the captain's right hand. Never has there been a man alive more intimidating than Dupre. Known around the grove as the man too large for doors, he has to duck and turn slightly to fit between the jambs.

Captain Wren's voice calls from within. "Detain the girl."

The fear that spears through me turns to shock as Dupre uses shackles from his belt to ensnare Aurora's wrist. She doesn't fight it, face set in fierce determination as Dupre pulls her other hand behind her back, chaining them together.

"Send her to the brig. Stand by until I'm done here."

Aurora doesn't speak a single word, doesn't demand answers as to why she's being detained. She simply allows Dupre to usher her out, hard gaze lingering on Messer the longest as if to say *I told you so.*

Kai takes the lead. "What was that about?" he asks his father, appearing infinitely more at ease than Messer or I do.

Captain Wren is seated in the chair across from the settee. "I'll ask the questions first," he says, a drink in hand.

We file in as we await our fate.

Kai's mother, Faline, enters from the galley and rushes to sweep her son into an embrace. "I've been worried sick," she says, voice breaking.

Kai gives her a reassuring pat on the back. "I sent word back every other day just as you asked."

"It should have been every day," she says with more

steel in her voice, pulling him to arm's length to get a good look at his person. "Like a thoughtful son would do."

"It would have unnecessarily tied up extra birds," the captain drones from his chair, face in the crook of his hand. He appears at ease with a tiny, endearing smile gracing his features as he watches his wife fret over their son.

"What's a few birds in relation to my peace of mind," she says, smiling at Messer and me.

We both share a look of mild relief, tension easing from our shoulders. Faline steps in front of me, giving the two of us gentle squeezes on our upper arms in a maternal gesture before taking her place beside her husband. Kai's mother has always been kind to me.

The captain lifts his wife's hand, kissing the back of her knuckles. "Nothing besides him actively breathing in your presence will ever do anything for your peace of mind when it comes to our only son."

She smiles, not refuting his statement.

Her hair is pulled back in a clip, the exact shade of Kai's, but that's their only common attribute. Every other source of Kai's features comes from his father, identical except for the decades between them.

Returning his attention to us, the captain motions for us to sit. "I've gotten the messages, but I want to hear it from you three. What exactly transpired?" His eyes land on me first.

I take a deep breath and force myself not to look to Kai as I explain my side. I tell them about the soldier following me, his accusation of calling me a thief and attempting to remove my hand. I skip mentioning the wall or the singeing pain and run through the sequence of events, ending with the explosion Aurora set and gaining our escape.

"And you didn't take anything you didn't purchase?" the captain asks.

I don't look away from his stern and unyielding stare. "I did not."

He may not believe me given I don't have the best track record, so I don't blame him for the unsure look on his face, but he moves forward with Kai.

His perspective mirrors mine, coming upon the soldier and ordering him to let me go. The helplessness Kai felt in that moment is tangible even though his voice doesn't waver as he retells it. It's obvious to all of us that he didn't like not having the ability to stop them.

Messer repeats the same version of events except for the part where he had to admit to hitting the soldier who detained me. Committing violence against a person of Kenta breaks the peace treaty completely. We're trained to react in defense, and only if provoked.

"Did you feel like they were a threat to you?"

Messer fidgets. "Not to me, personally," he says, eyes shifting to me. "But to *B*."

The captain turns his attention my way. "And you, Brynn? Did you feel like you were forced to defend yourself when you used the Kenta soldier's weapon against him?"

I've had a lot of time to think back on how I sliced through the soldier's leg. I acted on impulse, but I nod, knowing there's no other answer that's acceptable given the situation.

The captain absorbs the information we've provided, silence settling over the room as we await his next words.

"Through all of this, no one has explained to me why Brynn was alone in the first place. You're supposed to stay in groups to prevent instances like this from happening."

I look at Kai. We prepared a suitable excuse, but he doesn't look away from his father when he says, "I asked for Brynn's hand in marriage."

Faline's quick intake of breath echoes through the room, and Messer shifts in place. I don't have to look at him to know he's shocked by the revelation.

The captain looks toward me then back to Kai. "And?"

Kai looks uncomfortable. "She hasn't said no."

I narrow my eyes on him. *Thanks for throwing me under the boat, asshole.*

I haven't said *yes* either.

All eyes land on me, and embarrassment burns up my neck and into my cheeks. I'm mortified. The last thing I expected to have to explain myself for is why I'm not jumping at the first chance to marry their son.

"I needed a moment to...*process*," I say, drowning out my racing heartbeat.

The captain sighs, as if annoyed. He stands, pacing a few steps. "What I'm about to divulge to you will need to remain between the people in this room, understand?" He waits for us to give a nod of acknowledgment. "We suspect Aurora is part of a small uprising here in Alaha. We think she went to the Market with the intention to create a disturbance to break the peace treaty."

We all still at the same time.

Then Messer leans forward in his chair. "Are you sure?"

"Yes," the captain says. "She hasn't mentioned

anything to you three about wanting to cause a rebellion in Alaha?"

Aurora tolerates me on a good day, so my answer is easy as I shake my head. Kai does the same.

Messer's response is more hesitant. "She's never made it a secret how much she hates the Kenta," he says. "But a lot of people voice their distaste for having to rely on Kenta as we do."

The captain folds his arms across his chest as he leans against his desk. "If I could find a way for my people to be more self-sufficient without war, I'd do it. After going back and forth, they've agreed to uphold the peace treaty on one condition: we turn over the two perpetrators who orchestrated the attack against their people, Brynn and Aurora."

Kai goes rigid in his seat. "Not happening."

"Kai," the captain reprimands.

"No," Kai says again, no room for barter in his tone.

Faline jumps into the conversation. "Listen to your father."

Kai bites his tongue, waiting for his father to continue.

"I don't want to do that, knowing your feelings for her, and that's why I've already informed them it's nonnegotiable considering she's betrothed to my son. They can ask for whoever they like, but the future leader's wife is not one of them."

My heart stops at the implication. I guess that settles the answer to Kai's marriage proposal.

"Plus, we're operating under the narrative that we acted in self-defense. I'm not turning over anyone yet."

"And if we don't?" Messer says.

"Kenta wants assurances that an uprising isn't

happening. I asked them to give us a chance to uncover if any is within our ranks so by the time the next trade comes around, it happens without incident. Which will be two years from now, instead of one."

I suck in a breath. "They're going to starve us out."

"We've stocked up enough supplies and food for the next year, and a lot can change in the coming months, so let's not get ahead of ourselves worrying." The captain's displeasure with the Market's events seem outweighed by his son's knee pressing into mine in an effort to soothe my fears. "Besides, we have a wedding to plan."

Messer chokes on his own spit, covering it with a cough when I shoot him a dirty look.

"Go. Get some sleep," the captain says, dismissing us as he walks back around to his side of the desk. "I don't need to remind you that everything we discussed stays inside this room."

It's not a question, just a simple statement of obedience, and we all nod in agreement.

"Good. See you tonight."

We're halfway out the door when Messer stops and says, "And Aurora? What's going to happen to her?"

Wren takes a healthy gulp of his drink and says, "That depends on her cooperation."

Knowing we're not going to get more than that, we don't speak until we're outside with the door closed behind us, checking to make sure there's not anyone nearby.

Kai scrubs a hand through his hair. "It could have gone worse."

"Speak for yourself," Messer says. "Aurora might get exiled."

"She knew the risk when she decided to ignite a war. Literally."

Messer sighs. "Knowing Aurora, she'll keep her mouth shut. I don't know if it'll end up helping or hurting her in the end." He shakes his head, features clearing as he looks to Kai then me. "I'll see you two love birds at the party?"

It takes everything in me not to punch him right in his smug face, and he laughs as he strides away. Kai, on the other hand, has the audacity to appear apologetic.

"I'm sorry," he says, pushing the hair off his forehead.

"For what? Your parents' disappointment that you asked me or the fact that it's obviously not my choice to make?"

His brows come down to form a frown as he shakes his head. I look away from him, taking in the bustle of the endless stream of people coming and going along the spider web of bridges.

"I need sleep," I say quietly.

He looks as if he means to argue with me, but whatever expression I have on my face makes him think better of it. "Later. We'll talk later."

I leave him without another word. I'm too exhausted and confused and angry to speak. As it stands right now, I can either marry Kai or hand myself over to Kenta as an Alaha rebel.

I suppose either of those options is still better than being exiled, but they're somehow equally as unnerving.

# CHAPTER 5

It's dusk when I wake.

I somehow manage to trudge my way underneath the spigot of my shower in the corner of my room, the water blessedly warm from the sun's heat. I take my time scrubbing the layer of sweat and dirt that's accumulated for weeks and weeks. I drain the rain reservoir on my roof to wash my hair—twice.

My bed looked too inviting to bother with bathing when I first got in, so I stripped down to my undergarments and fell face first into my pillow. I'm glad I have four coppers to my name because I'll add my bedding to the pile of clothes I need to take to the laundress.

The sky is dark by the time I'm done and dry. A caw of laughter comes from beyond the curtains of my window, and I hurry to push them open.

I'm surprised by his quick appearance. "Hey," I say, voice soft.

The bird answers with another squawk, head tilted in invitation for me to give him a scratch.

I oblige. "There's no way you missed me in that short of time," I joke.

He scoots closer for me to get his favorite spot. His feathers are black as night, but when they catch the sun just so, they shine the most gorgeous pearlescent rainbow of colors underneath, blue being the most prominent.

"Oh great, you're back." Leaning out of her window one room down from mine, Grenadine's gray halo of curls peeks out as she looks up at me. "I'm going to have to listen to this bird squawking at all hours of the day again."

As if offended, the bird opens his mouth and caws, the sound similar to a menacing laugh as his gullet bounces up and down.

Grenadine doesn't find it amusing, the wrinkles of her face compressed tight in indignation. "Your *pet* is a nuisance."

The word pet is exaggerated on purpose, considering the punishment for owning a pet is rationed food for a month. Food is meant for people, not rodents.

I retrieve a copper coin and toss it to her. "For your troubles."

Like the bandit she is, Grenadine snaps her curtains closed with a scowling smile.

Music begins to play from deep in the grove. The lights of the lamps hanging in windows and along the walking paths reflect off the ocean's surface, creating fiery dots atop the rippling black glass below. Voices carry with the wind as people start heading down to the celebration.

I grab my pack and climb out the window and onto my roof. I have a view of the grove in almost its entirety, my shiel being the highest point in the city. I've always found beauty in its complexity, felt pride in our people for surviving in such brutal conditions. But for some reason I can't pinpoint, it feels less impressive looking at it now.

Pecking pulls my attention from my melancholy

thoughts, and I find the bird attempting to break into my pack.

"You *are* incredibly needy," I tell him, pulling the dried fish he must smell from the bag. "You can have it. I'll be happy if I never eat another fish in my life."

This leads me down an even more unpleasant chain of thoughts, because if we are banned from the Market for two years, there will very likely be lots and lots of fish in my future.

Retrieving my sketchbook, I flip through my drawings. There's a memory that's been nagging me since we left the Market. I've been fighting the constant desire to sketch it, but I was too afraid while being in such close quarters and wanted to be able to take my time with it, to lose myself in it entirely.

I drew the details a little at a time instead, hiding them in my other drawings so I wouldn't forget them. In between the dresses of the Kenta women, lackluster in black and grays across the paper. Between the outlines of vendor booths and flags, in the margins sit the eyes and neck and hands of one man. Even as fresh as my recollection was when I drew them, they don't do his true memory justice. Even so, I have to get it out, regardless of how disappointing I know the end product will be.

I flip to a clean page and close my eyes, allowing myself to relive the scene in my head. It's the briefest of images in the middle of the chaos of action, a flash of a moment when I looked over my shoulder and my eyes met his as I ran toward Messer...when the dark-eyed soldier's gaze implored me to stop.

I open my eyes and place the charcoal of my pencil against the fresh page...and I begin to draw the soldier on his knees. The bird shuffles closer, finding a spot to roost on my bent knee before falling asleep like he does most times he visits me.

Eyes are the hardest. I can get all the other features in perfect proportion—nose, cheeks, chin—but if the eyes fall flat, it's all a waste, so that's where I start. Dark and devious, they look up from underneath the heavy slant of his brows. Anguished and helpless. Angry. Broody. Dangerous.

My first rendering doesn't come out too bad, and I expand onto the bridge of his nose and lose all track of time. It's not until the bird takes flight that I snap out of it.

Kai's head emerges over the lip of my window.

"I was wondering if he was hanging around," he says, pulling himself up.

I close the notebook in my lap. "How are you here?" I ask.

"Everyone is at the celebration, so I was able to sneak off." He sits with his forearms braced on his knees next to me, gaze weary as he takes in my appearance. "Did you get some rest?"

I fight a yawn. "What time is it?"

"A little before midnight."

I look him over: dressed in clean linens with his sword on display on his belt, hair that appears to have been combed into some semblance of order at one point but is currently hanging over his brow.

"How'd it go?"

He shrugs. "I spent the better part of the night looking over my shoulder, waiting for my best friend to arrive."

"Kai—"

"It's okay," he says with a half-smile. "I was just worried about you. I would have come to check on you sooner, but my father called me in for a meeting."

"Another? More news from Kenta?"

He shakes his head. "They've gotten nowhere with questioning Aurora since we arrived this morning, and instead of losing the information by pushing her too hard, they think she'll lead us right to the uprising if we let her back in with the population."

I raise my eyebrows, surprised.

"You think it's a bad idea?"

"You don't?"

He runs a hand through his hair, the culprit responsible for its disarray. "I think it's risky but can yield high rewards if we're lucky."

"She's a loose cannon."

"She's probably the only reason you're not in Kenta's hands as we speak."

He's right. It could have been Kai, or Messer, or any one of our people, but I think of the vendors with kind eyes and passing smiles and can't shake the guilt. Gathering the courage with a deep breath, I open my mouth to speak, but Kai's already shaking his head.

"No," he says, the same as he did to his father.

I push anyway. "It makes the most sense to turn us in."

He looks back out at the water, jaw set in unyielding determination. "If we give in this time, we'll have to give in every time. We'll be in the same position next year with someone else."

"You don't know that."

"I'm not willing to gamble with your life to find out."

"My life is insignificant compared to the Alaha as a

whole. I'm just an urchin."

A flicker of rage ignites behind his eyes, body twisting toward mine. "Stop saying that."

Kai's anger is rare. He's always composed and articulate and patient. His emotion makes me want to leave the conversation where it is, hating confrontation, but I'd never forgive myself if I didn't plead my case. I need to know I tried.

"Children, Kai. Children are going to go hungry if we don't do something."

"My father will find a way."

"And what if there is no other way?" I say, exasperated. "In a few months' time, if there haven't been any successful talks with the Kenta, then will you consider it?"

"It won't come to that."

"But—"

"Is the thought of marrying me so abhorrent you'd rather turn yourself over to them instead?"

It comes out like a physical blow, knocking the wind out of me and him both. The dejection and hurt are plain in his eyes.

I slide my hand over the fist he has over his knee, my fingertips an unspoken invitation gliding over his knuckles, and he opens his hand, allowing mine to weave into his.

"Marrying you wasn't part of the plan."

The anger and hurt from moments before are replaced with hope as he moves closer. "The plan doesn't change."

There's a hitch in my breath as I attempt to rein in the excitement beginning to course through my veins. "What about my place on the guard and finding a way onto land?"

I always hoped I'd be one of the few selected to make the annual trip to the Market. It's a fool's dream, but I wanted it nonetheless.

"Everything will be the same as before, except..." He lets out a breath, a tentative smile tugging at his lips. "We'll be together."

A tinge of happiness takes root in my chest from the magnitude of what he's saying. "But Kenta..."

"We'll figure it out," he says, leaving no room for argument.

I nod.

He rakes his eyes over my face as if allowing himself to look his fill. I do the same, marveling at the man before me—my best friend. Handsome and kind. My future match.

My gaze falls to his mouth, and he follows, eyes landing on mine in turn. I don't dare move, but I need him to do something, anything to put me out of my misery. He brings his other hand to my cheek, angling my face toward his.

We've snuck kisses for years. Never consistently or spoken of afterward, but often enough that I'd always anticipate another while unsure if it would ever happen again. He'd catch me off guard, here on my roof or while swimming or behind a corner. Some slow and languid, others a quick meeting of lips.

But this is different from all the ones before. There's purpose and intent in his eyes. His lips meet mine in a gentle touch before he pulls back.

"Breathe," he says, a wry smile on his lips.

So I do, sucking in a lungful of air. Once, twice. Again. He's witnessed my blush enough that I'm not self-conscious about it with him. "Try again?"

He doesn't wait this time, smiling when his lips touch mine, firm and searching as our breaths converge. A spark of desire cuts through all my trepidation, and I open my mouth up to his, giving him permission.

A noise escapes my throat of its own volition and Kai slides an arm around my waist, pulling me further into his body, his breath as heavy as mine. If I'd had an inkling of an idea of how good this would feel, there would have never been any answer but yes when he asked me to marry him.

I know now, and it's like an echo in my head as we kiss.

*Yes. Yes. Yes.*

# CHAPTER 6

"You think the hard part is over because you're almost to graduation?" Gramble strides across the arena, retrieving the cache of wooden swords. "You've gotten complacent. The trip to the Market spoiled you, spending all day playing cards and sneaking ale while on the ship."

We stand in line, heaving from the last set of conditioning.

He tosses a sword into each chest as he walks down the line. "Yes, I know all about your transgressions." He's baiting us, damn well aware the voyage was anything but luxurious. "Attack your left. Whoever goes down first has to run laps." He stands on the furthest side of the line of trainees to observe. "Begin!"

It's an all-out battle.

I swing the sword with my left arm, aiming for Lawson's exposed kidney, my right in a fist above my head to block the blow I know is coming from my right. The sword may be wooden, but it's polished and sharpened to perfection. The task is assigned on the regular as punishment for insubordination, and the edge of the makeshift blade sends fire down my forearm.

Lawson spins away, the tip of my sword a mere scrape against his back. My attacker, Paul, is quick to disarm his assailant, his attention solely focused on me now.

"Didn't know they let traitors stay in the guard," he sneers in my face.

I abandon being the aggressor as I take up the defensive, sword against sword to meet Paul's onslaught. He's bigger and stronger than I am. I use it to my advantage, getting inside his reach as I spin into his chest. With my back to him, I jam the sword into Paul's gut behind me. It's a fatal wound, and he's forced to fall back.

"You were saying?"

He throws his sword to the deck as he accepts defeat. I scan the arena and spot Lawson, who's taken the defensive position against Aurora, retreating back a step with each blow she advances. It's almost too easy to sneak up behind him, my eyes meeting Aurora's over Lawson's shoulder. Without tipping Lawson off, she angles her next blow to send him right in my direction, and I slice the sword across his throat.

He growls out a frustrated yell, and Gramble instructs him to quit whining and start running.

"Thanks," I tell Aurora, but she's already moved on to her next target.

I gulp down water from my pack, grateful to be done with today's hellish training session. I do not envy the felled guards who are already running laps around the arena. There are only four people left sparring—Messer against two, Aurora and Philipe—and it appears they have teamed up against Messer in a temporary truce. He's the best swordsman in our class, so it's a smart decision.

It doesn't take long for Messer to take down Philipe in a quick juke and slash to the back of the knees. Aurora, on the other hand, seems out for blood. Her attacks become feral with little rhyme or reason behind her movements, operating on nothing more than blind instinct to strike Messer somewhere, anywhere.

Messer meets her blows but doesn't counterstrike, and it's obvious he's letting her wear herself out. And, sure enough, her swings begin to lose momentum, and he's able to disarm her. Swordless, she stands before him, chest heaving from exertion. They stare at each other for long moments before Messer picks up her sword, holding it out for her in a show of peace.

It feels like everyone waits with bated breath to see if she'll leave him looking like a fool, but Aurora never looks away first. It goes against everything she stands for. Instead, she yanks the sword from his hand and waits for him to walk away before putting up her sword and beginning her laps.

Clapping comes from the entrance of the paddocks, and everyone turns to look as the captain, Dupre, and Kai emerge onto the arena floor. It's evident they've been monitoring training from the clock tower above deck.

We're on the most northern point of the grove, the easiest place to house the livestock after offloading from the ships. It's also where, if an ambush ever were to happen, it would be most visible.

The trainees stand at attention, including the runners, stopping midstride to pay their respects. Kai's eyes go straight to mine, and I do my best to appear unfazed by his surprise appearance. We've been sneaking around the past few weeks, finding any hidden moment we can to be alone, to hold hands and look at each other without prying eyes, and to kiss. Lots and lots of kissing. It's reckless, we know. I'm pretty sure his parents are aware, but they're willing to play ignorant as long as we don't get caught. The captain wouldn't be able to ignore our indiscretions if it became public knowledge.

"You may resume," Captain Wren says, releasing us. "You've done well training this bunch, Gramble."

Our instructor basks in the praise. If he had feathers, they'd be fluffed to their full glory.

"They've been a stubborn lot," he says in jest.

Kai takes in the victors. "Any in particular?" he asks, eyes sliding to mine. He's goading me.

Gramble, missing the connotation, declares all of us as problem children.

"How about one more demonstration," the captain says. "Your two best swordsmen."

Everyone perks up as Gramble turns his attention to us. As expected, he points to Messer. "You." He does a quick perusal before landing on Willard. "And you."

A fair match, at least as close as anyone can get to Messer's skill level. Willard is decent.

They move to gather their practice swords, but Dupre stops them, removing the sheath of leather from his back and unrolling it to reveal brand-new swords, real ones with handles made of varying shades of copper and bronze and double-edged blades, shiny and sharp.

"Choose your weapon," he says, voice full of gravel.

They each look over the selection and pick, Messer preferring bronze over copper.

"In the ring," Gramble instructs.

We all follow them to the sparring circle carved into the wood on the arena floor.

"You know the drill. First to submit or step over the line concedes the fight."

Everyone is silent as we watch the two opponents enter the ring. The stakes are different with real swords. It's not that the wooden ones aren't damaging in their own right—I have the scars and bruises to prove they are—but Willard has a tendency to be ruthless in his sparring, and being armed with a sharp blade adds a dose of danger to the mix.

Messer balances the weapon in his hand, flipping it to and fro in his palm to get used to the weight then readying his stance across from Willard. Gramble holds a hand outstretched between them, dropping it in a fist as the signal to start.

Willard initiates. Messer expects it and deflects, blades striking with a loud clank of metal. He follows it up with a quick returning swing that Willard hurries to match. Each flurry of movement has me holding my breath, waiting for the final ax to fall, and praying it's Messer's. It goes on like this for what feels like forever as the runners trickle in to watch the match when they finish their laps.

Eventually, battled into exhaustion, Willard loses a step that Messer's able to put pressure on, forcing Willard to concede another step to regain his balance. Messer doesn't relent, attacking with fast strikes that push his opponent over the line, and cheers erupt. I cup my hands around my mouth to celebrate his victory.

Captain Wren steps into the ring with Kai, and when he raises a hand, the applause dies down. "Each class needs a commander," he says, hand falling to Messer's shoulder in pride.

Kai unstraps the additional holster buckled across his chest, revealing a sword unlike the others. A snake is carved into the golden pommel, its forked tongue splitting into the crossguard where the blade meets the hilt. He holds it across both palms as he bows his head to Messer.

Messer looks at the captain then at his friend and the sword outstretched before him. He must be in shock, staring at the weapon with wide eyes for what feels like an eternity as everyone waits for him to accept his new position.

An awkward amount of time passes before the captain says, "Go ahead. You've earned it."

Messer swallows. Stretching out a hand, he runs his fingers over the golden snake then removes them. "With all due respect," he says, angling his body toward the captain and then Gramble. "No I haven't."

A flurry of murmurs zips around the circle.

"If I'm going to be the best, I have to beat the best."

Kai inspects his friend. "And who do you consider the best?"

Messer turns his head in my direction. "Brynn." The murmurs turn into a shower of voices, and Gramble shouts for everyone to be quiet. "You're the only one who's ever bested me," he says.

"Only because you were going easy on me," I counter.

Smiling a little, he shakes his head. "You know that's not true."

Do I? The two times I was able to defeat him felt like flukes, him making simple mistakes because he wasn't putting in all of his effort.

"A rematch then," Kai says, placing the sword against his back again.

I shake my head. "It wouldn't be a fair fight when he's already winded."

"Oh, I'm still going to win," Messer says, cocky,

swinging his blade to his side. "But at least I'll earn it this time."

Captain Wren gives Messer's shoulder a shake. "Very admirable, son." He motions for me to step forward, and I force my trembling legs to comply. It's not until I'm standing before Messer that I realize I don't have a sword.

Without having to be told, Kai pulls his personal weapon from his waist, gaze reassuring as he holds it out to me by the blade.

The chatter from our classmates falls silent. This isn't done. Swords are personal to each guard. They're never shared or traded, the most sacred of belongings to an Alaha. For Kai to offer me his as commander of his own fleet, as the future captain, says more than words ever could.

I grasp the gold hilt, the tree embossed along the handle foreign in my palm. It's heavier than I'm used to, and I run through a few practice techniques, shifting it from hand to hand to familiarize myself with it as quickly as I can.

I'm here despite managing to surpass every challenge designed to weed out the weakest links, and yet I've fought to defend my place in the guard since I joined at twelve. I've been met with skepticism from all sides, from Gramble and my peers to the old hag down the walkway from my room.

Taking a deep breath, I meet Messer's stare. An air of mutual respect radiates between us, and I decide, right here and right now, to quit trying to prove myself to people who don't care to know me. Maybe I wouldn't have gotten here without Kai's influence, but I know I've earned this fight. The fact that Messer thinks I'm worthy is more than enough for me, no matter the outcome.

Gramble puts his outstretched hand in the ring between us, looking to each of us for a nod of approval, then closes his fist and drops it.

I run through attack scenarios, but I know all his countermoves, and he knows mine. We circle each other, smiling cause we're both thinking the same thing. Even so, one of us has to make the first move.

He fakes a juke in my direction, smile growing wide when I don't even flinch.

"Come on, B," he taunts. "Show everyone what you got."

I suck on my teeth. "You're the one who invited me here. Are you scared?"

"Of what? Your back—" He deflects my jab with a spin, smiling at the narrow miss. "I was going to say backhand, but the jab is a nice start."

I swing left then right, and he blocks both, pushing me back with his blade against mine. I attack again, high, low, looking for a gap, but he parries every move. It's annoying.

I'm not going to let him take the easy way by wearing me down until it benefits him to counterstrike. I twist into what he wants me to give him, throwing all my strength into my backhand. He throws up his sword in just enough time, arms shaking from the reverberation when our blades meet. I keep the pressure, teeth bared as we stare at each other, mere inches separating us.

"Thought you weren't going to go easy on me."

He fights a smile over clenched teeth. "As you wish."

A sharp ting sounds as we push away with our blades, and it's the beginning of an unceasing melody of metal against metal. He doesn't relent, striking and dodging and counterstriking. We flow from one side of the circle to the other in an endless barrage of movement. There's no thinking or planning like it's often easy for me to do against other opponents, only instinct and reaction, my purest form of training taking the lead.

It's euphoric.

We break after some time, chasing air with every breath, and I realize I'm smiling as wide as he is before going back in. I switch hands, giving my dominant arm a break, and he does the same. Left, right, up, back. The blade never stops ringing in my hands. I'm mid-spin, throwing the sword back to my right, when I feel it— the opening I gave him. The resulting sting of the blade meeting the inside of my upper arm isn't surprising. I don't stop my momentum, elbowing him in the ribs instead and swinging back around to jab for his exposed side. He pushes me with a forearm to the chest, and I stagger back a few steps.

I'm forced to hold my ground against his onslaught. I'm tired. I have to concede a step to stop him from getting past my defenses, and like a shark smelling blood in the water, he advances. Grunting with every block, I defend again and again as he heaves all his power and might behind his weapon. I don't need to look behind me to know the line is at my heels. If I don't do something, he's going to bully me out of the circle.

In a last-ditch effort, I leap to the side, rolling into a stance. Hair falls from my braid, blocking my vision, but I don't dare waste the energy to move it. I'm in a battle of survival at this point, the thin edge of his blade looming closer with every pass.

I'm going to lose.

His strength and endurance wouldn't be as unshakeable if he just wasn't so damn good. I have only one option, a frenzied last chance to push him out of the ring. Mustering all the strength I have left, I let him come at me, blades connecting in a cross between us as he pushes me toward the line with all his might.

I let my knees buckle and release my hold on the sword, sliding to the ground so the momentum topples him over. He predicts it and jams his blade into the ground to stop his body from going over. Feet planted on either side of my shoulders, blade shoved into the boards above my head, he looks down at me.

I'm trapped.

Defenseless without my weapon.

Defeated.

I didn't expect to win, but it's a bitter feeling to come so close. If there's a consolation prize, it's the fact that Messer looks like he's been to hell and back with me. Sweat pours from his hair in streams, face and neck a deep red, shirt slashed in a multitude of places, panting from exertion. I can only imagine what I look like in turn—I feel like literal shit.

He reaches a hand down, and I debate the merits of living down here forever but accept it. It hurts.

Messer's smile is soft when he says, "I told you I'd win."

I push him, but it's a feeble shove.

No one cheers like they did when Messer won his first match. Only Kai enters the ring to greet the victor this time. He eyes me but focuses on Messer, once again presenting him with the sword fit for the new commander.

"*That* was an honorable fight."

Messer takes the sword in its sheath. "To be Alaha."

Kai nods. "To be Alaha."

I retrieve Kai's sword from where I abandoned it on the dock. The metal is scorching hot. I hold it out to him in the way he offered it to me, by the blade, apologetic.

He accepts it but doesn't let go, using it as a rope to pull me closer. "I am proud to call you my match." Then he kisses me, in front of everyone, rules and decorum be damned.

Whatever punishment awaits, we'll suffer it together. It'll be worth it.

# CHAPTER 7

It was not worth it.

We spent the night in the brig. The cells are enclosed on all sides with mangi stones mined from the ocean floor, the door a single wooden plank with iron bars in the window so the guards can check on their captive. There are four cells spaced along the perimeter of the grove located at the bottom of each watchtower, damp from the sea water that slaps against the stone walls. It's cold and loud and wet.

The captain took the time to escort us to our respective cells himself, first Kai, then myself. His frown was nothing short of telling as he shut me in. He's furious at Kai's defiance, but it burns extra hot because it's with me.

There's always that one couple who gets caught breaching the no-contact rules of engagement, but they usually get kitchen duty or mucking stalls. They also don't usually do it in front of the captain's face either, father or not.

The true punishment comes in the form of the extra weight of all of Alaha's eyes on me. The whispers and stares follow me everywhere. The taunts have grown quiet during training, but they've been replaced with cold avoidance and harsh glares. Gods forbid the adored and precious son of the captain chooses me as his match.

Messer slaps his breakfast down in front of mine as he takes his seat. "If you needed to know the secret hideout I use for moonlight trysts, you should have just asked."

Aurora rolls her eyes. "Everyone knows about your spot behind the tanner's shop."

The only reason Messer's never been caught is because everyone avoids the hide shop like the plague, including the night guards. The stench of urine seems to cling to anyone who draws near and is next to impossible to wash out.

"Beats spending the night in the brig." Messer shoves a pile of eggs into his mouth and grins around the bite. "Besides, I haven't had any girls complain."

"It brings into question the type of girls you're into," Kai says, sliding into the seat next to me. "Good morning."

I smile at his unkempt appearance. "Is it?"

"It's my last morning mucking stalls, so I'd say yes."

An added punishment Wren issued to his son. He knew the real reason Kai made such a public announcement of his intention to marry me: it makes it more difficult to walk back on once it's public knowledge. Wren needed to give Kai a reminder of his place—beneath his father's thumb.

Kai surveys the veranda, checking to see if the guards on breakfast duty are watching before squeezing my knee under the table. They're meant to keep a close eye on anyone attempting to swipe food or cause a disruption, but their attention lingers around Kai and me ever since our transgression, undoubtedly on Captain Wren's orders.

"How's your arm?"

I lift the underside for him to see. "Almost healed

thanks to the ointment you sent to my room."

"You can thank Messer," Kai says. "He offered to pay for it."

This is news to me, but Messer shrugs it off. "I felt bad after I defeated you so easily."

I scrunch my nose at him. "How very humble of you."

Kai leans closer, eyes darting to the guards patrolling, voice low when he speaks. "Two went missing last night."

Dread fills my stomach.

"Who?" Aurora asks.

"Drago and his son," Kai answers.

Messer cusses, pushing his plate away. "That's the third vessel to disappear since the beginning of the year."

Kai nods. "My father is talking about pulling all the fishing exhibitions."

"For how long?" I ask.

His eyes reveal there's not a definitive answer.

We all pick at our food, appetites gone after Kai's news. It's not uncommon for a boat or two to go missing every year, but it's increased tenfold the last three years. We honor our fishermen. Their jobs are dangerous enough. Disappearing at this rate can only point to a predatorial problem.

Something is taking our people.

After, Messer invites us to a game of poker on the Main, which we all decline, but he says he might meet a girl later, anyway—to fill the void of his dull friends, he says. Kai tells me he'll see me later, which means he'll find me after his shift in my usual spot on my roof. Aurora doesn't tell us her plans at all.

I grab my lantern and sketchbook and climb onto my

roof with my bounty. I've been trying to train myself back into my routine, finding joy in the simple things I did before the Market. I used to be satisfied with my charcoal drawings. With nothing to compare them to, I was proud of the odd sketch here and there. But after seeing the art of some of the vendors, I see everything my drawings lack, like extra color to add depth and dimension where I want it most.

Even the deepest of blacks can't convey the darkness of the soldier's irises. I've drawn and redrawn them over and over, so many times that I'm starting to think they're more of a figment of my imagination than actual memory. I flip to my previous renditions of him to compare, each unfinished and as disappointing as the first.

A sound vibrates the air, a heavy baritone that rattles the breath in my lungs. It's a sound I've never heard before but recognize in an instant.

The horn from the watchtower signaling *incoming.*

I cut off my lantern and shove my things into my pack, launching myself back through my window. I tuck the black blade into my waistband and shove my feet into my boots on my way out the door. People are already converging along the walkways outside their homes, eyes turned toward the north tower...the tower that faces Kenta.

I run.

It's almost dusk, and lanterns fill the open doorways and bridges along the paths. I'm on the opposite side of the grove. It's going to take me an hour to reach the other side and almost another to reach the bottom story.

Unless...

I eye the distance between my bridge and the one running perpendicular below it. It's doable. I think...

It's either that or jump, but it's as daunting of a swim. I climb over the railing and shimmy until I'm hanging by my hands. Taking one last glance at the drop, I squeeze my eyes shut and let go. The landing rattles my teeth, but I'm fine otherwise. I drop at the next crossing and the next until I hit the Main, then I run the length of it. Other guards are headed in the same direction. People keep to the sides to stay out of the way. They're following protocol to hunker down, a sense of panic in the air as people rush to their homes.

When I reach the bottom of the northern watchtower, the guards on shift are standing along the bridge and down on the dock, past the brig, where more off-duty guards are congregating. I see Kai standing with his father and Dupre, back toward the gathering soldiers as they face the open water.

I squeeze through the line of guards only to be met with a disgruntled commander. "No trainees allowed."

"I just need to speak to Commander Kai."

He points over my head. "Go home before I report you."

I ignore him and yell for Kai. His head snaps in my direction, his father following his line of sight. The captain says something to his son, giving me a nod before turning his gaze back toward the ocean.

Kai pulls me to the side. "Brynn, you can't be here."

"What's going on?"

His eyes dart to the closest guard to make sure he's out of hearing range. "There's a Kenta ship on the horizon."

"What?"

"It looks like they're sending in a dinghy. As of right now, all we can do is wait for it to get here."

"They didn't send word they were coming?"

He shakes his head. "Go back to your room and wait."

"What if I watch from the paddocks? I'll be out of the way."

Sighing, he takes inventory of the guards and how high the paddocks are. I can tell he's close to wavering, so I tack on a please for good measure.

"Stay out of sight," he relents.

I nod. "Be safe," I tell him, wishing like hell I could touch him. By the way he fists his hands when he turns away, I can tell he wishes the same.

The paddocks are clean after being scrubbed by the workers or whoever was granted the task as a punishment, and I claim a spot overlooking the dock. I spot the Kenta ship dead on the horizon, sitting where the sky meets the water, the place where the water starts to blur with the setting sun.

A small boat with one lone figure in it rows toward us, the person resembling a man with short hair and nothing more. Darkness falls before he makes it to the dock, but still we wait, all eyes trained on the small portion of ocean lit by the reflection of the lights throughout the grove. We wait and wait and wait until a single shot of light travels into the sky in the distance, exploding into white sparks above.

A signal from the Kenta ship that they come in peace.

As if on cue, the small boat slowly comes into focus, and my heart stops, comes to a complete halt because...

No.

There's no way it's him. I'm imagining things. It's dark. All men look the same in the dark.

Except this man is unmistakable in his stature and beauty. Even with just a glance at his profile, I know it's him.

Five guards await as he pulls his boat to the dock. He hands up a rope to tie off, hands raised into submission before even stepping onto the dock. The guard's voice can scarcely be heard on the wind as he orders him to his knees.

All the while, my heart is in my throat.

There's no way he'd come all the way here for a knife...would he? If I'm caught with it, I'll actually be the thief he accused me of being. I have to get rid of it. I swear I can feel it hum against my waist, as if it's reacting to its owner being so near.

And, as if hearing its call, the Kenta soldier's head snaps up, eyes landing on mine in the same breath.

Kai knows what's holding the soldier's attention, not needing to look up to verify. He stalks toward the man on his knees—the man who held my hand to the wall and has haunted my thoughts ever since—and stands before him, demanding his attention.

The soldier doesn't so much as blink. The other guards take notice, heads beginning to swivel up to see what's caught his attention. Kai leans over to intercept his line of vision. I see the soldier say something, lips moving as his eyes remain on mine.

I gasp when Kai punches him across the face.

The dark-eyed soldier's head whips to the side, and he spits on the dock before finally giving Kai his attention —and his smile.

The guards haul the soldier up, placing shackles around his feet and wrists. They direct him to the captain, who speaks to him. Whatever the soldier says

71

back doesn't sit well with Captain Wren, his face turning stern with anger. He ushers the soldier the rest of the way to the brig.

They pass directly underneath the paddocks, and the soldier's gaze once again finds mine, a single moment of meeting before disappearing into the cell, but the lingering look stays with me the entire walk back home. He wasn't outright smiling, but something akin to one pulled at the corners of his eyes, bright as they met mine.

Like he finds this...amusing.

Finds *me* amusing.

I spend the night in and out of restless dreams about the soldier and the wall at the Market and wildflowers in a meadow, grass whipping in the wind like a sea of green.

# CHAPTER 8

Messer's gaze locks on mine as soon as I step onto the veranda, and we each make a straight line for the other. My eyes shift when I spot the deep purple bruise shading his jaw, the mottled skin continuing beneath the collar of his shirt.

"Messer," I utter, taking him in.

He shakes his head, eyes going to guards nearby before pulling me into the food line. We carry our plates to the furthest part of the veranda overlooking the ocean, giving us a perfect view of the Kenta ship still moored on the horizon.

I wait until a guard walks past before pinning Messer with my eyes. "What happened?"

"He caught me sneaking out, but I'm fine." He stabs the eggs on his plate. "Have you spoken to Kai?" he asks, stepping over the conversation about his father.

I'm surprised he admitted as much. It's been three days of no training, so there's nothing to blame for the injuries like he usually does. I can't say there's anyone I harbor hatred for as I do for Messer's father.

Messer's eyes all but beg for me to let it go, so I do, forcing myself to take a bite of food and swallow before answering.

"No. Have you?"

He surveys the crowded veranda, lips thinning in worry. "I haven't seen Aurora either."

"You haven't…heard anything from your father?" His father is third in command, next in rank to Dupre. He's definitely in the know as to what's going on.

He shakes his head. "He's not exactly happy with me right now."

"There are what, thirty? Forty men on that ship?"

He eyes the blurry silhouette on the horizon. "If that."

"They'd be cut down before ever stepping foot in the grove."

"I don't think they're here for retribution," he says.

"They've been sending out birds every day. Do you think Wren was being honest about the terms Kenta gave us?"

"I don't know what to think," he says, glancing up at me. "But I know they're keeping a tight perimeter around the north tower, so they still have him in custody."

Another guard makes his round, passing by our table.

"You know how I used the soldier's blade?" I don't need to elaborate.

Messer loads his fork and shoves it into his mouth, nodding without looking at me.

I keep my eyes on the food as I speak under my breath. "I may still have it."

There's a definitive pause from his side of the table before he's able to regain his composure. He takes a swallow from his waterskin before addressing my confession.

"Get rid of it," he says, voice absolute, no room for negotiation.

I know any of the excuses I'd give him for not having done it already would be feeble. I've spent every waking moment since the Kenta soldier's arrival worried sick about Alaha guards storming my shiel and finding evidence of my thievery, but I haven't been able to make myself do it.

It doesn't matter that I admire the black blade and the craftsmanship that went into it. It's not a keepsake or mine to begin with, so I dip my head in acquiescence.

We eat as slowly as we can while waiting to see if Kai will appear for breakfast, but time runs out and we have to report for training. Although the grove is attempting to return to some sense of normalcy, people congregate in clusters, their whispers floating through the leaves of the trees and on the wind. The Main is open. Shop doors are propped open, but no one is shopping today. The clerks linger in the doorways as people pass by.

There's a game of piranha happening. Kids giggle and scatter from the two chosen as the attack fish. They'll tag others in a bid to grow their school of fish of hunters, but as we descend upon the group, the lack of enthusiasm is evident, their voices quieter, laughter less joyful. Messer leaps into the fray, throwing his arms around a few of them at one time, causing a ruckus of screams to break out. He uses them to chase down the remainder of the free fish until there are none left.

Shirlane, the primary school teacher, comes to admonish Messer and the children, her coiffed hair and steely eyes as scary as they were when we were children. Bowing his head, Messer dips out, but not without a smile hanging from his lips.

His deviation causes us to have to rush the remainder of the way to the paddocks. The bell of the north tower clock chimes nine times, indicating the changing of shifts and the end of breakfast.

Gramble is already barking orders when we reach the

top step. "Give me a hundred for being late," he says, pointing to the dirty paddock deck.

Due to the temporary lockdown on the grove, no one has scrubbed the paddocks in days, but there's no time to contemplate the dung and urine coating the ground as we fall straight into conditioning. I give Messer a less-than-pleased glare, muck sliding through my fingers on every down movement. He at least looks repentant.

I'm thirty-seven pushups into my set when Gramble calls my name. Sitting back on my knees, I look up to find him and Dupre standing at the entrance. The scary-looking commander gestures for me to come with a wave of his hand.

Messer lifts a questioning brow at me, and I shake my head in response. I concentrate on picking up my pack and placing one step in front of the other. Dupre doesn't speak a word as he turns and leads me down the stairs of the paddock.

Captain Wren awaits at the bottom. "Brynn," he greets me. There's a polite smile on his face, but there's a note of seriousness underlying it. "I apologize for having to pull you from training, but I'm in need of you."

"Sure," I say, hoping I seem amenable despite the desire to flee coursing through my veins.

"This way."

I'm ushered to walk in front as we take the path toward the north tower. Kai comes into view outside the brig, and his scowl doesn't do anything to ease my quivering nerves. The captain stops me with an arm on my shoulder, and I fight the urge to step out of his reach. He turns me toward him while we're still out of hearing range of the cell.

He senses my hesitation. "No one is in trouble." He smiles, giving me reassurance. "I've brought you here because I need you to speak to the soldier."

I'm taken aback. "Me?"

"Yes. All inquiries we've sent to the Kenta ship have gone unreturned, and the soldier is adamant that the only person he'll speak to is you."

I look back at Kai, but he gives nothing away.

"All you need to do is go in there and listen to what he came here to say," says the captain, drawing my attention again. "He might try to manipulate or bait you into getting emotional, but don't let him."

"To be clear," I say, holding his gaze. "You want me to go in there and...listen?"

By the slight pause in his expression, I can tell there's more before he speaks again. "The Kenta have an armada of ships that we need the location of."

"You think they're headed here?"

"I don't know," he says, eyes going to the lone ship on the horizon. "But we need to know if this soldier and the soldiers on that ship are rebels of their own making, or...or if we need to be prepared for something else at work here."

This is a lot of pressure. The thought of speaking to the soldier sends a fissure of equal parts excitement and unease down my spine. My chest is tight and my heart pounds, but I can't possibly say no, not to the captain's request or for my people.

"Okay," I tell him.

Captain Wren smiles. It's so rare to see that it stuns me for a moment, but there's no time to soak it in before I'm marching toward Kai.

He's dressed in his commander uniform. "I'm going

in with you."

I nod, relieved.

"If you want to leave at any moment, say so and we will."

I can't find any words, so I simply nod again, hiding the shake in my hands as I fist them at my sides.

Kai reaches for the iron door handle, but the guard stops him with a hand on his chest. "No weapons inside."

Confused, Kai looks down at his sword, then at his father. Captain Wren gives him an affirming nod to obey, and Kai unbuckles the weapon from his waist and hands it over.

"The other one, too," the guard orders.

Kai goes still, as do I when I watch him lift the material of his shirt from his less dominant side and produce a dagger.

It's a prohibited weapon.

Wren looks less than pleased by his son's insubordination, but no one says a word as Kai holds out the sharp side of the dagger for the guard to take.

Reaching for my hand, Kai laces his fingers with mine. "Ready?"

I let his steady presence center me, taking a deep breath before nodding to the guards. They open the door and Kai steps in first, body angled in front of mine as he leads me inside.

The smell hits me first, worse than the paddocks. The kind of stench that seeps into every pore of your lungs, a constant reminder of the human condition.

Nothing could have prepared me for the stark difference between the last time I saw him and now. One eye is nearly swollen shut, the other bloodshot around the pupil with a deep cut slashing across the brow. His nose scabbed over where his nose ring once was.

It hurts for me to lock eyes with him.

He smiles, teeth stark white against his skin. "It's nice to see you again." He phrases it like it's meant for Kai, but we both know it's for me.

*Only* me.

The familiar bang of the cell door closing sounds behind us, locking us in with the soldier.

I do my best to put on a brave face. "Wish I could say the same."

His nostrils flare, eyes heating as he looks from me to Kai. "The Alaha work their young guards with the animals?"

"Be careful casting judgment." Kai's words are coated with ice. "We're limited on space, so we're forced to use the paddocks as a training arena."

His stare lingers on Kai. "Can you explain why this cell was covered in her scent when I arrived here?"

Shock registers through my system. He could smell —surely not. A guard had to have let it slip, or he overheard a conversation. I look to Kai, but his gaze remains on the soldier, glaring at him like he's little more than scum on his boot.

"We're not here to justify ourselves to you."

"That's right. We have a deal." The soldier turns his dark eyes back on me. "I wanted to apologize." His voice is level without a trace of hidden meaning behind it, or it's hidden very well.

Either way, it's unsettling.

"I didn't mean to hurt you that day in the Market. I've never experienced that pain myself, but I've heard stories of it, and none of them are pleasant."

I think about it all the time. How it felt like something living, like another entity invaded my body for the split second of connection I had to the earth. It's strange, because it happened so fast it almost doesn't seem real anymore, like maybe it never happened at all.

"It couldn't be any worse than if you'd taken off my hand instead."

He lifts a brow. "Or worse than what happens to you here."

He severs the connection between us, eyes going to Kai, and my gaze follows, realization dawning.

"Kai?" I step forward so he's forced to look at me. I grab his arm.

He stops me with a hand over my grip on his shirt. "He's manipulating you, Brynn."

The captain warned me he'd do this, try to get in my head and confuse me. Embarrassing, really, to let him do it so easily. I turn my attention back to the disheveled prisoner. He's watching Kai and me closely, eyes lingering on the way Kai's hand covers mine.

I release my hold, suddenly eager to get out of this cell. "Where is the armada?"

The dark-eyed soldier settles back against the wall, head propped against the stacked stones. "The largest portion is moored in Oldtide Bay. They keep a ship or two at the Market, then the few remaining are out at sea. They routinely switch out, but it's difficult to say when that'll be."

Well, that was easy. Too easy...

But Kai seems satisfied, already leading me to the door by my elbow, knocking to signal the guards outside we're done. I dare a look at the soldier before I'm ushered out. I'm either more gullible than I thought or there's something like unfettered concern in his eyes as he watches us leave.

"Until next time, *Brynn*."

The way he says my name, the last letter lingering on the tip of his tongue, sends a spike of fear through me.

He says it like he's not finished with me.

# CHAPTER 9

I'm careful to keep to the shadows underneath the shiels. Guards have been rotating shifts, issuing warnings to anyone not obeying the curfew set in place. They've caught a couple of adolescents sneaking around, but they were spared from the brigs.

Lucky them.

I stop on the first story next to the southern watchtower. It's been raining on and off for days, but there are thankfully no white caps on the water. I double-check my surroundings before making sure the blade on my hip is secure. Then I step off the ledge and plunge into the ocean, keeping my arms and legs together to minimize water disturbance.

I swim to the ladder hanging from underneath the Main. It's slick and covered in barnacles and algae, but I manage to get onto the structure of beams that make up the underside of the bridge. The beams aren't in any better shape. My feet slip with every step, the darkness swallowing up the space within a couple feet in front of me. I consider turning back. The bridge spans the entire width of the grove, and going at this pace, I might not make it there before daylight.

Still, the endless worry in my stomach pushes me to take another step, to get answers, but also to help. If I can.

I spend the next couple of hours shuffling along the

crisscrossed beams. One side of the bridge to the other, praying every step isn't going to plunge me into the ocean below. It's not a far swim to the fishing docks, but they're one of the most patrolled areas of the grove.

It's not until I'm within arm's length of the brig that I realize I've made it. By the grace of the gods, I've made it.

Bracing my hands against the mangi stones, I allow my muscles a moment of reprieve. I don't, however, remind myself I still have to make the trek back and am already on borrowed time. The sun can't be but an hour away from peeking over the horizon, which means I'm two away from having to report to training.

I peek through the cracks in the stacked stones. Light from a lantern hanging on the other side of the wooden door comes through the bars of the window, outlining one of the guards standing nearby. My eyes land on the figure leaning against the opposite wall facing me.

His knee is bent, chained arms hanging over the top. He appears to be sleeping with the back of his head braced against the wall. The light flickers along one side of his body, casting the other in darkness. He looks devastatingly handsome, even in his roughened exhaustion.

His eyes open.

There shouldn't be any way he can see me, but his gaze seems to land on my exact position. Holding my breath, I sink onto my haunches, mere inches of wood to balance on between the stones and the water below.

His eyes follow my movement. "Look who it is," he croons, though it takes effort to get past the gravel in his voice. "The little thief herself."

"I'm not a thief. I never took anything from the vendor at the Market."

"But you did take something."

"*That* was an accident."

The brig is nothing more than a box. If he were to lie down widthwise, he wouldn't fit. The chains around his wrists and ankles clang together as he leans closer, his face gaining clarity in the shadows despite moving away from the light.

His eyes are alert, surprising considering the state he's in. Clothes and skin covered in smut from the stones and moisture, blood dried across his skin, the bruises somehow nastier than they were a day ago.

A lascivious smile tugs at the corner of his mouth, his eyes holding mine through the gaps of stone. "Was detaching the back of my foot from my leg *also* an accident?"

I match his smile. "No."

There's a flash of teeth when he says, "You seem to be prone to defiance."

"Based on acting in self-defense?"

"Based on you being here right now."

He's not wrong.

"You wanted my attention," I say. "Now you've got it."

"Let me guess," he says. "The boy told you."

My hackles rise. "The boy," I spit, "is the future leader of Alaha, and you can at least feign respect when speaking of him."

"Is that how you always refer to him? *The future leader of Alaha...*"

He's mocking me.

"Why did you come here?"

He's really smiling now. "For you, of course."

A shiver runs down my spine. Although I'm mostly concealed by the stacked stone walls, I feel as if he's able to see every inch of me. His words cause a visceral reaction. One of fear or disgust, I don't know.

"What do you want with me?"

His smile remains but somehow loses the bitterness underneath, shedding the condescending edge. He cocks his head to the side then returns to his original position, relaxing against the wall.

"I can't tell you."

"What?" It comes out too loud, and my eyes flit to the bars in the door, checking the guard's position. The shadow remains unmoving against the flickering wall. "You wanted to speak to me," I seethe, quieter. "So speak."

He shakes his head once. "I don't trust you yet."

"Trust me?" I repeat, incredulous. "What does trusting me have to do with anything?"

He eyes me for a long moment. "Brynn." My name comes out like more of a question than a statement, as if he's playing with the vowels in his mouth. "Doesn't feel like it suits you."

I'm positive he is irritating me on purpose. "What's your name?"

"Acker," he declares.

"Do you have a family name?"

He ignores my question. "I hope you didn't receive a tongue lashing because of me."

He may be in the cell, but it's obvious I'm stuck abiding by his terms in this conversation. "Kai doesn't speak to me like he does to you."

"That's good to know." He shifts his weight when a wave breaks around us, sending water into his cell and spraying the stones. "Considering what he *is* willing to do to you."

"If you're referring to my time in this cell, rest assured I deserved my punishment."

And there it is—that smile he uses like a weapon. "Oh, I'm sure you did." He shuffles toward my side of the cell, chains clinking as he moves. "But that's still not what I'm referring to."

I swallow, half afraid to ask.

He's as close to the stones as he can get. "Tell me, what do you remember of your childhood?"

It's not uncommon amongst the Alaha for children to follow in their parents' skill set. Fishermen bring their children along early, sometimes taking them boating within days of being born. From what I've been told, my parents often liked to take me out with them on fishing expeditions.

After not returning from a trip, a search party found me in the boat—alone, not a single hint as to where my parents went or what happened to them. It helped perpetuate the folklore of the giant squid, but the most likely reasoning would be that they were spearfishing and forgot to tie off to the boat. Then by the time they came to realize their grave mistake, the boat had drifted too far out of reach.

I remember the days following, the way the pretty lady held me close as I cried and cried and cried—Kai's mother, Faline. She's my earliest memory, her and the gray-eyed boy who had a hard time reeling in his curiosity as he looked up at me in his mother's arms.

A gradual feeling happens inside of me, a yawning cavern door I haven't opened in a long, long time.

"*Why are you so sad?*" he whispered to me as his mother dozed with me in her arms.

I whispered, "*I don't know.*"

Looking back, I recall how frustrating it was that tears no longer came despite the gnawing pain in my heart. I recall the strangeness of the woman who attempted to soothe me and my desire to go home.

But I can't recall a single thing about my parents.

"Kai's parents took me in after my parents died, but... I don't remember anything prior to seven," I tell him.

He wouldn't have asked if he didn't already know. He doesn't have to voice it for me to see the confirmation in his eyes.

"The only way they agreed to bring you in to speak with me was if I made certain..." He tilts his head as he sorts out his words. "Gave *assurances* that I wouldn't reveal too much, so you're going to have to ask the right questions."

"What do you mean?"

He holds my gaze. "You know."

And I do. He's speaking of a blood oath, a binding between two people through blood—a myth like the black squid. Our ancestors weaved stories of monsters and superstition and people with magical abilities...

More folklore.

"The oaths you speak of aren't real."

He lifts one brow in response.

"They're folly," I say. "Kai and I would pretend as children. We'd prick our fingers and swear on our lives, and we never keeled over and died when we broke them."

He shakes his head. "You were missing a vital piece, the glue that makes the promise hold."

I think back on the old wives' tale and the rhyme that went with it: *Blood to blood, trust to trust, we plant this soil...*

"Dirt."

He nods.

"But we don't have any."

By the way he remains silent, I'm going to assume that's not true.

I release a knowing breath. "The captain has Kenta soil in his possession."

We're inches away, separated by a thin barrier of rock, and our eyes meet through a crevice.

"The dirt was old. Centuries old, if I had to guess, so the oath will wear over time. I can already feel the binds loosening. The more you're able to piece together, the flimsier it becomes."

"Let's say I believe you," I say, dubious. "If magic and blood oaths and gods know what is true, why make a pact that could kill you if it's broken?"

"I knew they wouldn't let you speak to me alone and they'd likely send someone to accompany you for protection." He tilts his head to the side in contemplation. "I needed to see it while it was happening."

"See what?"

He's quiet for a moment, which tells me the oath is stopping him from revealing too much.

He lets out a breath. "Do you love him?"

I'm confused and kind of irked by his invasive question. "That's a little personal, don't you think?"

He remains silent.

"Yes, I love him," I tell him. "He's my closest friend."

He shakes his head, chuckling through an exhale. "That has to be the worst proclamation of love I've ever heard."

"I didn't realize you were wanting me to recite poetry

about his eyes."

"Closest friend," he repeats, as if he's got all the time in the world to ponder my statement. "I'd be mortified if those were the words my match used to describe me."

"Fine," I say through clenched teeth. "Tell me about your match. What do you love about her?" That's assuming he has one. Considering his looks—the kind of handsome that's hard to stare at—I'd say yes, but his personality is very off-putting.

His smile fades into something sadder. "She has beautiful eyes," he says softly, like he's lost to memory. "They're brown and green and amber, like every color of every season. I've looked everywhere for eyes like hers, and nothing has ever been able to compare."

I actually hate how genuine he sounds. "Touching," I say, letting the annoyance seep into my tone. "She must be worried about you."

He shakes his head. "I worry more about her, I assure you."

"Lucky her."

"Careful," he draws. "You sound a little bitter. Is it because you realize you have zero romantic interest in your match?"

"The reason I was in this cell," I say, embarrassment and spite running away with my tongue, "is because we broke the Rule of Boundaries. Do you know what that is?"

He's no longer smiling. "I've heard of the Alaha's covenants. They're a mockery of our traditions, enforced to maintain control over one's people."

Any remaining intent I had of being nice evaporates into thin air. "The captain isn't a dictator. He's kind. He took me in when I had no one."

The fire in my eyes ignites in his, each feeding off the other. "And what about your real parents? Where are they?"

"Dead."

"You've seen their bodies?"

"It doesn't matter what happened to them. They're gone."

He clicks his tongue, a look of disgust on his face. "I can't help you if you want to keep your head buried in the sand."

"Help me with *what*?"

He shakes his head. "That's not the right question."

If I could reach through the wall, I'd strangle him.

"When you accused me of stealing in the Market, were you trying to..." I trail off, hesitant to speak my suspicions if I'm wrong. "Were you trying to help me?"

"Yes." There's a touch of eagerness in his voice.

"Because you think I'm in danger?"

He allows his silence to answer for him.

"From who?"

Waves are coming in faster now, the tide rising with the moon. It feels like an omen for what's to come. My parents, my past, my lack of memories of it...he's insinuating something big. I swallow past the lump in my throat, because I'm not...

I'm not Alaha.

I didn't need him to tell me. I've known for a very long time, the feeling of *other* I've held in a sacred place inside of me. But it's something else to face it from an outside source, for it to be reflected back to me by a stranger.

Panic engulfs my lungs and chest, sending me teetering on the small ledge. "We're done here."

He smiles without teeth but doesn't attempt to change my mind or bait me. Draping one arm over a bent knee, he dips his head in a nod. "Rest assured, *Brynn*, all will be revealed in due time."

There's an implied message somewhere in his words, a riddle he wants me to solve between the lines. It feels like a game.

One I'm not interested in playing.

"Enjoy your time in Alaha." I push to stand. "It looks like you're going to be here for a while."

It's a long trek back to the south tower with the conversation replaying in my mind. I thought speaking to him without the hindrance of witnesses would alleviate my curiosity, but it seems to have done the opposite.

I remind myself of Messer's voice when I get to the end of the bridge. Pulling the dagger from my waist, I run my fingers over the dark blade and worn handle, committing it to memory. With my heart in my throat, I hold it out over the water and drop it.

It disappears almost instantly into the dark abyss.

# CHAPTER 10

Commander Johannes, Messer's father, shakes Captain Wren's hand then Kai's, looking as self-righteous as the bastard can get. "I hear congratulations are in order." He looks at me, taking in my newly appointed guard uniform, then turns his attention back to the men at my side.

His wife, Danuh, on the other hand, takes my hands in hers. "I look forward to seeing you on the committee," she says, referring to the group of commanders' wives who plan all of Alaha's activities.

I hadn't given it much thought, but it makes sense that it would be expected of me to participate. Pasting on a smile, I thank her, grateful when she releases her hold on me.

It's graduation day. The Main is becoming more and more crowded the closer it gets to the start of the ceremony. Graduates are escorted by their families. Due to my lack of relatives, Kai invited me to arrive with his parents. It would have been rude to say no.

Messer grins at me, his eyes raking over my uniform. "Looks good on you."

I tug on the material, hating how tight and itchy it is. "Yours too. Your sword looks extra shiny."

He looks down at the hilt exposed at his side with a proud appreciation in his gaze. "My parents had it polished and sharpened for me as a graduation gift."

Then I see it again, more bruising down the side of his neck in the perfect shape of fingerprints. I clench my teeth and look away, my eyes landing on Messer's mother. It wasn't what I intended, but the anger and disgust must radiate from my gaze, because Kai bumps me with his elbow.

"You're coming, right?"

I shake my head, catching up to the conversation about the dinner following the graduation ceremony on the veranda. "I can't. I have a meeting with the dressmaker."

I'm late getting fitted, so I'm cutting it too close to miss.

"If there is dinner," Commander Johannes says. "Callom raised the blue flag this morning."

"Oh no," Faline mutters.

Blue is the worst of the flags, meaning a terrible storm is coming.

Danuh waves a hand in the air. "Callom is a worrywart. He often puts up warnings out of an abundance of caution."

Faline doesn't look convinced. "We can only hope," she says, looking to the overcast sky. "The Matching Ceremony is in three days."

Of course that's her biggest concern. A blue flag alert doesn't just warn of wind and rain, but rather the kind of storm that often causes the sea level to flood the bottom story of the grove, sometimes two, and the brigs are sure to be the first to go under.

"I'm sure everything will be handled before then," Captain Wren says.

He sees another high-ranking commander and excuses himself and Faline, but his words hang in the air as I watch him walk away. We mingle for a while longer before taking our place.

My class is lined up across the middle of the Main. Our family and friends stand opposite us, applauding after each student is called to receive their pin. It's a circle of metal we'll affix to our shoulder while we're on duty to signify the history of the armor the Alaha would wear during battle.

Every inhale feels like a feat in itself.

Captain Wren calls the next student, Joel, and my eyes trail my classmate's movements, gaze colliding with Kai's on the other side of the Main. All seventeen of the high-ranking commanders stand shoulder to shoulder to shake the hands of each graduate after they're pinned. Kai stands last as the youngest until Messer takes his place next year alongside him.

Wren has to all but yell over the howl of wind as it picks up strength. The sky above is turning darker by the minute, and I swear I feel a raindrop or two pelting my skin every now and then.

Wren's comment about everything being handled before the Matching Ceremony leaves a sick feeling in the pit of my stomach. If Callom is right, which he often is when it comes to his predictions, there's not a chance Acker will survive in the brig. I don't think Wren has any intention of letting the Kenta soldier go, not with the way the guards removed Kai's weapons before letting us in to see him. They're scared of him. It'd be too risky to let him out.

Aurora elbows me in the side. "Pay attention."

My eyes snap to Captain Wren's, and I realize he's said my name at least twice by the look on his face. My stomach churns as I force my legs to move. If I were to unclench my teeth, I'd hurl in front of everyone.

"Brynn," the captain says, smiling when I stand before him. He slips the pin onto my shoulder, and I pray he doesn't feel my heart pounding through the fabric of my shirt. "Congratulations."

I dip my head in acknowledgment, not trusting myself to open my mouth. I continue on to the commanders and begin moving down the line. Most of the handshakes are half-hearted, a formality they're forced to endure, but a few make a point to at least look me in the eye. Kai's presence looms larger the closer I get.

Then I'm standing in front of him, meeting the gray eyes so like my own. Open and inviting and warm. Familiar. Like home. He holds his hand out, and I try to hide the shake in mine as I slide my palm into his.

"Congratulations, Brynn," he says, gaze steady.

Calm washes over me, easing the tension in my teeth. He holds my hand longer than necessary, but I don't let go, welcoming this moment of comfort from him. I've waited for this day for what feels like my entire life, and I can't escape the feeling of despair hanging over me.

I somehow manage to make it through the rest of the ceremony. The captain finishes his speech, and the crowd disperses. Kai and his father are swarmed, and Messer finds me leaning against the bridge's railing.

He nudges me with his shoulder. "Everything okay?"

I shake my head. It's not possible to describe exactly what it is I'm feeling, but I know for a fact not everything is okay.

Releasing a breath, he clasps his hands over the rail, looking out over the water. "My parents finalized my match," he says.

"Oh, yeah?" I say, trying to gauge his emotions. "And?"

"It's Aurora."

I'm speechless.

I don't know what I was expecting, but it wasn't this. Not Aurora, the daughter of a fisherman with no history of the guard. They have no rank and no money, nothing of value to negotiate a marriage of Messer's notoriety.

"Are you…happy…with it?" I stutter out, shocked.

He gives a little shrug. "I suppose I'll never be bored." Looking at me, he smiles, but it's dimmer than usual. "I'm just looking forward to getting out of my parents' place and into my own."

Understanding dawns, and I smile back at him. "You deserve to be happy, Messer."

"As do you, B," he says with a sad and knowing smile.

After the Matching Ceremony, I'll be forced to leave my shiel on Urchin Row to live with Kai in the center of the grove. It's a sacrifice I'm required to make to create room for any unmatched after the ceremony, but it also means losing my favorite spot.

I enjoy spending my nights drawing on my roof. It may not be much, but it's mine. Well, mine and the bird's, and I don't want to share him with the new occupant of my current home. If they don't scare him away, that is.

A strong gust of wind comes off the sea. Decorations strung between the trees snap, sending their strings and banners into the branches and leaves. People begin to depart to avoid the incoming weather.

When I look out over the churning water, I spot something different. "The boat," I say, looking at Messer.

"It's gone."

He follows my gaze north to where the ship was posted, the space now vacant.

We make a beeline for Captain Wren and Kai and point out the missing ship. Wren isn't pleased, face flushing with annoyance as he asks his third in command why no one informed him. Messer's father doesn't have a good answer, which only serves to anger Wren more.

"Dinner is canceled," Captain Wren declares. "Everyone gather whatever food and supplies they may need to make it until morning. It looks like we're in for a rough night."

Everyone is prompt in their departure. Messer leaves with his mother, but I wait for Kai to finish conversing with his father and fellow commanders by the nearest stairs. We don't speak until we're safe from someone overhearing, pausing on the empty path where it forks in the direction of Kai's home and continues on to mine.

"He's going to kill the soldier," I say.

"He hasn't said it, but yes," he says, tendrils of hair breaking loose from their tie. "He's instructed all the guards to vacate their post once the swells reach ten feet."

By the look of the water now, that'll be within a couple of hours.

"Did you ever gather any more intel from him?"

He shakes his head. "Nothing more than what he revealed to you."

I don't like it. Letting him die...for what? "Surely he didn't come all this way just to apologize," I say.

Kai cocks his head to the side, eyes going to the horizon through the trees before he looks back at me, defeated. "Go back to your shiel. Close your shutters and hunker down. It looks like it's going to be a doozy."

We wait for a family to pass before sneaking a quick kiss, making plans to meet first thing in the morning.

Today should have been full of celebration and excitement, finally accomplishing what I've worked for since the age of thirteen, but a heavy weight sits on my shoulders. It's like the clouds were an omen from the moment I woke up. The ship is gone now and there's nowhere safe to hide a fugitive in the grove. Not without getting caught.

*Wait.*

I stop within feet of my door at the realization. There's exactly *one* place no one will look.

No. I couldn't possibly. I mean, there's no way I trust him enough to hide him with me.

Turning back toward the path to the south tower, I contemplate my options. There's a chance I won't even make it in time. Hell, there's a chance I won't make it at all with the size of the white-capped waves below. But the alternative...

*Dang rabbits.*

I sprint to the tower, telling a guard I run into along the way that I'm making a last-second run to get lamp oil. Thunder rumbles in the distance, and I strip off my uniform vest when I finally reach the end of the grove. The water looks angry, but I'm confident in my abilities to reach the ladder to the cross sections under the Main.

I do so without issue, but the real problem is the slickness of the beams, which are coated with a thin layer of seafoam. Some of the waves cover them long enough for me to lose sight of my steps, so it takes me twice as long to reach him.

With a foot of water already flooding the space, he trudges to my side of the cell, fingers gripping between the stacked stones. His expression is unreadable.

I slap my hands on the stones in an effort to stop myself from sliding from the ledge. "Tell me something, anything to convince me to help you."

He shakes his head. "I can't."

I groan. "Because of this alleged blood oath?"

"No," he says, voice tired and hoarse. "I'm never going to tell you something just to benefit myself."

"Not even if it means saving your life?" I ask, stunned.

He shakes his head again. "No."

A wave rolls high enough to reach my waist, and it takes all the strength in my fingertips to keep hold. I brace my forehead against the stones and consider my options, knowing there are only two outcomes.

"Look at me."

The command in his voice compels me to meet his gaze through a gap in the wall. He has his palms braced against it, putting him eye level with me. Nothing but patience and understanding shine back, his expression at complete odds with the storm raging around us.

Judging by the panic filling my lungs, one would think it was my life on the line, not his.

"I don't believe you came all this way to watch me drown."

I hate the small shake of my head I give to him in answer.

"Then we're wasting time." He says it as collected as ever, as if he has all the time in the world and is waiting for me to catch up.

This is madness.

"I'll try," I tell him. I'll try to break him out.

The ocean surges up from below, a deep rolling wave that forces us to become buoyant, treading water to keep our heads above the surface. It sends me careening back, the current wanting to drag me out to sea, but I swim against the stirring water to the other side of the brig.

It's only seconds but feels like eternity before the water recedes and I'm able to climb onto the dock. It takes longer for the water to drain through the gaps in the cell. Acker is trapped within the surge until the water finally leaves, dropping him to the hard ground of the brig, his chains rattling against the stones.

I yank on the iron handle of the door, but the latch doesn't budge.

"The dagger," Acker says, wobbling into a stance. "Where's the dagger?"

I open and close my mouth before I'm able to spit it out. "I threw it in the ocean."

He nods, quick to accept the truth, like he expected as much. "It's okay. You can call it."

I don't have time to ask him what the hell he's talking about before a rogue wave overtakes us, covering our heads this time. I clutch the handle of the door to stop the wave from sweeping me away, holding my breath for nearly a minute before it finally recedes.

For Acker, it's longer, and he sucks in a large breath when he emerges from inside his cell. "You can call it because it belongs to you." He stumbles into an awkward stance, chest expanding with each intake of air. "I can't explain right now, but it will answer your summons."

A smaller wave makes us float for a few seconds before dropping back down. We're on borrowed time.

Once the tide comes in, this entire story will be underwater within minutes.

Acker's shackled hands land on mine, gripping the bars in the window of the door. "It's a part of you, but not. Close your eyes."

I obey without question.

"Feel for it. Reach out like you're picking it up from where you dropped it, like it's right there before you."

This feels insane, but I pretend I'm standing on solid wood that's not covered in three feet of water. It just feels silly, like I'm wasting time instead of figuring out a way to break the latch on the door. I can feel another wave coming, and I hold my breath so I can continue my search underwater. Floating inside the wave without the roaring wind or Acker's piercing gaze, I find a semblance of calm within my mind and cling to it, encasing myself in it.

Everything becomes still. It's like time stops and the sea calms and I'm able to see the ocean floor. In my mind's eye, I skim over the sandy bottom, sending fish scurrying into the pitch black. It's desolate and barren. My lungs begin to burn. Silt clouds my vision as I hurry, as if I'm actually walking on the ocean floor, but there's —

There it is.

Lying on its side, half covered in sand. I reach and pick it up, closing my fist tightly.

I gasp when the water falls, marveling at the actual dagger in my hand, excited when I meet Acker's awaiting eyes. "I found it."

His answering smile sends a spark of emotion through me. Despite the hunger and exhaustion lining his features, he's still handsome.

"Use it to break the seal on the door."

The *what*?

Another wave pulls us under. It goes on for so long it begins to feel like the world has no end and the sea has no bottom. It takes longer this time, and we both suck in greedy air when it drops away.

"What seal?" I ask as soon as I can breathe.

"There's a seal on the door, but the stone of the blade can break it."

That's all he gets out before we're under water again. I don't know what to do, but I open my eyes and find the crack between the door and the cell wall through the haze. Sticking the blade in the gap, I search for something tangible like a latch but come up empty.

Anxiety takes over when my lungs begin to burn. Acker's hands closed over mine are the only things preventing me from letting go and kicking for the surface.

Letting go would mean I'd be leaving him for dead. It's not an option I'm willing to accept. For some reason beyond my understanding, I know I could never live with myself if I didn't give everything I have to save him, even if it costs me my life in turn.

The water takes longer to drain from the brig, and I wait with bated breath for Acker to break the surface. He's not able to hold his as long as I can, and his gasp is punctuated with desperation.

His fingers tighten over mine. "Jovie." He forces it out between breaths. Water coats his eyelashes, falling onto his cheeks. His skin is alabaster, the rich color of his cheeks that day in the Market long gone, making his already dark eyes all the more intense. "That's your name, your real name—Jovie."

There's goodbye in his tone.

I shake my head.

Then he starts to peel my fingers away from the metal bars.

"No." If I'm saying it to him or myself, I'm unsure, but I keep returning my grasp to the bars. Another wave and impossible wait ensues, and it's dark and cold under the water.

Acker's fingers are adamant now, pulling my hand away as I put up an equal fight, refusing to let go. I keep my eyes open, focused on the task at hand. The blade swings back and forth in the crack, but I can't find the latch. Pressure builds inside my head as I fight the instinct to suck in a hopeless breath, knowing I'd kill myself within seconds when my lungs filled with salt water instead of air.

Acker slams his hands against mine, but I hold on, jamming the blade in deeper.

*There it is.*

Like striking swords, the metal vibrates from the impact. Then the door gives, the force of an underwater current pulling it the rest of the way open for us. We reach for the other in our desperation before swimming for the surface.

Up and up and up.

My intake of air is a loud cry of relief. Acker's even more so, but there's no time to relax. We struggle our way onto the roof of the brig, and only then do we allow ourselves a moment of reprieve to breathe.

Acker hacks up water, basking in the oxygen flooding his lungs with the next inhale. Howling wind tears through the trees, sending leaves down with it. The wall of storm clouds is rolling in like it's bringing the night itself with it.

I eye the chains around his wrists.

Noticing the direction of my thoughts, he holds up the shackles and pulls, muscles straining as he struggles. Metal splinters apart and into the water. He falls forward, catching himself on his hands.

I'm stunned, unsure how that's even possible.

I eye the surf. "How good of a swimmer are you?"

He looks out over the rolling sea, chest still heaving in exertion. "Guess we're about to find out."

# CHAPTER 11

My hands are shaking.

I ball them into fists then relax them, taking a deep breath. The storm passed early this morning, and it's only a matter of time before they discover our prisoner is no longer inside his cell. No body, dead or alive. And they'll begin looking.

But first, food.

Acker is thin, too thin for a sea voyage. He collapsed when we reached the south tower last night. To his credit, it was an arduous swim on a normal day. During a cyclone and not at full strength? Damn near impossible.

I said as much when we climbed onto the platform, the water shoving us onto its planks.

*"I didn't think you were going to make it."*

He didn't have the energy to open his eyes when he replied, *"Me neither."*

I debated the merits of letting him rest there, but we had a better chance of getting him to my shiel unseen during the storm while everyone had their windows and doors boarded up. He didn't complain, not once as I looped his arm around my shoulders and climbed to the tallest story of Alaha. He hit the floor of my shiel with a thud and didn't wake.

Still hasn't.

He needs food and water, and that means I have to

venture to the mess hall for lunch. It's better to keep up appearances anyway.

I do my best to appear normal, like I didn't break out the enemy prisoner from his cell last night and am now hiding him in my room. Standing in line for my meal, I'm anxious as fish stew is ladled to me by a kitchen worker. My stomach growls and I grab an apple, tucking an extra under my arm. I turn around to find an awaiting Grenadine standing behind me, and I nearly leap out of my skin.

There's a knowing grin on her face. "You look like hell."

Calming my racing heart, I step around her.

She follows. "The storm kept me up all night too," she says, unfazed by my rudeness. "I hate feeling the trees sway."

The upper stories shift the most in the wind. During cyclones, the bridges and shiels groan under the tension between them. There have been instances of lines snapping.

"You could always request to move to a lower story," I tell her.

*And away from me.*

"And leave you all alone up there?"

I pick up my pace, but she manages to keep up as I take the stairs.

"But you're not alone, are you?" she whispers, eyes gleaming.

I come to a screeching halt. "Excuse me?"

She waits for someone coming down the stairs to pass between us before leaning closer. "Your pet is the only company you prefer to keep anyway, isn't it?"

The air rushes out of me, and I resume my ascension.

"I prefer the quiet."

"That bird is anything but quiet."

She departs at the next cross section, and I sigh in relief, but it doesn't last very long.

Vibrations under my feet travel up my legs as the bridge begins to shake. Twenty or more guards march throughout the shiels, departing at every cross section along the way. Their voices carry down as they knock on doors and order people out of their homes so they can inspect inside.

I don't wait around and watch like the others. As inconspicuously as possible, I hurry up the stairs, stomach in knots as I spot guards spreading with each passing story. Barreling through my door, I freeze, almost dropping the tray of food to the floor. The blade with the J inscribed on the hilt rests against my throat.

Then, just as quickly, the blade is gone.

Acker steps out from behind me. "Oh good, you brought food."

Without apology, he scoops it from my hands. He drinks straight from the bowl, throat bobbing with every swallow. He's shirtless. Water droplets cling to his skin, hair still damp from the shower he must have taken in my absence.

He grimaces after the fourth gulp. "This is terrible."

I ignore his comment. "The guards are searching for you."

He spots the apple and shoves the bowl back into my hands, snatching the fruit instead and taking three large bites out of it in rapid succession. He raises his eyebrows as he chews, eyes casting to the far side of the room, toward the Main.

"I assumed as much."

I rush to the window and throw open the curtain. "You need to get to the roof."

His gaze turns on me. "Where did you go this morning?" His eyes are steely, accusing.

I harden my stare in return. "Why would I save your life just to turn you in?"

He stares at me a moment longer, legs closing the distance as he encroaches on my space. I hold my breath, trepidation coating my lungs—or is it fear as his height and muscle tower over me?

My heart skips a beat when he reaches for my hand, placing the blade in my palm. "Scream if you need me." Then he shoves the apple in his mouth and climbs out the window, stopping when his eyes catch on my waterskin on the table beside my bed and taking it with him.

I release the breath in my lungs. "By all means," I mutter, closing the curtains.

I shuck off my clothes as fast as I can and douse my head under the shower to wet my hair. I'm able to throw on one of my long sleep shirts in just enough time before a quick rap sounds at the door.

Kai's voice comes from the other side. "Brynn," he calls. "Are you decent?"

Steadying myself, I crack the door open a smidge. "Kai? What's going on?"

Two guards stand at his back.

Kai takes in my appearance through the gap. "Can we come in?"

"All of you?" I say, making a point to look down at my dress, practically transparent in its thinness.

"Every shiel must be inspected," says the higher-ranking guard behind him. "Future captain's match or not, there are to be no exceptions."

Kai looks regretful as he pushes the door open, forcing me back a step. I cross my arms over my chest and do my best to appear confused. The guards march around my room, overkill considering how small the space is. Kai gives me an apologetic look before turning his back to me, a shield to cover the sliver of modesty I have left.

My heart stops in my chest.

Acker's shirt is lying in a ball underneath the sink, like he was disgusted by it when he tossed it away without looking. Covered in blood and sweat stains, it's easy to identify.

I try to conceal my near nakedness and shuffle to the other side of the room. "What is it you're looking for?"

One of the guards inspects the wet drain on the floor, the other lifting the lone blanket on my bed to peer under it. He moves to the window, using a finger to flip the curtain back, head swiveling up and down before letting it fall back into place.

They turn to look at Kai, giving him a nod before departing. Kai shuts and latches the door behind them.

"The prisoner escaped," he says, eyes snagging on my hands white-knuckling the hem of my shirt. There's a pregnant pause. "Someone had to help him escape. Someone from Alaha."

He runs a hand through his hair as his eyes wander around the room. He doesn't like this turn of events. He's stressed.

I grab Kai's hand and pull him toward me. I don't have to fabricate the worry in my gaze. He cradles my face in his hands and brings his lips to mine, the kiss tender and comforting, loosening the tightness in my chest.

Kai pulls back, eyebrows scrunched together as he continues to stroke my cheeks with his thumbs. "I love you," he says, eyes holding mine.

Warmth blooms in my chest and I blink against the onslaught of moisture in my eyes. He's never said those words to me, nor I to him. Matter of fact, no one has ever said that to me, not that I can remember. I never thought about it much, but I realize they hold weight with me. They mean something.

They possibly mean everything. I can feel it in every stitch of my being that I am meant to be loved, and loved by him.

I don't trust myself to speak without my voice cracking, so I use a hand against the nape of his neck to bring his mouth down onto mine. This kiss is anything but tender, his grip on my cheeks bruising in the best way. It's heat and desire and frustration, my front pressed against his, the evidence of his arousal between us.

He tears his mouth from mine, going back in with one more longing swipe of his tongue before releasing me. He looks as pained as he is flustered. "I have to go."

I nod, feeling as if a cold bucket has been tossed over my head.

"Everyone has been instructed to stay put for the time being." He kisses me on the cheek, a safe option before opening the door. "I'll be sure to send someone with dinner later."

Then he's gone.

As soon as I have the door latched, Acker swings back into the room, landing on his feet. His dark eyes are clear and focused as he rakes them over me, nostrils flaring. He's angry.

Yeah, well, so am I.

I reach for the balled-up shirt and throw it at him, hitting him in the chest where he catches it. "You're going to get us both killed."

"He—" He stops midsentence, jaw ticking as he wrestles with the words he wants to say.

All of a sudden, I'm exhausted. Too exhausted to argue, that's for sure. I crawl onto my bed.

He says my name. Not Brynn, but the other one, the one that sounds foreign and familiar all at the same time as I lie with my cheek flat to the mattress.

He cusses. "He overdid it."

I fall asleep within seconds.

# CHAPTER 12

There's a stranger in my shiel. He's still here, very much real and present, and he's doing pushups on the floor beside the bed.

Sweat coats Acker's back, his muscles contracting with the controlled motions. He finishes his set and sits back on his knees, drawing my attention to the way his muscles pull taut with each breath. Rest and hydration have done his body well.

The past two days come into clear focus as the fog of sleep dissipates. "What time is it?"

"Early morning. The sun will be up within the hour."

I gape at him. That means I slept for…over fifteen hours.

He swigs from my waterskin and points. "There's food."

Stew and a torn-in-half bread roll sit on a tray at the foot of my bed. On cue, my stomach grumbles, and I drag the food into my lap. I shovel a spoonful into my mouth.

Tension fills the space. It's not that Acker looks particularly perturbed by yesterday's events, body on full display as he stands and leans against the wash table, but I can feel the judgment rolling off of him.

"Thanks for saving some." Impressive considering the level of hunger he's been contending with.

"We can call it even."

"Cold soup as payment for saving your life," I say, lifting a brow. "When you put it in perspective, couldn't you have at least saved the whole roll for me?"

He quirks a sardonic smile. "After hearing my captor profess his love for you? I would have rather died."

And there it is.

"I don't owe you or anyone an explanation," I say, standing to place my dishes outside my door for pickup. I notice a guard a story below, patrolling, and latch the door behind me.

He tilts his head to the side as we stand facing each other. "I saw the realization in your eyes. I know you know you're not Alaha. Does it not change anything?"

A shot of anger flushes my cheeks. "This is still my life. What is it you want me to do? Leave everything I know?"

He raises his voice, looking at me as if the choice is clear as day. "Yes!"

I shush him. "Grenadine will hear you."

He makes a face before whisper-shouting back, "Who's Grenadine?"

"My neighbor, you moron. And there are guards on patrol."

He takes a deep breath, speaking softer. "These people took you from your home, from your mother."

A headache begins to thunder behind my eyes and the room begins to spin. I fall onto my bed, placing my palms against my forehead in an effort to stifle the pounding.

He scrubs a hand along his jaw. "What do you know about the history of Alaha's exile?"

"Your people—" I stop myself, shaking my head in frustration. It takes me a moment to continue. "The

Kenta," I amend, looking up at him, "didn't want to share their resources and land anymore, so they exiled us to the sea."

"You know of Kenta, but there are many territories. Each is ruled by families who are chosen by Mother Nature, if you are to believe in such a thing, and given gifts as a reward for taking care of the land and its people."

"Gifts," I say, looking up at him. "As in…"

"Magic," he says.

I laugh, but the steely hold of his gaze stops it from fully forming. "Magic isn't real."

He cocks his head to the side, eyes roaming my room with judgment in his eyes. "How would you know?"

It's an effective argument to shut me up.

Reclining against the side of my bed, he braces an arm over a knee. "The Alaha were gifted the natural ability of influence, meant to provide comfort to the fearful or calm to the vengeful, a gift designed to prevent war and strife. But the leader of the Alaha used his gifts to benefit himself. He persuaded leaders to hand over their riches, casting their own lands into poverty, and he built armies fueled by rage against any who were able to withstand his persuasion. He conquered land after land after land."

"That's why we were shunned?"

He nods and looks over his shoulder at me. "That leader is who you know as Captain Wren."

I shake my head. "That's impossible. That would make him hundreds of years old."

"Three hundred and seventeen. The lifespan of an Heir is shortened by the distance from land, but it's normal to live well past a century or two. Someone as powerful as Wren could live for millennia."

"Heir?"

He opens his mouth only to snap it shut, teeth clenched as he shakes his head in answer. I suppose the oath somehow still clings to him a little.

Licking his lips, he takes a deep breath before trying again. "His power of influence knows no bounds. He can convince men of depraved things and women of undying love."

"And you think Wren is capable of these things?"

"Not him," he says.

Acker nods when I begin to shake my head.

"He would never do that to me," I say, adamant. "Kai doesn't even have magic."

He dips his head in answer. "He does."

"You said magic was gifted by Mother Nature, but how? She's not, like, a real entity."

"In many texts, she was once. There are stories of her passing her magic by blood to her loyal Heirs, but after she deemed her creation self-sufficient, she gave herself to the land to carry on through the generations to come."

"Other than at the Market, Kai's never been within an inch of land," I say in defense.

"When you touched the wall at the Market, he tried to compel me to let you go. His father was smart enough to smuggle a little bit of soil before he was exiled to have it on hand when his son came of age."

I reach for my boots to shove them on.

"It's the very soil he used when we created the blood oath," he continues. "Kai's power is weak, but it's there. He's been using it on you. For years, I believe."

I'm overtightening the laces of my boots with every

angry pull. "You're wrong." Standing, I push past him to get to the wash bin to brush my teeth.

He follows close behind me. "Where do you think you're going?"

"Training."

He scoffs. "You're wasting your time."

He's standing entirely too close to me, but I pretend it doesn't bother me. "And why's that?"

"Because Wren believes women have their place, and it's at his feet."

"Kai would—"

"—never do that to me."

I spit into the sink and spin to face him. "You have a lot of nerve."

"At least I have something. Better than not having a backbone."

I react without thinking, my hand poised to strike him in the face before I realize, but he catches it before I make contact.

"Let go of me!"

He shushes me. "Grenadine is right next door, remember?"

Now I'm seething. "The Matching Ceremony is in two days. It'll be the best time to commandeer a boat without anyone noticing. And then afterward, we can forget we ever met."

The grip he has on my wrist tightens as he pulls me closer. "If you think I'm going anywhere without you, you're mistaken."

Our bodies are inches apart, his scent filling my lungs. It's nothing I can put a name to but masculine in every way. Heady, almost. Something akin to a genuine smile tugs at his lips, drawing my attention to his mouth. I force myself to meet his eyes, but it kind of feels like staring at the sun.

"You're delusional if you think I'd go anywhere with you."

His eyes skim down my body, assessing. "I'll hogtie you if I have to."

I rip myself from his grasp. "Then be prepared to fight, because I'm not going down in a sinking ship."

# CHAPTER 13

"Deal me in?"

Everyone's heads swivel up at me in surprise, Messer most of all with a smile spreading across his face.

"You heard her," he says, slapping the deck of cards in front of Lawson. "Deal her in."

I've never accepted Messer or Kai's invitation to play cards on the Main before, but I'm desperate to avoid my shiel at whatever cost, even subjecting myself to the awkward looks between the players as I take a seat.

Lawson shuffles the cards. Ophelia, one of the commander's daughters we were in primary with, accepts the cards he slides across the smooth, wooden table. "Does she know how to play?"

Messer opens his mouth to reply, but I cut him off. "*She*," I say, inspecting my cards, "knows enough to get by."

"Enough to put a wager on it?" Lawson says, licking his fingers as he lifts his own cards off the table.

"I'm not wasting my coin on a game."

Messer smiles. "That's not our kind of bet."

Ophelia rolls her eyes. "They've been going back and forth on how they're going to ruin the ceremony tomorrow."

"Ruin how?" I say, narrowing my eyes at Messer's grin.

As we sit, the committee is setting up the stage to be

used for the Matching Ceremony in the evening. Blue and white streamers hang from the maypoles where a dance for fertility will take place after everyone is matched—well, the ones who are lucky enough to be chosen.

"Whatever it is you two are scheming, please don't," Willard says from the other side of the table.

"You just don't want to delay getting back to your shiel with your match," Messer says, grinning. "Who you've yet to reveal, by the way. Scared I might swoop in and steal her?"

"Yes," he says, dead serious. "You're just enough of a spiteful bitch to claim my match as your own for shits and giggles."

Messer feigns offense, a hand against his chest, falling away with a full dimpled smile. "I'm flattered you think I could steal your girl."

Ophelia, the only other girl at the table, rolls her eyes. "You have your pick and you know it. Half the girls available would die happy if you picked them."

"Sounds like you're speaking from personal experience," Messer says, turning his charm on her.

I watch as a blush overtakes Ophelia's cheeks. I've never met a girl who wasn't immediately enamored by Messer—hell, any female of any age, Grenadine included. Even the Kenta women in the Market reacted to him. If there's anyone with influence, it's Messer. I've always chalked it up to his build and dimples, but perhaps...

I've spent the last few days refusing to acknowledge the constant hum that radiates from below my breastbone. A futile endeavor since I've been made aware of its presence, but I tap into it now.

"Thank the gods Aurora isn't the jealous type," I say, eyeing him over my cards.

It's a poor attempt at flirting, but I hope I do a fair job of conveying my intent without being too obvious. His smile falters for a split second before he's able to mask it.

He matches my tone. "Should she be?"

I don't know what I'm looking for or if it's possible, but I send a net out from my magic like I did when retrieving the blade, searching for something with it, anything from Messer.

And feel nothing.

The only thing I sense is his confusion, and that's less to do with my magic and more to do with being familiar with Messer's personality.

We play late into the night. It serves as a needed distraction, and I'm surprised to discover I'm not half bad. It helps that none of them are acquainted with me enough to know when I'm bluffing or not. It's enough of an advantage that it knocks out a couple people early in the game.

The players dwindle until it's just me, Messer, and Lawson. The committee has long since dispersed after decorating for tomorrow.

Lawson throws his cards down. "You're a damn cheater, that's what you are."

Smiling, Messer slides the chips to his pile stacked before him. "How many months of kitchen duty do you think you'll get for streaking through the ceremony?"

I give Lawson a look. "More than it's worth."

"He doesn't have a choice." Messer shuffles the cards, folding them over in his hands to make them cascade into order. He lifts a brow at Lawson. "Unless you want to up the stakes."

He sighs, shaking his head before scooting his chair back. "I'm calling it a night."

"Yeah. It's probably a good idea to get a good night's rest. Might be your last for the foreseeable future."

"I suppose the brig is a better alternative than being forced to watch the matching ceremony and move into Urchin Row."

Lawson's father is a fisherman and his mother is a laundress. He's already moved ahead in class by becoming a guard, but boys outnumber the girls by two to one for the last three generations. He's ordinary in looks and social standing. A chance of a match would have come by now.

Messer and I share a pitying look.

Lawson shrugs as he stands. "Maybe I'll get lucky and score a young widower in the next couple of years so I can bed a woman before twenty-five."

Messer chokes out a laugh. "If you're still virginized by then, I'll do you a solid and suck you off myself, mate."

Lawson gives him a taunting smile. "I'll hold you to that."

We watch him walk south toward his parents' shiel on the other side of the Main. Despite his humor, there's a slouch to his shoulders as he walks past the night guards stationed out tonight. This shift is relegated to the guards without a match or children to go home to. They live a solitary life besides their brotherhood. Lawson's future, undoubtedly.

Would have been mine, too, if the day at the Market hadn't changed that.

"He's a good guy." He deserves more.

Messer nods in agreement, mouth in a firm line as he watches Lawson's retreating figure until he's out of sight. "Want to play one more round?" Messer says.

I shake my head. "I have a meeting with the dressmaker, then I'm meeting Kai." Anya has been working overtime to finish some last-minute alterations on my dress. The clock tower reads ten minutes until midnight. I need to leave now if I'm going to arrive at our scheduled time.

"Risqué. I like it."

Smiling, I push from my chair. "Thank you for letting me win."

"I don't know what you're talking about." He does a terrible job of hiding his smile. "I'll beat you next game."

We share a smile.

The rest of the shops along the Main are closed for the day, but Anya's store is lit from within when I enter. She's sewing a delicate flower design by hand on fabric draped across her table. Looking up over her spectacles, she erupts in a smile.

"I just finished," she says, laying her current work to the side to retrieve the red gown hanging behind her. "Try it on so I can get a look at you."

I take the garment from her and duck into the section cordoned off by drapery. It feels wrong to slip it on. The material is soft, but I can't help but note that it's nothing in comparison to the softness of the dresses the women wore at the Market.

Simple but rich in color was my only request to Anya. It swoops across my collarbone and stops inches from my feet, hugging my figure, but not too tightly to be considered inappropriate for a captain's wife.

Stepping out, I blush at Anya's overinflated gasp of

delight. "Gorgeous girl. Absolutely gorgeous." She leads me to stand in front of the mirror, placing her specs on top of her head to see me better. "I can tack it a little here," she says, tugging on the neckline. "Just so we don't give anyone a show."

I smile at her. "That would be great. Thank you."

She turns to grab her pincushion when the bell over the door signals someone's arrival.

It's Kai. He takes a hesitant step inside. "Pardon. May I come in?"

If Anya is surprised by the future captain's arrival, she doesn't show it. "You are going to get me in trouble, boy."

He smiles as he closes the distance. "I don't think I'm the one who's going to cause all the trouble." His eyes rake over my dress, sending another wave of heat to my cheeks.

"What are you doing here?" I ask, glancing at Anya before lowering my voice to a whisper. "I thought we were meeting later."

"I'm here to pay the tab," he says, pulling coins from his pocket. He drops them in Anya's hand, adding an extra gold with a final clink. "Could you give us a minute, Anya?"

She bites the coin and winks at him. "I can give you a few." Then she disappears behind the counter.

Kai comes closer and slides his arms around my waist. He laces his fingers under my breastbone, smiling as he meets my eyes through the full-length mirror.

"I wanted to see you in your dress before the ceremony tomorrow," he says, perusing my figure. "And I can say that I am not disappointed."

Relaxing into his hold, I lean into his embrace, letting

myself have this moment, just the two of us. "This is better than being in front of hundreds of people."

We're swaying gently, our heartbeats setting the rhythm. "Remember the time we fell asleep playing hide and seek?"

I smile. "In the pantry."

We were eleven. Messer was it, and he got bored of searching fifteen minutes in. It sent the entire grove into a panic, and it wasn't until the kitchen staff reported for dinner that our hiding spot was discovered.

"That was the day I told my mother I was going to marry you when it came time to pick a match." He loosens his grip, letting me spin in his arms.

I wrap my arms around his neck and pull him down for a kiss. It's a kiss edged with a desperation neither of us have expressed before, all heat and untapped desire. He frames my face in his hands, deepening the connection, and I'm barely able to stop the moan from slipping from my mouth.

Pulling away, Kai's eyes are smiling as he looks at me. "I couldn't have picked a better bride."

Swallowing past the surprising knot in my throat, I bring his hands to my mouth, kissing the back of his knuckles. "I am honored that you chose me."

He tugs me in for another kiss. "I'll see you tomorrow."

I nod. "Okay."

Then, as if he tries to stop himself but can't, he kisses me one last time. It leaves me breathless and wanting and nearly bursting at the seams with adoration for the man before me.

My eyes follow him out the door, smile falling away

once I'm sure he's gone. Tears sting my eyes and I fight to keep them in check as Anya comes back out, fretting over the new wrinkles in the fabric.

The realization burns like hot coals in the back of my throat the entire trek back to my shiel, the first tear slipping past my defenses when I enter my room.

Acker's gaze is careful as he takes me in. "What's wrong?" He stands from the floor, movements slow like he's scared to spook me.

I shake my head and sit on the edge of my bed to unlace my boots.

"Jovie."

Again with the other name, not Brynn.

I can't stop the tears as they overflow and drop onto the top of my shoes. Kneeling in front of me, Acker stops my jerky movements with hands over mine. This is the second time he's touched me.

I squeeze my eyes shut, and more tears escape. "What does it feel like?" I pull my hands from his, not wanting his comfort. "What does it feel like when someone uses their power on you?"

He sucks in a breath and leans back, only his knees visible as I stare at the ground. "It depends. Most powers are easy to detect because they're rooted in the physical world: water, fire, sheer brute strength. But anything relating to the psyche is more difficult. Why? What is it you think you felt?"

Placing my palm flat against the spot under my sternum, I find the courage to meet Acker's gaze. "It was screaming," I whisper.

His eyes move from where I'm holding my hand against my body to my face. "Your magic wants to protect you. It can react on instinct."

There's more to it that I can't find a voice to explain yet, the invasion of smell and taste, like Kai became condensed into a sensation of brine and softness and love.

I wipe the wetness from my face. "I need a shower."

Concern lines Acker's face, but he stands to give me space. "I'll be on the roof. Take all the time you need."

I wait until he's gone to get on my knees and dig out the tin wastebasket I keep all my old sketchbooks in from under my bed. They're labeled by age, and I sort through them until I find the one I'm looking for. I unbind the twine holding year 14 together and flip through the pages in search of the drawing, a specific drawing of Kai. Past the pages of fish and boats and trees, all of them as dull and lifeless as the ones before. I stop when I find what I seek: my first sketch of a human. Of Kai.

He'd convinced me to stay, to sit on the limb to watch the sunset while everyone else swam back to the grove. A handful of us had spent the day climbing a broken and fractured hull of a tree to the lowest limb, leaping from its height and into the ocean, thirty feet or so below.

It was a good day. I remember being happy. No... *content*.

But it all changed with one touch of his hand on mine. My stomach was in knots as we watched the sun sink lower and lower over the horizon. I was seeing him in a...*different* light. His hair and cheeks and nose and lips were something to really look at. I tried not to stare but failed. He caught me sneaking glances and didn't bother hiding the smile tugging at his lips.

And he kissed me. Just at the corner of my mouth, as chaste as a kiss can be.

All my drawings prior to this were of nature or random objects, but never of people, too intimidated by the emotion and proportions human faces carry, but after that day, I was determined to figure it out.

My strokes were too heavy and lifeless, the brows too large and eyes too small. I run my fingers over the terrible drawing, hating my tears as they fall onto the image, smearing the charcoal.

For the first time since I was seven, I cry and cry and cry.

# CHAPTER 14

Head propped against his spare arm, Acker's eyes are trained on the twirling blade balanced on his middle finger as he lies on the ground beside my bed. It defies logic, watching the blade spin upright, its point somehow not digging into the pad of his finger.

He was there when I awoke hours ago, and we've been lying in the quiet ever since, him doing magic tricks with the weapon and me going through my old sketchbooks. Most of them are terrible, but a few catch me by surprise.

Not this one though. I tried to draw a replica of an animal from one of our textbooks, and I think I added one too many legs.

I slap the notebook shut and turn my attention to Acker. "What is your power, exactly?"

He looks up at me, the blade remaining atop his finger. "I'm what they call an elemental. I'm able to wield anything with metals. Iron, steel, brass." He tosses the blade and catches it in his palm, holding it out for me to take.

I reach for it and run a thumb over the point, nicking myself. A wry smile pulls at his lips.

Sucking the blood from the pad of my thumb, I give him a look. He's done well not being a snarky asshole all morning. No need to ruin it now. His growing smile seems to reflect my internal musings.

"Tell me." I run a finger over the initial inscribed on the hilt. I dare a look at him, gaining courage from the openness in his eyes. "Tell me everything you can."

He nods once, turning his attention to the ceiling. "Your family was visiting Kenta when you went missing. You weren't in your bed when your mom went to wake you, and after scouring the coast and surrounding woods, they suspected you ventured into the ocean on your own." A pinch of worry creases between his brows.

"You were there," I say, realizing he's recounting his own memories.

"I was," he says, glancing at me. "I was tasked with finding water elementals in town to help search the sea. The few we found worked together to push the tide back, searching for your body."

Foolish hope swirls inside me. "My parents?" I inquire, unable to finish the question.

The worry smooths into a tender sort of joy in his gaze. "Your mother is alive."

Something between a hiccup and a gasp escapes my mouth, and I hurry to cover it with my palm.

"She took your absence the hardest. There've been whispers and sightings of you over the years, rumors about neighboring lands taking you. She sent sentry after sentry to hunt down any information they could find, but they never came up with anything substantial. Your father thought a funeral would help her come to terms with your disappearance, but she never gave up hope. I'm currently unsure of your father's whereabouts."

There's sorrow in his gaze. It's strange to look into his eyes and see pain reflected back at me.

"We were close," I say in understanding.

He nods.

"*We* were close," I clarify further.

He nods again.

"Friends even?"

A small smile overtakes his lips. "If you can believe it."

I shake my head. "I can't."

He chuckles, eyes crinkling at the corners.

"Is that how you recognized me at the Market?"

He tilts his head to the side to look at me. "It was your blade."

I've been curious as to why he had it strapped to his person that day in the Market but haven't had the guts to inquire about it.

"It calls to you as you do to it."

I turn it in my fingers, looking at the cracks and divots with new eyes. "Is it magic?"

Grinning, he sits up, placing his back to the bed. "You made that blade with your father's help," he says. "He wanted you to be comfortable with a weapon early, and it's seen as a rite of passage for children to forge their first blade by hand, so they have an appreciation for the skill and effort it takes to make them."

I try to conjure an image of my father, but nothing emerges from the recesses of my mind.

"Whenever a weapon is handmade from the hearthstone of the land, it is magicked to belong to you. Axes or swords or even a battering ram—whatever it is will always answer the call of the person who made it. It's why most blacksmiths are blood-oathed. Only the most righteous are trusted to forge for others."

"Where's yours?"

"Sitting in pieces on my mantle at home, if I recall

correctly. Splintered in half on a walnut not long after my eleventh birthday." He holds out his palm, pointing to the scar between his thumb and forefinger.

"How did you end up with mine?"

"Your mother gave it to me when I joined the army, to have during my travels. It hummed when I saw you in the Market." His eyes hold mine, searching for something in the depths that I'm unable to see. "I looked for you. In every market and podunk town, in every corner of every land, I searched each face for yours."

I'm without breath. Without words, really. Overcome with an unnamed emotion, I bite my tongue out of fear of saying anything at all.

He swallows and lets his eyes fall to the floor, but I get the sense it's more out of reprieve for me than it is for him. "And I had quit looking. I had convinced myself you were dead as the years went by, and I wore the blade in honor of your memory, having long since lost its original purpose. That's why I couldn't believe it was you when the blade signaled your presence. Even when I saw you with my own eyes, like a ghost in broad daylight, I refused to believe it. Because…" He trails off, looking up at me. "Because it meant I gave up on you."

His shame is palpable. It sends a sharp pain through my chest. For the friend I didn't get a chance to grow older with or for having no way to appease his guilt, I'm not sure.

I quickly remind myself that he's still Kenta, still a soldier of a ruler who exiled an entire population of people just because of one person's deeds—assuming everything Acker has told me is true.

I hand the blade back to him, both to give him something to alleviate his shameful thoughts and simply because I like watching him play with it. "So," I say, balancing my chin on my hand. "What's my title?"

He lifts a brow. "Thinking a little highly of yourself, are you?"

I roll my eyes. "The Alaha wouldn't breach enemy lines to steal a child of a commoner."

He smiles, all teeth and pretentiousness. "You are Princess Jovie of the Maile."

I laugh. "No, really. What am I?"

He doesn't blink. "The Maile have been ruled by your family for the last century. Longer than the Kenta, even."

My smile falls away when he doesn't smile back. "You're serious."

"Deadly," he answers.

I flop back on the bed, at a loss for words. Maile. *Maylee.* Not Alaha or Kenta, but Maile—and a princess at that.

"I don't understand. Why would Wren kidnap me? For what?"

"It started a war. There was a lot of finger-pointing, many accusations thrown around. It's probably exactly what Wren was aiming for, to cause infighting between the remaining territories in hopes that he could pick off the weakest and commandeer the land."

"Well, it obviously didn't work."

Morning light filters in through the curtain of the window, casting streaks of golden light across his shoulders and hair, highlighting the russet in his eyes. They shine up at me.

"I'm starting to wonder if it's more sinister than that."

I roll onto my side and face him. "What do you

mean?"

"You know Alaha's version of a match," he says, eyeing me. "But a true match isn't chosen—it's gifted. Just like your magic." Acker's gaze flickers as he considers his next words. "They're rare, a bond like no other. If Kai was able to convince you that you are truly his match, he could claim half your territory."

I don't understand. "But I would have found out once we were on land."

"You're greatly underestimating Kai's powers. What you've been exposed to here is a fraction of what it would be at full power on land." He makes a face like he already regrets what he's about to reveal. "And his magic already mimics the same characteristics of couples who are matched. It becomes more potent through physical connection," he says, voice tense. "Touching, skin to skin. Or, as you probably know, mouth to mouth."

I stop him from continuing. "I got it."

"By the time you would even be made aware of who you are and what they've done, you wouldn't care. The person you are would cease to exist outside of what Kai influences you to think or feel."

Doubt lingers in the back of my mind. The idea that someone—me—can lose all sense of self, all sense of free will by someone else's hand, magical abilities or not...

Acker stands abruptly. "Someone's coming."

"It's probably the breakfast Kai is having delivered."

He's unmoving, head tilted as if he's listening, for what I'm not sure considering he's attempting to hear through walls.

"Wha—"

He reaches for the blade and shoves the hilt in my

hand, motioning for me to be quiet with a finger over his lips before pointing at the ceiling. A knock sounds at the door. I glance in its direction then back toward Acker, but he's already disappearing through the window. I shove the blade into the back of my pants and cover it with my shirt.

Taking a deep breath, I unlatch the door and open it. "Faline," I say, unable to hide my shock.

"Good morning," she says, beaming. "I wanted to bring your dress." She lifts the arm the fabric is draped over. "Can I come in?"

A guard stands behind her, looking bored. "Sure," I say, fully aware I can't deny her entry.

Her dress flows around her ankles as she breezes past me, hair in intricate plaits with flowers woven throughout. She takes in my small abode, eyes lingering on my bed, the wash bin, and the toilet in the corner. I would have once been humiliated in the face of her perusal, but I keep my chin held high when she finally meets my stare.

"Today's the big day," she says, masking her acuity. "How are you feeling?"

I blow out a breath. "Sick to my stomach."

She smiles with the epitome of understanding and kindness. "That's normal. Kai misplaced his sword twice this morning."

There's a beat of awkwardness when I don't reply. The mention of Kai reminds me of the open wound beating inside my chest.

"There's no need to be nervous. The day will go by fast. Before you realize it, you two will be together by sundown."

I nod. This is awkward on so many levels.

"Anyway," she says, placing the gown on the bed. She tugs and pinches at the fabric to avoid wrinkling. "I also wanted a moment to speak with you."

We sit on the edge of my bed with the dress between us. She tucks a hair that isn't there behind her ear, and I realize she's the one who's nervous.

"I don't know if you remember when your parents died, but there was a time you came and lived with the captain and me."

I nod, a slow dip of my head. "I remember."

"You were inconsolable. Day and night, I held you in my arms as you cried, trying and failing to give you some semblance of comfort. That was...until Kai took a liking to you." A soft smile pulls at her lips. "We'd kept you apart, not wanting to overwhelm you. Kai was a bit of a hellion at that age, but he managed to escape his father's eye and came into our room one night when I was attempting to rock you to sleep. He saw you and somehow knew to be gentle as he creeped closer to get a look. You locked eyes with each other, and it was the first time you quit crying in weeks." Tears form in her eyes. "From that point on, you two were inseparable."

I swallow past the lump in my throat.

She dabs under her eyes with a finger. "I'm going to be a sobbing mess today, aren't I?"

Reaching over, I place a hand over hers. "Thank you." I'm not sure what I'm thanking her for, but it feels appropriate at the moment.

She squeezes my hand between hers. "I should let you get ready for the ceremony."

I've stood to escort her out when an idea occurs to me. "Before you go," I say, holding the door open. "Can I ask you a favor?"

She's taken aback but smiles. "Of course."

"It's a little embarrassing, but it's customary to give your match a gift after the ceremony. And, well, I haven't received my official pay as a guard yet—"

"Say no more," she says, cutting me off. Digging into the coin purse hanging from her hip, she deposits a handful of mixed coins. I manage not to gawk at the number of gold and silver in the mix, and she winks at me before walking away.

In the time it takes me to shut and latch the door, Acker is back in my room. He eyes the dress on my bed, gaze swinging to me. It really is a pretty dress, the nicest I've ever owned. I suppose that's what I could have been thanking Faline for.

I toss it on the floor. "We'll wait for the Matching Ceremony, then we'll sneak away in one of the fishing boats. It's the only time it won't be guarded."

Acker smiles, but it's straight filth when he says, "Shame. I was kind of looking forward to tying you up."

# CHAPTER 15

I wait for as long as I can, but the bird never comes. He's been scarce since Acker's arrival, but I leave a bowl of dried cheese and nuts anyway. It won't last more than a meal, but it's all I have to offer as goodbye. I climb back through my window and into my room for the last time.

Acker finishes refilling the waterskin, eyeing me as he stuffs it into my bag. Music drifts in on the wind, signaling the beginning of the ceremony.

Acker asks, "Now?"

I nod. But first...

I pull the first sketchbook from the stack by the bed and open it to the page I bookmarked earlier. It's the one numbered for age eleven, when I first began to keep my journals, and I lay it open on the mattress.

Then the next bookmarked journal, age twelve.

And thirteen.

I repeat the process until there's a blanket of drawings across the surface of my bed, all of the same image, the last being from this morning. Rolling hills of grass as far as the eye can see. The same hills and waist-high weeds I've dreamt of my entire life as an answer to why I left and where I'm going.

*Home.*

I feel more than see Acker's deep intake of breath.

Taking in one last look at the place I've found solace in most of my life, I open the door. The crossways are empty, but the sounds of congregating voices and instruments float up from below. It's dusk and the lanterns are alight along the way. A strong breeze whips errant strands of hair from my braid.

"Stay behind me," I instruct.

Not that there's any way to hide Acker's stature. He's at complete odds with the traditional Alaha features, dark hair instead of light, brown eyes instead of gray. The Kenta clothes he scrubbed and dried to a semblance of cleanliness don't help either.

We've taken all of two steps past Grenadine's when her raspy, ancient voice stops us dead in our tracks. "Where are you sneaking off to?" She's leaning against her open door, an all-knowing and delighted smile on her wrinkled lips.

I do my best to appear unfazed by her appearance, avoiding her question. "Why aren't you at the Matching Ceremony?"

"Eh." She waves a hand. "There's no good food this year, so what's the point?" Her eyes go to Acker then come back to me. "He's very handsome. I'd jump ship, too, if someone who looked like him took a liking to me."

Wary of saying anything to piss her off, I don't correct her, biting my tongue. Instead, I reach into my pocket and retrieve one of the smaller coins, then two more, and hold them out to her.

Her smile grows, stained teeth showing. "You've always known how to speak to my heart." She takes the three gold coins and winks at me. "I'm looking forward to a good night's sleep without you two bickering nonstop." And with that, she shuts the door in our faces.

Acker lifts a brow at me. "I told you to yell at me

quieter."

We continue to the cross section, and I go first, hanging and dropping down onto the crosswalk of the story below. Acker follows close behind. We make it to the next story before we come across a group of people who are running late to the ceremony, and we lie on our stomachs so they don't see us when they pass below.

The sounds of the party are in full swing by the time we reach the third story. We're officially on borrowed time.

"We'll jump from here."

He eyes the choppy water below, probably remembering the swim through the swells of the storm during his escape.

"We'll climb onto the underbelly of the Main until we're closer." I motion for him to hand over the pack, which I secure around my waist. "Keep your legs and arms in line with your body. And point your toes."

He doesn't voice any trepidation if he has any, nodding in response to my instructions. I jump first and tread water when he leaps, a perfect student as he disappears into the water before reappearing again. We swim for the ladder and pull ourselves onto the cross beams below the Main.

The first time I crossed the underside of the Main, it took me hours, but I've figured out a method to step across the barnacles and moss-covered beams. We zigzag toward the boats, quiet as we concentrate on our steps.

"We're almost there," I tell him.

The wharf comes into view, the dock in the dead center of the Main and directly below the ceremony. I stop Acker with a hand and signal it's time to jump. The music and chatter cover the sound of our bodies hitting the water. Acker pulls himself onto the dock first, arm outstretched to lift me out. He's the first to leap onto the nearest fishing boat.

Untying my pack, I throw it to him and bend down to undo the dock line, hands shaking. The sound of lumbering feet and music is almost loud enough to block out the pounding of my heart.

I'm busy looking down when Acker calls my name—a warning I'm not able to heed quickly enough. Then hands are on me, the sharp edge of a sword at my neck.

Acker lifts his arms in surrender. "Easy," he says, eyes locked on the mammoth of a man behind me.

"Don't move." Chills skate down my spine at the realization that I'm in Dupre's hands. He instructs someone out of my view to go get Kai. "Onto the dock," he orders Acker.

Acker follows the instructions, hands remaining high for everyone to see, stepping over the side of the hull and onto the dock. Dupre takes a step back, forcing me onto my tiptoes to avoid the blade.

Acker's eyes focus on my exposed throat. "Easy," he repeats, a deeper warning in his tone.

Kai steps into view. "Or what?" Two guards follow along with him. He looks me over, disappointment and resignation in his gaze, tilting a chin at Dupre. "At ease."

Dupre lowers the sword, and I suck in a deep breath of relief.

It doesn't last long.

I can *hear* the power of his gift lacing the words when he says, "On your knees."

Acker lowers himself to one knee then the other, eyes raging against his calm movements. It's the first time

I've seen Kai use his gift on anyone, and a newfound fear takes root inside me.

The two guards close in, placing shackles around Acker's wrists. All the while, his stare doesn't leave Kai, rage simmering under the surface.

With Acker momentarily taken care of, Kai runs his hands through his hair, stopping with his hands on his hips as he turns his attention toward me. Sorrow and anger flit across his face, like he's torn between the two. "Everything I've done to protect you."

"Protect me?" I choke out. "You're who I need protecting from."

He shakes his head. "You have no idea."

I all but snarl at him. "Enlighten me then."

His voice comes out low and cold, eyes despondent. "It was me or my father."

Stunned by his words, I stumble back into Dupre. Kai reaches out to help steady me, but I jerk away from his touch.

Irritation sparks in his eyes. "I could sense your magic reacting to mine in the dress shop."

"Why didn't you stop me then?"

"Because I was hoping I was wrong." He throws a hand up in defeat. "I never wanted you to find out like this."

I sneer. "Let's not pretend you ever had any intention of telling me."

"I did," he argues. "I didn't know when or how, but I knew a day would come when I'd have to be honest with you."

"Yet here we are."

He reaches for me again, stopping short when I tense. "Brynn," he pleads.

There's a long moment as I swallow past the sorrow in my throat, the urge to cry forcing me to keep my mouth shut.

When I don't respond, he says my name again. "Brynn."

"That's not her name."

All heads swivel to Acker, whose words were spoken with an eerie calmness. It's unsettling enough to give the men pause. But Acker's attention doesn't deviate from Kai, gaze hard and unyielding despite the compromised position he's in.

"You have no power here."

Acker smirks, arrogance growing. "I have more than you."

Kai doesn't take the bait, turning his back in dismissal, but there's a noticeable unease behind his eyes when he sets his sights back on me. "I only ever fed emotions back to you, emotions you were already feeling."

I shake my head. "Nothing you say can justify manipulating me for your own gain."

Kai's face becomes hardened, anger tinting his cheeks with indignation. "Why do you think I never bedded you?"

Humiliation burns through my veins, tingeing the unshed liquid in my eyes and the heat in my ears. I know at this moment he's no longer my friend, but it feels like a low blow. Too low.

"I wanted it to be your choice, without the influence of my magic. I wanted you..." He trails off, almost as if he doesn't want to admit what he's about to say. "I wanted you to love me when you gave yourself to me."

I don't need my magic to know he's being honest.

"That's the thing, Kai," I say, voice quiet for just him to hear. "I did love you. You were my best friend and you *betrayed* me."

It takes a few heartbeats, but his reaction morphs from agony to resignation. "I have a plan in motion, but I can't let you leave." Holding my gaze, Kai keeps his back to Acker when he says to the two guards, "Kill him."

I reach for Kai, but my legs are kicked out from behind me, and I land on my knees. One of the guards grabs Acker's hair, angling his head back to expose his throat while the other pulls a sword from his belt.

Acker's gaze slides to me, eyes hooded, neck tight from the unnatural angle his head is forced into. There's a breath of time where he holds my stare, almost as if he's wanting to convey something to me, something like…regret, maybe?

Then he moves.

Swinging the chains from his shackles over his head, he catches the guard behind him by the neck, twisting the metal into a strangulation device. He finishes him off within moments. The other guard lunges for him but stops mid-attack. The sword that was in his hand is now in Acker's, and he plunges it deep into the guard's chest. Stunned, the guard stumbles back, gargling on the blood filling his lungs.

Dupre regrips the sword against my neck as Acker's attention turns in my direction.

"You won't kill her." He's not the slightest bit winded as he stalks forward.

Kai unsheathes the sword on his hip. Acker has the audacity to smirk, not missing a beat as he kicks off a dock post, bringing down a fist right into Kai's face. The fight is over before it starts. Kai falls to the dock with a heavy thud.

Dupre pushes the blade to urge me into standing, using me as a last line of defense against Acker.

Picking up Kai's fallen sword, Acker tests its weight, inspecting the weapon in his hands. "Let the girl go and I'll consider not killing you."

I've heard less than five sentences from Wren's most trusted guard, but this is the first time I've heard him cuss. "Go fuck yourself."

Acker looks up from the blade. "I'm starting to think the Alaha are all inbred. It's the only explanation for your level of stupidity."

There's a surprising shake in Dupre's hands, and I hiss against the sting of the blade.

Acker goes stock-still, losing every stitch of humor.

"I'm not scared of you—"

In one singular motion, Acker spins and launches the sword like a javelin. I squeal, squeezing my eyes shut as the weapon hurtles toward me. The sound of metal cutting through flesh and bone reverberates in my ear. Blood sprays over the top of my head. The sword at my neck slowly slides away as Dupre's large body falls to the dock with a loud thump.

Acker grabs me by the shoulders. "Are you okay?"

I squint up at him. "Yeah."

Wiping the blood dripping into my face away with a palm, he rubs it against the leg of his pants. "I'm sorry."

I let out a deep breath, trying and failing to stop the shake in my hands. "We'll call it even."

He sputters on a choked laugh, a smile pulling at the side of his mouth...but then it's gone, deflecting the incoming blade in the nick of time. It misses the intended mark, but Kai's still able to bury the blade halfway into Acker's side before ripping it free.

Blood blooms from the spot.

Kai jabs the blade again, but Acker stops it with embarrassing ease. He uses his other hand to grab Kai by the throat, an eerie calm settling over him as he takes the blade and points it at the hollow of Kai's throat.

"Don't kill him."

Kai's gaze swings to me, but I'm not looking at him.

I place a hand on Acker's shoulder. "Acker." It's the first time I've called him by his name, and he's slow to turn his head toward me, eyes void of any emotion when he meets my gaze. I swallow against my fear, knowing this is a big ask considering Kai just tried to kill him. "Please," I beg.

Taking in a deep breath, his eyes come back to life a little at a time before he pulls the sharp point away from Kai's neck. Kai's relief is short-lived when Acker jerks him close, wrapping his forearm around Kai's neck and cutting off his air. Kai fights, but Acker maintains his hold until Kai's face turns a nasty shade of red, then white, before his eyes fall closed. Acker drops Kai, letting his body hit the dock.

"Thank you," I tell him, but he isn't interested in my gratitude. He inspects Kai's dagger before lifting his shirt to pocket it in his waistband. I only get a glimpse of the fresh cut in his side before he covers it.

My heart finally slows to where the sound of music registers in my ears again. It seems the same happens for Acker because we both burst into motion.

I finish untying the boat from the dock and Acker retrieves the paddles, handing me one as we push off from the dock. A flurry of motion catches my eye, and I spot the guard with chains around his neck stumbling to his feet.

"I thought you killed him," I say to Acker, getting his attention.

The guard shoots us a murderous glare as he turns to the stairs leading to the Main. Standing, Acker slides the dagger into his hand. He adjusts his grip on the weapon then slings the dagger toward the guard. There's a discernible zip as it cuts through the air, followed by an abrupt smacking sound when it slices into the back of the guard's head.

Teetering on a middle step, he spins in place, giving us a view of the weapon that's projecting from an eye socket. He wobbles into a complete turn before falling down the remaining flight of stairs, landing face down.

Acker clicks his tongue against his teeth, stretching out his arm. "Aim is off."

I watch in astonished horror as the dagger dislodges itself from the dead guard and flies back toward Acker. He grunts when it smacks into his palm, as if the retrieval taxed him, and wipes the weapon on his pant leg.

Neither of us speak as we each grab our oars and begin to row the boat out from under the grove. The light of the Main highlights the surrounding water, and we work overtime to move into the shadows.

Music follows us for miles and miles as we row into the night.

# CHAPTER 16

A clatter jerks me out of my mindless rowing. Acker's oar hits the deck a split second before he wretches over the side of the hull. I move toward him, but my legs give out, so I crawl across the deck to my bag and to retrieve my waterskin.

I hold the skin to his lips. "Drink."

He's pale and drenched in sweat, eyes closed as his head lolls against the side of the boat. He groans but manages to tip his head back to take a few swallows.

"Let me see your side."

He groans again when he moves to give me access. His shirt is soaked with blood and sweat as I lift it. The gash is wet, bright red seeping over the dried blood around it.

"I need to clean it. Don't move."

He manages to speak. "Wasn't going anywhere."

I get my feet underneath me and to the hatch where the medicine kit is kept in case of emergencies. While gathering the clean dressings and a tin of salve, I'm grateful to find an extra skin of water someone must have left from their last excursion.

I bring everything to Acker and settle on my knees at his side. "This is going to hurt," I tell him, uncapping the water.

"Wait." He tries to sit up, and blood gushes from the wound—more blood than he can afford to lose.

"Woah, I told you not to move." I place a hand on his

shoulder to stop him.

"You," he says, eyes cracking open to look at me as he reaches for the water in my hand. "You drink."

"After I clean your wound."

He attempts to sit up again, abdominals clenching from the effort.

"Okay, okay." I maintain a firm hand on him to ensure he doesn't move while I bring the water to my mouth with the other. My lips are cracked and water dribbles out of my mouth, but I find myself taking large gulps when I mean to take only a few sips.

Acker finds a way to look smug even when he's half dying from blood loss. I don't bother warning him when I tip the rest of the contents on the cut.

*Dang rabbits.*

Upon opening the salve, I discover it's empty but for a smidge coated along the rim. I gather as much as I can and pack it into the open wound. He sucks in a hiss of breath, but the little bit of medicine seems to do the trick to staunch the blood flow. I make him drink the rest of the water from the second skin while I wait for the wound to clot.

"We need to wrap it," I tell him.

He's able to keep his eyes open for longer than a few seconds. "I'll heal much faster on land." Every word out of his mouth is coarse around the edges.

"It's going to be a while before we see land."

We are well and truly off course and fucked. We had to abandon our flee north. They sent all of Alaha's armada after us. White sails littered the water in our wake, so we had to make an abrupt turn west, a direction to nowhere. We rowed and rowed and rowed. When we were unable to row anymore, we rowed some more, unable to raise the sails out of fear we'd be too visible, too easily spotted against the dark water.

"My people have been waiting, keeping their ships moored out of sight," he says. "If we're lucky, we might run into them."

I don't voice my doubts. We went west because it's the least likely of paths we would have taken, and it's the least likely place anyone will look for us, whether Alaha or Kenta.

I place the gauze against the wound, using my other to bring it around his waist. My nose is inches away from his upper stomach as I pull it behind his back to tie the bandage, ignoring his gritted teeth when I tighten it and tie it off.

I look up at him. "It had to be done."

He tries and loses the battle to remain focused on me. I help him lie on the dock, and he passes out in an instant. The sky is gray, the rising sun within an hour of cresting, and when I push to stand, my knees shake. Hell, *I* might pass out.

It takes all my remaining strength to get the head sail off the front mast. I stretch the oars across the width of the hull and drape the sail over it, creating a makeshift canopy for shade. There's just enough room for me to lie on my side next to him, and I allow the exhaustion to win.

# CHAPTER 17

The sound of low, rolling thunder pulls me awake. The boat rocks on the ocean, Acker asleep next to me. I check his breathing with a palm on his chest and am relieved to see more color in his cheeks.

I climb out from under the sail and spot black clouds hovering in the distance. The weathervane atop the mast stutters, but the wind is steady. It's far enough away to not be a threat. It's difficult to figure out how far we've drifted off course with clouds blocking the stars in the darkening sky.

The boat is meant to be manned by two, but it's possible with one if they're experienced enough. Given the lessons we had as guards at thirteen, I'm not an expert, but I've helped and watched Messer and Kai fish plenty to get by.

I ransack the fishing supplies. There are poles and lines and a variety of tackles for attracting different kinds of fish, bobbers and hooks and weights, but we're really in need of a system to catch drinking water.

Finding what I'm after, I use my blade to cut an individual fiber from the fishing net and unbraid it from the woven pattern. Once I get a long, single strand, I tie it around the mast and stretch it to one of the livewells in the hull. Rain will hit the mast, then the line, and follow it down into the well—a basin for drinking water.

Lightning cracks overhead and it must wake Acker up, because a loud thump sounds, followed by a colorful array of curse words.

I pull back the makeshift shade cover. "Good morning, sunshine."

He leans on an elbow, squinting up at me before taking in the sky and the sea around us. "How long have I been out?"

I shrug. "Your guess is as good as mine. I woke up not long ago."

"You've been busy," he says, noticing the supplies I've dragged out.

I step down from the side of the hull and kneel beside him. "How do you feel?"

Without me having to ask, he lifts his stained shirt to reveal his dressing. I prod it a little, satisfied by how well it slowed the blood flow. Thunder claps on the horizon.

"How worried should we be about that," he says, eyes on the monstrosity of a storm miles away.

"Not very," I tell him, pulling his shirt back down. "But we should use the outer winds to our advantage. We've been drifting for a while." A very long while.

He sits up before wobbling into a stance. "Tell me what to do." He's either masking it very well, or the salve is working miracles, because there's not a trace of pain on his face. I'm suspicious, but I can't put the mast back up without his help.

Working together, we roll the sail back into position. I demonstrate how to tie it back to the bow, then to the mast, knowing we'll be repeating this job often. With a lot of tugging and pulling and cursing on both of our parts, we're able to get the jib in place, then I climb the mast to hoist the canvas into place. The weathervane begins to spin as the storm shifts positions.

"That's good," I tell Acker, handing him the halyard for the main sail. "Pull this while I steer."

Sitting with my back to the stern, I keep a hand on the tiller as Acker heaves the rope, pulling the mainsail up with each downward motion. Then we're moving, cutting through the water as the sail balloons.

I point to the standing end, a handle on the deck. "Tie the rope there."

He repeats the knot I taught him, and I smile, impressed by how quick he's picked up on it.

"Get down. I'm going to swing the boom."

Acker sits on the opposite side of the cockpit, facing me, legs wedged against mine.

I shift the rudder, and the boom swings to the side, sending the boat into a heel. Water kisses the top of the side of the boat as we turn. I keep my eye on the compass and the sails, finding the perfect combination of wind and direction. With the bow turned northeast, the boat loses some of its pitch, and we're cruising at a decent speed.

I did it.

Closing my eyes, I allow myself to bask in the wind. I'm doing it. I'm going to get to put my feet on solid ground. At least, if we make it. There've been deserters before, and there's no telling if they ever saw land. Kenta is a long way to travel in a small fishing boat, but it's the best we have.

When I open my eyes, Acker is staring at me.

"What?" The word escapes my mouth like a barb more than a question.

A small smile flares across his face, gone as quick as it appeared. "I'm impressed. That's all."

I'm ashamed of the blush trying to flood my cheeks. The solitude of the boat and the vast sea make it all the more difficult to withstand the intensity of his attention. "So easily fooled, are you?"

He scrunches his nose, playfulness in his expression. "I heard the guards talking about Kai's match being surprisingly good with a sword."

I cringe. "Don't be so sure about that. I'm nothing compared to you."

"Is that a compliment?"

"No."

He laughs.

After a moment, I say, "If you could fight like that all along, why didn't you just...escape?"

He shifts his head from side to side. "I could have, but I needed to get an idea of how ingratiated you were, how deep Kai's hold went. And I needed you to trust me."

It's presumptuous of him to assume I trust him now, but he's got a fair point. I got in this boat with him despite watching him take down four grown men by himself. I'm either stupid or desperate. Maybe a little of both.

"You fight like you've been to battle."

My assertion causes a shift in his demeanor. It's slight, almost unnoticeable, but definitely there just behind the eyes. "I joined the army when I turned thirteen, and I saw battle that very same year."

The image of a young, wiry boy with dark hair fighting against grown men makes my stomach turn. Only desperation teaches soldiers how to kill with that type of savagery. There was no hesitation when he killed the Alaha guards, and there was no humanity in his eyes when he was about to kill Kai.

"Why? Were they so desperate for warm bodies that they'd sacrifice their youngest?"

He doesn't react to my blatant distaste for sending children to war. "The Kenta you saw at the Market weren't an honest portrayal of how our people have fared. We've been in and out of conflict with a neighboring territory for decades. It's not uncommon for kids to join the service young, to begin training in adolescence. My friend joined, so I went as well."

I struggle to contain my disdain. "According to your logic, all war and conflict should have ended when you exiled Wren."

A flicker of anger surfaces in his eyes. "It did. For a hundred years, we lived in peace. It wasn't until your abduction that it fell apart."

My voice is laced with sarcasm when I reply. "Oh, well, in that case, my apologies for getting myself kidnapped."

"Are you always this difficult?" he asks.

"Only when I abandon everything and everyone I know to venture to a new land that is riddled with conflict and I'm stuck on a boat with you, it seems."

There's a tick in his jaw as he looks out over the water, gaze pensive. "Osiris, the leader of Roison, admitted to taking you, and your mother killed him."

But, as we now both know, he did not.

"I haven't figured out why he would have confessed to something he didn't do," he says, "knowing the outcome would mean his death. When his brother, Chryse, seized the throne, he reignited the call for a revolution, having been a sympathizer of Wren's from the war."

There's a period of time where there's nothing but the sound of the waves beneath the boat and the catch of the sails between us. We spend the majority of the day in our own thoughts, in our own tiny space on our respective sides of the hull.

When a rogue wave causes the boat to dip, he winces in pain. I tie off the tiller so the rudder remains in position and gather the bandage supplies, folding myself into the space next to him. He lifts his shirt without question. His side is coated in sticky blood, a mixture between old and new.

"Why didn't you say anything?" I attempt to pull away the gauze, and he sucks air in through his teeth.

"Oh, I have no idea," he says, voice laced with pain and sarcasm.

I smile. I can't help it.

I reach for my blade, and he goes still as I maneuver the tip underneath the bandage, pulling with a swift motion to cut the fabric away from his body. Fresh blood drips from the wound.

"It needs sutures."

He nods, like he already suspected as much.

I retrieve what I'll need from the fishing supplies: a line and a hook, more salve. I begin to shut the hatch when a dark bottle rolls out from under the hull, knocking against the wood. Smiling, I hold it in the air as I look at him. "Look what I found."

He holds out his hand for me to give it to him. He uncorks it and brings it to his nose, making a face of abject horror. "Are you trying to kill me?"

"Mead is considered to be contraband in Alaha, so there's no telling how long it's been hidden in there."

He takes one last sniff before taking a swig, face contorting as he swallows. Then he lifts the shirt clean from his body and pours the liquid right over his stab wound. He groans through his teeth, veins popping out of his neck and chest as he waits for the burning to pass, releasing a sharp breath when it does.

He lies flat on his back, looking up at me as I cut the excess line off the hook with my blade. "Do your worst."

My eyes pause on a scar in the shape of a V below his ribcage. I focus my attention to the wound and bring the hook down to the top of the gash. "I'll see what I can manage."

He huffs out a small laugh, but it's cut short when the tip of the hook sinks into his flesh. His stomach goes taut as I press hard enough to get the hook back through the other side.

"One down."

He releases a breath and says, "Tell me about your childhood." I can feel more than see his eyes on me as I tie the line into a knot, readying another stitch.

"What do you want to know?"

"What was it like?"

Realizing he needs a distraction, I tell him. I describe living with the captain and Faline for the first few years. They treated me the same as Kai, the same schooling, the same chores. We spent summers swimming and fishing and playing hide and seek across the entire grove. Then I tell him about the trouble we got into, the stealing and pranks and overall havoc we caused as preteens to the point that we had to be separated.

I was given my own shiel, located at the top of the grove with the other parentless and unmatched individuals. It did a number on me at first. No one my age wanted to be seen hanging with the kid who lived on Urchin Row.

It was lonely, but I grew accustomed to the solitude.

Once I was old enough to enter the bid to become a guard, it gave me a sense of purpose. I lived to train and formed friendships with Messer and Aurora. Or, looking back, I realize I became friends with Messer, and Aurora tolerated me. Which shouldn't be discounted, because Aurora tolerates no one.

Tying the last stitch, I look up at Acker. He inspects my work and must deem it satisfactory, because he sits up to give me better access to dress it. After I'm done, he places his hand over mine, stopping me from pulling away.

He doesn't remove his hand. "I spent years hoping you died that day. The alternative only left space for me to imagine the worst things happening to you. I'm glad you have good memories there, even if I wish they would have been at home instead." There seems to be more he wants to say, but he releases me.

"My childhood wasn't perfect, but I've known peace living in Alaha." It's more than he can say for himself. There's something that's been bothering me though. "Why did you make me put my hand on the stone wall?"

"I knew if Alaha kept you this entire time, you missed your awakening."

"What do you mean *awakening*?"

"When someone comes into their magic. I knew the only way I could be sure it was you was to get you to touch the land."

"You knew it would hurt."

"Yes," he says, apologetic. "That's why I followed you. I told myself it wasn't possible. It would have been stupid of Wren to allow you back if he was the one who took you, but I couldn't convince myself to let you go without being sure."

I realize my hand is still against his side when I feel the shift of his muscles under my palm. Self-conscious, I pull my hand back, and he follows the movement with his eyes, but he doesn't draw attention to it.

"Why does it hurt? The awakening..."

"It's like growing pains hurt during adolescence. You just weren't introduced to it over time, so you got the full dose at once."

"So this is it," I say, tossing the blade into my other hand. "The power to call a single blade."

"No." He smiles, shaking his head. "That's child's play. Your true powers won't be revealed until you finish the awakening."

My stomach falls. "You mean what I felt at the Market wasn't it?"

He shakes his head. "I've only heard stories of people who've experienced a late-in-life awakening, and from what I've been told, it's painful but over within a day or so."

I jab the knife into the hull of the boat. "Let me get this straight. You're leading me to land where I'm going to have to experience the worst pain I've ever felt for an undetermined amount of time?"

He makes a face. "More or less."

Clenching my teeth, I call the blade into my outstretched hand. It zips the short distance into my palm. "It better be a damn spectacular gift."

"I have a feeling it will be."

After checking to make sure we're still headed in the right direction, I return to the stern. It's quiet for a long time, hours it feels like, both of us lost to our thoughts and the pull of the sea.

Then a thought occurs to me. "So you're telling me

if I whittle a spoon from the hearthstone," I say, eyes narrowed on him, "and I use said spoon to gouge a man's eyes out, I'll be able to call it back to me?"

He rolls his eyes, but a smile begins to form at the corners of his mouth. "I guess it depends on if you whittled it with the specific intent to gouge people's eyes out with it."

I'm contemplating what other weapons I could disguise as an everyday object when I feel Acker's eyes on me.

"For what it's worth," he says, face lined with regret, "I am sorry."

I take a deep breath and let it out slowly. His apology isn't worth anything, but it's a nice sentiment anyway.

I shrug. "Me too."

# CHAPTER 18

Acker snaps the fishing line with his teeth as he continues to set the hooks at the end of the fishing rods. We took turns keeping watch last night. First him, then me, and he woke up hungry. We're both thirsty, but neither of us voice it, knowing it's wasted breath.

The fishing gear is meant for smaller prey on the reefs east and south of Alaha, but that also feels like a needless fact to point out. They're what we have, and we'll catch what we can.

Hopefully.

There's not much wind today, so it's slow going. I keep checking the compass and adjusting the tiller, but it's never by much. I can't stop my eyes from going back to Acker. His arms and chest are on full display, shirt hanging from the boom and drying after an attempt to scrub the putrid blood from it. My eyes track his hands and fingers as they tie a knot. I blame it on sheer boredom and the lack of anything else to stare at.

"Who taught you to fish?"

He bites off the line with an audible snicking of teeth. "My best friend, Hallis, mostly. We'd fish any time we traveled with the army. Freshwater fish. Streams, lakes. Stuff like that."

I realize I know so little about him when he seems to know everything about me. "Is he the friend you followed when he joined?"

"Yeah." He smiles up at me. "Much to my father's dismay."

This garners my interest. "I figured most noblemen would be proud to know their sons wanted to serve."

"He'd have preferred I spent my teenage years under his wing, gaining political notoriety with the court."

"And your mom?"

He furrows his brow, struggling to get the reel to set on the pole just right. "She died when I was twelve."

"I'm sorry."

He shakes his head, letting me know my apology is unneeded. "My sister mothers me plenty."

I pretend there's something more interesting to look at on the horizon. "And your match?"

"My match?" he repeats, glancing up at me before continuing the task of winding up a reel.

"Yeah. You said they're rare. What's she like?"

"Well," he says, shaking his head with a smile, "she's... *stunning*." The way he says it makes it undeniable, like he means it with every fiber of his being.

I can't control my eye roll. "Yeah, I got that with the details about her eyes. Tell me about *her*. What's she like? What does she do?"

He scratches his chin, about to speak when he notices something over my shoulder, eyes growing round at what he sees. I hear the flapping of wings before I turn in time to see a midnight blue bird land on the stern of the boat.

He squawks, and I gasp, a smile overtaking my face. "How did you find me?"

As soon as the question is out of my mouth, Acker is pulling me back with an arm around my waist.

"Hey!" I kick my feet in protest. "What are you

doing?"

He pulls me as far as he can from the bird and shields my body with his, reaching for his dagger. Having seen how lightning fast his reflexes are, I do the only thing I can think of...

I tackle him.

He lands on the deck with an audible *oof*. "What are *you* doing?"

"I don't care how hungry you are," I yell. "You're not eating my bird!"

"What?" He looks over his shoulder, not quite meeting my eyes from his position on his stomach. "I'm not going to eat it. I want to *kill* it."

"So you can eat it!" I keep my body weight securely on his back.

"It's more likely to eat *me*."

"You—what?" I look up at the bird, and he's watching us, head tilted to the side with a sense of keen understanding. He scratches his head with a tiny talon, leaving a single feather askew.

Acker groans underneath me. "You do realize I could easily overpower you if I wanted to, right?"

"Promise you won't kill my bird?"

We both watch as the bird spots a wood ant by its feet. He pecks at it, chasing it along the edge of the hull.

Acker rolls his eyes with a groan. "I promise."

I'm slow to rise, and Acker is just as cautious, eyes trained on the bird as it hops across the side of the boat.

"Calm down. He's harmless." I step around him and hold out my hand for the bird to hop onto my wrist. He tucks his head in and rubs it in my palm, begging for scratches.

Acker shifts closer, taking only the tiniest of steps.

"And how, may I ask, did you gain an eyun as a *pet*?" he says, like the term of endearment hurts him to say.

"He flew through my window. Or fell, more like it. His wing was injured, and I nursed him back to health." He flips over my wrist and dangles. "What's an eyun?"

"They're mythological creatures, birds of prey that can devour men whole without leaving a trace. And I've seen more than enough illustrations to know that *that*..." He points at the bird. "Is an eyun."

"Curious," I say, eyeing the water around the boat. "Sounds an awful lot like the stories of the giant squid we were told in Alaha."

"There are tales of demon creatures that scoured the earth when the Second Sun burned out."

The bird's talons tighten around my wrist, the only warning I have before he takes flight. Acker ducks as he flies over his head to land on top of the mast.

"Grenadine was a hag to him and the bird never tried to eat her."

"I am definitely a more tempting meal than Grenadine," he says, some of his playfulness returning. He takes one last look at the animal before checking the fishing rods. "What's his name?"

"We weren't allowed pets in Alaha, so I never gave him one. I don't even know if he's a he."

Acker looks at me then the bird. "Well, it looks like he's gotten attached to you regardless."

I think about it for a second, marveling at the bird who flew across an ocean to find me. "Blue," I say. "I like the name Blue."

He taps the lines, checking for tension. "Blue it is."

He smirks, about to say something smart no doubt, when one of the rods across from us begins to curve. He rushes to the other side of the boat and jerks the pole out of its holder, reeling in the spool. I reach for the line and tug, excited by the decent-sized pomper fish that breaks the surface of the water.

We work in tandem to get the fish close enough to the boat for me to lift it out of the water and over the side of the hull. It flops at our feet. Acker pinches it by the mouth and removes the hook, holding it up to show it off, his smile stretching from ear to ear.

A loud screech comes from above. Our heads jerk back in perfect time to miss the bird's—Blue's—incoming talons as he snatches the fish from Acker's grasp in one fell swoop. He lands on the stern and, in the span of a few seconds, stretches his beak open to the point of distorting his entire body, fitting the entire fish into his gaping maw before swallowing it whole.

Acker and I stare at each other in shock, mouths hanging open.

I look back at the bird, afraid to take my eyes off of him. "How did it fit all of it in there?"

He shakes his head, as disbelieving as I am. "Magic." We meet eyes again, and Acker points a finger at me. "Keep it away from me." He swings his finger in the bird's direction. "And keep away from my food."

Blue squawks.

I crouch low in front of him. "You must have been hungry after flying all this way."

He stares back, eyes black as obsidian holding mine.

"I'll make you a deal. We'll portion food for you as long as you don't steal our catches." I narrow my eyes at him, hoping we're at a new understanding. "And you can't eat Acker either," I tack on for good measure.

I don't know if it's possible, but I don't want to take

any chances.

He clicks his beak in rapid succession, and I'm going to assume that means he's in agreement.

# CHAPTER 19

Thirsty doesn't begin to describe it.

It doesn't matter how often I lick my lips or how often I swallow; there's no reprieve for the split skin and scratchy throat. We would be in worse shape without food and the little hydration we've received from the raw meat of the fish we caught over the last couple of days.

Acker hasn't said much, but I haven't either, I guess. It's hard to think of anything other than thirst and the desire to reach our destination. There's been near constant cloud cover, day and night. It's a nice reprieve from the heat of the sun during the day, but we also haven't been able to pinpoint our location at night.

Blue flies overhead, wings outstretched on the wind. We've remained steadfast in our move north, switching shifts to keep an eye on the sails and any possible ships on the horizon. The days somehow come and go with the slowest torture, yet they've passed in a blur, so many I've nearly lost track. We've settled into a rhythm: wake, eat, sleep, repeat.

Acker dozes, the lull of the ship in full effect, and I yawn for what feels like the hundredth time. We're moving slow enough for me to take a cooling dip in the water and relieve myself. It'll also give me the chance to check for barnacles that might've attached themselves to the bottom of the boat. If we wait too long, they'll reduce our speed from the weight of the drag.

Acker doesn't wake, his chest rising and falling in a steady rhythm as I strip down to my undergarments. I sit on the side of the boat and tie the mooring line around my waist, slipping back into the water. I relish the cool ocean water. It's like a balm on my overheated skin and as I float on my back.

After a while, I call my blade and dive underneath the boat. There are a few clusters of barnacles at the stern in the beginning of their growth, so they come off easily enough. I keep hold of them a handful at a time, feeding them to Blue when I come up for a breath.

I repeat the process enough that I lose track of time. It's a nice respite, focusing on something other than how miserable I am. As much as I know leaving Alaha was something I had to do, it doesn't stop me from being homesick. I've missed my small shiel and bed and the security of knowing what the day will bring. I miss Kai, and Messer. Maybe even Aurora, but that's probably the dehydration getting the better of me.

I come up to feed Blue. He waits on top of the water in between feedings, preening his feathers.

"I'm glad you're here," I tell him.

He gobbles down the barnacles and shakes his feathers. I wonder what he's able to articulate inside that birdbrain of his.

Then I feel something wrap around my ankle a moment before tugging me underneath the surface. I scream under water. I get my blade at the ready, heart beating furiously in my chest as I prepare to fight, possibly against a giant squid.

When I'm able to break free and pivot, I'm greeted by Acker's smiling face. I kick at him with my spare foot and swim to the surface, coughing up the water clogging my airway. Blue takes flight when Acker emerges.

He shakes the water from his hair, spraying droplets in every direction, and I throw any and every cuss word I can think of in his direction. He laughs, eyes sparkling with delight in being on the receiving end of my temper. It only serves to make me angrier.

I splash water in his face. "I could have hurt you," I say, holding up my blade.

"Wouldn't have been the first time, now would it?" he says, not even the tiniest bit repentant as his smile stretches from ear to ear.

"Ugh." I'm exasperated.

I turn toward the boat then register the sensation of water hitting the back of my head.

*He did not.*

I'm slow to turn and look at him, seething with every breath. "Do it again," I tell him. "I dare you."

He lifts a brow, pure bravado as he says, "Or what?"

I don't deem his question worth answering. I think it's obvious it'll be something very, very bad.

Light reflects off the water on his face, highlighting the droplets clinging to his eyelashes and hair. His skin has gotten darker, losing the red from the first few days out at sea, and it somehow makes his smile that much more lascivious.

Confident he won't splash me again, I turn for the boat. I untie the moor line around my waist and retie it to the cleat, fashioning a dip in the rope to use as a step up. I stab my blade into the hull and am about to step onto the line when Acker grabs me from behind and throws me back into the water.

*Bastard.*

Murderous thoughts fight for dominance in my mind as I kick away from him and make for the surface. He appears right after me, and I jump on top of his shoulders, forcing him back underwater. It's so satisfying, getting him back, that I splash him as soon as he comes up for air.

There's a predatory look in his eyes that sends me diving under the water. I know I'm a better swimmer than he is, so I dip under the boat to get away, emerging on the other side. I keep an eye on the water under me, on either side of the boat, waiting for a dark figure to emerge.

I tread for so long I start to wonder if he gave up, then a shadow falls over me. I wasn't expecting him to come from above, and I look up to find him smiling like the devil. I swim back to put distance between us, but there's no use. He leaps into the water, engulfing me in his arms in the span of a breath.

I kick and fight to get free, twisting in his hold, laughing when his fingers graze over the sensitive area of my stomach and ribs. His front is pressed to the entirety of my back, bare skin against bare skin, thighs and legs brushing along the length of mine. He's hot to the touch.

He pulls me under the water with him, but it doesn't stifle the burning heat of the hand splayed across my belly or the other banded across my chest. It evokes inappropriate sensations that flood my system.

It reminds me of the way it felt to be under Kai's influence, when Acker was hiding on the roof of my shiel after the guards searched my room and Kai used his powers on me. It's like my body is not my own.

There's no control or thought or reasoning to it, just feeling. Touch and the desire to be touched. Drawn to the warmth radiating from him.

And it's not something I should be feeling with Acker.

I manage to maneuver in his hold to where we're face to face. He must see the panic taking over me because his smile dims, arms slackening around me. I use my hands to push off from his chest and swim to the surface. The boat is already a distance away, and I push my arms and legs to catch up. It was reckless of us to leave the boat untethered.

My back is to Acker when he gets aboard. I unbraid my hair and run my fingers through it, pretending to be too preoccupied to look at him, pretending there's not a new thread of tension between us as we get dressed.

He's first to break the silence. "I didn't mean to upset you," he says, voice low and unsure.

I'm too embarrassed to meet his gaze. "It's fine," I say, not wanting to discuss my internal freakout—an internal freakout that's still very much underway.

Wind whips my hair around my face, and I look at the weathervane, the cloudy sky overhead, then the sails as they bow in and out. It's been hard to tell where the change in wind pattern is coming from.

I adjust the rudder, turning the boat until the sails straighten. I check the compass. "There might be a storm nearby. Up ahead, if I had to guess. We can divert around it but get close enough to catch some rain if we're lucky."

Acker sits across from me, dipping his head into my line of vision so I'm forced to look at him. "Do you want to eat in case the conditions worsen?"

I nod, grateful he's let the moment go.

He scales and guts a fish. Blue is a bottomless pit, we've discovered, and he's quick to catch the scraps in the air when Acker tosses them over the side of the boat. Fileting the meat into strips, he offers me a piece on the blade of his dagger.

As I reach for a slice, I realize something horrifying, hand pausing midair. "Have you been using this blade this entire time?"

There's a look of confusion on his face. "Yes," he says, but it comes out more as a question.

Bile rises in the back of my throat. "You've been feeding me with the same dagger you put through a man's eyeball?"

He narrows his eyes at me. "Would you feel better if I said no?" After a beat of silence, he takes my hand and slaps the raw meat into my palm. "I cleaned it with the leftover mead. It's perfectly fine."

That's it.

That's the final straw.

I launch the fish at him, satisfied by the wet smack when it hits him square in the face.

He blinks and wipes a hand down his face. "You have the only other knife. What do you think I've been using?"

If I was smarter, maybe I would heed the simmering calm in his voice, but I can't stop the revulsion from spilling out of my mouth. "I didn't think anyone in their right mind would ever use a literal murder weapon as cutlery."

He sucks in a breath, slow and measured like he's using the seconds to calm his own anger. "Says the woman who talks about gouging men's eyes out with spoons." He stabs the dagger into the side of the hull.

"Starve. I don't care."

He doesn't have any qualms about it, and we sit in stony silence as he eats. I do my best to ignore the hunger in my belly, hoping the lapping of water against the boat disguises the rumbling.

I think I feel a single drop of water land on my nose but come up empty when I feel for it. I tilt my head back and inspect the gray blanket of sky overhead but see no sign of rain falling. It must have been a stray drop of ocean water. I resume my task of pretending Acker doesn't exist then I feel it again, this time on my hand. Then one my forehead.

I blink against the falling drizzle. Acker feels it too and looks up, eyes lighting up, and he grins when our eyes meet. Within moments, it's a downpour. We're drenched almost instantly. I'm mesmerized by the way the water catches along the mast and glides down the string and into the well. I open my mouth and relish the sweet taste of nectar from the gods themselves.

When I open my eyes, Acker's gaze is upon me. His expression gives away none of his thoughts.

The rain casts a veil around the boat, reducing the visibility. I angle us eastward to avoid any worsening weather ahead, on a steep heel as the boat cuts to the side, the bow lifting over the white caps forming atop the water. The rudder jerks in my hand with each hit, but we remain steadfast for a long while.

We needed this after sitting stagnant for days. If we can ride this wind, we'll make fast headway. As soon as I think that, the winds shift. The sails lose their billow, hanging like wet drapes.

"Shit."

Acker leans forward to yell over the pounding rain.

"What is it?"

I shake my head, too scared to voice it, as if saying it out loud will make it more true. "The storm changed course."

It's no longer moving to the west but coming straight for us. The boat volleys back and forth as I fight the rudder.

"Should we turn back?" Acker says. "Try to outrun it?"

Blue calls out, taking flight as he leaps from the mast, feathers rippling in the wind. I misjudged the severity of the storm in favor of catching rain, and it might cost us our lives.

"We can try," I say, meeting his gaze.

But it might be too late.

# CHAPTER 20

It's pitch black. I've lost all sense of time and direction without my sight. The wind and waves batter us. The pitch of the boat is at the mercy of the sea.

We use our bodies to create tension against the side of the hull, keeping hold of each other, an unspoken agreement to not lose each other in the dark. For hours that feel never ending, we withstand the storm.

Every so often, the ocean bottoms out underneath us, and my stomach roils in protest. Water jumps over the side of the boat in one dip only to funnel back out the next. All we can do is hold on so it doesn't take us with it.

The temperature has dropped. Each intake of water in the boat feels like fresh ice against our trembling skin. If the amount of water collecting inside the hull doesn't sink us, the lack of heat will be what does us in.

Over and over, wave after wave comes. We don't speak. Words aren't going to save us.

Then...the roaring starts.

A low, thunderous vibration permeates the air, drowning out the sound of water and breaths and even the heartbeat inside my chest. I don't need to feel or hear it to know my heart has stopped beating altogether, because I know what's coming.

I've only experienced the middle of a swirling sea storm once before, but it's a memory I can't forget. The way the air became violent, rattling my eardrums and the trees and the entire grove, only for the piercing silence to follow when the water rose and swallowed half of Alaha. Many lost their homes that day, some their lives.

I reach for Acker. He doesn't hesitate to wrap his arms around me.

Placing his lips directly against the shell of my ear, he yells so I can hear him. "Don't let go! No matter what. Don't let go."

He brings me in tight against his body, tucking my head under his chin, using his legs and the arm not holding me to bracket us inside the boat.

Rain no longer falls but whips through the air like tiny needles. The hum of the roaring grows with the force of the wind. Lightning, the first we've seen in hours, spears from the sky. A sharp clack of thunder splits the sound of roaring like a whip. Acker tightens his arm around me. It's a painful embrace but one I'm grateful for as I clench his soaked shirt in my fingers.

Then, like blowing out a candle, the wind and rain stop. Acker's and my sharp breaths fill the stillness. The stern of the boat dips forward. Acker reinforces the tension in his arm and legs to stop us from falling forward with the tilt. The bow nosedives headfirst on the downside of a wave, and we're in freefall.

I squeeze my eyes shut and wait for the inevitable crash of wood slamming into the water below when our boat will splinter apart and we'll meet our end.

But it never comes.

"My gods." Acker's voice is barely a whisper, but it resonates in my ear nonetheless.

I open my eyes and lose all my breath. Flashes of

lighting come from every direction, like arms reaching across the sky and into the sea and everywhere in between. It provides light to see the churning water and the wall of clouds and rain we just passed through as waves the size of what I assume mountains to be roil in the heart of the storm.

A bolt of lightning hits one of the waves, illuminating the water underneath the surface in bright blue before it's black once more. The air is electrified, and despite being soaked to the bone, all the hair on my body stands on end.

A jagged line of electricity comes down from overhead as it seeks the path of least resistance before striking the water not far from our boat, illuminating the water around us.

I gasp.

Acker curses.

Long, dark tentacles surround our boat, winding around us in the churning water. The bottom of the wave I'm expecting to be our final blow seems to never come as we begin our ascent up the next swell, almost like we're floating above the water's surface.

Almost like we're being carried.

Acker doesn't let go of me. Not in the center of the storm and not when we breach the veil of the storm's eye. Not when the boat feels like it's going to be ripped apart at any moment and we're going to go overboard. He never lessens his hold, not even when his arms shake.

He never lets go.

# CHAPTER 21

It's a memory.

I'm aware of it within my dream, the same dream I've had for weeks now. A bed made of down and pillows shifts to rolling hills of grass as far as the eye can see. There's a soft breeze, my pale blonde hair fluid around my vision as I intertwine the stems of wildflowers in my hands.

I can feel the cool, damp ground beneath my bent knees, and the smell of earth is strong. My dress is yellow with white trim as I add another flower to my creation in my lap. A crown fit for a queen. My mother, of course, is going to love it. She loves everything I make her.

A golden butterfly alights on the back of my hand, so I freeze, remaining perfectly still as it opens and closes its wings.

"Hi," I greet it. "How are you today?"

Golden butterflies are my favorite.

Stomping feet stumble through the tall grass, revealing one boy then a second as they come to a stop before me. The butterfly flutters away.

The only feature of the first boy I can identify is his freckles. They're prominent across the bridge of his nose and onto his cheeks, but I can't distinguish anything else. His body is like a vague mirage in the sunlight, but I know he's scowling. I don't need to see the expression to know it's true. He's always mad about one thing or another.

I try to hide my crown from his view, but he clocks the movement and swipes it from my hands. "Making more of this rubbish, are you?" He places the crown on his head and turns to the second boy. "How do I look?"

The second boy comes into view. Brown hair and brown eyes and a full mouth, piercing in his beauty. He shoves the freckled boy. "Like a twat."

"I think I look rather distinguished." He prances backward and trips over a stick, hitting the ground with a choked sound.

The brown-eyed boy bursts into laughter, walking past him. "Serves you right, you dimwit." He winks at me over his shoulder. The freckled boy, now grumbling, follows close behind until they disappear over the hill.

I open my eyes.

The familiar rock of the boat is the first thing I recognize, the soft creak of its hull. Then the blue sky and too bright sun. I turn my head toward Acker. My cheek is against the inside of his arm, and I marvel at the sight of life within his chest, every breath visual evidence of our victory.

We made it.

Blue squawks from high in the sky.

Acker's eyes open and he blinks up in annoyance, scowling as the bird circles the boat overhead. Then Acker blinks, as if coming to the same realization I just did, and he turns his head to the side so his gaze meets mine. It's the gaze of the brown-eyed boy from my dream, just older and wiser, his life experiences gathered within their depth.

"Hi," he says, voice soft yet rough around the edges.

I can't prevent the emotion entering my voice when I reply, "Hi."

He wraps me in a hug, and I don't allow myself the space to think about it too much as I bury my face in his chest, relishing the utter relief that we made it. We're alive. Looking worse for wear, but alive.

We release each other at the same time, sitting up to survey the ship. The mainsail is halfway unrolled from the boom but intact. The headsail, however, is dangling from its post and ripped in two. The mast and boom appear to be solid, and there don't seem to be any imminent leaks. With only the mainsail, we'll be slower moving but operational. It could be worse.

I inspect the belongings we stored in one of the fishing wells. Everything is soaking wet, but that's to be expected.

Acker scrubs a hand down his face and over his chin. "I feel like I spent the night downing pints."

I retrieve the waterskin and drink half of it before passing it to Acker. "Do that often, do you?"

He finishes the bottle, throat bobbing with each swallow. "I've had my fair share of fun. What about you? Fancy a helping of wine? Gin?"

"Alcohol isn't permitted in Alaha, but Kai did steal his father's mead once. We puked our guts up during morning conditioning."

He smiles. "I've had similar experiences of my own. Swore off drinking more times than I can count. Unlike me, Hallis hasn't had a drop to this day."

I begin to work on fixing the sails, tightening the halyard. "Is he still as big of a twat as he was as a child?"

Acker goes still at my words, eyes locked on me as he comes to a stand.

Keeping my expression blank, I retie the rope to the sail, satisfied with the new knot. "He picked on me a lot," I say, meeting his gaze before moving on to the next.

Acker leans a forearm on the boom. "He had a crush on you. Just didn't know how to express it properly."

I make a face. "And what about you?"

"What about me?" he says, careful.

"You weren't much better, so what's your excuse?"

He doesn't answer, silence stretching between us as I begin to raise the sail. It lasts until we have everything rigged and ready to go, then he blocks my path to the rudder, forcing me to give him my full attention.

"When did you start getting your memories back?"

This conversation is already exhausting, and I kind of regret mentioning anything. "Maybe since the Market. I've been having these weird dreams. At first, I thought they were nonsense, but they keep getting more vivid. Like I'm reliving certain memories."

He studies me, as he's trying to figure out if I'm withholding information. "I've wondered if your memory would return once we're back on land, but whatever hold Wren had on them might be slipping as you get further away from him."

"I don't always remember them. Sometimes I wake up and the dream is...fuzzy."

With the strangest face, he says, "What have you dreamed about me?"

I'm surprised he skipped out on the chance to tease me with that question. I lift a brow at his inquisition and convince myself I'm not disappointed. "Not much, really. Only this memory of you and Hallis stealing my crown of flowers."

A crease forms between his brows. "A crown of flowers..."

Of course the one memory I have is so inconsequential to him that he doesn't remember it. "That and the one time you professed your undying love for me."

Color leaches from his face, so much so that it gives me pause. His face morphs into annoyance when he realizes I was only joking, and I can't help the laugh that escapes my lips at his embarrassment.

He turns away. "I was nine."

I follow him to the stern of the boat. "What did you say? What did *I* say?"

He pulls the fishing rods from the hull and begins inspecting them for damage. "I'm fairly sure I said you were the prettiest girl I'd ever seen." I swear the tips of his ears are pink when he glances up at me. "You laughed in my face." He glares. "Feels a little reminiscent of right now."

I struggle to tamp down my enjoyment, sobering my features the best I can. "I'm sorry."

He gives me a look that clearly says he doesn't believe me, but a smile twitches at the corner of his mouth. "You're kind of beautiful when you lie."

I'm stunned into silence, caught off guard by his admission.

He gives me his back as he works on getting a rod set up for cast. "It was the day before you disappeared actually."

I've watched him enough to know how he likes to string the lures, and I work alongside him to ready the rest of the poles. "Perhaps I did run away then."

I can see his smile in my periphery. "I'd be lying if I

said it didn't cross my mind a time or two. But let's be honest, no girl would run from my pretty face."

I roll my eyes. "I was seven. And from what I can remember, you were all gangly limbs and messy hair. I'm fairly sure I thought you had cooties."

"I did have cooties. I grew into them. Now, they're devastatingly handsome cooties."

"Devastatingly *humble*," I murmur under my breath, tone dripping in sarcasm.

He casts the first line and sets the rod in the side of the hull, turning his attention to me. "I'm glad we agree on both accounts."

I can't stop the heat from flooding my face. "I agree," I tell him, careful to keep my expression blank as I stare into his undeniable beauty. "You are also beautiful when you lie."

The gloating tease in his eyes narrows into confusion.

"Your match," I say. "She isn't real. You lied to make a point about my feelings for Kai."

He doesn't so much as blink at my accusation, a hint of a smile still poised on his lips, only a smidge sharper. "You mean your lack of feelings for Kai."

I roll my eyes again. I finish my rod and hand it to him to cast as I begin on the next. "How am I supposed to trust anything you've told me?"

He doesn't reply until I'm handing him the next rod. He doesn't take it from my hand, instead placing his grip over mine so I can't let go, forcing me to meet his gaze. "I haven't lied to you. I *am* matched."

The honesty seems to ring true as his eyes hold mine, unwavering under the heavy glare of sun overhead. I'm unnerved by the sinking sensation in my stomach. I tell myself it's from hunger and dehydration, not any unjustified feelings of disappointment. None at all.

"I didn't take you for a man who'd be indecent with another when you're already claimed."

Another crease forms between his brows. "Are you meaning the other day in the water?"

I don't need to nod for him to know that's exactly what I'm referencing.

He releases the hold on my hand, taking the rod from me. "I was wondering what upset you," he says, casting the line and relieving me of his fierce gaze. "I figured it had something to do with your lingering feelings for Kai, but I'm pleased to know you're concerned with my loyalty."

"Someone should be," I say dryly in admonishment.

I leave him to the rest and take my position at the stern. I don't know what's worse, thinking him a liar or a cheat. Both are untrustworthy in my eyes. I suppose I don't know why I had any expectations of him at all.

He finishes setting up the lines and takes his usual position across from me, back to the nose of the boat. It's early morning, but sweat already dampens his hairline, the moisture creating a sheen down to his throat.

"My match hasn't claimed me," he says. "We haven't married, so there's not a covenant to break. I'm free to do as I wish, as is she."

I lift a questioning brow. "With the way you spoke of the rarity of matches, I figured you wouldn't be so casual to dismiss it."

"I've waited a long time for my match to claim me," he says, expression pensive as he scratches the stubble that's been accumulating along his jaw. "Long enough, I think."

The words are spoken like he's sorted through the dilemma that has been plaguing him, like the decision has been lifted from his shoulders. He doesn't elaborate on why his match has not claimed him.

I tilt my head to the side, looking at him from a new angle. "And you said no girl could run from your pretty face."

He laughs, and it's pure delight. "I appreciate the lesson on humility."

# CHAPTER 22

"Would you rather...never eat bread again or only have bread to eat for the rest of your life?"

The fish seem to have been sucked up into the storm, because there hasn't been a single bite in days. We're out of food and on our last dredges of water. Clouds have closed in on us once again, and we're sailing without an accurate course. I'm trying my best to be optimistic, but it's difficult when my empty stomach is determined to make its presence known every waking minute of the godsdamned day.

Acker grimaces at the options, eyes closed, head propped up with a folded arm. "That's worse than the snake-arms ultimatum."

"Well, which is it?"

He peeks at me through one squinted eye. "I guess I'd never eat bread again."

I am outraged. "You're a masochist."

"Who needs bread when there's steak?" He resumes his lounging with a smile on his face as he closes his eyes again. "Would you rather be hairy all over or no hair at all?"

I groan at the reminder of the state my hair is in right now. I've tried my best to keep it in a plait, but the saltwater and wind have whipped it into a frenzy. "Who needs hair anyway? You have to wash it and brush it and it's *always* in the way."

"I bet you would swim really fast without it. Like a fish."

I recast one of the lines. "I change my mind then. You might actually mistake me for a fish and eat me."

"Joke's on you. I'm plenty hungry enough to eat you now, with or without hair."

There's a beat of silence where the connotation takes on a whole other meaning, and my skin burns a fiery red color. I don't look over my shoulder at him, pretending the innuendo went over my head.

"Should I throw the net out?"

Acker snorts. "You said it yourself, the net isn't going to drag deep enough as it's meant for fishing near the reefs. Plus, it'd only slow us down. You'd just be exerting more energy than you have without the substance to fuel you." He turns over like I assume he'd do if he were in a real bed. "Matter of fact, you should rest."

"I'm not tired," I lie.

I dare a look at him, and he's staring at me with lazy eyes. He knows I'm exhausted. He feels it too. The ocean has a way of doing that to you, sucking the life from your bones a little more every second. I can't imagine the anguish we'd be in if the sun was out in its full glory. Small graces from the gods, I suppose.

"Wake me for rotation?" he says after a moment.

I nod.

The day gives to night, and the clouds don't move. It feels like there's a heavy blanket over the earth. Acker doesn't shift an inch as he slumbers on the deck. The air is thick and humid, making each breath harder to take in than the last, and I'm so fucking thirsty.

I keep my fingers on the lines. With the barest of reflection from the moon to see by, there's a chance

I could miss the pull or dip of a line, so I rotate between the few we have cast. Every so often I check the compass, making adjustments on the tiller when needed. Time kind of runs on forever and quickly at the same time, so much so that I'm surprised when the clouds come into focus little by little with the morning light.

I nearly leap out of my skin when Acker breaks the silence, voice hoarse from sleep. "I slept the day away."

I reach for the waterskin and hand it to him. "Actually, it's morning."

He freezes mid reach, eyes becoming clear as he looks from the sky to me. "I slept through the night?"

I shake the waterskin for him to take it. "Like a baby."

"Why didn't you wake me?"

"You needed sleep."

He sits up. "And so do you."

I drop the container in his lap. "How's your side?"

He doesn't bother to look. "It's fine."

The quick dismissal isn't convincing. "I saw it when you got in the water yesterday," I tell him, revealing the truth. "It's not pretty. Have you been putting the salve on it?"

He knows he's caught. "I used it all." Uncapping the waterskin, he takes a miniscule sip before handing it back to me, its weight no different than before. "You've been sneaking glances at me while I'm undressing. I'm flattered."

I take my own miniscule sip and ignore his attempt to divert the conversation. "It's infected."

"I don't think the mead was top shelf," he jokes.

"Let me see it."

"Trying to get me undressed?" When I don't so

much as blink at him, he loses the pretense, expression becoming serious with his next breath. "It's not as bad as it looks."

"Then why won't you show it to me?"

He stands up, towering over me in the next instant. "Because you're worrying for nothing. It'll heal the moment we get to land."

"You act like it's right over the horizon," I say, growing frustrated by his nonchalance. "We might not see land for weeks. What will you do when the fever sets in?"

He shakes his head once. "It won't."

"How do you know that?" I all but yell, voice cracking from my unshed emotion.

He has the nerve to smile at me. "I've survived far too many worse things for an itchy wound to take me out."

I choke on the scoff attempting to escape my throat. "Your arrogance won't save you," I seethe.

"Neither will your worry." The softness of his words sucks all the fire from my veins, leaving a hollowness in its wake. He's slow to lift a hand to tuck my wiry hair out of my face, like he's afraid it'll provoke me. "You need to rest. The mind plays tricks when it's been restless for too long."

I know he's right. The desire to close my eyes pulls at me. I've been fighting it all night, and as if our argument has doused any energy I had in my bones, the yearning for sleep becomes more potent by the second.

I nod, giving in. There's a noticeable slackening of his body, like my submittal eases his own worries.

He grins. "Good."

His one-word answer feels incomplete, like he intended to say more and stopped. But I don't have time to ponder it as I lie down and close my eyes, propping my head on my pack. I'm out within a minute.

# CHAPTER 23

I think about Kai and what he's doing. It's difficult not to. When I came to the decision to leave, I told myself I wouldn't look back. I'd focus on moving forward, where I've always wanted to go—home.

It's a place that now feels like a myth. Maybe the ocean never ends. This is the hell I've heard of, not fire but an endless, fruitless reservoir.

I wonder if Kai thinks about me at all or if he's too busy constructing his own plans. Moving his chess pieces. Doing Kai things. Conniving.

The hunger is gone. That's a nice reprieve. Every now and then a stabbing sensation will shoot through my abdomen, but other than that, all is good. Well, other than the unrelenting thirst, but I'm only allowed to think about that every other swallow. I've forbidden it.

Even Blue is less interactive. He has to be even hungrier than we are. Surely, he would fly to find food if it became dire enough. Unless...unless he does intend on eating Acker. I look up at him perched on the weathervane and find him sleeping, head tucked under a wing.

Good gods, I'm in the early stages of delirium. I've heard stories of sailors who went mad. Messer told a story passed down from his grandfather about a fisherman they found after being lost at sea for half a year, said he ripped all his hair out. Maybe I *will* be hairless.

My gasp jerks Acker awake.

"Oh, hey. I'm sorry," I whisper. "Didn't mean to wake you."

He leans on an elbow to get a better look at me in the dark. "What are you doing?"

"Contemplating pulling my hair out."

He makes a face, half amusement and half confusion. "Please don't. Contrary to what I said, I rather like your hair."

I smile and run my fingers down the fishing line. "I'm just waiting for a bite."

There's a stretch of quiet where all we can hear is each of us breathing and the gentle sway of the boat. That is until he utters two words that stop my breathing altogether.

"Come here." His voice is deep and heavy between us. He motions for me to come with a wave of his hand. "You're not going to catch anything tonight, and I don't trust you to wake me to switch out."

I whisper my darkest thought. "Sleeping feels like giving up."

He huffs out a breath and shakes his head. "I'd wager quite a bit on the number of times you've ever given up on something," he says, a dry grin on his lips. "It's less than five, undoubtedly."

It's my turn to breathe out a laugh.

After a moment, he demands, "Come *here*."

"The tiller—"

"Isn't going to move. Look at the sail."

It hangs limp from the mast, not a trace of wind to ruffle it.

"I stink," I warn.

"I know. I smell you from here."

I shoot him a murderous glare, but it only serves to widen his smile, and I cave. I release the line and scootch in beside him, careful to leave space between us as I lie down on my side. There's barely enough room for one fully grown adult, let alone two, and I contort my arm to create a makeshift pillow. After the third shift, Acker extends his arm in my direction. I stare at the inside of his forearm, pondering my options.

"I'm not going to bite you," he says. "Not today, anyway."

His teasing provides enough levity for me to use his arm as a cushion for my head without it feeling weirder than it needs to be. He also smells alarmingly better than I do. First thing on the agenda tomorrow is a dip in the ocean.

"You said you could smell me."

He rolls his eyes. "I'm sure I smell just as pleasant as you do. Kind of cancels each other out."

"No. Back in Alaha, in the brig," I clarify. "You said you could smell that I had been in it."

"Ah. It's the iron in your blood."

"You can distinguish between people?"

He thinks about it for a moment. "Sometimes. It depends."

"On...?"

"How familiar I am with someone, I suppose. It can be as unremarkable or as memorable as any scent." He leans in and inhales, nostrils flaring wide with a kiss of smile in his eyes. "You smell like wildflowers. The kind that grows on the hills of Kenta."

I can feel the course of my flush reach from the top of my head to my toes. I try not to appear as affected as I am, but it's hard to do when he's smiling at me with his stupid mouth and stupider teasing eyes.

He makes a face. "Underneath the stench, I mean."

It breaks the spell I'm under, and I swat him in the chest with my free hand.

Laughing, he traps my hand beneath his between us. "Sleep, Jovie. You can enact your retribution on me tomorrow."

I don't need his permission to sleep, but I can't deny I'm comforted by Acker's insistence. I feel like death warmed over. If he doesn't see the harm in both of us getting some rest, that's plenty convincing for me.

I trust him, I realize. Not fully, not yet. But I think he's smart and loyal. To some degree, at least, which is more than I can say about most people back in Alaha.

Then I close my eyes and dream.

It's the same one where I'm in a comfortable bed full of pillows, a bed fit for a giant it's so large. I'm waiting for the transition to the meadow where I'm making a crown of wildflowers, but it doesn't come. Instead, I'm fighting to remain asleep. I like the bed and I don't want to wake just yet, but something keeps tugging at my shoulder.

"Jovie."

I awake to Acker nudging me, his expression full of excitement and urgency.

"Look," he says, eyes darting up.

I look up and stop breathing.

Stars.

Coating the sky instead of clouds, pinpricks of light reflect off the flat plane of the ocean as far as the eye can see. The water is so still, a tranquility I've never seen before, converging where the sky and water meet to create a sphere of unknown origin in every direction.

The boat is unmoving, as frozen as the water beneath it, and it's as if we're a part of the sky. I lean over to get a better look at the reflection on the surface of the water. It feels like I could dip my hand in and touch a star, the mirror image from above unwavering.

"Have you ever witnessed anything like this before?" Acker whispers.

I shake my head. "Never."

"Can you make anything out of them? Any of the constellations?"

There are more stars than sky. I can't make out any sort of configuration or shape I've studied before. I shake my head. If he's disappointed by my answer, he doesn't show it, his gaze as wide as mine. He stands and pulls the fishing lines from the water, sending the stars' reflections scattering in every direction.

I stand too. "What are you doing?"

He stashes the rods in a hurry and pulls his shirt over his head. "I'm going to swim with the stars," he says, as if the answer should be obvious. He shucks off his pants just as quickly and stands on the side of the boat. "What are you waiting for?"

Then he winks at me and dives in, sending the illusion into ripples of light. He emerges and shakes the water from his hair, smiling ear to ear. I can't help but follow.

Past the point of modesty, I strip to my undergarments and slip into the water. It's cooler than I expect, and a shiver racks my body. I try to keep my movements to a minimum under the water to preserve the reflections.

Blue caws from above before taking flight. There's no

wind for him to rely on, so he only makes a circle once before returning to the post, as if he, too, wanted to experience flying with infinity. I lie on my back and Acker does the same, floating next to me. We don't speak. There's no need to.

We stay like that until our skin is wrinkled and our exhaustion takes over. It feels like hours have passed by the time we climb back into the boat. We're too tired to wait to dry and dress, so we lie without a care for immodesty. The night air is perfect against my damp skin. It's the calmest I've felt since...

I can't recall a memory before sleep claims me.

# CHAPTER 24

"Thought I'd never see the day he would turn down food," Acker says, throwing the guts of his latest catch into the water.

Blue fluffs his feathers and continues to preen on the bow of the boat.

"Perhaps he's tired of fish." I know I am. The thought of eating another bite makes me nauseous, but so does the starvation. "He might go for some barnacles. The hull probably needs to be scraped anyway. If you want to take over the tiller, I'll dive down."

He shakes his head. "I'll go," he says, rinsing his hands in the water.

It's just a flicker of pain, but I catch the wince he tries to hide when he stands. He strips off his shirt, and I glimpse the purple, mottled skin on his side before he shucks off his pants. Even with the lack of meat on his bones, his muscles flex with every movement. From the power in his thighs to the smaller muscles along his ribs, his strength is still very much evident in the lines of his body. He ties the rope around his waist and steps off the boat into a dive. It's pure grace.

After the night where the stars and ocean became one, the fish returned in plenty, as did a smattering of downpours that allowed us to get a little bit of water in our well. But with that came the sun, high in the sky and blistering for vengeance.

Acker comes up with a handful of barnacles. He wipes the water from his eyes and swims to the side of the boat. He clicks his tongue at Blue and places the crustaceans along the edge of the hull one at a time. The bird flies down, landing a few feet from Acker, curious but cautious. Acker treads back to give Blue some space as he hops to the nearest shell. He inspects it, head tilting this way and that, picks it up with his beak, and hops a little closer to Acker.

Then he proceeds to throw the barnacle in Acker's face. It pings off his forehead before splashing back into the water. Blue squawks at him before taking flight, knocking over half of the remaining barnacles in the process. I'm stunned speechless. I look at Acker, who looks just as astonished as I am.

"That's the last…" He trails off, eyes caught on something over my shoulder.

I turn just in time to watch Blue on the tail of a seagull. He yells a battle cry and opens his mouth, gaping maw looming as he dives for the bird, which is oblivious to its impending doom. Gull captured, he lands on the stern…and swallows.

A muffled squelching can be heard from inside the tiny bird's body, and I blanch at the wet sound. "Sick."

Acker's excited gaze meets mine as he treads water. "We're close to land."

My lips thin, eyes scanning the horizon. There are a lot of small islands and reefs scattered between Alaha and Kenta. They're teeming with food, so birds frequent them, but I cling to hope anyway. It feels better than the endless barrage of misery I can't figure out how to escape.

Acker finishes scraping the bottom of the boat. We're

quiet for the rest of the day, but there's a noticeable energy as we work, our attention constantly returning to the horizon. It's like we don't want to curse our luck by voicing our doubts.

I'm in the middle of slicing a filet of fish for drying when the first wave of nausea hits me. I don't think much of it. The heat is brutal, so I make a conscious effort to ration my water more frequently.

It's dusk when Acker takes another dip in the ocean. I think it helps the heat radiating from his infection. I haven't brought it up again out of fear of rocking the mild truce we've cultivated. Plus, he's right—there's nothing to be done about it. Not until we're back on land.

A dizzy spell hits me like a wave, and I have to squeeze my eyes shut to stop the world from turning on its side.

Until it happens again.

And again.

I have to put down my blade and breathe through the bile threatening to creep up my throat. When I steady myself, I look up and spot the dark smudge of land in our direct path. We're too far away to tell for sure, but it stretches far enough to possibly be more than an island.

I lean over the side of the boat. When Acker surfaces, I'm able to speak one word and point to the horizon. "Land."

Then I puke my guts up.

# CHAPTER 25

Acker keeps his sight fixed on the shore as it comes into view. Black rocks frame a small beach of black sand, and seagulls nest along the boulders framing the outcropping. As the land looms closer and closer, Acker becomes more and more tense.

"There's only one place with black beaches like this." His mouth is set in a grim line. "This is Roison territory."

The map we were shown in Alaha was simplified. There weren't titles or boundaries, only the topographical markers labeled with dotted lines, but the black sand beaches were evident on the northeastern edge of the landmass. The east of Kenta is where Roison resides. We literally passed up our destination.

Acker curses under his breath. "We should turn west, head back toward Kenta."

I jerk my head back. "Absolutely not."

He tears his gaze from the shore, eyes homing in on me. "Chryse, their leader, has allowed rebels and bandits to have their way with the land. It's the worst place for us to venture into."

"What if we get caught in another storm or blown off course? We've been surviving on scraps for weeks and you want to turn your back on the first land we see? No. It's too risky."

"Jovie, you're already feeling the effects of the awakening. It's going to be ten times worse once we reach land, and you want to encroach onto enemy territory?"

"We won't survive at all if you succumb to the sickness in your veins," I tell him, pointing to his side. "You said you'd heal on land. Well, there it is." I swing my finger to the beach. "Right there."

He clenches his teeth. "There's a peace treaty, but it's fragile. If Chryse finds us in his territory, it could be at the cost of reigniting the war."

A piercing pain begins to pulse behind my eyes, and I squeeze them shut, opening them once it abates. "We should swing the sail if we're turning around."

Acker pulls me in by my elbow. "How bad is it?"

Terrible. My head is screaming and my stomach wants to revolt and there's a flashing light in the corner of my vision that I've been ignoring.

"I'm fine."

He's not convinced but releases his hold on me anyway. I turn to untie the boom then hear his loud sigh.

"Stop."

I look at him over my shoulder in question.

"We should take it down and row the rest of the way to shore. Less of a chance of being spotted."

I stand up straight. "Are you sure? You said—"

"I know what I said," he mutters. "Just promise me you'll follow my orders once we touch down."

"You have my word."

He is somehow even less convinced than before.

We take down the flag and gather everything we can bring with us. It's not much but plenty to weigh down the pack. When the waves begin to break, we row with our backs toward the beach. It takes fortitude not to look over my shoulder with every stroke. It feels wrong to put my back to the enemy.

It's nightfall by the time we make it close enough to the beach to disembark. Acker jumps first, then I follow suit. The water initially feels freezing cold before it shifts to a scorching temperature against my skin. Like touching a hot stove, a shock of ice before the burn as if I've been thrown into a pot of boiling water.

I yell as I flail to stay as far above the waves as I can. The beach and rocks and lack of vegetation should have been a warning. The water is obviously uninhabitable. I reach to find purchase on something, anything to save me, only to be met with nothing but searing pain as the water passes through my fingers.

One look at Acker tells me everything I need to know. He's not struggling. The water is fine.

It's just me.

He swims toward me, worry on his face, but I don't wait for him to reach me. I swim for the shore with all my might. I need to get to shore. There'll be relief once I'm on dry land.

But I'm wrong.

So very wrong.

My knees hit the sandy bottom of the shallow water where the waves break, and I yelp. I stand, but my legs immediately give way from the pain lancing through them. I realize there's no escape. I tread the water, tolerating the searing pain. There's no way out of this.

"Jovie," Acker yells, stomping through the crash of waves to get to me.

I can't disguise my pain, my fear sending me into full-blown panic. A day of this, maybe two, he said. "I can't," I cry, unable to make myself leave the water.

He doesn't bother asking my permission before reaching down and placing a hand under my legs, the other under my back to lift me from the water. It offers mild relief, but it doesn't last long. Each step forward brings another level of torture as we travel further onto land. The blinding light that was in the corner of my eyesight grows to encompass everything.

We reach the rocks lining the shore then move past them as the sand turns to grass. Blue swoops overhead, staying low as Acker marches with me in his arms. He, too, knows the importance of being discreet.

I can't tell how long it takes, but we reach a wooded area where trees loom over our heads. They're not like the trees of Alaha. These are thin with smaller leaves and sparser.

Acker stops in a small clearing. "We should have enough coverage to wait here for your awakening to pass."

He kneels, and I cling to him. "Please." *Not the ground. Please don't put me on the ground.*

"Jovie," he says, breath brushing over my hair. "The only way through it is through."

I know he's right. There's nothing I can do to prevent the inevitable, but I'm tempted to beg him to take me back. Back to the boat. Back to Alaha. I know I'd hate myself for it, so I bite my tongue until I taste blood.

"I'm going to set you down now," he says, soft but stern.

I nod, releasing his shirt from my tight grip. The moment the ground meets my back, I scream. Acker cups his palm over my mouth, hand cradling my skull as he lowers my head back the rest of the way.

I can't stop it. My body contorts itself in an effort to escape the pain. I can't hear what Acker's saying. All I can see is his lips moving, but there's no sound. All that exists is the pain, like lightning through my veins. My heartbeat is my very own death march, each thump fueling the fire.

His voice breaks through the roaring in my head. "Please, Jovie," he says, desperate.

I struggle to remain focused on his face. His mouth moves, but his words are garbled, face warped as he continues to speak—no, plead. He's pleading with me.

"I need you to quit screaming. Please."

I clamp my teeth shut, groaning through the release begging for escape.

Acker's chest heaves as he lets out a gust of breath. "I'm sorry," he says. Over and over, he apologizes. "I'm going to try to find something to make it better, okay?"

Tears stream from my eyes, but I manage a nod. I urge my body to relax, trying to unclench my muscles, but it's next to impossible. Each breath and pulse of my heart feels like an attack against myself, like my own body is revolting. I feel the magic beneath my sternum. It's swirling and changing, reveling in the agony I feel.

This doesn't feel like a gift. It feels like a punishment.

I sense Acker's presence before he speaks. "Chew this well before you swallow it." He holds a leafy plant to my lips. Acker cups the back of my head, settling it on his thigh as he brings the waterskin to my mouth.

Most of the water spills over my mouth and down my chin, but I somehow manage to get a couple of swallows. Acker pushes my hair from my forehead, running his hand over the area again and again, a soothing gesture. I fall into an open pit of slumber.

# CHAPTER 26

Everything is convoluted.

The sky is purple and the grass is red and the trees swirl in the wind. I'm eating a pastry at the table in the kitchen, looking through the open door to the tilted world outside. Mother brushes my flyaways back behind my ear as I kick my feet under the table.

She's smiling, but I can't make out her face through the rain. It's pouring inside the house, soaking the table and floors and walls without touching us. I'm upset, but I don't remember why.

"Go see him," she tells me.

I brush the crumbs from my hands and get up to walk toward the doorway. The rain disappears when I step outside, the sky a deep shade of plum as the sun dips over the horizon. I reach for the pail on the stoop when I spot it. The one thing that's crystal clear in my mind, like it's been plucked from another world: a crown of wildflowers sits on top of the pail. I reach for it...

And I jolt awake.

The sky and trees looming overhead are back to normal shades of greens and blues. My stomach rebels, and I groan as I roll onto my side, hacking up what little remnants there are.

Acker comes into view as he kneels beside me, face pinched with worry as he pushes my hair away from my face. "How do you feel?"

Like shit.

I retch again. His lips thin as he takes in my appearance, holding the waterskin to my mouth so I can drink.

The ground rolls like the sea beneath me. "Why is the ground moving?" I say, voice weak.

"It's not. The saigon root I gave you can cause fever dreams, sometimes hallucinations. I was hoping to give you enough to sleep through most of the pain, but you burned through it quicker than I thought you would."

Yay me.

I have a spotty recollection of Acker shuffling me from one area to another, but I have no sense of time or place. The trees all look the same. The sky is clear, so it must be midday. The sharp edge of pain isn't as prevalent.

"The pain," I say. "It's better." Not gone, but no longer eating me alive.

Acker looks at me, skeptical. "You look terrible."

I huff out a broken laugh. "Thanks."

I suppose, in comparison to his appearance, I look like I'm on the brink of death. Where the land seems to have sucked the life out of me, it breathed new vigor into Acker. The hair falling onto his brow seems to be shinier, eyes brighter, shoulders...wider? I swear his skin is glowing.

"We can't stay here for much longer. The boat ended up capsizing south of here. It's drawn attention to the area. We're going to have to travel further inland than I'd like."

Blue lands on his shoulder, and I really *must* be hallucinating because he fluffs his feathers and chirps, settling in like they're not mortal enemies.

"He's been keeping a perimeter, checking for rebels."

The bird hops off his shoulder and onto the ground, chasing a beetle between the leaves. Our safety is in great hands, I see. Great feathers. Whatever.

Acker reaches into the pack and tears off more leaves, holding them up to my mouth.

I shake my head. "I can wait it out."

"There's no sense in you suffering for the hell of it."

I dig my fingers into the soil at my sides, resistant to the offering in his hand. But even in my fingertips, I'm made all too aware of how feeble I am. I despise this, hate being the weakest link. Blue is more helpful than I am right now. When Acker threatens to shove the leaves down my throat, I shoot daggers at him with my eyes, but he only lifts a brow in response.

"Try me," he dares.

I open my mouth, and he feeds the torn pieces onto my tongue. I use what little energy I have to snap my teeth down as hard as I can despite the slice of pain it ignites behind my eyes. He jerks back, but not quick enough, and I'm able to nip the tip of a finger. He hisses, returning my stare with a vengeance.

Hand braced on the ground beside my head, his anger morphs into a cunning smile. Like a snake in the water, smooth and precise.

"Sweet dreams," he says, eyes alight.

Maybe pissing him off when I'm on the verge of losing consciousness wasn't a good idea, but I fall asleep without an ounce of worry or fear for my safety.

# CHAPTER 27

"Put me down."

He doesn't listen.

"Put. Me. Down."

I'm hanging over Acker's shoulder like a child. This gets added to my list of least favorite ways to wake up.

I don't want to tell him, but…

"You have vomit on your shirt."

"I'm more than aware," he says, stepping over an uprooted tree.

The ground tunnels in and out of focus with the movement, and I'm grateful there's nothing else left in my stomach. I lift the material, inspecting the knife wound on his side. No longer open and discolored, the area appears healed, but the skin is mangled.

He shudders from the touch. "Stop it."

I drop the material. "It's your fault for forcing me to eat the plant of nightmares."

The dream lingers in the back of my mind. I was being chased by a giant bear with glowing red eyes and claws the length of my arms dragging the ground, which continued to shift and move like the ocean. If it's a memory from my past, it's not one I'm eager to get back.

"You can't hold me against my will," I say, putting as much conviction into my voice I can muster.

I can feel more than hear his huff of annoyance before he shifts my weight off his shoulder and I'm flipped upright. My legs give out from under me, and Acker lifts me up from under my arms to steady me.

He gives me a look. "That's what I thought." This time he cradles me against his chest when he picks me back up.

"It's been three days," I say, head bobbing against his chest as he walks. "You said the awakening would have passed by now."

"Four days," he corrects me. "It's been four days."

"Four?"

"You've been in and out. At first I thought it was the saigon root, like you'd had an adverse reaction of some sort, but you shouldn't still be in this much pain."

He looks down at me in his arms, worry etched around the lines of his eyes. He doesn't need to say it for me to know something isn't right. I feel it, inside me where the magic lives. It's made itself small, like it's hiding. From what, I'm not sure. It's almost as if it's...

Scared.

"A band of rebels have picked up our trail. Blue has kept an eye on their movements, but it's sporadic. I've been trying to shake them off the past two days without much luck. Every time I lose them, they backtrack to pick up our scent again."

"How many men?"

"The last Blue reported was twelve, but that's assuming we can trust a bird's ability to count."

Despite my extra weight, Acker stalks through the woods on sure footing, quiet but strategic as he avoids twigs and wet ground. He's been doing this for days with no sleep, and it hasn't deterred him in the slightest. It magnifies how useless I am, literal dead weight in his arms.

And I threw up on him.

We're on a slight decline as Acker marches downhill. The forest floor is littered with a carpet of dead leaves, but tufts of vibrant green peek through the layers, moss and fawns and leafy bushes.

We were taught about the land in Alaha—what each part of the continent's ecosystem consists of and where the native plants and animals live and thrive, which are poisonous and which are edible—but seeing the illustrations in a book is nothing in comparison to real life. The sounds and smells and sensations, birds and fresh blooms and humidity. There's a desperate sort of urge to fall to the ground and dig my fingers into the soil and *feel* the very essence of the earth in my hands.

Acker comes to a halt.

"Wha—"

He shushes me.

Head cocked to the side, he's...sensing something, I realize. Then he begins walking in a new direction. I can't tell if we're going toward or away from something until there's a break in the trees up ahead and I hear it— running water.

We emerge onto an embankment of rock with a rushing stream flowing before us. We're in a gorge, snowcapped mountains visible between the treetops in the distance, so far away they're hazy around the edges. There's a bend in the stream going the opposite direction.

I gauge the safety of crossing the rushing water. It's white and foaming, angry looking. I have no reference for how dangerous the current is, but it may be the only chance we have of shaking the people off our tails.

Flying in from above, Blue comes into view, black and

rainbow feathers reflecting in the sun as he lands on a rock beside us.

"Any change in their movements?" Acker asks. He speaks as if the bird understands every word out of his mouth.

Blue shakes his head, feathers puffing out before settling again.

"How many?"

He clicks his beak…ten times.

"Down by two now," I say, getting the gist of their communication.

"They could have split to follow a false trail I planted."

We turn to look at the foamy water. I don't have the strength to make it, and I don't think Acker can carry me without the water taking us under. He twists the hand I have my legs draped over, fingers pointing toward the opposite bank, eyes searching for something.

No, *feeling* for something.

I'm not sure what until I see the specks of tiny rocks ascending from the river. Acker points his fingers down the embankment, rattling a few as he passes over them with his magic. He's searching for any rock laden with heavy metals.

He looks at me. "Can you hold on to me if I put you on my back?"

I nod. Even if I can't, I will. There's no other option.

I wrap my arms and legs around him, and he grabs me under each of my knees and shifts me higher on his back. Then, widening his stance, he stretches out his hands toward the river.

Palms upright, he pulls, fingers curling in. It takes a moment, but then I see them. My breath catches at the sight of shards of rock and raw metals arising from the water. Some as small as a pebble and some as large as a coconut, they glint in the afternoon sun.

Veins bulge up Acker's arms as he concentrates. As if pulled by an invisible hand, the sediment converges into a floating bridge before us. Acker keeps one hand before him to maintain the structure, the other under my knee, and places his first foot onto the bridge. Freezing cold water splashes at his feet, the bridge dipping slightly under his weight, but Acker doesn't stop. One foot in front of the other, we cross the angry rapids until we reach the opposite embankment.

Acker drops his hand and the bridge falls, causing a rain of rocks to disappear under the white rapids, leaving not a trace of our path behind.

Acker's chest rises and falls, concentrated effort releasing along with the tension in his muscles. "Are you okay?"

I'm shaking from the energy it takes to maintain a hold around him, sweat coating my skin. "Yes," I reply, in awe.

"Good." He returns his grip to the back of my legs and holds me against him. "We need to put distance between us and here, so I'm going to move quickly."

It's the only warning I get before he takes off in a jog through the trees. He runs until the sunlight begins to fade, and I lose my fight for consciousness not long after.

# CHAPTER 28

This time I know for a fact the ground is moving beneath me before I wake.

We're nestled in the crook of two fallen trees. Based on their state of decay, they've been here a long time. Blue sits atop a broken limb, head tucked under a wing as he sleeps. The sun is low in the sky, telling me I've been out for a while.

Acker's chest rises and falls in a steady rhythm. He has an arm draped over my legs, which are curled in his lap, his other around my back, palm flattened at the top of my spine to keep me locked against his chest. I don't move, afraid to wake him. His heart beats steady in my ear, and a sudden bout of loneliness hits me.

I've left everything I know, everyone I know, to travel to a place I've never been before. Not just any place, but a home I've only caught bits and pieces of in my dreams.

Acker's not my friend.

He's a man who's been with me along the way, who risked his own life multiple times to protect me. A friend from a previous life, a life that could have been, maybe, but he's only here due to a promise he made to my family, to my mother.

I don't know how much longer it'll take us to reach Kenta, but our time together is coming to an end.

I take a moment to take note of my pain level, ignoring the slight ache in my chest. Wary, I reach out a hand to touch the dirt on the other side of Acker; it feels cool. Lifting my fingers to my face, I scrub the pads of my fingers together, feeling the grit of the dirt between them. I have a strange urge to taste it. I bring the tip of my finger to my tongue, which I regret instantly. I hurry to scrape it off, regret hitting me hard as I bite down on tiny grains of sand.

My head bobs from Acker's silent laughter, alerting me that he's awake. Probably been awake, if I had to guess. His chest jerks as he struggles to keep his laughter contained before he loses the battle, a rumble of sound pouring from his mouth.

I can't help but smile in return. "I don't know why I did that," I admit, embarrassed.

My comment only serves to make him laugh harder, and Blue's head pops out from his wing. I don't move from Acker's lap, but I lift a hand for him to perch on. He's been such a good help, communicating with Acker while I've been sick. He's deserving of some neck scratches.

He makes the short leap to my hand and bends for me to get the pesky spot behind his head. He blinks at me and flies away.

Rejected, I pull my hand back. "That was strange."

Acker runs a hand down my back in a soothing gesture. "He's been keeping the perimeter for days. Hasn't boded well for hunting. He's probably searching for breakfast."

That's fair.

I turn my attention to Acker, looking at him for the first time since waking. His eyes are soft but alert. A few hours of sleep did him good. I don't think I'll ever get used to being under his sole attention.

He continues to rub his hand along the length of my spine, sending goose bumps down my legs when he reaches the dip in my lower back. "Any more dreams?"

"A few, but they were too confusing to make sense of."

Eyes searching mine, he says, "Tell me about them."

"Well, there was this raging bear. It had blood-red eyes and ran on its back legs as it chased me."

Acker pauses then bursts into another round of laughter. The sound is somehow even more lovely than the one from a moment ago.

I smack him in the chest. "It's not funny! It was terrifying."

That only makes him laugh harder. Annoyed, I shove away from him. He reaches for me, but I bat his hands away. It's not until my torn pants expose my knees to the moist soil underneath that I realize I'm kneeling on the ground between Acker's legs.

He notices at the exact same moment I do, his laughter dying in his throat, eyes steady as he takes in the sight of me before him.

"How do you feel?"

I make a face as I struggle to put into words the feeling in my bones. I lower my hands to the dirt, palms flat to the earth.

"It feels…" I'm scared to say it, but I can't think of any reason to withhold the truth from him. "Strange," I say. "But there's no pain."

He doesn't react like I thought he would. It's not that I was expecting an outburst of some kind, but I wasn't expecting the blank expression on his face, like he's lost.

Shaking his head, the smile returns to his face, smaller but there. "Hallis used to scare you with stories of a bear he called Fang Hands who waited in the woods for little girls in pretty dresses to walk by."

I scowl at him. "I don't have many positive thoughts regarding your friend, Hallis," I say. "Sounds like a rightful pri—"

Acker leaps to his feet and pulls me up with him, my back to his front a split second before men pour into the space around us. Like the fish that camouflage in the reef, they flow in from between the trees, swords and bows aimed in our direction from all sides. Dressed in foliage, they match the terrain with dark smudges under their eyes.

It's nine against two. I've seen Acker take down four men with ease, but nine?

I haven't used my legs in days, and I feel like a newborn calf as I gain my footing, Acker's arm banded around my waist to help steady me. I note the soldiers with swords. I'd need to get close enough to wrangle one from their hands, but I'm much too spent to perform that miracle, let alone wield a weapon.

A tenth man strides into the makeshift circle. He's tall with light hair, eyes a stark blue. It's eerie how similar he looks to the Alaha in appearance.

"Hold on to your weapons." He speaks to his men without looking away from us. "We have the Soldier of Chaos amongst us."

A frisson of unease flits around the circle, but none of them move, only their hands as they tighten the clench on their weapons.

The man dips his head in acknowledgment. "Ace," he says, eyes on Acker.

By the tightness of Acker's posture behind me, it's obvious he is well acquainted with the man before us. "Vad. Desertion looks terrible on you."

The threadbare shirt and ripped pants don't temper the steel in Vad's gaze. "You don't look too well yourself." I do my best to not appear as feeble as I feel, but something tells me he can see straight through my facade. "And what do you have here?"

"Nothing you or your men are interested in," Acker says firmly. "I assure you."

"Mmm. I think you're wrong."

Acker's tone goes chilly, but I can tell there's a coldhearted smile on his face without looking at him. "I'm never wrong."

"You're in the wrong now, being across treaty lines."

"Spoken as a man of treason," Acker says.

"Cut the morality bullshit, Acker. We both know who's the most bloodthirsty here."

Acker doesn't speak or move behind me.

"There's no need to worry." Vad's eyes flick to me for a brief moment. "She's run through multiple scenarios of you killing every man in this clearing. She's not scared of you. Quite the opposite, actually."

I freeze. Impossible…

"I'm an oracle, darling," he says. "How did you think I managed to ambush your elemental friend? You'd be smart to remember that now you've returned home."

It's Acker's turn to go stock-still, nothing but solid muscle ready to spring at my back. Vad knows who I am and where I came from.

"Jovinnia, the lost Princess of Maile. Or do you prefer to go by Brynn?"

I haven't given my name much thought. Neither of them feel right. I suppose, if I had to choose, it would be Acker's version.

"Jovie it is," Vad says with a smile.

Acker damn near snarls in reply.

Vad lifts a hand in complacency. "If your goal is peace between our lands, we can forget I ever saw you. No blood needs to be spilled today."

The pointed look Vad gives me sends a chill down my spine. The blade at my waist gives me little reassurance.

Acker moves his arm across my upper chest, his breath a warm caress against my cheek. "You don't have to make me out to be the bad guy, Vad. I have no problem playing my part. And, as you've already discovered, she doesn't mind."

In the deep recess in the back of my mind, I feel Vad's power like a single lick of flame in the darkest night. There is no barrier, nothing to stop him seeing whatever it is he desires. The flame passes over and through my memories, inspecting them. Searching, searching, searching.

I can't stop the shake in my bones. I've known fear, but never like this. I pretend my mind is a well to douse the fire in my brain. I imagine the water overtaking the magic invading the space, but Vad's power evaporates any chance of keeping my innermost thoughts private. He can see and hear and feel anything he pleases. My mind is weak, weaker than I ever knew.

His smile only grows at my realization as he relishes my secrets. "Anything you'd like to know?" he asks Acker.

"Get out of her head," he seethes.

Vad is unfazed. He lifts a knowing brow at the man behind me. "I know you're curious."

Acker's nearly vibrating with anger. "*Now*," he demands.

Like blowing out a candle, the flame turns to smoke in

my mind, leaving the residue of soot behind.

"She finds the idea abhorrent," Vad divulges. "Sending children into battle. Matter of fact, I'm sure she'll agree with turning herself over to spare the same happening on her behalf."

Nausea rolls through me. I can't tell if it's from the invasion of privacy or the awakening. "I have no desire to be anyone's sacrifice," I declare, correcting him. No matter what he can gleam from my mind, I want him to hear the truth. "I would rather die than go anywhere with you."

I can feel Acker's smile against the shell of my ear. "Do women express that sentiment to you often, Vad? That they'd rather *die* than be in your presence?" He makes a clicking sound with his tongue. "Embarrassing."

Vad smiles. "You've always been a cocky son of a bitch."

"Tell him to back off," Acker says. One of the men to our right has been inching himself toward our flank this entire time.

"I don't have any authority over these men, Ace."

"And yet you've led them to their death."

Vad shakes his head. "You're not going to kill any of these men."

There's obvious familiarity between the two of them, and something in the way Vad holds himself gives Acker pause. I can feel his hesitancy behind me.

"How do you figure?"

Vad takes a step to our left, and each of the men follow, creating a counterclockwise motion around us. "Because she's dying."

I blink. I must have misheard him, because I thought he said...

"You've suspected it." Vad takes another step. Then another, his men following the same pattern. "You knew her body was probably too weak to make it through the awakening without a healer. You wanted to turn back to Kenta, where you knew a healer would be on standby the moment you made landfall."

Acker doesn't adjust our position, letting Vad disappear behind our backs. They're closing in on us, but he doesn't make any moves. As firm as a tree, his feet are planted to the ground. Still. Lethal.

"But she pushed, and you conceded. She was miserable on that boat, and you hated watching her break down a little more and more each day."

Acker's voice comes out low and cold. "That's enough."

"Tell me," Vad says, reappearing in our peripheral. "Is it different to witness on land? Does it make it easier to tolerate?"

"I said that's enough." An imperceptible quiver travels through Acker's body, barely concealed rage desperate to get out. I further relax into his hold, hoping to communicate to him to remain in control, to remain calm, my own emotions notwithstanding.

"I don't need to see inside your mind to know the truth." Vad completes his circle, stopping before us once again. "That's a symptom of being a mind reader since I was twelve. It leaves little mystery as to the human condition. People are..." He thinks on it a moment, eyes going skyward before returning with renewed energy. "Boring."

Each breath feels more labored than the one before. I focus on keeping a steady rhythm, afraid to let on how worn down I am from standing alone. Even with Acker to lean on, my strength is waning.

By the look on Vad's face, I don't think I'm doing a good job disguising my feebleness. "You've been practicing your mental defenses. I'm impressed at your ability to keep me out."

Acker doesn't speak. From the looks of the men surrounding us, it makes them uneasy, eyes shifting between them, uncertain of what is to come next.

"I'll make you a deal." He snaps his fingers and shoots one in Acker's direction. "I'll tell you the location of a healer here in Roison if you let me inside your memories for thirty seconds."

Acker laughs, a quick chuckle of disbelief. "You're delusional."

"Am I?" Vad makes a face. "It's more than a day's ride by horseback to the border."

Before Vad can utter another word, breathe another breath, a whiz of air being pierced sounds through the clearing. It's unmistakable. In the next instant, I'm punched in the chest. I look down. A wooden reed is protruding from the side of my sternum. Acker pivoted us in the split second before impact, having seen the incoming arrow, causing it to miss its mark. Sticking out from between my ribs, the reed pulses with the beat of my heart.

Acker growls, voice erupting as he throws out his hand. Weapons fly from the holds and straps of the men and into the necks and sides and bodies of the men standing next to them. Half of them are dead before they hit the ground.

There's another zip in the air, another wooden arrow narrowly missing Acker's jugular as he angles us away from its trajectory.

"Stop!" Vad shouts.

His men listen.

Acker does not. He calls his blade from one of the felled corpses into his spare hand.

"If you kill me or anyone else, you'll never know where to find the healer, and Jovie will die before you're able to get to the border."

Liquid bubbles up my throat, and I cough. Red flecks of blood splatter onto the hand I have pressed around the entrance wound. I'm grateful for Acker's hold. My legs would give out otherwise.

"Fine," Acker spits. "My mind is open."

Vad shakes his head, smile returning, taunting Acker as it grows. "You'll only kill us after. No. I want a blood oath of you swearing not to harm us."

Acker doesn't hesitate. He lifts his hand and uses his magic to swipe his blade across his open palm. "With this blood, I swear to do no harm to you or the men here today as long as Jovie doesn't die." He squeezes his fist and lets the blood drip to the ground along with the weapon.

Vad seems less pleased with Acker's terms, but he doesn't voice them.

Acker speaks through clenched teeth. "On with it."

As he tilts his head to the side, Vad's eyes zoom in on Acker before going blank. The arm Acker has banded around me tightens, but his body goes stock-still behind me. I concentrate on breathing. Each inhale feels tighter than the last, and the taste of metal coats the back of my tongue. I know it's only thirty seconds, no more than the same number of breaths, but it feels like a lifetime before Vad's eyes focus again and life returns to Acker's body. Whatever knowledge Vad was able to garner from

Acker better have been worth it.

"There's a brook that cuts west. Follow it through the woods until you come across the trees covered in moss. There's a cottage tucked between the trees. It's disguised, so keep your eyes peeled."

"How far?"

"Twenty minutes," Vad says, eyes falling on me. "If you run."

Acker cradles me to his chest. I cough again, and I can feel the blood hot on my chin and neck.

A man's scream comes from high in the trees. From the archer, I presume.

"What is that?" one of the men on the ground asks, fear in his voice. "You said you wouldn't harm us."

Acker turns his back on the men as more screaming ensues. "I didn't say anything about the bird."

"Bird?"

I can't see Blue, but I hear his battle cry a moment before the shrieks turn into garbled moans, then choked silence. There's a long pause before the sounds of the men fleeing for their lives echo behind us.

But Acker doesn't look back or wait. He runs.

# CHAPTER 29

"We should kill him and turn his head over to the king."

Another male voice chimes in. "He can kill you without moving a muscle, boy. I suggest you keep your mouth shut."

Acker's voice is laced with rage. "I'll kill you both if you let her die."

Every breath is a struggle. Fluid gurgles into my throat and mouth with each inhale. I want it to end, but death doesn't seem willing to make this quick for me.

An older, female voice says, "Who's at the door?"

There's a stretch of silence, the only noise my shallow breathing.

"You're the healer," Acker says, losing the hardness in his tone, desperation seeping through.

Cold fingers trail my cheek. "She isn't fully awakened," the female says. A moment passes before she continues. "She can't be healed without going through the awakening. I'm sorry. There's nothing I can do for her."

"Try," he demands, a weak order as his voice breaks on the single word. "Please."

There's a deep breath of consideration before she orders the other men to gather oils and herbs from her apothecary cabinet.

"We'll go to the temple."

"There's no time for your fanatical bullshit," Acker spits, anger returning full force. "Here. Do it here."

"You don't know it all, metal slinger. You will do what I say, and threatening me with death will do you no good," she tacks on.

I sink in and out of consciousness. There's a hot poker shoved through my chest, but I feel removed from it, like I'm separate from my body and I only exist in my mind. Memories stack on top of each other. Not just from my early childhood as my father tucked me into bed, a blank space where his face should be, but from my time in Alaha, when Kai began teaching me how to hold my breath for long increments under water.

The recollections volley back and forth, over and over like my soul is trying to mesh the two histories together. Then I'm catapulted into the real world, screaming from the searing pain when the arrow is ripped from my body.

"Hold her down," the woman yells.

Hands pin my arms and legs to a hard slab of rock, my eyes locking on Acker's above me. He's sweating, eyes wild and teeth mashed together as he holds my shoulders down. I can't stop screaming long enough to formulate words, but I'm begging him.

*Stop this. Let me free.*

He looks away, toward the woman as she begins to speak. "Do it."

Then she puts her hands on my chest. It's worse than the awakening, worse than the reed that pierced my chest, indescribable in every way. Pure agony. My body bows away from the table. I've lost all control. It fights to get away.

Shouts breach my muted senses, not mine, but of the

225

people holding me down. One of the men begs a god I don't know for mercy.

The woman barks commands. "Close your eyes! Don't open them unless you want to go blind!"

I don't know what she's talking about. I can't see anything. Endless nothing before me, behind me, in every direction. I can only feel the hands on my bare skin, hear the words of the woman as she resumes the task at hand.

Acker's hair tickles my brow, and I realize his forehead is pressed against mine, his hands the most prominent on my shoulders. I'm teleported into a memory, different from the ones I've dreamed of before.

I'm standing on a cliff overlooking the sea as I turn to face Hallis. His appearance is clear for the first time, but he's grown. A man stands before me with deep auburn hair, freckles blending with the tan of his skin.

"What if she's too far gone," Hallis says.

His golden eyes pierce my own, steady as he gives me time to consider my answer.

No, not my answer.

*Acker's.*

"I can't abandon her."

His thoughts string through me like they're mine. No one has gone to Alaha and returned to tell the tale. Mercenaries and spies, killed under a veil of secrecy. Wren has crafted a persona as a doting leader. The body parts we've received by messenger bags beg to differ.

I'll arrive in broad daylight. It's the only way to prevent Wren from killing me outright. His power is muted over the ocean, so he can't persuade the minds of that many people in his favor if he kills a man in cold blood. Weather permitting, we'll embark in the morning.

Hallis nods. "The galleon will release a peace flare when you arrive."

I reach for the blade strapped to my outer thigh and come up empty. I feel incomplete without it, but it brings me solace that it found its way back to her.

"Send word to her family. No matter the outcome."

Hallis nods and places a hand on my shoulder. "May the next time you two reunite go better than the first."

I shove his arm from my shoulder, trying to disguise the strain in my walk as we head back to port. My ankle aches despite the healer's touch, but a smile pulls at my mouth in anticipation.

I'm going to get Jovie.

# CHAPTER 30

Acker sits in a chair at the foot of the bed, head propped against a closed fist like he fought and lost the battle to stay awake. His upper chest and arms are bathed in dried mud and blood and god knows what other gunk, his hair crusty from where it's matted against his forehead and temples. Light pours in from the lone window behind him, outlining his body in a silhouette of gold.

He's in sharp juxtaposition to myself as I pull the clean lace gown away from my body, inspecting the pink scar that spans the space between my breasts, a singular line from where the arrow peaked out. I'm in a small bed in the center of the bedroom.

The creaking of floorboards sounds from the other side of the door, followed by a knock that snaps Acker awake. He stands when the door opens, the top of his head nearly touching the roof. The woman steps in, slow and measured as she looks toward Acker. There's a tray of food in her hands.

She looks at me and dips her head and upper body into a bow. "I brought food."

Acker shifts on his feet as the woman approaches the bed, settling the tray at the foot. My stomach growls at the smell of the chicken and rice and green vegetables. Acker's nostrils flare, his stomach undoubtedly doing the same.

"There's plenty for you both. There's more where it came from if you're left unsatisfied."

This is...odd. She's acting as if we're guests of honor. How much time am I missing? The last thing I can recall was...

Being held to a stone slab. I wasn't just healed but also forced through the last remnants of the awakening. The memories of screams that weren't mine...

She must sense my discomfort, or maybe it's Acker's. Neither of us is demonstrating common manners.

I force a smile. "Thank you."

She returns the smile with a much more genuine one. "Fia," she says, introducing herself.

I don't hesitate. "Jovie."

"You two are welcome to stay as long as you need." She gives a pointed look in Acker's direction. "The washroom is free if you'd like to use it." Then she bows again before walking back out the door.

Acker lets out a breath and runs a hand over his face, sinking back in the chair. His eyes scan the length of my body, scrutinizing every inch of me as if he's checking to make sure I didn't sustain any further injuries while he was asleep. "How do you feel?"

I shrug. "Normal."

He drops his gaze. "Just normal?"

Well, now that he mentions it, my magic...

It feels...*alert.*

"Like I'm going to die if I don't eat my weight in food."

He smiles a little. "It's a consequence of exerting your energy. Magic always comes with a price."

I hold up my hands, inspecting them for a sign of my new gifts. Narrowing my eyes on him, I throw an arm in his direction, aiming for the dagger at his waist.

Nothing happens.

His smile tilts to one side. "Nice try."

I make a noise of disappointment.

He shakes his head once. "You're not an elemental."

"Then what am I?"

Breathing deep, his grin lessens a degree. "I'm not sure yet."

"But you have an idea."

Elbow resting on the arm of the chair, he bites the pad of his thumb as he further inspects me. He's so far away. After being attached to his person for weeks now, the eight feet of space between us feels like a chasm, like I'm being forced against my will to remain in this bed when I have the strongest desire to climb in his lap.

Then I realize his hands are clean. Too clean in comparison to the rest of him.

"Who bathed me?"

He doesn't miss a beat. "I dressed you."

I blink in surprise.

"It wasn't..." His brow furrows in the middle. "It wasn't like that. You had...you had burned all the clothes from your body."

"I—what?"

"During the awakening," he says, struggling to find the words. "You lit up and were... bright. Like the sun. And your skin became hot enough that you disintegrated your clothes from your skin. Burned away all the blood and dirt along with it."

I'm struck speechless.

He looks down at his open palms. They're scorched pink. "After Fia was able to heal you, I carried you here, back to her home, and got you covered."

I try and fail to digest the information he's given

me. It doesn't feel real, doesn't sound real if I'm being honest, but I trust Acker. Call it my gut or magic, I don't care. I just know it to be true.

"Thank you," I tell him.

He doesn't respond.

"I assume burning your clothes off isn't a typical reaction to the awakening."

He breathes through his nose, exhaustion lining every inch of his face and body. "It's hard to say. The descriptions of late awakenings are few and far between. I've never encountered someone who's experienced it themselves."

I'm afraid to ask, but I must. "Could it...be my gift?"

"If it is," he says, brow still furrowed, "it's unlike anything I've seen before."

That's not reassuring.

After a moment, he motions to the tray of food and stands, moving toward the door. "Eat."

"Where are you going?"

"To bathe *myself*," he says with a playful smile.

But...I have so many questions.

"The sooner we get moving, the better."

He shifts his eyes toward the hall outside the door, and I understand everything he isn't saying. Fia has been accommodating, but we're still in enemy territory. No one is to be trusted. There's a pregnant pause before he places my dagger on the tray at the foot of the bed. I give him a single nod in understanding.

He turns to leave but lingers with his hand on the door handle. The urge to go to him comes back in full force. Not just to go to him, but...for him to pull me into his arms, like he did through the storm.

Acker breaks the spell first, finally walking away. I

lean to peek through the open door, and I have a direct view of him speaking to Fia in the kitchen, their muffled voices filtering down the hall. He asks for a change of clothes and follows her out of sight. When he reappears, I see he's carrying a folded set before he disappears into another doorway.

Fia stops at the end of the hall. She smiles before moving away.

I've never given death much consideration, but I can't deny the gratitude I feel to be alive. I pull the tray of food toward me and am equally as grateful Fia can cook a decent meal, although I'm sure anything would appeal to my empty stomach right now. I open my mouth to shovel in as much food as I can then I blink and the poised spoon is gone.

Everything is gone, I realize. I'm in another room. It's a washroom. There's a basin filling with water and a sink and—

I don't have control over my hands or where I look. I'm sitting on the edge of the basin as I bend to untie my boots.

Acker's boots.

Not my hands, Acker's hands.

I watch as he takes off his shoes and places them under the sink, one next to the other. Unlike the memory of him and Hallis, I'm not privy to his thoughts and emotions. Just a voyeur behind his eyes this time.

He stands and unbuttons his pants, shoving them past his hips.

In a panic, I attempt to squeeze my eyes shut, and I'm thrown back into my room, back into my body. I'm staring into empty space, breathing hard as I calm the panic racing in my chest. The food that was on the spoon in my hand is now in my lap, the warmth of the meal seeping through the gown.

I shake my head.

I'm imagining things. Lingering effects of the root Acker gave me, undoubtedly. I need to fill my stomach with something more substantial.

The food is *divine*. I scarf down the entire plate and am licking the remnants from my fingers when Fia appears in the door. She has another set of folded clothes in her hands.

She motions to my chest. "May I?"

Nodding, I slide the blade under the fold of the blanket under the guise of making room for her to sit. She sets the clothes down as I remove my gown, shoving down my worry of propriety. According to Acker, she's seen it all already.

"I was spent by the time I finished healing the vital parts. I didn't have the energy to seal the wound as well as I would have liked." Her fingers are cold against my chest as she inspects the flesh. "Would you like me to remove it?"

It's angry and red but no longer than my smallest finger. "Will it hurt?"

"It would be mild, but there would be some discomfort, yes."

I shake my head. I've had enough experience with pain as of late. "I'm fine with it."

She smiles. "As you wish. Here is a change of clothes. You're close enough to my size."

I retrieve the trousers she brought me and stand. They're light as a feather and a deep russet color, reminding me of the dresses on the girls at the Market. I slide them on, relishing the softness of the material.

The brassiere and tunic are just as delicious against my skin. My frame has thinned a considerable amount, but the clothes fit well.

Fia smiles when I'm done. "That color suits you," she says. "It brings out the color of your eyes beautifully."

My stomach rumbles.

Fia smiles. "There's more food in the kitchen. Come get a second helping."

I hurry to pocket the blade and follow her out of the room. The home is modest, but as small as it is, it's warm and comfortable, inviting even. The food is left on a spindle table in front of a window overlooking the dense forest beyond.

"I wanted to prepare enough to send you two on your journey back to Kenta," she says, noticing my attention. "Fix whatever you like."

I pick a slice of bread from a loaf cooling on a cutting board. It's almost too hot to consume, but I can't seem to stop myself.

"When was the last time you had bread in Alaha?" Fia asks.

I'm not sure what Acker has revealed to her regarding who I am versus what she may have pieced together herself. It's obvious she knows who Acker is. He is known by more than one name, it seems, but I don't want to volunteer information.

So I rip off more bread with my teeth and shrug.

"Smart girl," she says, fixing herself a plate. She sits at the table, unconcerned as I inspect her home.

The kitchen makes up the majority of the main living area. Tapestries hang from various walls, ranging in colors and designs. The far wall is lined with shelves of vials filled with different liquids. Feathers and strips of leather hang from the doorways. I peer through a window on the other side of the kitchen.

"We're a little less than a day and a half's trip from the Kenta border. There are not many homesteads between here and there due to the years of conflict within the area, but the region's full of soldiers. Best to stay away from the windows."

I nibble on another bite of bread. The door to the washroom opens, and a fresh Acker pauses in the doorway, head swiveling from the now empty bed where he left me before finding me in the opposite direction. Hair wet and skin clear of debris, he looks amazing in a pale blue shirt that offsets his features. Handsome doesn't cover it.

I tear my gaze away first this time.

"May I?" he says, motioning to the assortment of food.

"Of course," Fia says, pointing to a cupboard. "Bowls and cutlery are over there."

I keep my back toward them as I continue to peruse Fia's home and trinkets. It's more out of a need for distraction than actual interest, and I still can't help but keep an ear on Acker's movements. The chair as it scrapes the floor, the clinking of silver against a plate, the gnashing of teeth, the bliss when the spices hit my tongue—

I spin in place.

Two sets of eyes look up at me, addled by my sudden movement.

I don't hear Acker enjoying his food; I *feel* it. *Taste* it.

Acker does a quick scan over my person before returning his attention to his meal. It's the first time he's been able to eat real food in weeks, and he manages to not look like a scavenger as he sticks a modest portion of meat in his mouth and chews. He's even using a fork, for gods' sake.

There's no denying I'm jumping inside Acker's head. My powers might be manifesting of their own volition. My gifts might be more reminiscent of Vad's—the oracle in the woods—than Acker's like I was hoping for, and Acker's mind must be the easiest to leap into considering he's who I'm closest with. I can't imagine a worse gift.

That's a lie—not having control over my body igniting itself until it's hot enough to obliterate my clothes from my body would be the worst gift. Being an oracle is a close second. A very close second.

The door to the cottage opens, revealing an older gentleman and boy I deduce are Fia's husband and son if Acker's lack of concern regarding their arrival is any indication.

"Good news." The older man who comes through the door halts when he spots me standing in the living area. He pivots with a hand to his chest and bows in my direction, deeper and longer than Fia did, and it sends a tendril of trepidation down my spine, like I'm missing something. "Name's Jorgen," he says as he straightens. "I'm happy to see you're doing well."

Unsure of the custom, I bow in return. "Thank you."

His son is less enthused, his greeting a mere dip of his head, and for that I am relieved.

Fia stands to greet her husband with a kiss on the cheek then directs her son to eat. He can't be more than sixteen but has the appearance of a man. He's blatant in his dislike of Acker and me as he skirts by us.

"Tell me about this good news," Fia says, pulling a

chair out for her husband at the table.

He shakes his head and removes the knit cap from his head, using his fingers to push the errant strands of gray hair back down. "We found a couple of horses."

That gets Acker's attention.

Fia is skeptical. "Found?"

He gives her a look as if to say, *Don't ask because you won't like the answer.* Sure enough, her responding *tsk* is pure displeasure.

Acker tears off a piece of bread and dips it in the drippings. "What's the bad news?" he says, popping the bread into his mouth.

"Word has spread about the boat that crashed offshore and the rebels that were found dead in the forest." He shares a look with his wife, conversing with his eyes. "Ten men. Half of them were mutilated. Their eyes and tongues were plucked out."

There's a stony silence between them.

Acker's eyes dart to me. That means one managed to escape, and it means Blue is a special kind of terrifying. Acker lets out a slow, growing smile as if to convey a big, fat *I told you so.* And, if I'm not mistaken, something like pride shines through.

"Some of the townspeople have gathered together to send out a hunting party. There's fear of Kenta invading again."

Again?

He delivers the last bit of information like it should be concerning to us, but Acker doesn't so much as blink at the news as he continues to sop up sauce. "Technically, we did," he says, giving Jorgen a look that says something along the lines of *Let's be real.* "We'll only take one horse, and we'll be gone by nightfall tomorrow."

Jorgen cocks his head. "That's if you're not caught."

"We won't be."

"Mighty sure of yourself considering the state she was in when you brought her to us yesterday," Fia says. "You should let Jorgen and Sven accompany you the rest of the way."

"That was before Jovie had completed the awakening. We're in better shape, much thanks to you and yours, but we'll fare just fine by ourselves.

Jorgen braces his hands on the back of Fia's chair. "You're headed into the king's most guarded territory. It's not a matter of if you encounter problems, but when. If you're not clocked by sight, they're going to know who you are just by being alone with one girl. It'll be less suspicious if we travel as a group."

Acker wipes his mouth and pushes his chair back. "I mean this with no disrespect, but you'll only be a hindrance."

"We promise to carry our weight."

"You're confused," Acker says, holding the man's gaze as he stands from his seat. "I don't need the added worry of whether or not I'll need to kill you or your son in case one of you decides to do something stupid while my back is turned."

Jorgen's face turns red at Acker's accusation. His son, Sven, smirks.

"The metal slinger is right," Fia says. "That's why you'll both give blood oaths to do no harm to either of them."

Sven begins to argue, but Acker cuts him off with a hand. "I don't care for sworn fealty."

"You can't deny the truth—there's a better chance of

you two making it to Kenta if you travel with us," Jorgen says. "The oath alleviates any of your concerns."

"And, with all due respect," Fia says, turning her attention to me, "it's not your decision."

# CHAPTER 31

The air is divine. Crisp, and green somehow, like the trees are breathing life into the world around it. Each step I take is cushioned by the moss-covered ground. Bending down, I run my fingers over the soft surface.

"You can pet the lawn another time," Acker says, strapping a knapsack to the horse in front of him. He manages a smile, but there's an urgency in his body I don't think I've witnessed before.

Jorgen and Sven emerge with Fia on their heels. Acker motions for me to come closer, but I eye the horse. It's ginormous, bigger than the cattle we had in the paddocks in Alaha and stacked with muscle.

"Jovie," Acker says, impatient, hand outstretched as an offering to help me onto the creature's back.

Its dark eyes watch as I approach, as if the animal knows I'm intimidated by his imposing size. He knows I'm afraid, and he likes it.

Fia's inhalation of breath comes from behind me, but I'm too nervous to turn my back to the horse. Acker's brows furrow in the middle as he maintains his gaze on me. He says my name again, this time in warning. I still can't tear my gaze from the horse, its nostrils flaring, muscles twitching.

Acker yells. "Jo!"

I meet his gaze, confused. He's looking at me as if he doesn't know what to do with me.

"You're glowing," he says, answering my unspoken question.

Lifting an arm, I suck in a breath at the light emanating from my skin like a lantern without a flame, glowing without any fire. "What in the... Is this part of the awakening?"

"It's your gift," Fia says, coming from behind. "You're a light wielder."

There's a reverence to her words, but I don't dare pull my gaze from Acker. "What does that mean?"

"I think your gifts are reacting to your fear," he says. "You need to control it."

"I...I don't know how." And, as if my magic senses my panic, the light surrounding me grows brighter.

"Careful," Acker says, outstretched hand turning upright as he steps closer to me. "You don't want to burn through your clothes again."

"Or us," Sven says, a hint of fear in his voice.

I say Acker's name, a plea.

"It's okay," he says, hand hovering over my shoulder, eyes holding mine. "Close your eyes."

I don't want to close my eyes. I shake my head in protest, but all he does is nod back, slowly and deliberately, until I do. His hand makes contact with the dip of my shoulder, and I relish the comfort of his touch, the very sensation I've craved since I awoke this morning. I anchor myself to the feel of Acker's palm as it slides to the base of my neck, to the place where my collar meets my throat.

His thumb sweeps over the tender skin. "Your magic exists inside of you. Find it. Tell it you're not in any danger and to stand down."

I shake my head, not understanding.

"Mine is here," he says. Reaching for my hand, he places it on something rigid. His chest, as I realize by the rise and fall of his breaths and the warmth and tick of his heart. "Find yours."

But it's everywhere. From the shuffling of my thoughts to the tips of my toes, every piece of me feels electric. I speak to it from my mind anyway, telling it to obey like Acker instructed me to.

*I'm not in any danger. I'm not in any danger. Everything is fine.*

The flow of energy is hesitant, but it furls itself bit by bit, like the way a hermit crab sinks back into its shell.

"There you go," Acker says, voice low and soothing.

I open my eyes and am met with the full force of Acker's beauty. I'm so stunned my breath fails me, and I have to make a conscious decision to suck in a lungful of air. It seems to snap Acker out of his own stupor, and he takes a step back. I immediately miss the solace of his touch.

The sound of movement pulls my gaze behind me, and I lose my breath for a whole new reason as I find Fia and Jorgen on one knee, heads bowed. Jorgen's hat is in a fist to his chest. Then there's Sven, hard gaze holding mine until his knee hits the grass, losing the connection when his chin meets his chest.

My eyes flicker to Acker in an attempt to gauge the situation, but his face is set in stone, not a hint of emotion in his steely gaze. I lift my brows at him, begging him to do something, *say* something. I don't know the social etiquette here.

He breathes out through his nostrils and does a quick roll of his eyes. "Get up," he orders them. "You're making her uncomfortable."

The next thing I know, Acker's hands bracket my waist as he hefts me onto the blanketed back of the horse. I'm not scared of heights by any means, but the distance to the ground is daunting. The top of Acker's head is level with my thighs when he looks up at me. The horse shifts his feet, and I cling to the hair of its mane, throwing my leg over the side so I don't fall off.

"You're fine," Acker says, stroking the horse's neck but speaking to me. "He can sense your fear. Relax."

Fia hands Acker a knapsack and a roll of what looks to be bedding, and he shoulders it. I look to the family preparing for our departure. They respected my decision to trust Acker's opinion on traveling to Kenta alone, but their worry is evident on their faces.

I clear my throat so my voice doesn't break when I speak. "Thank you for saving my life."

Fia steps forward, a sheen of moisture puddled in her eyes. "You're going to change everything, girl."

I pause, unsettled by the warning underlining her words. It sounds more like a threat than a promise.

Acker grabs a handful of the horse's mane and uses it to leverage himself onto the horse's back. "If I'm able, I'll send payment," he tells her.

"You'd only be risking whoever you sent. Spare them."

He dips his head in acquiescence, and she pats my knee once in farewell. Jorgen steps forward next and bids his goodbye as well. Fia has instructed him to remove the other horse from the vicinity before the search party finds it at their door. They embrace. Jorgen says something softly to her, and she cups his face in her hands, kissing him.

Sven doesn't bother with goodbyes or pleasantries before going inside.

What I wasn't prepared for is how closely we're seated together. Acker's legs bracket mine, the inside of his thighs hugging my rear and outer legs, arms brushing my ribcage on each side as he situates the reins over my lap.

"We're directly west of the Dark Forest," Jorgen says. "I'd stick as close as you can to it. There are fewer sentries patrolling the area."

"Should we go north or south once we hit the tree line?" Acker says.

"South. Fewer trolls."

Excuse me? *"Trolls?"*

Acker smiles at my reaction. "They typically keep to themselves, but people avoid them."

Jorgen gives me a look. "The smell will never leave you."

Okay, yeah. South it is.

Acker clicks his tongue, and the horse begins to walk forward. I can feel the muscles of the animal stretch and contract, creating a deep sway back and forth with each step. I look back to wave goodbye, but the cottage is gone, like it faded into the ether, Fia and Jorgen along with it.

"It's magicked," Acker tells me. "Jorgen is an illusionist. He can make the eye play tricks on itself. He does good work. Nearly missed it yesterday."

Interesting.

I can't will my body to relax when Acker's front is in complete contact with my back. Every step the horse takes creates a soft glide of his body against mine. This is a special kind of torture. I can feel the heat of my neck and cheeks turning pink, but if Acker sees it, he doesn't acknowledge it, or the stiffness in my posture.

A soft flap of wings sounds before Blue lands on the horse's neck. The horse's ears flick back, but he doesn't slow or show any signs of agitation.

"Hi." I reach out to scratch behind his neck. Jorgen's description of mutilated bodies comes to the forefront of my mind. "Good job," I tell him. "And thank you."

Acker snorts, but even he reaches over to tickle the feathers askew on Blue's head.

We move like this for hours. Blue circling overhead, Acker and I remaining quiet. It's not until the sun is low in the sky and we're deep within the forest that I begin to lose the fight to keep distance between us. The surge of energy from the awakening has slackened over the day, and the ache to use Acker as support finally wins over my stubbornness.

He doesn't react when I finally allow my body to sink into the opening of his, keeping his gaze ahead.

"Has your stance on whether you live or die changed since you cheated death?"

*Oh.* He means what Vad divulged about me.

"I'm grateful to be alive," I say, settling back against him once again.

I feel the deep breath Acker takes against my back. "Good."

There's a flicker of a moment where I can see from his point of view, a flash of looking over my shoulder, at the reins he has draped over my thigh. But as quick as it comes, it's gone.

"Thank you," I tell him. "Not just for saving my life, but for...taking care of me."

His voice comes out gruffer than I expect it to. "Of course."

"But, also, fuck you for not telling me I was

actively dying. You could have divulged that tidbit of information to me."

"To serve what purpose?"

"I deserved to know."

There's a period of silence as I seethe to myself before he says, "I was afraid. I felt like if I said it out loud, it would make it real." He runs his thumb over my forearm. "I'm sorry. I should have told you."

His honesty douses any remaining anger I have at him. "Promise me you won't withhold information from me again. Not if it pertains to me," I clarify.

"I promise," he says, resolute.

"Good. Now tell me why in the world Fia and her family felt the need to bow to me."

He stutters out a laugh. "I think this is considered entrapment."

"You literally just promised."

"Healers are known to be zealots. They view someone who possesses one of the four main elements to be ordained by Mother Nature herself. The world was perfect by her design, a gift to her four children: air, water, fire, and earth. But legend says they constantly fought for dominance, and it created a world of chaos, not the stability Mother Nature intended. To protect the earth from total decimation, Mother slipped her own creations into the world—humans with gifts fit to control the elements."

A memory from when we were back in Alaha resurfaces. "An Heir."

"Yes." Acker pulls the reins to slow our horse into a walk when he sees the trickle of a stream cutting through the woods. He dismounts first and turns to help me down. "And the last time a light wielder walked the earth, she *ruled* the earth and the four elements within it."

I look up at him, aware of the fact that he hasn't removed his hands from my waist yet. "What was she like?"

He doesn't need to answer. I can see it in his eyes. Whoever the light wielder was, she was not kind. He tightens his hold on me before releasing me altogether.

Tiny fish zoom away when I kneel next to the spring. A long-necked bird takes careful steps further down the stream as the horse slurps from the spring with floppy lips. I cup the cool water in my hands to drink, and it's the purest water I've ever tasted. Pulling the hair over my shoulder, I dribble what I can from my palm to my overheated neck.

Then I see myself from behind—through Acker's eyes. I can taste the water he's swallowing from the waterskin as his eyes linger on the curve of my neck. I still have awareness of myself, like I'm in two places at once. I dip my hand in the water and pour it over my neck again, watching as the droplets of water trail down my neck, disappearing under my blouse.

I dare a look over my shoulder, cutting the connection as I meet his gaze. But his face reveals nothing as he strides toward me. Crouching down, he refills the now empty waterskin, eyes no longer on me but on the task in front of him.

I realize I prefer it when his attention is on me. "Is that why you didn't kneel?"

A smile grows on his lips before he caps the waterskin and looks at me. "Did you want me to kneel?"

My own smile threatens to reveal itself. "Not if you think I'm the incarnation of an evil ruler."

His smile deepens before disappearing altogether, face turning serious. "You're not the incarnation of anything, and you're not evil."

"How do you know?"

"Because I do."

We're less than a foot apart, and I realize a moment too late that I'm staring at his mouth. Color stings my cheeks when I meet his eyes again, only to find he's doing the same. His eyes flit back and forth, from my mouth to my eyes and back again.

He shakes the excess water from his fingertips then moves the stray hairs out of my face. "I believe you're going to bring a world of peace to Kenta."

# CHAPTER 32

The pile of dirt I've shaped and patted into place resembles a tiny mountain, like Mount Zallis that we learned about in primary school, the tallest point on earth, which magical creatures are rumored to inhabit. I stick a leaf in the top of the dirt, like I'm the first to reach its peak and claim the land.

Who knows? Maybe those creatures are real considering magic exists. It doesn't just exist—I harbor it. I'm considered an Heir, allegedly ordained by Mother Nature herself.

I crush the mountain with a fist.

"What are you smiling about?" Acker asks.

Looking up, I realize I *am* smiling as I watch him walk the perimeter of the makeshift campsite. He's been picking up random sticks, inspecting them, then placing them in specific locations in a circle around us.

"When that school of jellyfish surrounded you." He couldn't swim back to the boat any quicker if he had fins.

"It's a fond memory for you, is it?" he says, accent thicker around the edges.

Dusting off my hands, I fold my feet underneath me. "It's not my least favorite."

I catch a glimpse of his teeth as he tries and fails to hide his smile. He must deem the perimeter safe, or safe enough at least, because he issues me an order to stay put and disappears into the woods.

The last remnants of daylight dissipate, leaving the full moon to its full glory. Acker said a fire would draw attention, but he didn't say anything about magic.

I lift a palm face up. Taking a deep breath, I imagine it glowing like it did when I was afraid of the horse, but nothing happens. I close my eyes and search for that spot where Acker said magic resides and come up empty. Opening my eyes, I pout at the ordinary color of my skin.

A soft breeze catches me by surprise, and I shiver. Warmth envelopes me then, and I look up as Acker drapes a blanket over my shoulders.

"It's the Dark Forest," he says. "We're just beside its border."

It's obvious this forest and trolls are common knowledge that don't require explaining to most people. Acker settles on his bedroll, forearm braced over his knee as he picks through his own food reserves. They look even more abysmal than mine.

"It's a thatch of forest that sits in the middle of the border between Kenta and Roison." Goose bumps erupt along Acker's arms. "It senses we're near."

"Are you trying to scare me?"

He's picking through the dried fruit and berries until he finds one suitable for his liking. I find myself fascinated by the flex of his forearms, the tendons and muscles honed to perfection. Arms and hands used for killing, but also snacking.

"You're safe as long as you don't go in."

I can't help myself. I ask, "What happens if you go in?"

He crunches on a couple of nuts. "You don't come out."

I pull my blanket tighter. "Why?"

"No one knows. People go in to never be seen again." He shoves the handful of food into his mouth, done with the conversation altogether. He folds an arm behind his head, twirling his stolen blade with the other as he settles in for the night. "Try to get some rest."

I wipe the crumbs from my hands and take a swig of water. Another draft of cool air creeps over the small clearing, and I get as comfortable as I can considering the ground is as hard as a rock.

We've been traveling for weeks and weeks, and we're less than a day away from our destination. Everything feels foreign, like I'm out of place and every leaf and blade of grass knows it. Kenta isn't my true home.

I feel a tickle of awareness, and I open my eyes, finding Acker looking at me. He's on his back with his head turned toward me. His hair has grown over the weeks, and it hangs over his brow.

I've wavered on revealing the mind jumps to him. I'm unsure how he'll take it given the violation I felt when the oracle, Vad, dug around in my mind. I've done my best to stay out of his head, but I've come to realize physical touch obliterates any barrier I'm able to erect between his mind and mine. Riding a horse together does little to help.

It's a near constant bombardment of his perspective colliding with my own. He has a particular interest in the place where my neck meets my shoulder. There have also been more than a few views when he's adjusting the reins around my legs and his eyes linger on my thighs.

Otherwise, I'm just viewing the land and sky through his gaze, nothing noteworthy. With the way he's looking at me now, I'm convinced he knows I'm harboring a dark secret between us.

"Why did the oracle try to kill me, only to give you the location of a healer to save me?"

He appears perplexed. By my question or his answer, I'm not sure. "Vad has been trying to see inside my mind for years without success. My mother had me train with an oracle friend since childhood, so he knew he wouldn't get in without leverage. Hanging your life on the line was probably his smartest tactic yet."

"What is it he wanted to see?"

"He searched for this memory I had with my father. After my mother died, he…" He takes a moment to swallow before continuing. "He invited me to have my first drink with him. It was in his sitting room I was never allowed in. He gave me a speech about handling heartbreak with vigor."

"That sounds…painful to have to relive."

He shrugs like he's indifferent. "Vad's like that. He likes to poke and prod inside people's minds to satisfy his own sick curiosities."

"How do you two know each other?"

"He was in training camp with me and Hallis." There's a moment where I think it's all he has to say on the matter, but he turns on his side to face me before continuing. "He's a son of a farmer, so no one expected him to awaken. He didn't tell anyone of his gift. That is until he betrayed us by giving away our battalion's location to the Roison rebels. They ambushed us in the middle of the night. They would have slaughtered us if our leading officers didn't sacrifice themselves by fighting inside Roison's ranks with explosives strapped to their backs." He doesn't look away, doesn't shy away from the truth or the hurt he carries from the memory of it. "Only a handful of us survived. Whatever childhood we had we lost that day, but with it came a bond like no other. There's no one else I'd rather have at my back than those five soldiers."

"And Hallis?" I dare to ask.

"Alive and well." Then he smirks. "Less a hand, but he's learned to make do just fine."

I lift a brow. "I'm somehow not surprised."

"He's an advisor and sometimes an instructor for the new recruits, but he fares better than most active soldiers in a sword fight."

The thought makes me smile. "I'm sure he holds a certain element of surprise."

Acker matches my smile. "You could say that."

We settle into our bedrolls. Closing my eyes, I let my imagination run wild with what my future will look like, the possibilities that lie before me. There's a chance my life will span two, three, or four times longer than I've ever thought possible. If nothing ill befalls me, anyway.

Sleep never comes. Minutes turn into hours.

I think of a comfy bed, endless art supplies. I've never painted—couldn't afford to—but I'm desperate to know what it feels like to place a wet brush against a canvas.

My mother remains a mystery. I don't know what she looks like or how she'll react to my return. I vacillate between expecting tears of joy with a warm embrace and cold indifference or awkwardness. Neither seem like the right fit.

Yawning, I allow myself to open my eyes for the first time since I closed them last. The stars peek through the canopy of trees like pinpricks of light shining over us. Turning over, I look for the horse. It is unmoving and asleep while standing up, a fact that was not covered during the years and years of lessons on land animals in primary school.

I rub the chill from my exposed arms as I sit up. Acker's eyes are closed, and his chest rises and falls in a steady rhythm. I'm surprised he's able to rest, but I drop the blanket and stand as quietly as I can, unable to take another minute of lying here.

I've just taken a step when Acker's arm shoots out, hand wrapping around my ankle to keep me in place. His eyes are clear and void of any sleep as he stares up at me. "Where are you going?"

I calm my racing heart with a hand against my chest. "I need to relieve myself," I lie. "Is that okay with you?"

"I'll come with you."

"You absolutely will not."

He makes a face like I'm being ridiculous. "Are we just going to pretend we didn't live stranded on a boat together?"

"Yes," I tell him, refusing to acknowledge the least savory aspects of that time.

After a few beats of neither of us wavering, he releases me. "Three minutes."

"Five."

"Three or I'm coming with you."

I roll my eyes. "Thanks so much for your generosity."

He has the nerve to smirk at me.

There's just enough light to see by as I venture past the nearest tree. These woods are denser than the ones closer to shore. Leaves crunch under my feet as I scope out the area. Now I'm just wasting time so I don't give Acker the satisfaction of knowing he's always two steps ahead of me.

There's the barest layer of fog covering the ground. I kick at it, creating small swirls of clouds before they dissipate and are replaced by more tufts of vapor. Deciding enough time has passed, I turn to return and come face to face with Acker.

I swallow my yelp. He's standing close enough to touch me, and goose bumps spread like a wave down my body.

I straighten my spine. "What are you doing?"

He doesn't answer at first. His eyes jump between mine, visible with just enough moonlight to see by. "Do you regret it?"

I shake my head at him, totally confused by his question.

"Do you regret leaving Alaha and coming with me?"

I'm completely caught off guard by his inquisition, and it takes me a moment to find my words. "No. I couldn't stay. Not knowing what I know."

His dark eyes hold mine, worry etched into his calm facade. "But..." he says, voice quiet in the dark night.

I shrug. "I don't know what my future looks like here."

Acker breathes deep, chest expanding before releasing. "Do you...see *me* in your future?"

My heart leaps straight into my throat. "I don't know," I say, honestly. "I don't know what you expect of me."

His brow furrows, revealing his own confusion. "Expect of you?"

"I don't..." I pause to gather my nerves. "You made a promise to my family to return me," I explain. "But that doesn't make you indebted to be my friend forever."

"Is that what you think?"

"I don't know what to think."

He says my name on an exhale, part disbelieving and

part angry. "You still have no idea?" he says, almost accusingly. "I thought the awakening would make it evident." He licks his lips, a hint of nerves peeking through his demeanor. "I guess I'll have to show you."

*Show me?*

His answer to my unspoken question is to glide his hand from where it rests on my upper arm to the spot where my neck meets my shoulder, the spot I've caught him studying time and time again. My perspective leaps from looking up at him to looking down at myself, eyes focusing in on the way his thumb presses against the bottom of my chin to tilt my head up.

Then I'm back in my own head, but not by choice.

I was forced out.

Acker's gaze lingers on where he has his hand against the side of my neck. "How long have you been able to see inside my head?" His eyes ascend, meeting mine. There's not a hint of irritation in them, just an open vulnerability, asking me to be honest.

"During the awakening, I had a vision of you and Hallis, before you came to Alaha. You were both standing on a cliff, discussing strategy for how to get me out."

He recognizes the memory. "And since?"

I wrap my hand around his wrist, to balance myself, feeling off-kilter, but also to stop him from pulling away. "I've done my best to stay out, but sometimes... sometimes it traps me, like I'm in two places at once."

I can sense the thoughts running through his head as his eyes flit between mine.

"I was going to tell you after we got to Kenta," I say. "You said my powers were unlike anything you've seen before and—"

He cuts me off. "Jovie, I'm not mad."

I speak my biggest fear to him. "You don't think I'm like Vad?"

He shakes his head, so sure. "No. Not even a little."

I let out a small breath of relief.

He runs the pad of his thumb along my jaw, his eyes softening as he takes me in, gaze falling to my mouth. I stop breathing altogether at the realization he intends to kiss me. His eyes are questioning as he leans closer, and I have less than three heartbeats to decide whether or not I'm going to let this happen.

I shouldn't, right?

But also...*why not*?

My mouth opens of its own accord, all too willing to participate, then Acker goes still. He looks to the side, though it's too dark to see further than a few feet. I know him well enough to follow his lead. When he puts his finger to his lips and pulls me behind a nearby tree, I do it without question.

He sinks to his haunches and pulls me down next to him. It's uncomfortable, but every move creates a disturbance in the soil and leaves beneath our feet. The grip Acker has on my shoulders tightens, letting me know to not budge. By any means necessary, do. Not. Move.

Then I see it. An animal as dark as the night surrounding it, slinking close to the ground as it moves. It's eerily quiet. Its only giveaway is the reflection of the moonlight on its black coat. A large cat of some kind. A panther, I believe. Bigger than Acker and me combined.

It sees the horse first. Its golden eyes narrow as it continues to move closer to our bedrolls, nostrils flaring when it catches our scent. The horse sees the cat and whinnies, yanking its head back in an attempt to flee.

The panther stands on its back legs. The muscles and bones shift and snap into place, contorting back into human form. The black hair retracts to reveal the smooth, fair skin of a young man. It sends the horse into a fright. He kicks and jerks until the lead that's tied around the limb of a felled tree gives, and he scatters into the forest.

The man turns in place, and I suck in a breath at the sight of Fia's son. Inspecting our makeshift camp for the night, he lifts his nose to the wind, bare chest expanding as he breathes deep.

"I know you're near," Sven says. He steps over our bedrolls. Stalking as he searches the nearby brush, each step as quiet as his feline steps were. "I can smell you."

The boyishness I observed in him when we were at the cabin is gone. As his gaze shifts, the moonlight reflects off his eyes, revealing the truth underneath—an unfettered predator.

"You see, my parents are under the belief that if you put good into the world, you'll receive good back," he says. "But for that to be true, the same must be said for the bad. Life gives you what you're willing to take." His smile sharpens into something off-putting. "And you, metal slinger, have killed a hundred times for what your head is worth. Why should you get to live with so much blood on your hands?"

He prowls along the perimeter, eyes cutting in every direction. He's within spitting distance when his attention rises upward, up toward the midnight blue bird in the tree.

I cover my mouth with my hand, but it's too late.

His head snaps in our direction. "There you are."

*Shit.* I'm glowing.

Sven shifts again, but before he's able to return to all four paws, Blue dives in from above, changing course mid-flight.

Messer lands on his feet.

Acker and I cuss at the same time.

*Motherfucker. You've got be fucking kidding me.*

Messer spits out one word in our direction: "Run!" Then he shifts into a leopard that rivals the size of the panther.

The two cats pounce at the same time, colliding and rolling across the forest floor in a tangle of claws and teeth.

Acker jerks me to my feet. "We need to go."

But Messer—

The undeniable sound of claws tearing through flesh is followed by a piercing yowl.

I choke on his name. "Messer!"

The panther breaks free, his flaxen eyes fixating on us as he gets his footing, body crouched low in preparation to pounce. Acker all but shoves me out of the way right before the panther crashes through the thicket. It skids into a nearby bramble.

I look toward Messer. Streaks of blood line his body, but he's undeterred as he scales a tree.

Using our only chance of escape, we make a run for the border, or what I assume is the direction of Kenta. The forest seems to close in on us from all sides. Fog invades from all around. I keep my eyes on Acker and the leopard leaping through the cover of trees overhead, afraid I'll lose them if I look away. The chill from earlier returns with a vengeance.

"Halt!" Acker yells, throwing an arm out to stop me

from going further.

It takes me a moment to realize, to see the change in the trees. Bark as white as bone covers the trunks of the thin trees as they stretch high into the canopy, creating a divide from these woods and whatever lies on the other side. Dense fog pours out from between the stalks, which are barren of any leaves. Nothing but pitch blackness can be seen from the other side.

The waft of disturbed fog and mist forewarns us a moment before the panther makes his appearance. We turn left, running parallel to the Dark Forest, the sound of snapping twigs and leaves on our tail.

We can't outrun him.

Coming to the same realization, Acker slows to a stop. "Give me your blade." I pull the weapon from my waist, and he magics it into his palm the next instant. "I'll hold him off. Follow the forest until you reach the border. You'll know it when you see it."

I shake my head. "No."

He's angry, gritting his teeth at my stubbornness, but we both know there's not enough time to argue. He shoves me behind him with a growl.

Sven is closing in fast. He's running at full speed with no intention of stopping. I grip the back of Acker's shirt in my fists, preparing for what is to come next, and I realize I trust this man unequivocally. I'm pretty sure I'd follow him anywhere, including to my own death.

But whatever I was expecting, it wasn't for Messer to wait until the last possible second to attack. He leaps onto the panther's back, the action sending my heart into my throat as their interlocked bodies tumble forward, the momentum sending them both through an opening between the trees of the Dark Forest. Their pitched screams end in abrupt silence.

*No!* I stumble out from behind Acker. He reaches out a hand to stop me.

"He's gone," he says, firm and undeniable. "There's nothing you can do to save him."

I struggle to tug his hand from my sleeve.

"Jovie. Stop."

I somehow manage to free myself from Acker's grasp and slip close enough to the white birch trees that Acker freezes in place, eyes going wide when I look at him.

"I have to try," I say, voice breaking. "I can't just leave him."

Acker's chest heaves with each breath. "Jovie," he says, pleading, hands outstretched in a placating manner. "Listen to me. If you go in there, you'll never come out."

Tears flood my vision as I'm confronted with a choice. "Come with me."

Acker cocks his head, disbelief and helplessness mirrored back at me in his gaze. He says my name, the two syllables breaking along with his voice.

"I trusted you. I followed you here," I tell him. "Now I'm asking you to do the same."

He swallows. "And if we're stuck in there forever?"

I give him a small smile in return. "Then at least we'll be stuck together?"

There's an imperceptible shake of his head, like he can't believe he's even considering this. I'm going whether he comes or not, but I'd much rather not do it alone.

Then he snaps his mouth shut, making a decision, and he closes the distance between us. Without speaking a single word, he wraps his arms around me

and falls backward into the forest's open mouth.
   Into the pitch-black beyond.

# CHAPTER 33

It's not completely without light, but almost.

My magic snuffed out the moment we hit the ground. It's freezing cold, and it takes a moment for our eyes to adjust. It's as if the darkness is a fog itself, smothering life from the woods. The white bark of the trees provides the tiniest amount of illumination. I blink over and over again in a vain attempt to gain clarity.

Acker keeps a tight grip on my hand as we right ourselves. One look back tells us the break in trees we fell through has disappeared. There's nothing in every direction. If we were to take more than four steps away from one another, we'd be lost to the inky surroundings.

I open my mouth to call for Messer, but it's so quiet I almost don't want to disturb the silence.

"You think the people who went missing simply...lost their way?"

"I don't know," Acker says, voice matching the low whisper of my own. Like I am, he's peering into the dark abyss, but there's nothing to be seen beyond our reach.

After standing in silence for long moments, I can't stand it anymore and call out, "Messer!"

Acker's hand tightens around mine, but he doesn't stop me as I call again. Louder this time, trying to project past the stifling atmosphere. My voice only gets swallowed by an unseen weight in the air.

I hiss.

There's an alarm in Acker's voice. "What is it?"

I feel the back of my neck for the source of the sharp pain. I bring the hand up to my face. The liquid on my fingers is as dark as the night, but I don't need to see it to know it's blood. A wet sensation drips down my shoulder blades.

"Something bit me—"

Before I can finish speaking, a winged creature flies at my neck a second time. Latching onto my shoulder with talons or teeth, I'm not sure.

I scream. I claw at the thing as it digs deeper. Acker latches onto its body to wrestle it away, and my fingers dig into the leathery skin as bile coats my tongue at the disgusting texture. I don't need to see it to know it's grotesque.

As soon as we're able to dislodge the creature, another flies in for the attack. There's no time to react. This time it latches onto Acker. Then again, another. And another, to the point we're forced to release hands in a bid to save ourselves from the onslaught.

I brace my hands over my head to protect my face and neck. Pain sears through my forearms. They're being shredded. Razor-sharp teeth or beaks tear through skin and muscle. It feels damn near to the bone.

Screaming through my teeth, I grab one and chuck it as far as I can, only for another to take its place. Their wings beat a thunderous sound, overlapping in cadence as the horde grows in its attack. I stumble back and trip over something sticking up from the ground, letting out a cry at the slash of pain in my hand.

If possible, the roar of creatures multiplies, like they sense weakened prey and are descending on me like a wave. Acker yells for me, but there's no use. We're both going to die, and it's all my fault.

Anger unlike anything I've felt before fills me. I am *sick* of constantly being on the brink of death or an attack, sick of men who think they can control the world and everyone within it.

"Enough!" I shout, throwing my hands out.

With the gesture comes a flash of light, blinding as it illuminates the horrifying scene. Hundred upon thousands of rabid bat-like creatures hover above us. I'm burning them with my magic, and they begin a panic to get away. Their skin melts from their bones, wings disintegrating into nothing before they drop to the ground.

"That's it," Acker encourages, helping me to my feet.

Fueled by my anger, my attack is frenzied. I can feel my magic swelling below my chest, straining for the death of every single one of the creatures trying to retreat. An endless thrum of vibration sounds in my ears.

The forest begins to clear. My gift rages from my palms, swelling to cast light in every direction. We can see the trees and forest floor and...and bones. Blanketing the ground in various shades and stages of decay, including the one protruding from my hand.

"Don't let the magic control you," Acker says, eyes flitting around us, looking for an out, a direction. Anything to tell us where in this forest we are.

I yank the bone from my palm and magic flares, but I don't feel the pain, like my magic wants to protect me from the sensation. Nothing can touch me. I'm unstoppable.

"Jovie," Acker warns.

Annoyance spears through me.

"Rein it in, Jovie."

The creatures continue to fall to the ground like rain from the sky. The bubble of light expands around us, as if it's chasing the darkness back with each inch it invades. The dark is a writhing mass beyond, fighting the inevitable.

Because it is inevitable. My light *will* prevail.

Acker shouts my name, but he's so far away. He might as well be at the bottom of the ocean.

The sky breaks through overhead, my light meeting the afternoon sun like old friends. The creatures, out of room to escape, evaporate into thin air.

I can kill them all.

I let my power flow and push and chase and decimate the forest. A place of death and suffering now knows what true demise looks like, and I watch as my light threads through the trees and reaches the edges of the forest, not a stitch of shadow to be found, until the dark place is dark no more.

I'm tackled to the ground. My skull rebounds off it and my vision filters out for a few seconds before I'm able to focus again, the pain registering with it.

I cradle the back of my head. "Ow."

Acker's eyes are still squeezed tight, cracking open a smidge before deeming it safe enough to look. They're filled with equal parts relief and awe as he looks me over before quickly transitioning into anger.

"Are you trying to kill me?" The scratches and puncture wounds are beginning to heal across his face and neck, the skin stitching back together within seconds.

I struggle to catch my breath. "Consider it payback for

feeding me fish with a murder weapon."

"I—what? Are you serious right now?"

The lack of humor in his gaze does exacerbate the guilt already taking root in my stomach. Wielding my gift without the anxiety of needing to taper myself felt as natural as breathing, allowing the warmth to spread over my body and mind like a balm to my soul. I didn't want to turn it off. Ever.

"I'm sorry."

He lets out a sigh of relief. "Are you okay?"

I nod. He helps me to my feet, and that's when I'm able to fully process our surroundings. The Dark Forest is…no longer. The trees are smoldering. Leafless and singed, they stand without a winged creature in sight. There's no indication of direction or which way is Kenta.

We weave through the trees, stumbling over skeletons and debris. A lump of soft body is visible in the distance, and I make a run for it, Acker hot on my heels. It's the Roison shifter, still in his panther form. He's breathing but unconscious. Between the fight against Messer and the creatures, he's past the point of return without a healer to stop death from claiming him.

"Leave him," Acker says, urging me forward.

But I can't continue, not if there's a chance Messer is nearby. Acker sees the decision in my eyes. He growls out his annoyance under his breath. He turns in the opposite direction and begins to look for a being that may be wounded.

"Messer!" I call, again and again, Acker's voice echoing mine.

I'm the one to find him. Entire chunks of his leopard

flesh are missing. His breathing is shallow. Eyes closed, he has less than a minute left.

I call for Acker, and he comes close. I can tell by the look on his face he thinks there's no hope. I look up at him, tears in my eyes as I struggle to lift the leopard's head. "Help me. Please."

He orders me to move. I scurry out of his way. He lifts a leg in each hand and swings the mammoth animal over his shoulders. Blood runs like a waterfall down his back. He motions for me to go before him with a jerk of his head.

I run at a near sprint, not knowing if we're even going in the right direction, then the sound of pounding of hooves gets my attention.

"Keep going," Acker orders, his breathing somehow less ragged than my own.

That's when I see it, the break in the trees and the flow of soldiers coming over a hill in the distance, the Kenta flag flying overhead: green with a horizontal line down the middle, daggers fanning from it like rays of a sun on its side.

The ground turns to grass, and I nearly weep with joy when we emerge from the forest and into the open field of Kenta territory.

Acker halts the first soldier on horseback, laying Messer across the wither of the horse. "Get him to a healer."

"Yes, your highness," the soldier says, turning the horse back around.

*Your highness.*

I take a step, wanting to tell the soldier to hurry, but I can't make my legs or mouth cooperate. My vision blurs, everything going out of focus as I try to alert Acker that something is wrong.

The last thing I hear is him cursing as I hit the ground.

# CHAPTER 34

I'm in a tent. The canvas ripples in the wind, causing the door coverings to flap open, revealing the night air and the Kenta soldier standing outside before they fall shut again. The cot across from mine is empty except for a smattering of blood-soaked dressings littering the surface.

Sitting up, I inspect my healed hand, then my body. No aches or pains or remnants of clawed attacks. A fresh set of clothes sits on the table between the two beds, and I don't waste time changing into them. I've just pulled the green tunic over my head when someone sweeps a hand inside the door, pulling it back to reveal one of the most beautiful women I've ever seen.

"You're awake," she declares, entering the tent.

Her raven hair is coiled at the nape of her neck with a metal pin. Leather with a metal rope of some sort adorns her shoulders. It encircles her waist and hangs from her belt in a cinch. It's an impressive uniform. She's ranked, for sure.

She sets a pitcher and two glasses on the table. "I brought you water."

I don't move.

She pours into each of the amber glasses, eyes holding mine as she drinks from hers. "There's no need to be embarrassed," she says, smiling. "We've all done it one time or another."

I reach for the other glass, forcing myself to take a measured sip despite the desire to gulp it down. "Done what?"

"Burned through our magic." She settles her rear on the edge of the cot opposite me, gripping the railing at her sides. "It's why you fainted. The cost of using magic too greatly is that it causes our human minds to turn off. Kind of like running out of oil in a lantern."

"Good to know," I tell her. "Do you know where Acker is?"

She gives a halfhearted shrug. "Probably somewhere committing atrocities while being shamelessly good-looking."

I narrow my eyes at her. "Who are you?"

As if remembering her manners, she straightens before curtseying. "I'm Beau. Third in command and Acker's sister."

"*Sister?*"

"Please don't tell anyone I forgot to bow," she rushes out. "It'll be my ass."

I pinch the bridge of my nose and take a deep breath. "Our secret as long as you never do it again."

"I can't promise that, but you have my word to not do it again in private."

"Thank you," I say. "I'm glad the Kenta find women to be valuable enough for you to be so high in rank."

"Woman or not, it's impossible to deny my skills."

"I didn't mean to insult you," I say.

"No offense taken," she says, dismissing my worry with a wave of her hand. "You'll come to realize things are different on land. Much different."

"Do you know what they did with the shifter?" I say, motioning to the cot she's leaning against.

She glances at the mess. ".The Alaha boy? He's being held for transport. Why?"

I bristle. *Held?* "Transport to where?"

"To the Kenta dungeons." She says it like the answer should be obvious.

My heart drops, and I exit the tent before the next beat that follows. The guards standing outside my door startle at my sudden appearance, but neither of them make a move as I march past them.

Heads pivot in my direction, conversations dying as I descend upon the camp. Kenta soldiers are scattered about, playing cards and drinking ale, preparing dinner as nightfall approaches. Plumes of smoke fill the sky to the north and south, the tops of the tents reaching as far as the eye can see in both directions.

"Where's the prince?" I ask anyone willing to meet my stare. "Where's Acker?" Only blank stares answer back. I trudge through the maze of tents, asking again and again. "The prince—where is he?"

A voice cuts through the awkward silence. "I may be able to help you." Leaning against the post of a tent, hair bright in the setting sun, freckles lifting with his smile.

"Hallis," I say on an exhale. He holds my stare for a moment before he dips his head as if he's going to bow. I rush to stop him with a raised hand. "Please don't."

Surprise is clear on his face, but he's quick to mask it. "As you wish, princess." The way he calls me by my title, with a mocking undertone, feels familiar.

"Where's Acker?"

"I'll take you to him."

I follow a few steps behind his hulking figure. He's in military garb similar to Beau's, except the sleeve of his left arm ends with an abrupt absence of a hand. I look over my shoulder but don't see her.

Sound continues to fade away as we move through the camp. Some of the soldiers stop and stare, some look elsewhere. Very few are gracious enough to fake a smile or dip their heads in the Kenta greeting. If it's odd behavior, Hallis doesn't acknowledge it.

I don't need Hallis's confirmation of where Acker is when we come to it. The metal helmets of the soldiers stationed outside give it away. They nod their approval to Hallis, and he uses his available hand to hold back the material for me. "After you, princess."

I eye him as I step through. Then my attention shifts to Acker. I take in his appearance. It's as if my eyes can't drink him in fast enough. His hair is damp from when he washed up, eyes shining from the lamplight. The sleeves of his clean shirt are rolled up his forearms as he leans over a table with a map.

A smile quirks at the edge of his mouth, but he's quick to disguise it as he stands to his full height. "Jovie," he says, hand outstretched to one of the men with him. "This is the lead commanding officer of this legion. Rango, please meet the Princess of Maile, Jovinnia."

The stout man offers me a bow and a smile. "The pleasure is mine."

I don't know the appropriate response. I feel the weight of the eyes of the other four men around the table as I smile and nod in return.

"I wasn't expecting you to wake for another few hours," Acker says, rounding the table, eyes flitting over my shoulder. "I see you and Hallis have become reacquainted. I hope he was very accommodating."

Hallis isn't amused. "She's here, isn't she?" he smarts. "No thanks to her lack of survival skills as she marched through the camp demanding your soldiers give up your location."

Acker's gaze comes back to mine. "Did you meet Beau?"

"I did. She's...*pretty*." Hallis grunts, but I ignore him. "She told me Messer is being held."

Acker stares at me for a beat, his eyes appearing darker than usual, his lashes seemingly thicker, and heavier around them without natural light. Then he looks at Hallis. "Where's Beau?"

He shrugs. "The princess was alone when I found her."

"I left her in the tent," I tell him. "Why? Where's Messer?"

The commander—Rango—chimes in as though I didn't even speak. "She's probably scaring my men."

"Acker."

He gives a command to Hallis over my head. "Find her."

I clap my hands in front of him. Sparks of light erupt from the impact, but I'm too irate to pay it any mind, or the men who get their swords at the ready. "I'm speaking to you."

Holding up a hand, a silent signal for his soldiers to stand down, Acker finally graces me with his attention. By the clench in his teeth, I can tell he's pissed.

He speaks without looking away from me. "Have three thousand ready to move south by morning."

Rango bows his head in compliance, gathering one of the maps from the table along with his men. I keep my searing gaze on Acker as they pass by, but I feel their eyes on me the entire way.

Hallis lifts a brow, appearing as bored as ever. "It

appears not much has changed." Sunlight pours in for a brief moment before the door falls shut behind him, and then we're alone.

Acker lets out a deep breath through his nose, releasing with it the sharp edge in his jaw. "You can't undermine me in front of my men."

"*That's* your concern right now?" I say, stunned. "I didn't realize your ego was that fragile."

"You have no idea how delicate this situation is."

"Messer's—"

"Not him," Acker cuts me off. "*You.*"

I'm taken aback. "What?"

He walks around the table and waves me closer with a hand, turning to make room for me before the map. Round and detailed unlike any I've seen before, it shows the territories divided and labeled, prominent features marked and illustrated.

"We are here." Acker points to a wooden sword marking our position then slides the tip of his finger to the right. "This is the Roison border."

The land is twice the size of Kenta's, making up the majority of the right side of the continent's landmass. Ocean closes it in on all other sides, flat other than the shoreline to the north.

Acker moves his finger along the dotted line separating the two territories until he reaches the forest shaded with black. "This is the Dark Forest." It spans the entire border except for two short clearings along the north and south passages. "This forest has been plagued with dark magic for millennia. The most powerful of Heirs have gone in with the intent to break the curse and failed. But you," he says, "you single-handedly cleared it without blinking."

*Impossible.*

"All of it?"

"All of it," he confirms. "Every map that exists will have to be altered because of you. Every scroll and depiction will need to be reworked to show a new and open border."

"How?"

I don't realize I've said it out loud until Acker replies. "That's what my men want to know. They were stationed north of here when they saw the light. According to some of them, it eclipsed the light of the sun in the middle of the day."

"They're scared of me," I say, putting the pieces together.

He doesn't deny it. "The last thing I need right now is you marching around and appearing unhinged." He leans forward, invading my space enough that I can smell him. "It looks like I can't control you."

That last sentence snaps me into focus. "You *don't* control me."

"Godsdammit, Jovie." He slaps a hand on the table. "You know what I mean."

"*You* brought *me* here," I remind him.

"And *you* brought an Alaha shifter."

"I didn't do any such thing and you know it."

"Do I?" he says, eyes sharp on mine.

I snap my mouth shut, afraid I'll say something I'll regret if I don't calm myself first.

His eyes are unwavering. "Did you know?"

Did I know one of my closest friends was masquerading as a pet? Or that he would follow us in our departure from Alaha? Either way, the answer I give him is the same.

I don't dare look away. "No."

There's a stretch of silence where he holds my stare before he says, "Okay."

The underlying current of tension between us dissipates, the comforting gaze of Acker returning in full force, the eyes of a familiar friend. It feels nice to put a title to our relationship, although the moment in the woods comes to the forefront of my mind, the moment when I thought he was going to kiss me, challenging the idea of friendship between us. *Friend* doesn't quite measure up.

Acker reaches for a sash of knives on the table and belts it across his chest. The Kenta emblem is stitched into the leather at his shoulder. "Let's go talk to him, shall we?"

# CHAPTER 35

Eyes continue to follow me as we march through the camp, but only after heads bow in respect for their sovereign.

"So...prince, huh?"

"Since birth," he says, looking at me from the side. "But you suspected, didn't you?"

"It makes sense, given my title and the history of our families. Why didn't you tell me?"

"You wouldn't have trusted me," he says. "Considering the state of affairs between our people. You would have suspected I was seeking retribution." He notices the smile I'm biting back. "What is it?"

I scrunch up half my face. "Your arrogance should have been the first clue."

He discreetly jabs his elbow into my side. "Speak for yourself, *princess*."

We come upon the last group of tents along the camp's border. Set back from the rest, the structure is surrounded by soldiers dressed in full armor. It feels a little overkill, especially upon entering and finding Messer chained to the singular mast upholding the roof in the center of the space.

A helmeted soldier stands behind him. The deep eye slits of his head covering make me uneasy. It's strange to feel his eyes without seeing them in the low light.

Messer's on his knees with his arms stretched behind

the beam, healed, but not to completion. Bruises and cuts litter his form, and when he looks up at us, the evidence of fatigue lines his face and body.

I fall to my knees before him, hating the strain it takes for him to tilt his head back to look at me. "Is this how you treat those who risk their lives to save yours?" I ask, throwing a glare in Acker's direction.

He shoves his hands in his pockets. "It's how we treat probable spies."

Messer's lips tip up at the corners. "At least they gave me pants."

I can't help but smile at his attempt at levity. "Your eyes," I say, pausing as I take them in. "They're blue." No longer the gray common in the people of Alaha.

"Yours too," he says.

I reach to touch my cheek, as if to feel their change, to sense their new color. I look at Acker. He never mentioned it to me.

"It's what happens when you're separated from land for too long. The water bleaches them of their color."

Hallis shoulders through the tent's opening. "Found her," he says, tone droll as he holds the material back for Beau to enter. "She was, indeed, scaring the men."

Beau clicks her tongue and rolls her eyes. "They're scared of everything."

"They're battle-hardened brutes."

She cocks her head in his direction. "Exactly." As if she notices where she is and the presence of other people, she smiles. "What do we have here?"

Acker motions to Messer with a flick of his wrist. "You tell me."

She steps closer. Her eyes are dark and sharp, so much like Acker's as she assesses the situation. "Lovers, perhaps?" Her gaze turns inquisitive. "No, that's not it."

Realizing something is happening that I'm not fully privy to, I rise and take a step back. I look at Acker for some form of explanation, but he's not looking at me. His eyes are affixed to his sister as she circles Messer's kneeling form.

"There's love, but not of the romantic variety. Although," she says, arching a brow, "he has considered it before. From what I can tell, he's a bit of a philanderer."

Messer appears as alarmed as I am, but he hides it well, smile turning flirtatious when she stops in front of him. "Interested?"

Beau's smile is real entertainment. "Not in the slightest."

"Beau," Acker chastises.

She drops some of her bravado, focusing more. "He's loyal. Probably to a fault. He leads with his heart, but he's also a troublemaker. Duplicitous. Doesn't care for rules or decorum. Loves attention."

Messer is smiling as she rattles off his characteristics, like it's all the things he believes about himself and he appreciates hearing them out loud.

"Tell me something I don't already know," Acker says. "I was able to determine as much during the time I spent with him as an eyun."

"An eyun?" Beau says. "And where have you seen an eyun to know what to shift into?"

"My father," Messer says, looking at Beau, then Acker. "He has an illustrated book of creatures, those alive and dead, in his keep."

Acker looks to Beau for confirmation. She makes an affirming gesture, a tilt of her head that indicates what I assume to mean she believes Messer is telling the truth.

Acker continues. "Declan is your father, yes?"

Messer loses the flare in his smile when he responds. "Yes."

"Is he who exposed you to your magic?"

Messer is slow to shake his head. "No."

"Who then?"

He hesitates. It's plain on his face as he looks at me. The pause continues to grow, like the air is made of water. It's heavy and suffocating as everyone holds their breath out of fear of death, myself included as I wait for Messer to answer. Whatever Beau's gift is, it's nothing to tamper with.

"Kai," he says, eyes shifting back to Acker's hard stare. "My father knows nothing of my gifts."

Removing a blade from the strap across his chest, Acker twiddles it between his fingers, face contemplative as he digests Messer's answer. "Why did you follow us?"

Messer quirks a smile. "I couldn't let B have all the fun without me."

Beau snickers. When Hallis glares at her, she says, "What? I found the *one* who isn't afraid."

Acker is not as amused, jaw flexing as he lords over Messer's kneeling figure. "You overheard every conversation we've had the past several weeks. Every interaction, you listened in on." His eyes turn downright murderous. "You know damn well that's *not* her name."

Messer attempts a shrug, thwarted by his bound wrists. "Does it matter? She is who she is regardless of her name, regardless of her title."

Acker sinks to his haunches before him. "And who is

she to you?" he says, voice low and demanding.

Acker could kill him from much further without batting an eye, but something about him being so close to Messer with a sharp weapon at his disposal is disconcerting.

Messer meets my gaze once again when he says, "My friend."

He's been with me this entire journey. Even before, when he would visit me in my window in Alaha. We spent hours on the roof of my shiel just...*being*. Together, the two of us. Maybe he needed a place to escape his father, a place of respite from the hurt and mayhem, but maybe I needed him too, to feel less alone.

I take a step closer. "Why did you follow me?"

"We always said we'd make it to land together or not at all." Messer lets all traces of humor fall from his face, revealing the truth so few see underneath his lighthearted exterior. He's angry at me for leaving without him. "You went alone."

I shake my head. "I wasn't alone."

"I didn't trust him." *Him* being the man between us. "Kai told me what he did—how well he fought—and I knew I had to find you. I figured I'd scope out the situation and fly back once I knew you were safe, but then the storm happened, and I spent all my energy ensuring you two survived. I didn't think I could endure the flight back."

"The squid," Acker says, surprise lighting his eyes, lacing his voice. "That was you?"

Messer nods.

Acker's gaze shifts to Beau, then Hallis. "He was able to maintain his shifts over the open sea."

Messer likes Acker's impressed assessment and

manages a half-assed smirk. "You're welcome, by the way."

Acker doesn't take the bait. "Did anyone know of your intentions before leaving?"

"Yes," he says. "Aurora. And Kai."

Acker doesn't like that answer. "Did he tell you why she left?"

By the repentant look on Messer's face, it's very apparent what his answer is. He doesn't need to voice it.

"And you still consider him a friend?" Acker says. "After finding out what he was doing to her?"

"He always knew," I say, answering for him. "Didn't you?"

Messer shakes his head. Not in answer, but disappointment. "Kai hated it, but he felt like there wasn't another option."

Acker twirls the blade in his palm, a habit of his, fiddling when he's deep in thought. "Excuses."

"Spoken like someone who's never gone to bed hungry."

The blade in Acker's hand freezes, right along with his gaze. "Don't pretend the son of the third in command of Wren's guard has ever felt true hunger."

Messer matches Acker, teeth bared when he says, "You don't know my father."

Acker doesn't need to look at Beau for confirmation. The searing pain lashed across Messer's face is telling enough. His father is not a good man. He put Messer through plenty to make up for any ways he benefited from his father's status.

"Are you here to do any harm to Jovie?"

Messer shakes his head. "No."

"Are you here as an informant for Kai or his father?"

"No."

"Are you honest in your intentions?"

"Yes."

Acker looks to Beau, who nods her approval. He orders the helmeted guard to retrieve the healer. Then he looks at me.

"It's your decision," he says.

"About what?"

"It's either the dungeons or release." He continues to spin the blade from one digit to the next, over the back of his hand and into his palm again. It happens so fast I'm not sure if it's pure skill or the work of magic. "He's your friend," he continues. "He's chanced his life for yours, yet he doesn't appear to have an allegiance to any head. It makes him a potential liability to keep around. We could put him on a boat back to Alaha, but given his ability to shift, there'd be nothing stopping him from returning."

I look from Acker's intense gaze to Beau's mercurial grin then to Hallis as he stands without an offer of reassurance, stare dry as I presume is typical of him. All their eyes are locked onto me.

"Couldn't you just..." I struggle through the rest of my question, hating myself for thinking it. "Make him give a blood oath to leave and never return?"

There's a noticeable shift in the air, in the tiniest of movements between the three of them at my suggestion.

Beau speaks first. "Blood oaths are messy, especially when given under duress. The swearer has to make the promise without prejudice, or it leaves room for gaps within the agreement. They're not easy to outmaneuver, but it's not impossible."

"I could though," Acker says, eyes holding mine as he gives me the harsh truth. "I could banish him to a lifetime of the sea. Or I could simply make him swear his fealty so I could sleep better without having to worry about his treason, but at what cost when the only thing the man is guilty of is being questionable?"

"Not even Wren or his people were held to an oath when they were exiled," Hallis says.

It explains Acker's words to Fia about his distaste for sworn oaths. If I choose Messer's release, I'm essentially vouching for him, and I don't know if I can do that. Messer's chin rests against his chest, but his eyes meet mine through the stringy hair overhanging his brow, giving me what comfort he can offer through his gaze. He knows the predicament this puts me in, and I know without a doubt he'll understand whichever I choose.

"I can't send him to the dungeons," I say, hating the falter in my voice.

"Even with the knowledge that he knew of Kai's transgressions against you?" There's not any judgment or condemnation in Acker's gaze, simply a gentle reminder of Messer's part in all of this.

"I saw what Messer's father did to him," I say, refusing to meet my friend's stare. "I saw the bruises and never did anything about it."

Seeing the finality in my eyes, Acker opens the lantern hanging from the top of the mast and places the sharp end of the knife inside. A dark blade of stone, like my own. He paces to stand beside Messer. "Do you know anything regarding hearthstone?"

Messer shakes his head, but it's weak.

"It's mined from deep within the earth where rivers of liquid fire flow. It can be used to create the only weapon that can leave a scar that can't be healed. It's the only known matter that can kill an Heir's gift," he says, removing the blade from the fire.

The once dark stone is now an unnatural shade of pearl white. He places the searing point against Messer's chest, blistering the skin under his collar. Messer howls, eyes going wide in surprise.

Acker pins Messer's flailing head back with a fistful of his hair. "Tell me now if this is where your magic resides."

Messer growls through clenched teeth. I yell Acker's name, but Hallis halts me with an arm around my waist, pulling me out of reach.

"Last chance," he threatens.

Messer shakes his head, spit flying from his lips. "It's not there."

Acker digs the knife deeper, cutting past the flesh and into the tissue. Blood cascades from the wound when he removes it only to shove it back in, causing Messer to become rigid again before going lax when Acker pulls it out.

I recognize the V, identical to the one above Acker's hip.

"There are only four people other than myself who wear this mark," he explains. "It's notorious amongst our enemies, considered a coveted trophy for many who hunt us. If you're caught outside Kenta territory, you'll be tortured for information you don't have before dying a slow death. Wren included."

I shove out of Hallis's hold. "You could have warned him."

Acker cleans the blade with a cloth from the table against the far side of the space. "He didn't have a choice."

The soldier announces his return before entering. A female soldier with her hair cut close to the scalp follows in close behind. She doesn't pay any heed to the mood of the enclosed space or the circumstances as she goes right to Messer. She inspects the wound and Messer's overall appearance before sinking to her knees. Placing a palm on the front of his chest and the other on his back, she instructs him to take a deep breath.

Messer's choked sound of pain tapers off into a sigh of relief. The dark creases under his eyes vanish. His breathing returns to normal, and he's able to remain upright without fighting for air. The V is still very much there, the skin sealed back together but a stark reminder against the rest of his unblemished skin.

Acker thanks her for her service and bids her good night.

"Untie him," I demand.

With a nod of approval from Beau, Acker uses the same knife he defiled Messer with to slice through his bonds.

Messer rubs his wrists as he stands. "Any chance I can get a little something to eat?" he says, smiling as if he wasn't all but enslaved for his own free will. His stomach growls the loud evidence of his hunger.

Hallis smiles for the first time since laying eyes on him. "There are plenty of field mice if you'd like to favor a fox."

"Or a snake," Beau chirps.

The veiled analogy doesn't go unnoticed by anyone.

"We'll get you better lodgings as well as a hot meal," Acker says with a pointed stare directed at Hallis.

He's less than thrilled about the task judging by the

barely concealed roll of his eyes, but he leaves without protest.

Messer is still all teeth as he nods to Acker. "I appreciate your generosity."

Acker is unaffected by Messer's attitude. He returns the dark blade made of hearthstone to his sash. "I know trust is too great to ask from either of us right now, but I hope it comes in time." Acker's expression sobers. "And for what it's worth, I want to thank you. You protected us on the ship and on land. I can't say with certainty we'd be alive without you."

A thin layer of Messer's sarcasm falls away as his smile becomes more genuine. It's typical of Messer to move on so easily. He's never been able to hold a grudge. There's only one exception to that rule, and it's reserved for his father.

I place a cautious hand on Messer's arm to divert his attention. His smile radiates from him, and I can't help but think of those moments when he disappeared in the Dark Forest. The world was so close to losing one of its purest humans.

He pulls me into a tight embrace. We've never hugged before, but I'm grateful for the contact because I'm not sure my voice would work past the knot in my throat. As unexpected as it was to see him find our boat in the ocean, I'm grateful to know he was with me the whole time, but it's nothing in comparison to seeing his real face and perpetual smile.

With my chin tucked over his shoulder, I catch the glower in Acker's eyes before he's able to mask it. Beau doesn't miss it though. Her stare is scrutinizing as she looks from Acker to me. Then she...stops. She freezes as she stares between the two of us.

At Acker. At me. Back again.

Acker catches on to her sudden interest, giving her a shake of his head. A warning, I realize. It takes her a moment to fix her face. Something tells me not a lot is able to ruffle Beau's outer shell, but whatever she just saw caught her off guard.

She leaves without another word, and unease unfurls in my gut.

# CHAPTER 36

I look over the map, from the expanse of Roison to Kenta at the center of the landmass and then to Maile in the north, mountains bordering the territory. Further left, smaller but not by much, is Streau territory. I follow the span of ocean south to the islands dotting the coast, sliding the hilt of my dagger to where Alaha is marked, a lone pinprick of green with a wooden tree to identify it.

Acker strides through the open door of the tent, steps laden. He unbuckles the strap across his chest and hangs it from the post. "You should eat," he says, sitting in the chair across from the table. He begins to unlace his boots but seems to exhaust himself of it, leaving them untied as he settles into the seat.

After handling Messer, he left to help his commanders get men ready to move along the now open expanse of border. I don't know how he's made it this far after the day we've had. Morning is no more than a couple hours away.

"It's yours," I tell him, pushing the bowl of leftover gruel and carrots toward him.

He eyes the cold meal but doesn't make a move for it. "I see you've found your blade."

I hold the weapon up in the light, inspecting the point. "A boy brought it to me. Said he sharpened and polished it according to your orders."

The flicker of the lantern casts an orange glow over his features, somehow making him all the more enticing and dangerous in appearance. "He's not a soldier, if that's what you're assuming," he says. "He's a squire. Orphaned, most likely. However, some families send their sons as aid. It alleviates the cost of feeding them and the boys get a small wage to send home."

"Do they join the army when they come of age?"

"Most, yes." With an elbow braced on the arm of the chair, he props his temple against a closed fist, like the act of holding his head up is too great a burden to bear. "Perhaps this is a conversation to be had with Hallis. He'd be able to give you a better perspective of squirehood than I."

"He was a squire?"

"He was."

Interesting considering Acker's recollection of their first battle together and how poorly it ended. I wonder where on Hallis he wears his mark of victory.

"How did a poor boy and a prince become friends?" I say, rounding the table to get closer. "He is who you followed into the army, is he not?"

Acker's features tighten, his impossibly dark eyes holding mine. Fatigue lines every stitch of his body. "It's a story for another day, preferably after a good night's sleep."

But there are so many questions I need answers to. Messer's state of being, left unhealed to stop him from shifting. Then Beau's gift, a sight of some kind. Similar to Vad's, but not as invasive and assaulting. Acker's forced branding as a reliability measure. None of which was imparted to me. He walked me into a situation I was lacking in. It feels like a recurring theme with him.

Sensing my dissatisfaction, he speaks. "Say it."

I inspect the distance between our current position on the map and the sword marking the capitol. "How far are we from the palace?"

There's a stretch of silence. He knows it wasn't my original question, but he lets it go. "Three days if weather permits," he says.

We're in Kenta. We're safe. I should be grateful for small mercies.

I eye the cots on either side of the table. "Is there a bed you prefer?" I say, pulling my hair free of its braid. "The one closest to the door, I presume." I stop finger-combing the ends of my hair when I see the look on his face. "What?"

His eyes soften. "I've had accommodations set up for you," he says.

It takes a moment, but my cheeks flame pink as the mortification sets in. "I assumed..." ...we'd stay together.

His gaze is apologetic as he takes in my scorched face. "It wouldn't be appropriate," he says.

My eyes dart to the open door of the tent and the soldiers stationed outside, partially to check for any witnesses to my humiliation as well as in realization of why the doors were tied back when we returned.

"Of course," I say as I finish combing through my hair.

It's happening as I predicted. Acker holds no ties to me. I don't know why I'm surprised. I guess, for a moment there in the woods...I thought...

*I'm so dumb.*

I can't miss the look of contrition on his face, and it tells me everything I need to know; this *infatuation* I have for him is one-sided.

I slide my dagger into the back of my waistband and avoid his gaze as I navigate around his chair. "I'll let you rest."

He reaches out and grabs me by the wrist, pulling me onto his lap before I'm able to comprehend what's happening. I steady myself with a hand on the back of the chair to stop myself from plastering my body across the front of him.

"Once we're at the palace," he says, eyes darting between mine as he stares up at me, chin tilted at the perfect angle for me to watch the bob of his throat when he swallows. "I will sleep wherever you want me to. Whether it's on the floor or in the dirt or in your bed, I'll be there if you want me."

I suck in a breath, heart pounding at the mere mention of us sharing a bed. It sends a wave of heat through my body. An image of us tangled under bedding flares inside my mind, a place in my head where I no longer have to fight the desire to be near him like I have from the moment I came to after my awakening, where I can allow the growing desire to have his skin against mine without the addled shame that always follows right behind.

Acker's eyes widen, nostrils flaring as he clenches his teeth. I watch from his perspective as he cups the nape of my neck and brings my mouth down to meet his.

*No*—not a real kiss, but his longing for one, a fantasy I've peeked into.

I jerk back, unsteady as I get to my feet.

"Jovie." He sits forward in a bid to stop me from retreating, but I step out of his reach.

"What was that?" I say, palm covering my mouth.

Acker's shock mirrors my own. "What did you see?"

I pull my hand away and look at my fingers, as if I'll find the evidence of a kiss that didn't happen there. "You kissed me, but—"

My heart stops, blood stilling in my veins. Turning away, I snatch one of the blades from the sash Acker hung up. He says my name, but I ignore him as I hold the metal close to the lamplight, inspecting my reflection in the sliver of shiny metal.

My eyes—not the gray I've stared at for all my life, but a murky color. Hazel with variations of green and gold depending on the angle I tip the dagger in, letting the light shift and reflect off my iris.

*...like every color of every season.*

Gasping, I drop the blade.

He says my name, voice deep and demanding my attention. *Jovie.* He takes a small, measured step toward me. Cautious, like I'm a wild animal who will dart at the first sign of danger...

"You've known all this time," I accuse, spinning on him. "That's why I can see into your mind and no one else's."

It wasn't a question, but he nods anyway. "Yes."

Horror replaces my blood with ice. "Can you see inside mine too?"

He doesn't reply, but the answer is clear as day in his eyes.

"Oh my gods." I try and fail to recall every thought I've had about him for the weeks we've been together.

"It's not as easy for me. To see inside your head," he clarifies, eyes imploring mine. "Your mind is strong. Aside from a moment ago, I've only been able to see inside when you're drawing."

I can't dwell on what he saw a moment ago, knowing

it contained a vision of us with nothing but skin between us.

"I think…" He hesitates before deciding to continue. "I think that's when your mind is the most free."

The last time I sketched anything was back in Alaha, the day after I cried myself to sleep. I spent the morning in bed, inspecting my journals, my diaries over the years, documented in sketch form. He knew and hid it from me.

"Why didn't you tell me?"

"I didn't know how you'd take it, given what you went through with Kai. I thought it might be better for you to feel it after your awakening."

I shake my head. "Feel what?"

He watches me with rapt intention when he says, "The tether."

Like a bolt of awareness spearing through me, I know in an instant what he's referring to. The pull I've felt since the morning I awoke in the bedroom at Fia's. The relentless desire to be near him, to touch him. Like a strand drawn taut with tension between us.

I shake my head. There are too many thoughts and not enough time to sort through them, not with Acker's presence drawing me in like a moth to a flame.

"I need to think."

It's an obvious statement to make, but he understands, receding back a step. He sits on the arm of the chair, disappointment clouding his features before he's able to tuck it away.

He calls for one of the guards from outside. "Please escort Princess Jovinnia to her billet," he instructs the soldier, tone solid and steady.

It's careful and put on, like he's protecting himself

from me. I can't differentiate if it's the tether that reveals that to me or if it's because I've grown to know him well enough to see past the facade he sometimes wears.

As I follow the soldier out, Acker nods at me. "Good night, Jovie."

# CHAPTER 37

I awake to the midday hustle and bustle of camp with my stomach demanding to be fed. I ask the soldier stationed outside my tent what the fuss is about, but all I get in return is a blank stare.

My first instinct is to find Acker. It's a thought before I even realize it's there, the tether more prominent than ever. It tugs below my breastbone. I look south, in the direction it wants me to go, and turn in the opposite direction. I don't know where Messer is, but it'd be nice to have an internal compass that leads to him instead.

I amble through the camp until I spot soldiers with food in their hands and follow the trail back to an open-air kitchen. There's a line, but I'm hesitant to infiltrate. Unwelcome stares and turned backs greet me, but I spent the better part of my life secluded in the far reaches of Alaha. I've been gossiped about and shamed for being an outsider, and I sure as hell am not going to let history repeat itself. Plus, I'm *hungry.*

I step into place despite the glowers. The line is long, but it seems to move quickly. The man in front of me looks over his shoulder as if offended. I'm determined to not let them affect me, so I smile at the soldier, only for him to turn back around without returning the gesture.

*Rude.*

"It's quite the spectacle," Beau says, sidling up next to me. If the men behind me have an issue with her cutting, they don't voice it.

"What is?"

She's smiling, but her eyes never stop roving, absorbing as she peruses the comings and goings of the camp. "Seeing them nervous around someone other than me for once."

"I think you're confusing outright disdain for nerves."

She laughs, and the soldier before us looks over once again, this time to be met with Beau's disarming smile in place of mine. It stuns him, eyes growing wide as a flush fills the highs of his cheeks, and he hurries to turn back around.

"Trust me when I say they're bluffing."

We shuffle forward in line. "And how are you able to discern such things?" I ask casually.

"I see auras," she says.

"Like…colors?"

She waves a hand in the air, causing the chains around her shoulders to clink together. "Sometimes it's colors, sometimes it's vibrations. There's not any record of anyone having the same type of gift as me before, so there's no name for it. I just call it an aura because it's the easiest for others to understand."

I nod like I do, but I don't. I don't want to scare her off.

It's our turn to receive our rations, and I'm pleasantly surprised to find it's pork with a honied biscuit. There's a water station where Beau fills her waterskin from a barrel, and she offers to share with me. We find an overturned log to sit on a ways away from the camp's center while we eat.

Despite my hunger, I can't stomach more than half my portion before setting it down.

Beau nudges me with her shoulder. "Ask me anything," she says, sensing my apprehension. Or seeing it, I suppose.

She presents a good picture of an open book. It's either because she feels like she has to be considering what she's able to discern from everyone else, or because she just doesn't perceive boundaries the same as we do.

"Last night," I say, unsure if I even want to know. "You saw something between Acker and me…"

There's a curiosity in the way she tilts her head to look at me. "The majority of human interactions I see are benign. There's not a lot of overlap between friends or acquaintances or, say, someone you bump into in passing. But if there's strong emotion emanating from one or both people, it can flare in their aura."

"You're saying you saw Acker's aura…*flare*?"

"More than that," she says with a glint in her eyes. "I saw it *merge* with yours."

Her description makes it feel very intrusive.

"Acker's aura has always had a subdued quality to it. He has such acute colors with hardly any blemishes or waver to them, but they've always been muted, like viewing them through stained glass," she explains. "That is until last night, when I saw the connection between the two of you. You two are fated."

"I don't know what any of that means."

"What is it about the bond that unsettles you?"

"Truthfully? I'm sick of having no say in my life." There's release in finally voicing my thoughts out loud, in telling someone of the bitterness that has eaten away at me over time.

"Of course you do," she says, smiling at me like I'm

silly. "A matching bond is just that—a bond. It doesn't dictate anything you feel or do." She throws a hand out in front of her. "Pretend the bond doesn't exist if you'd prefer."

"Don't the...*colors*...or whatever reveal all truths or something?"

"It doesn't work like that because *humans* don't work like that."

I'm growing frustrated with the lack of well-defined answers.

"I can tell you Acker feels a great affection for you, if that's what you want to hear," she says halfheartedly with a shrug. "I can tell you he adores you and is proud you're his match, but it doesn't solve your real concern, now does it?"

I can't discern if she's being sincere or not. While the majority of me wishes for those things to be true, they don't appease the anxiety gnawing at my insides.

"What is it you see when you look at me?"

Her smile is equal parts empathetic and pitying. "I'd be doing you a disservice by telling you."

I'm somehow not surprised by her refusal to answer.

"Human emotions are fickle, Jo. Yours, mine, Acker's. They're nothing but a wave in the ocean. What really matters is what you decide to do with them." As quick as she imparts those words of wisdom, she points to my half-eaten breakfast and says, "Are you going to eat that?"

I huff out a breath of laughter and shake my head. "It's all yours."

We sit and watch the men as they meander about. She talks of them being scared of me, but there's a noticeable unease when they see Beau. They don't look anywhere near as uncomfortable when Acker walks through the camp.

Two, braver than all the others, sneak glances at us as they walk by. It's a different sort of attention but not any less menacing, especially when they break into laughter once we're out of earshot.

"What was that about?" I ask her.

She leans in close. "When it comes to men, Jo, it's best to just assume the worst."

Well, that's not reassuring.

Voices begin to carry over the chatter of the men like a tidal wave over the camp, growing in volume before crashing in an uproar. Men reach for their armor and weapons while others forgo them altogether and make a run for it.

South. They're running south.

Without speaking, Beau and I take off at a sprint. I ready my blade from my side. Beau's two steps ahead, metal rope in hand as she darts between the tents. She's fast, so fast I struggle to keep up. I'm out of shape from the weeks at sea, and I'm panting by the time we make it to the commotion.

Beau steps through the line of bodies standing on the outskirts of camp. The hillside dips, giving a wide view of the border. There are no telltale markings of where one land ends and the next begins, but there are two men on horseback. They're turning away from Kenta and back to Roison, lowering their white flag in their retreat.

Acker's figure marches up the hillside to the waiting band of soldiers. The wind lashes at his hair and clothes, and it only serves to outline the strength in his build. As if he can feel the appreciation in my gaze, his head whips up, eyes locking on mine.

*Acker is my match.*

The finality of that statement sends a spark through my chest.

He speaks with Rango, Hallis, and a couple other men I don't recognize before dismissing the band of soldiers. I can't tell if the consensus amongst the departing is one of alleviation or disappointment. I spot a few spoiled faces.

Acker's stare lands on me as he approaches. "That was Jorgen, Sven's father," he says. "When Sven never returned home from the tavern after the day we left, he suspected he learned of a bounty on our heads and came after us."

"Did you...tell him?"

He nods, remorseful. "He's upset, understandably. I promised to have the remains returned to him."

"It's a big risk to send a man into Roison just to give a grieving father solace," Beau comments.

"I owe his wife a life debt," he explains. "She saved Jovie's life. It's the least I can do."

Beau shakes her head, looking toward the border. "I'll leave you to decide which man you're sentencing to death."

"I have to send a scouting team regardless, so it's neither here nor there," Acker says, scrubbing a hand along his jaw. "Jorgen warned of rumors spreading. The people are of the belief we—Kenta—have destroyed the Dark Forest to get unfettered access to the border."

"You've been distributing men all along the border," Beau says. "What else are they to expect?"

"It's a lose-lose situation," Hallis butts in. "If we don't move our men, it leaves us vulnerable."

Beau doesn't seem pacified by Hallis's assessment.

"It's only a matter of time before Chryse sends his own troops," he says, looking at Beau. "The number of men he sends will determine if we need to be on the offense or defense."

Messer's voice cuts in from behind me. "I'll do it."

I turn and find him looking better than I've ever seen him before. His hair and skin have a glow to them that emphasizes his appearance. The shock of it sort of takes my breath away for a moment. The girls back in Alaha thought he was handsome before; they'd be dying to see him now that he's on land.

When I look back at Acker, he's not looking at Messer. He's looking at me. He then drags his attention toward Messer. If he's surprised by the offer, he doesn't show it.

"Are you sure?" Hallis asks. "Roison is littered with rebels and bounty hunters on top of their ever-moving military."

"I know the danger," Messer says, smile turning teasing. "Consider it a step toward building that trust Acker is so keen on developing."

Acker nods once. "You're better equipped to go undetected than anybody we send. Could you be ready to go by nightfall?"

Hands clamp onto my shoulders, and I suppress the knee-jerk reaction to flinch. Messer gives me a squeeze like it's perfectly normal for him to touch me so casually. Then I realize he's baiting Acker, testing his reaction.

Another squeeze. "I'm at your disposal," Messer says.

Acker isn't dumb. He knows Messer's messing with him. He looks up from the fingers Messer is drumming against my clavicle with a renewed sharpness. "Great.

You can start by retrieving the carcass."

All eyes fly toward the skeletal remnants of the Dark Forest in the distance and the blur of scavengers circling overhead.

"If you hurry, you might beat the maggots hatching," he smarts.

Hallis's grin mirrors his friend's. "Can't say the same for the smell, however."

Undeterred, Messer gives me a little shake before releasing me. "Do me a favor, would ya?" he says, eyes overflowing with glee.

"Yeah. Sure," I drag out.

He strips out of his shirt and hands it to me. "Hold these for me? I don't want the smell of rotting flesh to soil them before I leave on my death quest." He doesn't give me a chance to respond before undoing his pants and jerking them down. I avert my eyes, face coloring from embarrassment. I feel more than see him place his trousers on top of the shirt in my open hand.

Careful to keep my eyes above his chest, I glare at him. "Not funny." The stripping or the joke about his possible future demise.

"On the contrary," Beau says, smiling from ear to ear. "I find him rather hilarious."

He basks in her compliment, winking at me a moment before he sprouts wings, snapping into bird form in the blink of an eye. He shoots into the sky, a smattering of black feathers raining down behind him.

A nearby soldier shouts his dismay, some type of bellow regarding the eyun, and I can't help but smile at the fact that they are all stupidly frightened even though they're supposed to be big, bad warriors.

Beau and I share a knowing smile.

# CHAPTER 38

Any nerves I have evaporate at the sight of Acker's easy grin. He strokes the neck of the mare he's holding the reins to, eyes bright as I draw near. There's a peaceful quality to him today. It reminds me of our time on the boat. Everything was simpler when it was just the two of us. Even so, distrust lingers from constantly being left in the dark.

"Where are the other horses?" Beau says, eyeing the two before us.

Acker holds his hand out to help me onto the horse. "The battalion needs as much muscle as they can to disperse the camp."

She narrows her eyes on Acker. "Then I'm riding with Jo."

But he's already pulling himself onto the blanket behind me. "Hallis and I won't fit together. It is what it is, Beau," he says. "I don't make the rules."

Gritting her teeth, she all but stomps over to Hallis, who's smirking like the devil he is. "You do," she says, slapping away Hallis's offer of a helping hand. "It's your monarchical sovereignty. You literally make the rules."

I know her plight all too well.

Hallis leans forward, lips a hair's breadth away from her ear, and says, "I promise I won't bite."

She bristles. "Oh yeah?" She elbows him in the ribs. "I might."

He grimaces through his smile as he rubs the tender spot with his hand. "It's going to be a long three days."

I dare a look at Acker over my shoulder, and his eyes fall on me. The anger I've been harboring dims at the sight of him. From the line of his brow to his full lips, I'm entranced by his beauty.

I hate it. Especially his smell, like crisp air and woods with a hint of something sweet.

"Are you ready?" he says, eyes roving over me, assessing.

Am I? It's hard to see past the thought of spending the next three days on this horse with him, but when I stop and focus, excitement buzzes inside me. There's hope that whatever lies before me is better than what lies behind me.

"I think so."

He smiles, a hint of teeth peeking through. "Good. Every princess should know how to properly ride a horse." He takes my hand and places the reins in it, tightening his grip on my wrist before letting go. A small act of encouragement, but there's a sensual edge to it, a slow glide of his fingertips from my skin.

Or maybe it's just all in my head.

"Show me what you've learned," he says.

I shake my head. "I can't."

"You paid attention when we left the healer's," he says. "Every time I tightened or pulled on the reins, you made note of it. I saw you. You can do this."

I stare at the leather straps in my grasp, unsure of what to do. "I was just staring at your hands," I say, the truth escaping my mouth before I realize.

He leans to the side so he can get a better look at my face. "You what?"

I can't stop the blush from stinging my cheeks, and I shrug. "You have nice hands."

His smile grows until it's pure brass, and I roll my eyes, knowing I've just started something I'm never going to hear the end of.

Beau speaks under her breath, but it carries with the wind. "It's going to be a very, *very* long trip."

Acker is gracious enough to let it go—for now—and gives me basic instructions on how to steer a horse, when to tighten and give slack and adjust across the neck.

The camp is a quarter of the size it was when we arrived, just a handful of tents huddled in the large area of flattened and muddied earth. Acker lifts a hand in farewell to the soldiers who are left. We descend the hill and move up the next, where Acker instructs me to tug the reins low, stopping us.

Hallis lets out a low whistle.

Trees without leaves and white as bone stretch as far as the eye can see in one direction. The exposed forest floor looks like snow, a blanket of bright ash. Like a reverse birthmark on the earth butting up to the rich, dark colors of the woods and grass surrounding it. A forest, once dark, now light.

"You did that," Acker says, voice low, as if he's speaking to himself.

The magnitude of it hits me like a physical blow. I sink further in the saddle, my weight supported by Acker's chest as I come to grips with the power that's been tingling in my fingertips for days now.

Without another word, we depart. With the enemy at our backs, we kick off into a canter, whipping across the grassland in a way we couldn't through Roison's wooded valley. Acker keeps my hands in his as he helps me lead the horse. I remind myself that Messer will meet us at the palace in a fortnight.

We keep the swift pace for the better half of the day until we're forced to slow as we descend into a rocky hillside where boulders speckle the ravine. It creates a bottleneck effect, and Beau and Hallis are forced to our rear. The horse does most of the work by herself, but Acker's hands stay tight on mine with the reins, legs tense as we traverse the terrain. Trees shroud the crack of earth, casting shadows over us. It's a nice reprieve from the heat.

Beau's voice distorts as it reverberates off the winding hillside, followed by Hallis's deeper tone.

"What do you think they're arguing about?" Acker says, voice rough from the hours of unuse.

"Breathing."

He chuckles softly. "They've been like this since they were kids. I should probably feel worse than I do about pairing them together."

"So why did you?"

"Sadistic pleasure," he says, not the least bit repentant. "But really, I just needed a reason to get you with me."

I don't know how to reply to his confession, so I don't, but I note the sharp sensation his words elicit.

"To the left," he directs, showing me how to position the reins to steer the horse to the left of a downed tree branch.

Beau's voice carries over the sound of the horse's hooves on the rocks, a sharp insult ending their bickering, punctuating the resounding silence that follows.

"Okay, I feel a little terrible," he says.

I snicker. "No you don't."

After a few moments of quiet, he says, "You're no longer angry with me." It comes out more like a question.

I let out a breath. "I don't know."

I don't *feel* angry until I think about it. Then it burns that he kept the truth from me, but I can see his reasoning. I try to imagine him revealing our bond to me during different points of our...*situation*...and I can't find one where my reaction would have been any different. I'm fairly certain it would have been worse, actually.

The best I can do is garner more information. "When did you know?" I ask.

"Honestly, I think I knew when we were kids," he says, surprising me. "You always had these big emotions as a young girl and—" He stops to gather his thoughts, to figure out how to describe them. He lets go of the reins, and I turn enough to see him place his palm to his chest. "I swore I could *feel* them." His eyes are alight with the memory.

His description makes me sad. For the girl he's speaking of, a girl I don't know, and for the boy who thought he lost his match. He doesn't return his hand to the reins, letting it rest where our thighs meet instead.

"But I knew for sure when I placed your hand on the stone wall. I felt your magic then and I knew it matched with mine. Then whatever doubts I had left disappeared when I could see into your mind, when you were drawing in your hammock in the bilge on the ship back to Alaha."

I sketched a lot of the same during the trip back

from the market—the blade. Over and over and over. Until I got back, when my obsession switched from the inanimate object to him. "You saw me drawing you at the Market," I say.

"You seemed to struggle getting my lips just right," he says, teasing me.

I roll my eyes to mask my mild embarrassment. "Can you control the visions?"

"No. I've tried to get in while you're not drawing with no luck," he says. "You?"

"I can get out, but I don't have much of a choice as to when I get pulled in." I debate what to reveal to him, but I suppose it's best to go ahead and get it all out in the open at this point. "I think physical contact heightens the connection."

He takes a deep breath. "The matching bond is cloaked in mystery. There are so few who have it, and those who do keep it under lock and key. There is someone who may give us some answers in the capitol. For the price, that is."

"In Alaha, they made it seem like it was chosen, like a marriage pact."

"There are tales of Matches being common once upon a time, but they were never chosen. That's a tradition Wren adopted to further control his people."

We scrape by a wall of stone, misshapen and jutting from the hillside, and we duck to avoid the overhang of rock. The passage is narrow. Our legs bear the brunt of the squeeze at the tightest section before we're through.

Then my breath stalls in my chest at the sight before us. We're in a shallow valley filled with purple flowers, the stalks tall enough to reach our calves as we're mounted on the horse. The fragrance I've been smelling for miles quadruples in potency.

"Can we—"

Before I'm done asking, Acker has dismounted, landing on his feet in one motion. I follow suit, looking a tad less graceful.

Careful as I step between the flowers, I brush my fingers along the petals, relishing their silky texture. The tallest reach my waist. Bees and other insects fly to and fro, buzzing by without concern for the giant stepping into their domain.

As I get further and further into the valley, it opens on one side, revealing a view of rolling green hills that transform into mountains in the distance, white-capped and jagged as they point to the sky. The world, bigger than I ever could have imagined. It's breathtaking. Moisture coats my eyes as I try to take in every detail.

The swishing of grass turns my attention to Acker as he approaches. He holds up a parcel of food, waterskin in his other hand.

"Figured we could eat while we rest," he says.

Over his shoulder, I spot Beau and Hallis breaching the rock overpass, sour faces on both of them. Acker sees them too and tugs me to the ground with him, finger pressed to his lips. Hidden from sight, we hear them arguing over who's riding in the back for the rest of the trip. Beau asks where we are, which Hallis must ignore because silence follows until we hear Beau tell Hallis to *eat shit* when he asks for a share of lunch.

Acker and I snicker. He lies with his upper body braced by an elbow and hands me the food wrapped in wax paper. I fold my legs underneath me and unfold the

—

I gasp at the cut red berries and cheese. "I haven't had strawberries in years," I say as I pick a slice. The tartness of the fruit overwhelms my taste buds, and I eat a slice of cheese to combat it. "Where did you get these?"

Acker picks a berry from the bunch, pops it in his mouth, and chews. "Bartered with a soldier. His mother has the gift of earth magic and sends him the best care packages."

"Lucky him."

"Lucky us," he says, taking more.

We deplete the rations and take turns taking swigs of water. My eyes go to the mountains in the distance, amazed by the visible difference between temperatures there and here.

"I've never felt snow."

He follows my line of sight. "You did as a child. Maile is just beyond those mountains."

It seems so far away and yet so close at the same time. I shove the cap back on the water, and when I look up, I find Acker staring at me, eyes like molten ore. It feels intentional as he continues to observe me from mere feet away.

"Will you put your nose ring back in?" I say to break the intensity.

I don't know if it's polite to ask, but he doesn't seem surprised or offended by my question. "Do you think I should?"

I shrug, pretending to be impartial.

He smiles, but it doesn't quite reach his eyes. "Maybe I will."

I know we shouldn't waste daylight, but I move to lie next to him, and he extends his arm for me to use as a pillow without a word passing between us. I roll onto my side so I can look at him. He does the same, mirroring my position. My cheek is propped against his forearm, his other arm draped over the curve of my waist. This is how we slept while on the boat, but it somehow feels more intimate on dry land. Maybe it's just because I'm aware of the matching bond.

Or maybe it's because there's plenty of space for us not to be huddled so close together anymore, yet...here we are.

I touch the spot where the V is underneath his shirt. "You, Hallis, and three more?"

There's a look in his eyes I can't decipher, a heat that's in direct contradiction to our conversation. "You can count," he says, playfully pinching me in the side.

I manage to shove Acker's hand away from my ribs due to the lack of fight from his side as he spears his fingers through mine, interweaving them together between us instead. His plan all along, no doubt.

We fall into silence, letting the buzzing of bees and looming flowers create a cocoon around us. There's still so much unsaid, but none of it feels important right now. I can't recall the last time I felt more at peace. There's a small voice trying to break through the haze, trying to remind me of all he's withheld from me, but I shove it away.

It's not until I feel Acker's fingers threading through my hair that I realize I've dozed off.

"You've got to be kidding me. Get up," Hallis barks, face lined with frustration, so much so I'm halfway convinced he's never experienced joy in his life...*ever.*

"Good gods," Acker rumbles, squinting up at his friend through his own sleepiness. "Half a day of sharing a horse and you're already cracking."

"If you two weren't busy napping, you would have noticed the change in weather."

As if on cue, the sky falls out on us. Rain pours down despite the sun shining between white clouds, and we jump up to make a run for cover, the trees toward the bottom of the valley. Hallis cuts in the opposite direction, helping Beau get the horses.

It's a futile attempt at avoidance, evident in the grass and stray petals littering Acker's hair and skin, the fabric of his shirt clinging to his chest. He reaches out and plucks a leaf from my hair, holding it up for me to see, but I've only got eyes for him. He lets the leaf flutter to the ground between us. All I can think about is what the water dripping from his hair tastes like on his wet lips when he licks them.

He takes a step closer, forcing me to tilt my head back to look at him. "Jovie..." he whispers, bringing his fingertips to my cheek.

But the pounding of horse hooves pulls us apart as Hallis and Beau get closer, looking even wetter than we are, and angry. Both of them.

"It doesn't look like it's going to be easing up anytime soon," Acker says, eyes lingering on me before looking toward them. "Let's go ahead and set up camp for the night. We'll get an early start in the morning."

It's very apparent Hallis is unhappy about the turn of events, but he's smart enough not to voice it, not after Acker's remark about him *cracking*.

Beau dismounts and wrings out her hair. "Hallis needed a shower anyway."

I swear I can almost *hear* Hallis's teeth grinding in irritation.

# CHAPTER 39

"I knew you were taking the long way around," Hallis says, turning to Acker. "But setting up camp because of a little rain?"

They're under the awning we strung between the trees. Rain continues to pound on top of the canvas, drowning out the crackling of the small fire, its light casting an orange glow over the space. Acker sits with his back to a tree, forearm braced over his knee as he fiddles with a blade. My blade, I realize, the black stone impervious to the firelight. On instinct, I check my waistband, then remember I tucked it under my bedroll when...

I look to the shelter Beau and I claimed for ourselves and see two figures sleeping across from each other. Beau to the right, myself to the left. I watch my chest rise and fall in a steady rhythm.

"Her world has been turned on its side," Acker says, drawing my attention back to his and Hallis's conversation. He looks up at Hallis and I do my best to stay in the shadows, outside the boundary of the light from the fire. "She could use an adjustment period."

"You're wasting time we don't have," Hallis replies.

"War is war," Acker says. "A week's time won't make a difference."

Hallis's back is to me, but there's noticeable frustration in the way he shifts on his feet. "Come on,

Ace. Be real with me." He throws a hand out between them. "What are you doing?"

Acker holds Hallis's gaze for a long beat. "She lived in a hovel, Hallis. They kept her apart from the rest of them, isolated her to make her rely on Wren's son as her only confidant. As her lover." A look of barely concealed revulsion crosses his face. "She's been sheltered and conditioned to believe she's *less than*. The palace will tear her apart before she steps through the door."

"Don't feed me that bullshit," Hallis says. "She's proven to be plenty capable of handling herself."

"You know better than most how cruel the court can be."

"I do," Hallis agrees. "And she'll either adapt or—" Hallis stops mid-sentence, realization dawning. "You're scared she'll choose to return to Maile with her mother."

Acker doesn't confirm or deny Hallis's suspicions, allowing the silence to speak for itself.

"And you think making her fall in love with you will prevent her from leaving?"

Acker glares at him with a calmness that would make any other man fear for his life. "Contrary to what you may believe in that overinflated head of yours, you don't know everything."

"I know what I saw," Hallis says. "When you were about to kiss her, looking lovesick."

The blade that was in Acker's fingers is now embedded in the bark of the tree behind Hallis, missing his jugular by millimeters.

Acker's gaze is downright murderous. "Shut your mouth."

"You missed," Hallis says, not the least bit shaken by Acker's anger.

"Has it occurred to you that I may have feelings for her?" he says, more subdued.

Hallis sits on his bedroll across from Acker. "I know you do," he says. "But I also think the guilt you've carried around for years ties in with the responsibility her mother placed on you. And, with the matching bond, it's muddled things."

Acker pulls the blade back to him and resumes spinning it between his fingers. "You're wrong."

They stare at each other for long moments before Hallis gives in. "Okay," he says, situating himself for the night, head under his arm. "If you insist. But a word of advice?"

Acker lifts a brow, the perfect representation of boredom.

"You should tell her before we get to the palace. There are no secrets in court, and I don't imagine her taking your betrothal to the Princess of Strou well."

His *what*...?

I must be dreaming. It's the only explanation for how I'm in two places at once. I take a step back, and I don't know how, but Acker clocks the movement out of the corner of his eye, head snapping toward me. Our eyes meet.

"What is it?" Hallis says, reaching for his sword at the foot of his bed.

Acker shifts, and I take a step toward my sleeping body. Then I'm gasping as I sit up, head swimming as I come to, waking Beau in the process.

"Everything okay?" she says. "You look like you're going to be sick."

My eyes shoot across the fire, toward Hallis and Acker's shelter, and I find them right where I left them a mere moment ago. Then Acker's on his feet, face equal parts shock and determination as he marches through the rain toward me. I scramble to stand.

"When were you going to tell me about that nifty trick?" he says, and I'm surprised by the venom in his voice.

I'm instantly defensive. "Probably when you were going to tell me you're betrothed," I spit back.

"Yikes." Beau grabs her metal rope. "I'll just...be over there," she says as she sneaks past.

Neither of us pay her any mind.

"Tell me the truth, Jovinnia." That's maybe the most hurtful of all, him using my full name. "How long have you been able to do that?"

"Why should I? It's apparent you haven't been forthcoming with me," I counter.

"Are you working with Wren?"

I'm so taken aback by his question that I'm stunned into silence, mouth hanging open like a fish, baffled by his conclusion.

When I do manage to find my voice, it's lacking the fire it had before. "What are you talking about?"

Sensing my confusion, Acker releases a breath, nostrils flaring with an exhale, eyes losing the hardness behind them. But not all of it.

"You've spent the majority of your life in Alaha. Plenty of time for Wren to warp your mind and place you at the Market as bait, knowing I'd be there like I have every year prior, and knowing I'd come to save you if I saw you. You very well could have been playing me for a fool this entire time."

Shaking my head, I throw my hands up in defeat. "I'm not tricking you, Acker. I'm sure Beau can attest to the fact that I'm being honest. That's the reason she's here, isn't it?"

He has the wherewithal to at least look confused as his anger dissipates. "Then why were you eavesdropping? How were you able to do that?"

"I don't know! The last thing I remember is going to sleep, and then I was watching you and Hallis. It was like my mind manifested itself somewhere else. Somewhere..." I trail off, my voice losing its fire. "...near you." It's too pathetic of a confession to be anything but true.

Like a bucket of water was dumped over his head, a wash of guilt and shame overcomes his person, face and body going slack with the understanding that he just screwed up.

"Jovie."

I hold up a hand to stop him. It's tinged with a faint yellow glow that I hurry to shake from my fingertips.

"I've been betrothed to the Princess of Strou since I was thirteen," he says, despite my refusal to listen. "And before that, it was you."

I feel out of control, like a barrage of emotions is fighting for supremacy inside me as I turn away from him.

When I don't reply, he continues. "That's why your family was visiting mine when you went missing. You would come every summer, to renew the alliance."

An alliance I'm assuming went sour after my disappearance. The Kenta, the only people who share a border with Roison, an enemy with a lot of resources and the army to back it...it's easy to see why Kenta would be hungry for a political agreement with another territory.

"When are you expected to marry?" I say, facing him again but from a distance.

"By the end of the summer," he says, but he's quick to add, "But the wedding will be called off after we speak to my father."

"You'll lose the alliance."

"It doesn't matter," he says, scrubbing a hand through his overgrown hair, throwing droplets of water all over the place. "You're my match." He says it like the answer is simple.

"I don't know your customs," I say, fighting the blood wanting to crawl up my neck and into my face. I'm angry with myself, so naive and clueless outside Alaha. "Did you...*court* her?"

He hesitates but nods. "Since she turned of age, I've visited twice to establish a familiarity of sorts. Our families aren't close like yours and mine were, so I wanted to foster a friendship first."

"To make her fall in love with you," I say, remembering the words Hallis used.

He doesn't like the connection I've made. "Not necessarily, no."

"But not *not* necessarily, either."

The muscle in his jaw pops from the accusation. "I have a nation of people depending on *me* to save them..." He stops, head bowing before looking back up. "There's not a lot I wouldn't do to keep them safe."

I know it to be true, because he's withheld a lot from me to ensure that. I don't believe Acker wants to keep me in the dark for nefarious reasons. I believe his intentions are as close to good as they can get, but it doesn't make them enough.

"Who has the bigger army, Maile or Strou?"

Acker's eyes darken at my question. "It doesn't matter."

I demand an answer. "Maile or Strou?"

He swallows. "Maile," he says.

My chest almost caves in from the realization. "How convenient it is to procure a possible Maile alliance, an alliance with a more dominant army by making the heir fall in love with you..."

"Jovie," he says, voice harsh as he closes the distance between us.

I sidestep before he's able to reach me. "Don't touch me."

His hand closes into a tight fist. "Don't twist this around and make it something it's not."

I shake my head. "I don't know what it is, Acker. This could all be a gimmick, a magical trick to emulate a matching bond, if such a thing even exists."

He calls for Beau without looking away from me. "Come tell Jovie what you're able to read from me."

"Like she's a reliable source," I say, sarcasm dripping from my tongue. "You're her prince, her *brother.* She'd tell me whatever you told her to."

This time he doesn't let me escape when he reaches for me. Hands framing my neck, he brings his mouth down onto mine. I push against his chest but he jerks me into his hold, hand gripping my jaw to stop me from pulling my head back.

He bares his teeth against my mouth. "Stop fighting me."

His fingers pinch as they dig into my cheeks and he seals his lips to mine again, this time quick to dip his tongue inside my mouth. Something embarrassing escapes my throat, a noise that's half moan and half protest as I taste him. Desire licks up my body like a flame on a struck match, turning any of my objections into dust. The hands I was using to push him away moments ago now travel from his chest to his shoulders to where his neck meets his hair. I use his height as leverage to get closer to him, pressing the length of my body into his.

He sweeps his tongue in deeper, groaning as he devours me, and that's when it happens. Our magics, like two separate entities, touch for the first time.

No, not the first. That was at the Market, when my hand met the stone wall. But it's the first real introduction.

Like being lit from within, I feel Acker's power intertwine with my own. I can feel his strength and reach. Every speck of metal within miles vibrates with awareness, in the trees and soil and deep underground, as well as the heavier metals of human creation, like weapons and tools and Beau's metal rope. All mine and Acker's to wield and bend and expand to our wills.

Tearing myself from the kiss, I shove Acker back, hands searing through his shirt and marking his chest. He doesn't so much as bat an eye at the burn, breathing deep against the discomfort of being pulled apart. I feel it too, the yearning to reunite, to continue what we started.

"I don't trust you," I say, also struggling to catch my breath.

"I don't need you to," he says, scrubbing a hand across his mouth. "I just need you to trust yourself." He turns back toward the fire but spins back just as quickly. I hold my ground as he comes close, eyes blazing mad. "Mark my words, if I ever see him again, I'll kill him for what he's done to you."

There's no clarification needed. I know he's speaking of Kai.

Then he walks to his shelter and strips off his shirt. He says something to Beau, and she shakes her head.

I call my blade, knowing I'll sleep with it on me from now on.

Acker retrieves an intact shirt from his pack, pushing each arm in before scooping it over his head, covering the two handprints marked on his chest. He looks at me for a moment before kicking dirt onto the fire and pitching us into darkness.

Except it's not totally dark due to the slight glow of my skin.

# CHAPTER 40

"We'll pass through a small village before we reach the outskirts of the capitol by nightfall," Hallis says. "If we're lucky, we might be sleeping in a real bed this time tomorrow night."

I can't lie. The thought of an actual bed sounds borderline euphoric after the lack of sleep I've experienced the past few nights. I toss and turn, desperate for unconsciousness to take me under, but I can't escape replaying the events of the night. How I projected myself outside of my body, arguing with Acker, him accusing me of working with Wren.

And the kiss. Gods, that kiss...

Acker sits with Beau at his back, and I realize it's a less intimate riding arrangement and probably uncomfortable for all involved. When it was time to depart from camp, I made the rash decision to ride with Hallis. There was a noticeable pause where Hallis and Beau awaited Acker's reaction, but if they were expecting something significant, they were disappointed when all he did was adjust the halter on his mare and help Beau onto his horse.

I've yet to relax in Hallis's front.

"You chose this," Hallis says, exasperated.

I pretend to not understand what he means. "Chose what?"

I can almost hear him rolling his eyes. "You know

exactly what I'm talking about."

Antagonizing me when I'm already teetering toward volatility is not a smart move on his part. I decide remaining silent is the best plan of action. For his safety, of course. The handprints seared on Acker's chest are a clear indication of what I'm capable of when pushed.

I still can't make heads or tails of the fight. After overhearing his conversation, it somehow got turned back on me. His suspicions, Beau's station over me—all of it sheds new light on the situation. And while I know there's genuine merit to what Acker accused me of— being a secret ally of Wren—it doesn't change the hurt that came along with it.

Maybe hurt isn't an accurate description of how I feel. Maybe it's more along the lines of disappointment. Disbelief. Frustration at my own naivete for not seeing the writing on the wall. Acker could very well be manipulating me for his own personal gain. The promise he made to kill Kai rang with utter conviction. There wasn't an ounce of reservation in his words. It will happen whether I want it to or not. Acker spared Kai's life once for me, and he's made it clear he won't do it again.

We keep a steady pace the rest of the day. The temperature mellows as the sun dips toward the horizon, and a sea breeze wafts in every so often, telling me we're not far from the coastline. We come across a narrow creek. Our mare becomes skittish when crossing, and Hallis has to take the reins from me. He holds the leather straps between his fingers, using each digit to steer the horse with fine-tuned motions. It's impressive, especially since I can't do it with two hands.

We're halfway across the waterway when Hallis

speaks, voice low in my ear. "See, you're not the only one who is displeased with our riding arrangement."

I don't dare look up to see whatever it is that prompted him to make that statement, but I can *feel* Acker's attention on us. It burns like the sun itself. I keep my eyes locked on Hallis's handling of the reins, focusing on how he squeezes the horse with his legs to push her through her fear.

The weight of Acker's stare doesn't let up until we're back on dry land.

"If looks could kill..." Hallis mutters, a hint of amusement in his voice. "If you find me dead in the morning, you know where to look."

I find myself smiling in turn. "Acker isn't who you should fear. I've contemplated your death more than Acker ever has, I promise you."

Hallis's body goes taut behind me. "Excuse me?"

"Does the name Fang Hands ring a bell?"

"Fang Hands," he repeats with a hint of recognition. "The story I used to scare you with when we were children?"

I nod, and his body becomes relaxed once again.

"Acker said you don't have any memories from your life before Alaha."

"I've dreamt of some, but it's fuzzy. I regained the darling memory of Fang Hands after a particularly bad trip with a saigon root." My stomach churns at the memory.

"That must have been..."

"Terrifying," I finish for him.

"I am so sorry," he says with an undercurrent of sincerity that I recognize. "For what it's worth, I have my own experiences with saigon. I woke up naked and on the dinner table at my grandmother's house with her homemade jam smeared in…*unsavory* places."

I'm stunned by his admission. I didn't take Hallis to be the type to divulge much at all, let alone anything humiliating. "Your poor grandmother."

"Hey," he feigns offense. "It's not that bad of a sight to wake up to."

That only serves to make me laugh, and I'm smiling when I make eye contact with Acker. The look on his face takes me by surprise, so much so that my laughter dies in my chest. I was expecting the blank stare he's carefully kept in place, not the soft crinkle of a hidden smile in his eyes before he looks away.

"He told me you overheard our conversation." When I don't say anything, Hallis continues. "I may have said some things that could paint Acker in an unfair light."

It didn't do him any favors, that's for sure. "It's nothing I shouldn't have already suspected."

"He's loyal to a fault—a dangerous fault. The kind where he'd risk life and limb to save someone he cares about, to save his people." Hallis shifts behind me, and I get the sense he's uncomfortable discussing his friend, especially with someone he doesn't trust. "There are only two sides of Acker: people he's loyal to and everyone else. And trust me when I say there's a side you *never* want to be on."

"And where does the Strou princess fall in this equation?"

"I think that answer is up to you."

"I can find little difference between him courting her for political gain and what Kai did to me."

"If you can't see the difference then I'm not going to be able to convince you otherwise. You're allowed to hate Acker all you want, princess, but you don't need to make him the bad guy to do it."

Is that what I've been doing?

"Is there such a thing?" I ask. "For a bonded couple not to end in a true love match?"

"There have been tales," Hallis says.

"And?"

"They ended up destroying one another, along with everyone else around them."

Well then.

# CHAPTER 41

The dirt path we've happened upon turns to cobblestone outside one of the two entrances. Stone walls wrap the town, and guards stand outside, checking papers for anyone who enters.

Hallis leads the horse with his shorn hand in his pocket. "This is the first line of defense from the border. The town's been ransacked a time or two, so they're particular about who passes through."

Acker has pulled the material from his neck in the fashion of a hood to cloak his face. They've also hidden their weapons, and I've been instructed to keep my blade out of sight. When I asked why we needed to hide our identities, Hallis said it was to prevent the prince's presence from causing a ruckus with the townspeople. They don't get to see the royals outside the capitol's walls very often, and it usually creates a maelstrom of bodies. It's also to prevent word of our location from spreading in case Roison plans on retaliating.

"Papers," a guard calls when we approach. It's obvious we're not their typical visitors. The horses and saddles and clothing gives away our wealth in an area filled with farmers and serfs.

"We have no papers, but we have coins to spend," Acker says, shaking his fist to rattle the metal before exposing his palm.

The men lean in to get a better view, sharing a look

before the leader shakes his head. "The cost for passage has increased. Make it triple."

"Triple?" Hallis barks in outrage.

"Pay or go around. There's been word of a light wielder at the border, a lowly girl who's been rumored to look a lot like one of the two you're toting behind you," he says, pointing at Beau and me with a dirty finger. "And we don't want no trouble in our town."

Acker digs three more gold coins from his pocket. "Is this enough?" he asks, words clipped in annoyance.

"For you two," the guard says to Hallis and Acker. "The girls will be an additional fee."

"You've got to be fucking kidding me," Hallis all but shouts. "This is extortion. Does your lord know about this?"

"Lord Gravebriar is in the tavern if you'd like a word with him regarding our practices," the guard says, beard twitching when he smiles. "But first you'll need to pay."

Acker retrieves enough coins that I assume could buy an entire plot of land and slaps them into the man's hand. "They better have good ale."

The men shuffle out of the way for us to pass, smiling like the thieves they are and sharing silent laughs at our expense.

Once we're out of hearing range, Hallis pulls in close to Acker. "How much is left?"

"Not a lot," he replies.

The town branches off from the middle like spokes on a wheel, an old well as the centerpiece, where stray chickens and children are congregated.

"We need to split up," Acker says, handing Hallis half of what's left of the money. "I'll find a board for the horses. You three go check for lodging and whatever doesn't look like it'll give us a bout of food poisoning."

"Not happening." Hallis stops him with a hand on his shoulder, head tilting in our direction. "Pick one and we can call it even."

"Excuse me," Beau butts in. "Do we not get a say?"

Acker lets out a breath, eyes going to me. An offering for me to choose.

"I'll go with Hallis."

Beau isn't put out by my decision in the slightest and all but skips to take the reins from him. Acker tells us to meet back here in an hour, pointing to the clock in the center of town before we depart.

The buildings are old and worn down, brick facades crumbling and broken windows covered with boards. Many of the signs aren't legible due to weather and neglect, but we manage to find the inn with relative ease thanks to the vacancy sign in the window.

The doorway is propped open with a chair, and we enter the small parlor. It's empty of patrons besides one lone man sitting in a booth in the corner, a glass of dark liquor on the table before him. There's a bar near the stairs with an elderly woman behind it scribbling something into a notebook.

"We don't serve for another hour," she says, not bothering to look up from her book.

"How much for two rooms?" Hallis asks.

"Papers?"

"Not this bullshit again," Hallis mutters. "How much *without* papers?"

She looks over the brim of her reading glasses, eyes skimming us with sharp dexterity. "For the two of you and no papers?" she says, eyeing us once more. "Three silvers each."

Hallis assesses our funds and makes a face as he slaps all of it on the bar. "This is all I've got."

She fingers through the array of coins before sliding them into her palm and pocketing them in her chemise. "No violence or excessive drunkenness allowed. Keep it clean. Shared bathroom at the end of the hall on the right." Producing two sets of keys, she holds them with one in each hand.

Sounds reasonable enough. "Either of them have separate beds?"

She smiles at me and shakes the one in her right hand.

Hallis and I reach for the key at the same time, but I'm successful in grabbing it first. The number four is etched into its base. Hallis takes the other, less than thrilled by the prospect of sharing a bed with someone. There are only a few options as to who will get the pleasure of doing so, and I think we both know it won't be me.

"Name your price," Hallis says as we leave the inn.

"There's not a thing you could offer me that would suffice," I tell him, tucking the key into the fold of my blouse.

We return to the well before Acker and Beau. Hallis does his version of pouting, which is the best version, in my opinion, because it means he doesn't talk and avoids eye contact.

The town reminds me of the Main in Alaha, but seedier. There's a bakery and a shoe shop near the center and a tavern down the way. People carry packages wrapped in twine and paper from a nearby alley where the butcher resides. There are couples and families and men, but I haven't spotted a single woman out by herself, which is the most telling, along with the darkness that envelopes the town as the sun sinks behind the stone wall.

"Hallis?" He grunts in reply, and I point to the lanterns lining the street to get his full attention. "Why aren't they lit?"

He's quiet for a long pause, and I look at him to double check that he's not still ignoring me. Beau and Acker appear before he's able to answer.

"The whole town is crooked," Beau says.

"How much do we have?" Hallis asks.

Acker shakes his head, the only answer needed.

"If I'm going to bed on an empty stomach," Beau says, "at least tell me there's running water where we're staying."

Hallis and I share a look, which Beau's able to interpret, groaning at the lack of optimism radiating from us. We follow Hallis's lead back to the inn. If Beau or Acker are offput by the lack of light along the way, they don't voice or show it. Patrons line the dark alleyway as we pass by, and it seems the business has picked up since we were last here. A woman stands by the door, greeting people as they enter and...

...is she wearing negligee?

Hallis halts, the first to get a look inside the bustling establishment then up at the dilapidated sign.

Beau peeks her head past Hallis's shoulder and wheezes, "You booked us rooms at a brothel?" She smacks him in the shoulder.

Hallis's gaze goes to Acker, the last in our group. "I didn't know," he tells him, apologetic. "It was empty when we were here earlier and the lady who took our money was not..." He makes a face before looking to me for back up. When I don't offer any, he says, "She was *not* a lady of pleasure, if you get what I'm saying."

Acker sighs. "There's not a chance in hell we're getting the money back."

All eyes go to me, and it's obvious they're waiting for my reaction. I look to Acker over my shoulder to gauge his preference, then Beau says, "He doesn't mind a brothel, do you, Acker?"

He clenches his teeth but manages to keep his annoyance under control. "If you're uncomfortable, we'll go," he tells me. "None of us are strangers to sleeping on the ground. Another night won't kill us, and we'll be at the palace by nightfall tomorrow anyway."

But the money is already wasted, and it's too dark to situate a decent camp. Plus, I'm exhausted. "It's fine. Let's just get some sleep."

There's a noticeable sigh of relief between Beau and Hallis, and I wonder if they have any idea how alike they are.

Hallis is first to enter, and the lady at the door welcomes him with a smile and slow graze of her fingers along his forearm. He nods at her—the Kenta greeting—and passes by with curt politeness.

"Oooh." She does a shimmy at the sight of Beau and me dressed in little more than scraps of fabric. "I love women who are in touch with themselves. Maybe one of you could touch me later." She winks at me as I pass, her thick painted lashes accentuating the gesture. "Or maybe both of you."

Acker follows close behind, hand at the small of my back as we enter. "She definitely has a preference," he whispers in my ear, sending chills down my spine with his proximity.

The parlor is filled with men and scantily clad women. Perfume and liquor permeate the air. Everywhere I look, there's a woman drawing me in, their clothes and hair and makeup all a ploy to entice and evoke interest. Some have elaborate garments of shiny crystals and beads, others in nothing but a slip of lace as underwear, breasts bare.

And the two men in our party? Tall and handsome and wealthy, Hallis and Acker are prime targets walking through their establishment, leagues above their normal clientele, and they don't waste time before descending on them.

Hallis and Acker do their best to turn away their offers of service as politely as they can despite some of the women volunteering their time for free. There's even a mention of having a healer on staff in case any unsavory symptoms or concerns might arise in the morning.

By the time we manage to make it up the stairs, we're out of breath and disheveled, clothes and hair out of place.

Acker huffs out a breath and removes his hood, sending his hair in every direction. "I think we fared better escaping the Dark Forest."

I fail to hide my smile.

Beau scrubs at her eyes with the palms of her hands. "Everything is red."

Hallis studies her as he arranges his shirt back into place. "You okay?"

Dropping her hands, she takes a breath and nods, a smile returning to her face. "Yeah. A good night's rest will help."

I pull out my key and find the door with the matching

number.

Hallis does the same, stopping at the door opposite mine. "If you're rooming with Beau, we should get the double."

I hate that he makes sense, although the idea of Hallis and Acker sharing a bed does paint a pretty picture. "Fine," I say, accepting the trade.

"Keep your doors locked and don't go anywhere without someone with you," Acker orders.

"Yes, sir," Beau says with a mock bow.

He says her name in warning, and she suppresses an eye roll.

Hallis gets his door open and cusses. "The old hag switched the keys," he says, stepping aside so we can see the single bed in the middle of the room.

We all turn and watch Beau shove our door open, revealing the same exact layout inside our room as well: one single bed in the middle of the space.

"Looks like she hoodwinked you guys," she says.

I click my tongue at Hallis as I step backward into the room. "Don't be such a *princess*," I drawl.

Acker smiles at Hallis's annoyance.

"Sharing *is* caring," Beau agrees, shutting the door in their faces and locking the door. "Finally," she says, pulling a bottle of liquor from the folds of her pants like a magi. "Let's get drunk."

# CHAPTER 42

*Godsdammit.*

This is really, really annoying.

I'm standing in Hallis and Acker's room. I glance down and confirm I'm in what I wore to sleep, nothing more than my underwear and my blouse that kisses the top of my thighs.

Hallis sits at the writing desk next to the door, shirt off and scribbling something in a small notebook in the low lamplight. It's a book I haven't seen him with before, but from the scratched leather of its cover and frayed bindings, it's obvious it's well used.

Across the room, Acker lies on his stomach on the bed, head propped on a folded arm as he sleeps. Wearing only his pants with his boots hanging off the edge of the mattress, he remains motionless other than the slight rise and fall of his back.

Hallis hasn't looked up from his work. I take a hesitant step in his direction, noting the sword he has balanced against the table beside him. I peer over his shoulder and am surprised to find words on the page before him. His handwriting is messy, almost illegible, tiny scribbles that blur into the next line. I can feel the body heat radiating from his skin, but he doesn't look up. Testing the boundaries of my presence, I blow on the shell of his ear, and his head snaps in my direction.

I startle back a step. The words on the tip of my

tongue die at the way he stares at me. Well, not at me. *Through* me.

Eyes darting left and right, he looks toward Acker, who remains asleep on the bed. They narrow as he struggles to see into the darkness. After a long, tense moment where I think my heart is going to explode, he turns back around.

Releasing a quiet breath, I turn toward Acker. I've observed him sleeping many times over—in my shiel, in the boat, on the hard ground—but never have I seen him sleep like *this*, with abandon and peacefulness. Hair falling over his brow, lashes fanning across the tops of his cheeks, mouth slightly ajar. It brings a tightness to my chest that I can't identify, something as soft as it is sharp.

His strength is evident in the muscles of his back and arms, every dip and curve curated by training and fighting. The scar from where Kai stabbed him remains visible on his side. Skin that's gnarled together over time, unlike the wounds from a quicker healing that happens over land. The rest of his skin is a deep tan and flawless.

I wonder...

Leaning down, I run a finger over the smooth curve of his shoulder. There's no time to think or react before I'm flipped onto my back and Acker's fist is around my throat, dagger poised in midair and ready to strike.

Hallis shoots into a stance, weapon at the ready. "What is it?"

Acker's eyes clear of sleep, the haze dissipating as he takes me in. His grip loosens on my throat, and I accept the air with greed.

"What in the hell do you think you're doing?" he says,

ripping the dagger from the air and laying it flat on the bed with his palm over it. He leverages his body over mine, eyes morphing from the blank gaze of a calm killer to hot annoyance in the span of a few breaths. "It's Jovie."

Hallis's hold on his sword slackens, blade pointing toward the ground as he loosens the tension in his shoulders. "So that's what I felt a minute ago."

Acker's eyes take me in, trailing down the front of my blouse, eyebrows rising when he gets to my exposed underwear and thighs, which his knee is pressed between.

"You can't see her?" he asks, not taking his eyes off me.

"Not at all," Hallis replies, but I don't dare look away from Acker's heated gaze. "You look like you're pinning down a phantom."

Acker sits back on his knees, face unreadable. "Speak," he orders me.

I find myself smiling. I don't know why. "Speaking."

Acker's slow to look away, but I don't miss the slight upturn of his lips he manages to suppress before he looks at Hallis.

He shakes his head. "Nothing."

Acker returns his attention to me. "Are you sleeping right now?"

"The last I remember, I was. Beau was halfway through a bottle of brandy when I went to bed."

Acker cusses as he looks at Hallis. "Beau's drinking."

Hallis snatches his discarded shirt from the back of the chair before storming out of the room.

I look at Acker, confused.

"She only drinks when she's struggling with her

magic. With all the heightened emotions...it can be overwhelming," he says, careful to choose his words.

I'm finding it difficult to focus on what he's saying anyway. If he were to look down, he would have a perfect view of the thin fabric between my legs. I scoot up until my back is to the wall, and he catches the movement, eyes flicking down to where my thighs are pressed together then back to my face.

The obscene sounds coming through the thin walls all night start to sound seductive instead of fake as we hold each other's stares. Then I'm startled awake by the sound of glass breaking.

"You're so *gray*," Beau whines, dark hair a tangle around her head as she reaches for him.

"Why didn't you tell me the truth when I asked if you were okay earlier?" Hallis asks, cradling the back of her head. It's the softest I've witnessed him be, coddling Beau. "You know better."

Beau drops her forehead to Hallis's chest, knuckles white as bone as she grabs his shirt. "I'm sorry."

His anger dissipates in an instant. Cradling the back of Beau's head to his chest, he places the bottle on the small desk beside the door. Acker enters and takes in the scene, mouth in a tight line as he takes in Beau's emerging tears.

"Want me to take the first shift?" Acker says.

Hallis sighs and shakes his head. "It doesn't look like I'll be sleeping tonight."

They share a look, communicating without words before Acker dips his head in acquiesce. He looks toward me, holding out a hand for me to come. Hallis keeps his gaze on Beau as I get closer.

I'm at a loss for what to do. "Beau—"

"No," she cries, squeezing even closer to Hallis. "They're so bright, Hallis. Please don't make me."

I look at Hallis, concerned, but he just shakes his head. "Just go."

Acker nods in encouragement, and I let him lead me out of the room and across the hall. He locks the door behind us and places his dagger on the edge of the desk, the point of the blade toward the door.

"Does this happen often?"

"Not as of late. It was worse when she was younger." He removes his shirt and hangs it on the back of the chair. "I've never been envious of her gift. She'll be fine after she sleeps it off."

There's a heaviness lining his shoulders as he looks at me. It's obvious he's displeased by the turn of events.

"I'll take the floor," he says, stepping around me to reach the pack, dropping it in the slim space between the bed and desk.

He sits on the edge of the bed to unlace his boots, moving them out of the way. I stop him from sinking to the floor with an arm on his shoulder. He goes still. His gaze travels up from my exposed thighs until he meets my eyes.

"As much as it pains me to say this..." I grimace through the words I'm about to utter. "I think the floor is even too great a distance between us if I am to get any rest."

He looks toward the bed, chest rising on an inhale. A mirage of thoughts and emotions flit across his gaze. He must settle on one of them when he drags his weight onto the bed.

With his chest laid bare, upper body balanced on an elbow, he takes me in. I fight the urge to squirm under his gaze. I pretend my blouse isn't see-through. I wish it were just a smidge longer. I can all but feel his eyes dancing across my exposed skin, and for reasons I can't fathom at this moment, I let him.

"I hate that the first time we share a proper bed is in a brothel."

I climb onto the rough duvet. "You say that like there'll be other times in the future."

He slides into position, arm outstretched for my head to rest on. Grinning, he braces his forearm over the curve of my hip. "We're matched. It's a foregone conclusion."

A lick of anger races through me. "Can you at least pretend you still have to court me?"

His grin slips away, surprise replacing it, then frustration soon after. "Have I not proved myself to you yet? I risked my life to go to Alaha to save you. I protected for you. *Killed* for you."

Even through the darkness, nothing but the half-burned candle Hallis left on the desk casting light over the room, I can see the sharpness in his eyes as he looks at me. I don't like the wave of guilt that threatens to make my eyes water.

"Tell me, Jovie," he says, angry. "What more can I do?"

I shake my head, just the tiniest of movements, because I don't know. I don't know if there'll ever be anything he could say or do that would remove my trepidations.

He must see it too, because resignation settles over his features as he releases a deep breath. "You haven't slept in days."

I am so very tired, the kind that's rooted inside the bones. A cool draft sends shivers down my bare legs, and Acker pulls me closer, shoving his legs between and over mine to cover them. The exhaustion I've been chasing for three nights begins to ebb. I allow myself to find solace in his presence, if just to ease the tension in the length of the matching bond connecting us.

"You've been avoiding sleep so you don't visit me," he says, voice rough in the reprieve of the quiet room. "It didn't happen until after I quit letting you inside my mind, right?"

After I think about it, I nod.

"It's as if the bond is looking for a path of least resistance."

"Why is it only on my end?"

He takes a moment to consider my question. "Because you're opposed to it."

My breath sticks in my lungs as I come to the realization that my own reluctance may be the cause of my bond trying to find ways to close the gap. If it's true, I will never get a say in the matter. The bond will get what it wants regardless of my objections.

Taking a deep breath, I soak in Acker's scent. It's equal parts familiar and dangerous, enticing and comforting, like a midnight swim on a summer night.

He squeezes my hip. A gesture of reassurance or placation, I'm not sure. "Get some sleep."

"Easier said than done after that revelation."

He smiles, pulling me so close that his chin rests on top of my head. "Don't worry, Jovie. I'm going to court you so well you'll be begging to climb into bed with me."

I can't stop the smile tugging at my lips. His challenge touches the competitive spirit in me. I run my nose along the column of his throat, enjoying the goose bumps that erupt along the skin. Then I send an image of closing my teeth around the vital portion of his neck straight into his mind. Like pushing through a stuck door, I divulge *my* fascination with his throat.

He's unprepared for my intrusion, a shiver racking his body as he grips the hair at the back of my head, eyes roving my upturned face. "How'd you—"

"Or," I drawl, a tad bit smug, "my end of the bond is waiting for yours to catch up."

His gaze jumps between my eyes, inspecting them for any falsehoods or deception. Coming up empty, he angles his open mouth over mine. I freeze in place along with my breath as I await his next move.

In the space where his thigh is wedged, heat pools between my legs, a fiery longing seeping into my veins. The feel of his naked chest rising and falling against the meager material covering mine reminds me to breathe. I draw in a large rush of his breath, and it only stokes the fire inside me more.

He speaks against my mouth, lips kissing mine as his deep voice utters my name. "Jovie."

Then I feel it, his own desire, hard and pressing into my lower belly. His lashes cast a shadow over his cheekbones, irises dark as he holds my stare. I can't help the slight tilt of my hips as I seek some sort of relief or contact or friction, something to lessen the building desire burning me from the inside out.

He slides his hand from my lower back over the curve of my ass. He relishes each side before choosing one and squeezes. I'm all but about to beg him to kiss me when a smirk overtakes Acker's face, sending all my thoughts and blood to a screeching halt at the sight of it.

"Or maybe your bond knows what you want better than you do."

I slap his hand away and he untangles himself from me, chuckling in the face of my attitude. I'm glad it's dark enough to hide the searing heat tinting my cheeks. I can feel it all the way to my ears.

I flip over and give him my back. "You're a bastard."

Unperturbed, he slides a palm across my stomach, pulling until his front is flush with my back. The evidence of his arousal is still firm against the curve of my backside, but I don't move away, grateful for the warmth his body provides as he covers my legs with his once again.

At least that's what I tell myself, and my bond for good measure. The damn tether is practically purring in contentment at Acker's close presence as I drift off to sleep.

# CHAPTER 43

My mind has been running in circles since Hallis knocked on my door this morning. The space beside me was empty. Acker left to retrieve the horses from the farrier before dawn, which I came to find out when I returned our room key to the old lady at the front desk where Hallis and Beau were waiting.

While better than the last time I saw her, Beau looks like what I assume the epitome of the color gray feels. I wonder if she can sense her own aura. If so, I wonder what it looks like considering the massive hangover she's dealing with. I ask her as much when we stop for lunch.

"Depends on how long I'm willing to stare at myself in a mirror," she says, eyes toward the small village in the distance.

We've been weaving in and out of the outcropping of towns neighboring the capitol. Unlike the one closest to the border, none of them have any type of surrounding barricade, but we've steered clear of them for reasons unspoken to me despite it slowing our progress.

"Frankly, I don't care that much."

She takes a swig of water, skin pale despite the afternoon sun hanging over us. I don't know what happened after I left her alone with Hallis. I hate that I had the best night of sleep I've gotten in many weeks while she was fighting unseen demons with her archnemesis consoling her.

"Your blaring guilt isn't helping," she says.

I grimace. "Should I not have left you?"

"Not that." She makes a sound with her teeth. "The other thing."

I inhale a deep breath, turning my attention away so I don't have to look her in the eye. I've been shoving the feeling of betrayal down as far as I can every time the emotion dares to make an appearance since I awoke this morning. I've let my nerves run free, hoping they overshadow any other emotions threatening to break through. It's concerning that Beau was still able to discern the sense of disloyalty plaguing me.

"I didn't stop loving Kai when I decided to leave Alaha," I tell her, hating the shame coating my tongue. "Even though I knew it was the right decision—the best decision—it still hurt."

"That's normal, having conflicting emotions about someone. It can take a long time to sort through the heartache, to separate what once was from what is meant to be."

I shake my head. "I don't know if he even knew what a true match is."

"Would it matter?"

I brave a look at her, noting the sympathy in her eyes. At the end of the day, regardless of why I left Kai in Alaha, he's simply not my match. Acker is.

"You can never get loving people wrong, Jo. There's no shame in accepting your feelings for Kai, just like there's none to be had for accepting them for Acker." She lifts her brows, expression lighter than it's been all day. "Don't tell Acker I said that. I like my head where it is on my shoulders."

We're smiling when we walk back to the horses. Acker and Hallis both pause at the sight of our return.

"Everything okay?" Acker asks with a smile, eyes flitting to Beau and back to me.

I nod. If Hallis is suspicious of Beau's change in demeanor, he doesn't voice it, but his eyes never leave her as she brushes by him and mounts their mare.

The nerves return as we gather our stuff and continue our movement toward the capitol. I'm back to sharing a horse with Acker. It was an unspoken understanding between the two of us, which Beau and Hallis seemed to prefer for the first time since leaving the border.

When I awoke to an empty bed, the bond instantly protested at his absence. Like a strain under my ribs, the tether didn't lessen its stinging pull until Acker was within reaching distance. Then it only reduced itself to a dull tug.

Still, as my body is pressed firmly between his thighs, it doesn't feel close enough to satisfy the damned thing. Neither of us have broached the subject, but I'm dying to know if it feels the same on his end with the way he was able to end...*whatever* was happening between us last night.

I can't think about it too long, because the pulsing ache of desire comes flooding back with a vengeance. I can't stop the memory from progressing into a full-fledged daydream where Acker doesn't stop and we're the reason the wall behind our bed shook all night. Then comes the embarrassment when I recall the smug smile on his face and the shame that followed. I all but growl at my inner thoughts. I'm trying to give Beau a break, not add to her stress with my annoying emotions.

"What is it?" Acker asks, voice low enough so Hallis

and Beau can't hear.

"I'm nervous," I tell him.

While that is somewhat honest, there's no way in hell I'd admit I've actually been reliving last night in my mind at nauseam.

"Anything I can do to relieve some of your stress?"

"No?" I say, confused by his offer.

"Are you sure?"

The inflection in his voice catches my attention. "What are you getting at?"

He dips his chin close, lips grazing my cheek and ear as we sway with the horse's trot, sending shivers down my spine when he speaks. "The bond is *throbbing* from your end of the tether."

I all but gasp at the realization that he might be able to feel me through the bond. "What are you talking about?" I say with the driest tone I can muster despite blush coating my entire face and neck.

"You know what I'm talking about," he says, sending another wave of chills through me.

Then he does something I least expect. He drags his mouth to curve of my neck—the very spot he's been fixated on—and places an open-mouth kiss to the skin. This time I do gasp, head falling back against his shoulder to give him better access. I won't ever reveal this truth, but the fantasy I've been chasing all day doesn't compare to the real heat and feel of his tongue on my skin.

I release a breath that's somewhere between a sigh and a moan, and he places his palm against the flat of my stomach, pulling me against the hardness pressing into my lower back. He ends the kiss with a drag of his teeth over the sensitive area. I don't need to be able to feel the end of his bond to discern that the throbbing I feel is definitely coming from him.

All very much him.

"Feel better?"

I shake my head. "Not even a little."

He laughs and places a chaste kiss against my temple. The gesture leaves me feeling more exposed than the kiss of my neck did, and I sit up, needing some semblance of space between us.

We ride for hours without speaking. I surmise Acker's teasing did help. My mind mellows out, leaving a sense of expectation rather than nerves. Hallis and Beau are equally quiet, subdued as we pass more and more homes and farms littering the countryside.

The roadways become congested with fellow travelers, tradesmen and farmers moving livestock. Most of the people we encounter create a wide enough berth for us to pass, seemingly wary of strangers. It's not until we pass a family headed in the same direction as us that someone notices. The recognition on the father's face sends them all to their knees at his insistence. Acker places a hand on his chest in respect, but we pick up our pace not long after that.

The sun is touching the horizon after we circumvent one of the largest towns I've seen as of yet when a company of men on their horses are spotted at a distance. Acker holds up a hand to signal Hallis to stop behind us.

"Who is it?" I ask, noting the lack of flag with them.

Acker doesn't reply right away. Hallis halts his mare next to ours, eyes squinting in the distance.

"Can you get a read, Beau?"

She shakes her head. "They're too far away."

Acker places the reins in my hands and dismounts. "Stay here."

"Take Beau with you," Hallis instructs, holding his horse still as she also dismounts.

"No," Acker says, retrieving his strap of knives and buckling it across his chest. "I'll give the signal when it's safe."

"I don't think—"

Beau cuts Hallis off with a hand on his thigh. "Let him handle this."

Something in Acker and Beau's demeanor stops him from arguing, and it worries me.

Acker looks up at me. "I'll be right back."

We watch him march across the distance with the wind whipping through his shirt and hair with every step. I know Acker can handle himself, but there look to be close to ten men on horseback, and it feels a little like a fool's errand.

"Is that…"

Hallis's voice trails off when the band of men separate, revealing a man with long, blonde hair in their midst. It's hard to make out, but it's obvious they're discussing something. Unease spreads through my chest as one of the men gets down from his horse. I tighten my hands on the reins, urging myself to be patient.

Not until they separate and Acker turns to look back do I get a better look at the man. He begins to move toward us, Acker following close behind, and I recognize the markings on the leather of his uniform: a golden butterfly surrounded by deep burgundy. The emblem of Maile.

I dismount as they get closer.

"Princess," the man says upon his arrival, sharp eyes keen on me before he folds into a bow then a kneel, blonde hair free and cascading around his handsome face.

"Please," I sputter, my nerves getting the best of me. "Stand."

He smiles as he rises. "As you wish." He does a decent job of keeping it in check to remain polite, but something tells me he finds me humorous.

"This is General Samasu." Acker introduces him, drawing my attention from the soldier. "He's a sentry from Maile. Your mother sent him to intercept us."

The general cocks his head, eyes the color of wheat never leaving mine. "I'm here to take you home," he says, leaving no room for interpretation.

Acker's chin dips toward his chest, a grin forming on his face before looking up at the general then me. "Does the princess not get a choice?"

General Samasu doesn't so much as blink when he says, "No."

Acker's grin turns into a full-fledged smirk in reaction to whatever expression is on my face. He makes a motion to let me know this is my problem to handle, stepping around the general and standing close enough behind me that I can feel his heat on my skin.

I look at Hallis, strong and steady on his horse, sword laying across his lap. Then at Beau, who has her metal rope lassoed around a closed fist. Both prepared, not a stitch of fear or uncertainty in their gazes.

"Whose likelihood of survival are you assessing?" the general asks, eyes inquisitive on me. "Ours or theirs?"

"I don't wish any lives to be lost today," I answer in turn.

"I will not lie to you, princess." He glances at the man behind me and then adjusts the strap holding the sword across his back. "Most of my men will die here if you do not come willingly."

"And yet you still are willing to challenge this?" I ask. "All the while knowing it may cost you your life?"

My question makes him smile. "Oh, no. I will not die," he says, placing a hand to his chest. "But my men will."

And to support his statement, he disappears. Just... vanishes from existence, leaving nothing in the place where he stood a moment ago.

Acker catches on the quickest, spinning in place to face the general where he stands behind us now. Both Hallis and Beau lose their crafted semblance of calm. Hallis slides from his horse while Beau unravels a link of her rope.

"As I was saying," General Samasu draws. "There's no need to worry about me, but I appreciate the concern."

I step around Acker's tense back, but he stops me from moving closer with a hand around my wrist. It's a warning not to get too close.

The general clocks it. "If you want a true pardon, you'll hand her over to her mother."

Acker's body is drawn taut. I sense the tension rolling off of him in the pressure of his hand around my wrist. "What makes you think I want a pardon?"

"Why else would you retrieve the princess?" the general asks, eyes locked on Acker.

"Well, aside from the promise I made to Queen Evelyn to find her daughter myself," Acker says, sliding his hand into the palm of mine and intertwining our fingers, "Jovie is my match."

General Samasu freezes in place, completely

unmoving other than his golden hair dancing in the wind around him. "You're lying."

"He's not," I say, tightening my fingers that are interlaced with Acker's, letting him know which side of this I stand on. "We are matched."

He's not swayed, gaze narrowed between the two of us, assessing and calculating the likelihood that I'm not being manipulated somehow. "You better find a way to convince me," he says.

Acker and I look at each other. The only thing I can think of is the kiss we shared where our magic wanted to become one with the other, wanted to wield our gifts together like one weapon instead of two. It was the tiniest glimpse of what we could be together. If I had concentrated on the magic aspect over the taste of him, maybe I could have sensed the possibilities of our combined powers better. But other than attacking his mouth with mine, I don't actually know how to tap into it.

There's a smile in Acker's eyes as if he knows where my thoughts ventured to. "Give me your dagger."

Removing it from my side, I keep my questions to myself, not wanting to let on that I'm as naive as I am. I'm not prepared for Acker to bring our joined hands before us, and I'm especially not prepared for him to shove the blade into the space between our palms. I can't stop the flinch. It's mostly from shock, but I don't dare pull away despite the burn.

He looks up at me through his lashes, and I get the sense this is more for my benefit than that of anyone else present. "Jovinnia, Princess of Maile, is my match. With this oath, I swear to protect her until my dying breath."

Blood escapes through the cracks of our fingers and drips down my wrist. There's a shine to his eyes that I've never seen before. It makes my heart pick up pace, my breaths deepening. I swallow past the tightness in my throat.

"And," he says, licking his lips before continuing, "I love her."

Hallis barks Acker's name, a clear yet panicked warning that Acker ignores as he turns our hands to the side, letting our mixed blood splatter to the ground.

I don't know the implications of what has just been done or why he did it, but I couldn't fight the desire to kiss him if I tried. And, if I'm being honest with myself, I don't. I eagerly meet his descending lips with my own, my mouth open in invitation. Acker has enough wherewithal to keep it short, though he still coats my tongue with the taste of his.

A cloth smacks Acker in the side of the face, Beau's aim perfect on her intended mark. "You fool." Her insult isn't in jest. True anger shines behind her eyes. "Stupid, stupid fool."

Hallis is even more upset. All he can manage is a slow shake of his head, disgust lining his face.

General Samasu, however, is damn near ecstatic. "A fool, yes, but possibly the bravest man I've ever met."

"I think you mean crazed," Hallis says.

Acker isn't fazed by their reverie. In no hurry, he takes the time to clean the rivulets of blood already drying along my digits, eyes flitting between his task and my eyes. It feels like an apology of sorts, an act of contrition. He rips the fabric with his teeth, tearing it in two and using the better shred to wrap around my bleeding palm.

He looks back at the general. "Are you convinced?" he asks, returning to business.

I, on the other hand, am a quivering mess on the inside. My stomach is in knots, head swimming. I squeeze the makeshift bandage and focus on the sting.

General Samasu shakes his head, still in a mild state of disbelief. "I suppose I am." Then he all-out laughs. "The queen is going to need proof."

I motion for Acker to hand over my dagger and give it to the general. "Tell my mother I will send word when I'm ready to come home. I'll call for the blade in three days' time. Will that be enough for your venture back?"

He stares at the black stone dagger before meeting my gaze. "Dang rabbits," he mutters.

My heart stops at his use of words.

Shaking his head, he throws a hand up in acquiescence. "Go ahead and make it two. Anything more than a day and she'll have my head."

He smiles then, and I recognize it, the affinity between him and Wren. The way his lips part, the crinkle around his nose, the shape of his teeth. I keep the revelation to myself but return the smile.

He winks at Acker. "Good luck, boy." Then he blinks from existence.

We turn toward the men in the distance, with whom General Samasu now stands. The small battalion begins to retreat, the horses picking up pace and heading west.

Acker pinches my chin, angling my face to his, and places his mouth on mine, letting the kiss linger before releasing me from his hold. It's simple but feels like everything.

It feels like the beginning of the end.

# CHAPTER 44

The capitol is unlike anything I could have imagined. Stone walls encircle the city, shielding everything but rooftops from view. And the palace...it sits on a hill above all the rest, also made of stone with gold-capped spires that shine in the night, a beacon towering over the city below.

"That's your home," I say, trying to wrap my head around what it was like growing up in such opulence.

"When I was younger, yes. I haven't been back in over a year. Before that, nearly two when I was traveling with the army. I consider my home to be wherever my head lies these days."

*She lived in a hovel, Hallis.*

The time since I left Alaha is jumbled. I can't recount the days or weeks exactly, but it's been many since I had a place to call home. There are nights when I'd do just about anything to be back in that tiny room and lumpy bed.

The road widens to accommodate carriages and population. Buildings line the streets, curving outward from the entrance. They're gorgeous in their own right, made of stone but adorned with copper, exemplifying the gifts of their prince.

A small brigade awaits at the city gates to greet us. Iron and copper weave together in an arch stretching from either side of the wall, the posts manned by helmeted soldiers. They are the only soldiers who don't bend a knee at Acker's arrival.

"Greetings, prince," says one of the soldiers, dipping his head in acknowledgment. "I hope your travels were pleasant."

A snorting sound escapes me before I'm able to reel it in.

I can hear the smile in Acker's voice when he responds. "Pleasant enough, soldier. Do you have a briefing for me?"

"Yes, your highness. The city has been anticipating your arrival for days. The streets are a bit crowded, so your father sent a carriage to transport the princess in." He makes a motion toward the golden buggy loaded behind a team of horses.

"Not necessary," Acker says.

The soldier shuffles on his feet. "With all due respect, sir, your father—"

Acker cuts him off. "She'll ride with me."

The soldier heeds the statement, dipping his head and ordering the carriage to be sent to the palace.

"Beau and I will take the lead," Hallis says. "Send your men to the rear."

If he doesn't like that order, he doesn't voice it. Another soldier steps forward with a cloak. Acker reaches down to retrieve it, draping it around his shoulders and buttoning it at his collarbone. It's deep greenish-blue and made of velvet.

Acker leans in close, chest pressed to my back. "Ready?"

Taking a deep breath, I release it and nod. "As I can be, I suppose."

One of the guards blows a horn to announce our

arrival, but it's unneeded. When we turn under the arched entrance, there's a clear view of the crowded streets teeming with people, overflowing into alleys and rooftops, more people than I've ever seen in my life. In open doors and windows, everywhere I look are the faces of strangers staring back at me.

Acker said it's customary for the city to greet the return of a monarch, but this feels excessive. The crowd's anxious chatter grows to a thundering cheer at the sight of their prince.

"All hail the prince!"

Their shouts and praises overlap as people celebrate Acker's homecoming, but their excitement dims at the sight of me. The cheers fall to dull whispers before descending into silence. People stare with wide eyes, mouths agape like I'm a dancing monster from the sea with eight legs and a hat parading through their city.

I'm grateful for Acker's ostentatious cape so I can hide the grip I have on his arm underneath its cover. He switches his hold on the reins to free up a hand so he can intertwine it with mine while out of view.

We come to a town center. Instead of a well, there's a statue as high as the building around it of a woman with her hands open to the sky. Water flows from between her fingers in a rainfall to the basin she's standing in. Children stand in the water, eyes wide and joyous as their prince parades through the city, not getting the message that something is amiss. They wave with cheeky smiles on full display.

Someone blows another horn, shushing the crowd once again. As if they've been reminded of their manners, they begin to bow, knees touching the cobblestone one at a time. Like a wave in the sea, heads and shoulders sink to the ground.

The silence is deafening.

That is until someone yells from deep in the crowd, "She's cursed!"

An exclamation of fear and dismay ripples through the people.

Another yells, "She only brings bad omens!"

Then another. And another. Then the damn breaks. Voices come from every side, fingers pointed at me. Telling me I'm not welcome, I'm evil, the prince is walking death into his city.

I can feel Acker growing more and more angry behind me. I keep a stronghold on his hand, half out of comfort and half out of fear of what he'll do if I don't.

The nearest lamplight goes out, and it incites the crowd. Hallis barks orders to the men to pick up the pace, but not before the next one goes dark, removing the beautiful orange glow that highlighted the street and buildings around it. Then the next goes out, and the next, and the next, like a river of darkness toward the palace in the distance until the city is pitched into its depths with only the light from the occasional open window and moon to see by.

Acker releases my hand as we move into a gallop toward the palace. Everything becomes a blur as I realize the reason the small town we spent the night in didn't have lamps lit: in opposition to me.

The iron gates of the palace are within view when a tomato is thrown at me. I lift an arm to shield myself from the rotten vegetable, but it breaks apart and splatters down my person. Beau is quick to rope the offender, metal whipping around his wrist to hold him in place until a royal guard is able to detain him, but the damage has been done.

My gift unfurls and ignites across my skin. I urge it to calm down, but it senses my fear and heart beating furiously in my chest and refuses to listen. The horde of angry citizens screech in fear. As fast as their mob mentality ensued, they scatter at the sight of my glowing skin.

With the road cleared, we're at least able to make it to the gate quicker. Cages hang from the iron posts, and upon a quick glance, it appears there are moving animals inside. We enter the palace's courtyard, and Acker yanks the reins to stop, leaping from the horse's back.

"Where's my father?" he demands, holding his hands out to catch me.

A guard adorned with a multitude of insignias on the lapel of his uniform steps to Acker's side. "He thought it best to wait inside."

Acker doesn't like his answer, but he keeps an arm around me as he ushers me toward the steps. The rest of the men step out of our way, but their eyes follow me. At the top step, I turn and look out over the courtyard. The iron gates at the entrance are now shut, the city's bravest standing with their faces against the bars as they continue to yell their outrage.

"Jovie," Acker says, gaining my attention. "Let's get inside."

Beau is nowhere to be seen. Hallis's gaze is downcast as I pass by, and I can't help but feel like he knew this was going to happen. I think they both did.

There's no time to dwell on my thoughts or the shaking of my hands when I cross the threshold of the front door of the palace. We walk the distance of a long hall, each step against the polished floor echoing like a ticking clock counting down. We enter another set of doors, and my gaze is drawn to the ceiling first, gold and shined to perfection, causing our reflections to peer back down at us from stories above. It's dizzying, and I'm quick to return my gaze forward. Columns line the room toward the staircase at the opposite side of the chamber, and I can't help but feel like the design is meant to make anyone who enters feel...less than.

Helmeted soldiers line the room, the hilts of their swords braced against their palms, pointing to the ground. Loitering before them are men I don't recognize, but by the finery of their clothes and jewels, I'm going to assume they are the king's council. Some of them may be lords, having traveled from their provinces to witness my arrival. It appears their wives and consorts will have a viewing as well.

I follow Acker's lead, stopping at the foot of the dais. I'm quickly abandoned when the king makes his appearance.

Stepping out from the hall behind, Acker's father is nothing like I expected. I'm not sure what I imagined, but the medium height and build of this man was not it. Handsome, yes, but average in every other way. His cloak, more ornate than Acker's, drags the ground as he steps forward.

Smiling wide, the expression so similar to Acker's it hurts to see another man wield it, he lifts his arms in an open embrace. "Son," he calls, voice melodic.

Acker's eyes beam as he ascends the throne, throwing his arms around his father's shoulders. Even though his father is smaller in stature, he exudes authority as he pulls back to look at his son.

"Feeling a little lean," he says, adjusting the cloak around Acker's shoulders. "How have you been, my boy?"

Appearing more boyish than I've ever seen him before, Acker's cheeks turn a hint of pink under his father's appraisal. "I'm glad to be home."

The king nods. "Good, good." He ushers his son toward the twin thrones, gold and ornate and audacious in every way. Turning toward the parishioners, the king sweeps his cloak to the side, setting his eyes on me as he sits. "Kneel," he demands of the congregation.

A flurry of shuffling happens where every head and knee bend to the king's will. Looking to my left, I find Hallis on one knee, shorn hand braced atop the other. Acker remains standing before the throne beside his father. The silence is stifling.

I'm wholly alone before the stage. I look up at Acker, at a loss as to what is expected of me. He tilts his chin in answer, and distaste coats the back of my tongue as I drop my eyes to the marbled floor, my knees following right after, the stone bitingly cold through my pants.

There's a long period of waiting where the only sound I can hear is the beating of my heart and the thoughts racing through my mind. I dare to look up and watch as Acker takes his place on his designated throne.

Only then does the king give another order. "All rise."

There's a rush of opposite movement as everyone ascends. Well, everyone but myself. I remain on one knee. There's a look in Acker's eyes, a specific tip of his chin and sharpness in his gaze I've never witnessed before.

I've seen the soldier, seen the arrogance. I've seen

the fighter and the annihilator of a man trained to kill without a second thought, and I've seen the caring protector. I've even seen the boy who was seeking his father's approval moments ago.

But this is the first time I've seen the predilection for power lurking underneath. Sitting upon a metal throne, surrounded by his liege, in a palace coated in gold. The abilities he has could ravage this building and everyone in it.

I've never been more scared of him than I am now. My chest nearly caves at the realization.

"Jovinnia," the king says, finally requesting my attention. "You're so gracious. Thank you. Please, stand."

As if I've been waiting for his permission, my body rises of its own accord. "Thank you, your highness," I say, proud of the steadiness with which I'm able to articulate those few words.

I tell myself to not look, but the eyes of the people standing on either side of the room draw me to them. After experiencing the wrath of the town's people, I'm expecting the same hostility from the parishioners, but what I'm not expecting is the laughter in many of the men's gazes, as if there's a joke I'm not clued in on.

The king brings my attention back to his position. "I can't articulate how ecstatic I am to see you alive and in one piece after all this time. You have grown to be a stunning woman."

I somehow manage to paste on a smile. "Thank you, your majesty."

There's a pause as he looks at me, dark eyes roving. Only then do I discover I'm still glowing. I attempt to cover the exposed skin of my arms with my hands, making the strangers giggle at my expense.

"There's nothing to be embarrassed about, princess. We all struggled to control our magic when it was new." His eyes crinkle at the corners when he smiles, revealing the age behind his flawless skin. "I hope you accept my apology on behalf of my people. They can be overzealous at times."

I raise my eyebrows at his choice of description but keep my thoughts to myself. "All is forgiven."

Something in his smile tells me he doesn't quite believe me, but he bows his head in acceptance anyway. "That is very courteous of you." He looks at his son. "She makes a fine Heir."

Acker's returning grin is placating, eyes shifting from his father to me.

"Well, I'm sure you're exhausted after all your travels. Stassia," he calls, and a petite young woman appears from one of the neighboring rooms. "Will you escort Princess Jovinnia to her chamber?"

"Actually, father," Acker says, stepping forward. "Jovie and I would like council with you."

His father doesn't look away from me when he replies. "It has been a trying day, son. We must offer our guests time to rest. I'm sure it's nothing that can't wait for dinner."

I look to Acker for guidance, and he nods once, albeit with chagrin. Stassia, the waiting maidservant, motions for me to follow her. I struggle to make my eyes leave Acker, to make my feet move away from Hallis's presence, but somehow I do as I'm told.

I follow the girl out of the court, pretending the stares on my back aren't as harsh as they feel. We come to a staircase that branches off into two directions. We take the left, venturing down the main hall until it dead-ends into another sharp left. The same gold from the court's ceiling trims the doors and handles. Ornate rugs run the entire length of the hallway, and I feel terrible for walking on it with my boots.

Stassia, the young girl, stops in front of one of the doors. She speaks a breath above a whisper. "This will be your accommodations."

She opens the door for me to enter first and takes a step back as I pass. I'm fairly sure her hands are shaking, but I pretend not to notice.

The room is bigger than any shiels in Alaha, including that of the captain. Decadent is the only word I can think of to describe the rich tapestries and decorated walls, the oversized bed covered in downs and pillows, and the etched glass door that leads to a terrace outside.

"There's a bathing chamber just through that door," Stassia says from the threshold of the entryway. "I'll send up some soaps as well as a change of clothes. There's a bell if you need assistance." She points to the rope hanging from the ceiling beside the bed.

I don't get my full thanks out of my mouth before she leaves, shutting the door in her wake. Standing in the middle of the room, I take in my surroundings, afraid to touch anything for fear of soiling it.

As opulent as everything is, I find it all very grotesque.

The palace alone rivals the size of all of Alaha. The town is ten times as large, and I've never felt more alone. Fear and uncertainty threaten to push moisture to my eyes, but I chase it down with the reminder that I'm here for a reason. Many reasons. And there's no room for pity.

I decide it best to remove my boots before crossing the room to get to the terrace. Fresh air breezes in when I step outside. The city beyond the palace's walls remains dark, but all seems quiet on the streets below.

It's only in my mind where their hatred continues to echo.

# CHAPTER 45

Feeling sorry for myself evaporates the second I sink into the copper bathtub. The water is near scorching, and it does wonders to eviscerate the tidal wave of emotions I've been struggling to hold in.

The tub matches the bench stocked with soaps and towels next to it. Sniffing my way through the assortment, I settle on a purple soap that reminds me of the field of flowers Acker brought me to. I scrub every inch of my body and wash my hair three times before I'm satisfied with my work. Then I relax in the neck-deep water. I allow myself the reprieve, letting myself enjoy a luxury I never imagined I'd experience in my life. It puts the water reservoir I thought so highly of to shame.

After nearly dozing off twice, I step from the water with red and raw skin, no longer glowing to any degree, and wrap a towel around myself. It takes all my effort to make it to bed, where I throw myself down. It feels like I take the first real breath I've had in weeks.

"I see you're already enjoying the comforts of the palace."

I snap into a sitting position, letting out a sigh of relief at the sight of Beau lounging in one of the tufted armchairs. "Dang rabbits," I mutter. "You scared the hell out of me."

Legs thrown over the arm opposite the one her head

is propped against, she smiles, threading the metal rope between her hands. "Good. It'll remind you to never let your guard down." She settles the rope on the back of the chair. "Not here."

"What happened to you?" I tighten the towel around my chest. "You disappeared when we arrived."

She rolls her eyes, but it's not filled with her usual sass. "Had to deal with the farmer who believed you were a place to discard his rotten produce."

"Deal with...how?" I say, squeezing the excess water from my hair.

"You'll see," she says. She doesn't elaborate.

"What are you doing here?"

Sitting up, she points a thumb to garments hung over the other chair. "Delivering your wardrobe. Apparently, you scared poor Stassia half to death, to the point she has all the other maidservants in a tizzy, refusing to serve you. Hence..." She motions to her person.

It's my turn to roll my eyes. "I didn't do anything to her," I say in defense.

"I know that, but my father insisted I be the example, so I'll be the one escorting you to dinner and anywhere you'd like until further notice."

*Escorting me.*

"It'll be fun," she continues, exhaustion seeping through her demeanor.

It goes unsaid that she just needs a break, maybe some food and a decent night's rest before she can brave another day of people with strong emotions. Especially if she's going to be accompanying me of all people.

"Well," I say, sliding down from the obscenely tall bed. "I'm in no need of your services tonight."

I rifle through the heaps of clothes and find the

undergarments, pulling on a pair of underwear under my towel. It's the softest underwear to ever grace my bottom, that's for damn sure. Butter underwear.

Beau tilts her head at me. "Are you not wanting to attend the dinner tonight?"

"And be subject to more passive consternation regarding my return?" I give her a sardonic grin, a teasing, knowing look I hope she can decipher without me having to speak the words. "I'll pass."

A little sign of life sparks behind her eyes. "Acker will be concerned if I don't deliver you."

I shrug like I'm indifferent. "Let him."

She smirks in return, as if she likes that I'm not worried about Acker's need to know everything I'm doing at all times, but it's quick to lose its brightness as she fights a yawn. "In that case, you'll get no complaints from me."

I whip the nightgown in my hands at her. "Go get some sleep."

She slides her rope onto her wrist, the length reaching the crook of her elbow, and stands. We're the same height, but she has a way of making me feel smaller than I am. It feels like a test of sorts, a challenge to hold my ground.

After a moment, she smiles at me. "I'll be here first thing in the morning."

"Bring more underwear."

She laughs, turning to the door. "You've got it, princess."

When she exits, I make eye contact with the two soldiers who are now located in the hallway. They don't react to my dress or lack thereof, but there's something in the leer of the one on the right that I don't like. I shut the door and lock it.

At least the brigs in Alaha didn't disguise themselves as anything but what they were. I don't need my cell to be comfortable. I would actually prefer that it wasn't, but I suppose beggars can't be choosers.

I make quick work of hanging the garments in the armoire and moving the rest of the unmentionables and nightgowns to the chest of drawers. I test out the chair Beau vacated, throwing my legs over the side like she did. The ceiling is painted, I realize, clouds and bursts of sun rays mimicking the sky. It's a poor representation, but I can admire the artwork, even if it is a little lackluster.

My eyes begin to droop. I look to the bed. So very far away, too far away to get up when this chair is better than anywhere I've slept in so long. It'll do just fine.

I dream of rabbits. Lots and lots of rabbits at my feet. They stand on their hind legs to reach for the food in my hands. I hand them carrots and green stalks of kale. The sound of their munches brings a smile to my face.

Then there are too many sights and sounds and smells. I'm standing in a dining hall. The voices of the mass of people reverberate off the golden ceiling, causing a cacophony of conversation. Tables line either side of the room with an amount of food I've never seen before covering their surfaces, platters upon platters of fresh fruit and vegetables and meats. People loiter around them, picking through the helpings, while others sit for their meal. They pass by without a notice in the world for the girl who's half naked and standing in the dead center of the gathering.

The thicket of crowd parts, and I spot Acker standing amidst a small gathering of parishioners. They're all

vying for his attention. The men, yes, but the women...
they're unmatched in their endeavors.

He makes a point to look at whoever is speaking, but
they're all in competition to hold his attention, so his
eyes never land on one person for much longer than
a sentence or two. He seems engaged, nodding and
smiling at the right times. Someone cracks a joke, and
he laughs, eyes crinkling at the corners.

But none of it is genuine. I know this to be true
because all of it falls away when he sees me. There's a
noticeable jerk of his frame, eyes gaining clarity as he
takes in my exposed skin, my towel doing the absolute
bare minimum to cover the salacious parts of me.

The girl closest to him notices he's distracted, and
she looks over her shoulder to follow his gaze. Her
hair falls over her shoulder, revealing her beauty. She
looks left and right, brow pinching in confusion before
turning back to Acker, touching his forearm to gain his
attention. He snaps out of his surprise and looks at her
with dark eyes made to draw people in. It provokes a
sting in my chest I don't like.

I can't dwell on it.

No. Now is the time to test the limits of this bond, to
see what I can do within its confines.

I keep my eyes on Acker as I pad across the marble
floor with my bare feet. He hurries to dismiss himself,
skirting around the beautiful girl. As I navigate through
the crowd, our gazes meet and disappear between the
bodies. He's within hearing distance within a handful of
strides.

"I'm angry with you," I tell him.

He stalks through the ebb and flow of people. "Are
you?" he says, casually dismissing someone with a hand

on the shoulder when they try to stop him.

Sliding a hand along a table, I pick up a fork. "I am."

His eyes flit around, making sure no one sees the fork levitating as I stab a piece of melon. I bring it to my mouth, but it's snatched out of my grasp by Acker as he calls the metal with his gift.

"Tell me," he says, placing the speared fruit down on another table.

"It's a long list."

He's closing in, and it reminds me of all those weeks ago when we were at the Market, how he hunted me down and changed my life forever.

He picks up a goblet and drinks, using it as a prop to dissuade other people from approaching him, avoiding eye contact. "Start at the top."

"First," I say, sidestepping his attempt to grab me, "you marched me through your city like a prized horse."

"Better than being brought to the stable to be put down like a lame horse."

I stop as I reach the wall of stained-glass windows. The lanterns cast a glare on their colors, making it impossible to see out. My reflection shines back at me, including Acker's over my shoulder.

"You're doing a terrible job of apologizing."

He grins, placing a hand on the sill next to me. To anyone else, he's a man contemplating his drink. To me, he looks like one of the gods come down to seduce me. Flames flicker in the lamp above, casting lights and shadows that dance across his features, the shadow of his lashes fanning the top of his cheeks.

"I'm waiting until I've heard the whole list," he says, eyes trailing down my chest, then to the slit where my towel gaps at the top of my thighs. "What are the rest of my transgressions?"

"You stranded me before your father." I focus on keeping my breathing deep and even, not wanting to let on how much he affects me. "So I guess it's comparable to putting a horse out for slaughter."

This sobers him real quick, features hardening at my accusation. "Is that what you think?"

"Don't belittle me, Acker."

He swirls the dark liquid in the cup in his hand, jaw tense. "I understand you're unfamiliar with the ways of my people and I don't hold that against you, but everyone must stand before the king upon their arrival. It's customary."

"Oh, it was wonderful," I say, sarcasm heavy on my tongue. "Meeting my match's father, alone, covered in tomato before all of the royal court where I was laughed at for being juvenile in my gift."

He rises to his full height, drinking the remainder of the contents of his glass before setting it on the ledge beside me. "You're right. That wasn't fair."

I lift a shocked eyebrow at his admission.

"Nothing about our lives is fair, Jovie," he says, dark eyes holding mine.

The frank honesty in his voice catches me off guard. "I guess I just expected…" I don't finish the thought, too ashamed by the rest of the sentence to voice it.

But he catches it anyway, a smile softening the blow to my ego. "There's not a person in this court or on this earth you're not capable of standing before." He slides his hand along the ledge until he reaches my shoulder, drawing the back of his fingers over the skin without being conspicuous. "How's your hand?"

I lift my palm up for him to see the wound scabbing

over. He runs a thumb around the pink flesh, then he brings it to his mouth where he licks along the tender area with the flat of his tongue. It sends a bolt of lightning straight down my stomach and to my core. I dare a glance around us, making sure no one sees their prince doing filthy things with his mouth, but no one seems to notice with Acker's back to the masses.

He doesn't let go of my hand, trapping it between our bodies as he leans in close, placing his lips next to my ear. "I am a starving man, Jovie. Don't appear without clothes again."

"Or what?" I say, not recognizing the timbre of my voice.

Lips tracing the outer shell of my ear, he tilts his pelvis toward mine, revealing the truth of his arousal. "Or I'll make you finally confront the desire you've been so determined to pretend doesn't exist between us."

I suck in a deep breath, hating the way his words only add fuel to the fire wanting to rage inside me.

He pulls far enough back for me to see the same heat mirrored in his gaze. "Better wake up." Then he swipes the goblet from the window ledge and turns to speak with the man approaching, a pleasant facade back in place. It's as if the last few moments didn't happen.

I'm grateful for the out, taking swift steps out the massive hall's doors. I don't know where I'm going. The palace is huge, but I don't slow as I find the nearest stairs and take them two at a time. Their dark trim and handrails are nothing like the gold I remember leading to my room.

I've just reached the landing when I see a rabbit on the top step. It hops down one, nose turned up as it sniffs the air before continuing down. I keep moving, taking the first path I see, and stop dead in my tracks when I spot another rabbit. Except there are more. Three, to be exact.

How odd.

Stepping over the animals, I look up and see twice as many. They're multiplying. One hops to me, and I bend to pick it up, cradling the soft animal to my chest and scratching behind its ears. Then it exposes its mouth, revealing long and ghastly fangs, and I drop it.

I blink and I'm somewhere else entirely, a greenhouse covered in snow.

"Jovie," a voice calls.

I spin toward it and awake from my dream with a start, clutching at a rabbit I'm no longer holding. The room is dark, the oil in the lanterns burned out. And I'm alone.

I find the nightgown I had earlier and slide it on. The bed looks much more enticing now, and I slip between the sheets with a heavy sigh. I'm so tired that when the door opens, I don't even move. If someone is here with ill intent, I'll accept my death as a mercy. Or maybe I'm not afraid because I already know who he is by the outline of his figure. The tether responds with a dull ache.

Unlacing his boots, he kicks them off on his way to the bed. My eyes have adjusted enough that I'm able to admire the cut of his body as he strips off his shirt then his pants before climbing into the bed with me in only his underwear.

I somehow find enough energy to use my voice. "This isn't appropriate," I remind him.

He reaches for me under the cover, filling my nose with his scent as he pulls me toward him. "I told you once we reached the palace, I'd sleep where you sleep."

"I don't think that's how that was said."

He moans into the soft bedding, adjusting the blankets over the both of us. "I'm not going to let gossipers stop me from helping my match get better rest." He threads his legs through mine and rests his palm on my hip. "I would have been here sooner, but I was hoping to corner my father at dinner regarding the annulling of my betrothal."

I know I should feel bad for sharing a bed with an engaged man, but I can't find it in me. I'm pretty sure I never want to leave this bed. Ever.

"And?"

His sigh is answer enough. "He never showed. I asked his courtier of his whereabouts, but he wasn't forthcoming."

Hmm.

I place my hand over the hard plane on his chest. He stills at the touch. It's the first time I've initiated contact of my own accord. There's no hidden agenda or contention underlining my gesture, just a simple desire to feel him. I slide my palm up his chest, running my fingers along the dip of muscle where it meets his shoulder. Slowly, the tension in his body fades as I explore parts of him I've only ever been able to appreciate from afar.

He follows my lead, using my unspoken invitation to do his own exploring, hand at my hip gliding over the curve of my waist until he reaches the end of my nightgown. Easing his hand underneath the fabric, he takes a breath at the feel of my bare skin under his palm. There's a slow, agonizing pulse of desire coursing through my body.

"I wasn't going to put you in a carriage like a disgraced secret," he says, feeling along the small of my back.

It's difficult to concentrate on his words when his fingers are alternating between featherlight touches and deep pressurized points along the trail of my spine.

"My father may hold most of the power, but I have favor with the people. I wanted them to see that I am in favor of *you* and not ashamed to call you my match."

It feels like my heart is at the base of my throat as I absorb his words. I keep my eyes trained on my hand, avoiding the intensity of his gaze as I drag my fingers along his throat, across the bridge of his Adam's apple.

I can't disguise the hurt in my voice. "They don't even know that, and they seemed less than pleased by me riding with you," I whisper.

"There's not as much opposition to your return as it looks," he says, voice vibrating underneath the tips of my fingers. "It's a fraction compared to those who welcome your return. Give them time. The fearful will come around."

He's asking for grace for his people.

I drag my hand down the seam of his chest until I feel the steady beat of his heart under my hand. "Okay."

He snakes a hand under my pillow, sinking his fingers through the hair at my nape, tugging to angle my head toward his awaiting mouth. "And I'd like to parade my prized horse around a few more times."

I pinch the skin at his side, but all he does is smile as he tilts his head in for a kiss. There's no hesitation on my end as I meet him fully, using the sleep clouding my judgment as an excuse to indulge.

At least that's what I tell myself.

# CHAPTER 46

Beau strides into my room right as Acker finishes pulling on his shirt from the night before. "Ah, so this is what the maidservants were chattering about this morning," she remarks, smile downright mischievous.

"He was just leaving," I say, cringing at the panic in my voice.

Acker's cloying eyes cut to me still lounging in the bed. Even after the night of kissing followed by the deepest I think I've slept in my entire life, my cheeks burn. It only serves to make his smile grow.

"Yuck." She sticks out her tongue while making a nauseating gagging sound. "Get a room."

Acker is far less amused by his sister's antics. "You're standing in it."

Falling into one of the chairs, she lifts a brow. "Better?"

"You wouldn't happen to know the whereabouts of our father, would you?" he asks, taking the chair opposite her to put his shoes on.

"Not a clue," she says. "Haven't seen him since we got back. Thank the gods." The last line is uttered under her breath.

Acker doesn't like her answer, but he fixes a careful smile on his face. "Be good to Jovie today, yeah?"

Beau smiles. "I shall take her under my wing."

Although she means it to be a teasingly mild threat, I

can see the gratitude in Acker's eyes as he dips a nod to her. He stands and walks to the bed, leaning over with his hands braced on either side of my legs.

"Take today to rest. Explore the palace. Eat," he says, smiling at the low growl emanating from my belly. "Tomorrow morning, I'm taking you down to start training." He leans close, placing soft lips on mine. "I'm eager to see you with a sword in your hand."

I internally groan at the thought but let him kiss me anyway.

"Is that an innuendo?" Beau asks, face scrunched in disgust.

Laughing, I push Acker away with a hand against his chest. "Don't ask questions you won't like the answer to, Beau."

Beau gags again, maybe for real this time, and Acker laughs as he walks to the door. Her eyes don't leave him until the door clicks shut behind him, and I'm surprised by the worry in her expression when she looks at me.

She's quick to blink it away. "Are we staying in bed all day?"

As much as I love the prospect, my stomach is all but screaming at me to feed it. Beau waits while I use the bathroom and get dressed. The soft pants and matching blue top fit me to perfection. I find I'm unable to stop myself from running my hands over the fabric. Compared to the rough, simple cuts of fabric from Alaha, it's going to take time to get used to.

"Boys." Beau greets the guards outside my door on our way out. "Take off the rest of the day."

My least favorite of the two glares at me before departing.

Beau watches their backs retreat down the hallway

before looking at me. "What was that about?"

"I'm not sure," I say, honestly. "But I don't like him."

"You should tell Acker."

"Why?"

"They're his men." She turns and leads us in the opposite direction of how I was escorted to my room last night. "Our father wanted to put a suppressor on you, but Acker convinced him to let two men in his ranks keep watch over you instead."

"A suppressor?"

She touches the base of her neck. "A collar to dull your magic. Anyone with gifts outside of the palace is required to wear one, but your lack of control worries the regents. They think you're too dangerous without the proper training."

We pass a maidservant exiting one of the doors lining the hallway. She freezes, bedding pulled in close to her chest and gaze stuck on me as we pass, like she's scared to move out of fear of me. I'm quick to avert my eyes.

"Don't do that," Beau chides. "Don't cower."

I know that, logically, but I just...hate the idea of making anyone uncomfortable.

Beau stops, sharp eyes pinning me in place. "Their apprehension toward you isn't your doing and it's not your problem. Got it?"

I'm momentarily stunned by the sharpness of her beauty, smiling at the contradiction of her admonishment. "You're paying awfully close attention to my aura."

She rolls her eyes, but I spot the grin as we resume our pace. "It's extra loud today."

I don't need to clarify what she means, because I can practically feel the contentment radiating from me, knowing the cause for my bliss is due to who slept in my bed last night.

Beau takes me down to the kitchen, bypassing the breakfast being served in the dining hall.

"Full of braggers and tattletales," she says.

There's a noticeable unease in the kitchen staff, but they loosen up in Beau's presence. It's obvious they're well acquainted with her, and she inquires about the growing baby bump of one of the sculleries, which further alleviates the worry in the air. We're served full plates of eggs and sausage and these cakes with a sugar dressing that they call pancakes. A moan escapes my mouth, and they all titter at my reddening cheeks.

"This is the best thing I've ever eaten," I tell them.

Henry, the cook, slaps a rag against the butcher block counter before moving on to his next task. "You've yet to be truly amazed, princess. Just you wait."

I'm only able to finish a quarter of the portions served to me, but they don't seem to find it rude as they clear my dishes. Next Beau gives me a tour. We start in the state room, the place where the king greeted us upon our arrival. It branches off from there into four quadrants like a rounded-out square with a massive courtyard in the middle. My room, as I learn, is on the west end.

As we continue to traverse the corridors, I begin to discover that the majority of the palace is unoccupied. Rooms sit fully furnished but empty. It's nauseating in comparison to the condensed population of Alaha where it's one room stacked on top of another like fish in a can.

Beau explains how the king keeps his closest advisors at court year round, but lords and parishioners of Kenta only stay for periods at a time when needed. Most came when the king sent word of my pending arrival, so the palace is fuller than it's been in decades. We find the majority of the current tenants are congregated along the inner corridor.

Heads turn and watch as we walk past the onlookers. We could pass as vagrants in comparison. Dressed in opulent dresses and silks, the women and men look like they're dressed for a party, not to stroll along the promenade. Even so, I maintain my gait, keep my gaze forward, and remind myself of Beau's words.

The passageway gives a perfect view to spectate the soldiers training in the courtyard below. The clang of metal and grunts of men echo up the open palace walls. Set up in different stations, soldiers perform conditioning and strengthening exercises very similar to the ones we do in Alaha.

I scan the men, stopping when I spot Acker standing amongst the fray watching a sparring match in the center of the courtyard. He leans toward Hallis, commenting on the match, arms folded across the expanse of his chest. His skin is flushed, skin glistening with sweat in the midday sun. I swallow the excess moisture in my mouth.

As if he senses me nearby, his eyes rise in my direction, a smile tugging at the corner of his lips when he sees me watching from the veranda. Hallis notices Acker's diverted attention, eyes following to our location, and he also smirks when he spots us.

Beau huffs a breath of annoyance. "Men are insufferable creatures," she says, giving them her back. "Is there anything else you're interested in seeing?"

"The library."

It's a long walk to the uppermost level. The doors stand open as if inviting wanderers and scholars alike to step inside. The smell hits me first, assaulting me with ink and paper and worn leather. Books and scrolls line the shelves of the curved walls, drawing the eyes toward the spired ceiling above.

"Good gods," I whisper in awe.

A female voice draws my attention back to our level. "Don't forget about the bad ones too." Smirking over the gold rims of her glasses, the woman stands from behind the circular desk in the center of the space. "Everyone's always muttering about the good gods, but the bad ones are way more interesting."

Beau parks herself on the edge of the desk, metal rope clanging against its wooden top. "If you believe in fairy tales."

"I'm a librarian, darling. Of course I do."

They embrace, hugging for a beat before letting go. "Mother," Beau says. "Meet Jovie, the lost princess of Maile."

*Mother*...meaning Beau and Acker aren't full siblings.

"Jovie, please meet my mother, Greta."

Beau's mother walks to me, reaching for and clasping my hands in hers. "It is my utmost pleasure," she says, placing her forehead against the back of my hands.

It catches me off guard, and I look to Beau for guidance, but all she does is give a half shrug in response, not at all surprised by her mother's greeting.

"It's nice to meet you, too," I manage to say.

"My apologies," Greta says, releasing me and pushing the frames of her glasses up the bridge of her nose. "I can be a lot. That's why they sequester me in the library."

Beau's voice comes out sardonic. "That's not why."

"Hush," Greta spits out of the corner of her mouth.

My eyes catch on the necklace at the base of her throat, tortoiseshell and shiny in the light pouring in from the windows above. I realize it's made of mangi stone.

"What can I help you with?" she asks, eyes bright.

"Uh, I'm not sure, actually." My eyes go back to the book-lined walls. "I've only ever read about libraries, never seen one."

This horrifies Greta. Absolutely, profoundly horrifies her.

"Let me give you the grand tour," she says, grabbing my hand and pulling me behind her.

Beau smiles at her overzealous mother. "She's not big on personal boundaries."

"Not true," Greta insists, though Beau's face says otherwise.

Greta leads us up the staircase that lines the winding walls. Every few stacks there's a sitting space or desk designed into the shelves, like the reader is immersed in the library as they simultaneously bury themselves in the pages of books.

By the time we reach the top where a small seating area is, I'm slightly out of breath. The weeks of travel have done a number on my stamina, and I already know training is going to be a special form of hell in the morning.

"So," Greta says, waving her fingers about. "What will it be? Do you prefer mystery? Drama? Maybe a little romance?" She wiggles her eyebrows at the last suggestion, but none of the categories mentioned are what I'm hoping to find. I'm cautious, and Greta must sense my hesitancy, because she becomes more subdued. "I keep the erotica behind the counter."

Beau rolls her eyes at her mother, but it's all in fun. It's obvious she adores the woman, and now I can see where Beau gets her radiant personality.

Laughing, I shake my head. "Maybe another time. I'm looking for information regarding matching bonds."

Lifting a brow, Greta's gaze is curious but open. "I have that."

We descend the entire length of the tower. She yanks on a chain near the massive wooden doors at the entrance, sending a rumble of vibration through our feet as they swing closed, knocking some books from their shelves. She pays them no mind as she leads us to her desk, ushering us to its center.

"Here is where we keep the archives."

I'm about to ask where, only seeing half-bound books —and, indeed, erotica behind the desk judging by the illustrated spines—when she pulls a hidden lever under the counter and the floor slides away. I brace my feet, not wanting to slip into the darkness below.

Greta mumbles under her breath. "It's around here somewhere."

Then there's a tick of sound before light illuminates the staircase. Greta descends first, followed by myself and Beau. A fraction of the size of the main library, the room is a tiny replica of the one above it. Its confines somehow make it all the more daunting.

"This is where the archives are kept." Greta inspects the book spines until she finds the one she's looking for and hands it to me. "It is very old, so please be delicate with it."

"Of course," I tell her.

I run my fingers over the embossed leather. *Matching and Other Bonds*. It's heavy and twice the size of my primary school textbook in Alaha.

"Can I?" I ask, motioning to the desk.

"I would usually not mind, but I'm currently working on something myself. These are my studies here," she says, waving a hand over the open texts. "Anything you would like is yours to borrow as long as you promise not to tell anyone. Many of these books are forbidden." She winks at me conspiratorially. "Which is my favorite kind."

I thank her and ask if she has anything on the history of light wielders. She doesn't ask questions, just simply finds the text on a nearby shelf and hands it to me. I settle on the two books for now. "It should keep me busy for a while."

Finding an alcove with a desk in the main library, Beau retrieves a mystery to keep her busy as I dive into the weighty book on bonds. I spend the majority of the day scouring for any information I can find about matching bonds, but there's not much.

Greta sends up lunch sometime midday. A few stragglers come into the library, but none stay long after discovering my presence. It's almost as if I was gifted with repulsion *and* light wielding. I'm nearly convinced of it, except the text details that each Heir receives only one gift.

It also states they receive a single bond each, if they're lucky enough to get one. Or unlucky, depending on which text I'm reading. It's a collection of discoveries and observations over time, written by unknown authors. Some recount stories of matches who were connected at the hip, each not existing without the other nearby, but others speak of the devastation of matches who despised one another and the hardships they inflicted upon those close to them. There's a list of matches from before the war, all of them dead.

Sighing, I look up, and golden hair catches my attention on the first level of the library. It's the girl Acker was standing next to last night. She's somehow even more beautiful in the daylight. The crimson of her dress looks like blood pooling around her ankles. The collar of mangi stones shines as she shifts, her eyes meeting mine from below. She smiles, and I'm so taken aback by the kind gesture I have to remind myself to give the same in return.

I say Beau's name to get her attention.

"Hm?"

I motion with my chin. "Who's that?"

Beau looks over the railing then back at me, a strange sort of look in her eyes. "That's Irina."

I already know I'm going to hate the answer, but I ask anyway. "Who's Irina?"

"The princess of Strou."

My heartbeat fills my ears, and I can feel the reddening of my cheeks as I fight to remain unaffected, but my blood is boiling in my veins. There's no hiding it from Beau. Not with her abilities.

"He didn't tell you she was here?"

I shake my head.

She cusses then rolls her eyes. "He's an idiot."

I wait until Irina leaves before telling Beau I want to return to my room. Shock and adrenaline begin to morph into unfiltered anger. I want to pick up the old text and throw it off the stairs, but I keep my wits about me and shut it with a calm I don't feel. I manage to thank Greta once again, promising to return the book in a few days.

*After I murder Acker with it.*

The walk back to my room is silent. I'm sure I scare even more of the staff in my fuming state of dazed marching, each step more punctuated than the last. I barge into my room, coming up short at my made bed. The clothes I left dirty on the floor have been cleared away. Undoubtedly the maidservants' doing, waiting until I left to clean, but it's the parcel sitting in the center of my bed that stops me in my tracks.

I look to Beau for an explanation, but she only grins. I pull apart the twine bow on the wrapped parcel to reveal a sketchbook and charcoal pencil, the same as the one Kai's family gifts me every year. I flip over the note tied to it, air sticking in my lungs at the words scrawled in small penmanship.

*Draw me something. -Acker*

I throw it down on the bed and march into the bathroom to take a bath. It's the only thing I can think of to calm me down at this point. I turn the spigot, and while I wait for the tub to fill, I focus on breathing through the stinging in my chest. My hands are glowing.

Beau leans against the doorway, legs crossed at the ankles. "Your heart isn't the only heart you'll break, you know?"

I shake my hands, and they dim a little. "Are you telling me you predict the future, too?"

She smiles. "My mother does."

# CHAPTER 47

By the time Acker walks into my room, it's well into the night and my rage has returned with a vengeance. He's dressed in plain black clothes, hair clean and pushed away from his face. The nose ring has made its return, and I hate the way my heart skips a beat at his appearance. It only serves to further fan the flames of my anger.

I finish the braid of my hair with a tie. "Beau said you wanted to take me somewhere."

He saunters toward me, eyes holding mine in the mirror of the vanity as he leans down to kiss me. I give him my cheek, and a flash of hurt stutters across his face before he's able to mask it.

"Everything okay?" he asks, eyes following me as I stand.

I tell myself to calm my racing heart, to not let my emotions get the best of me, but the burning sensation in my chest is damn near impossible to ignore. "No," I say, meeting his gaze head on.

Crossing his arms, he leans his back against the armoire. "Okay. Care to elaborate on what's changed since this morning?"

"Irina is here."

Understanding registers on his face a moment before he dips his head in a nod. "She is."

"That's all you have to say?"

"I should have told you, yes, but I didn't find out until dinner last night. She came while I was away."

"You were in my bed all night," I point out.

He cocks his head to the side. "You were already angry with me. Why would I add to the list by bringing up Irina?"

Lightning burns down my arm and into my hand, and I sling it at his head. He ducks in time to miss my surge of power, and it singes the wooden front of the wardrobe, smoke billowing from the impact. Shock turns to fury as Acker levels his gaze on me. Satisfaction fills my veins knowing he feels an inkling of the fury I've been fighting with all day. I let my power settle in my palm, readying another throw, hand igniting in a yellow glow.

"Jovie," he warns.

Ignoring him, I fling the hot ball of light at him again. It's a narrow miss, but it snaps Acker's control and he storms toward me, eyes hard and furious. He grabs me by the neck, and I rise onto my toes in a bid to stop him from cutting off my air supply. It's a reminder of how much stronger and deadlier he is than I am.

"Use your magic on me again and I'll take it as an invitation to do the same."

My hold around his wrist scorches from the magic still burning through me. "You can't kill me. You swore a blood oath."

His smile is dry as he walks me backward to the edge of the bed. The gold filigree adorning the foot of the frame detaches and wraps around my ankles, causing me to fall onto my butt on the bed. With ease, he removes the grip I have on his arm and holds mine to the duvet, tying my wrists to my knees with the winding vine of filigree.

My chest rises and falls on tight breaths. Bracing closed fists on either side of my thighs, he leans back just enough to examine his work, eyes scoring down my restrained body. My neck and cheeks burn with humiliation. Well, that and other things I refuse to give credence to.

His eyes linger on the tinted skin, lashes flicking up as he meets my gaze directly. There's no mistaking the heat in his eyes. "Let's get something straight," he says, jaw ticking as his attention falls to my mouth for a brief second. "I will not hurt you." He darts a look over my bound body. "Ever. Not because of a blood oath I made out of necessity, but because I don't want to."

The last few words send my heart into the base of my throat. "Untie me," I demand, voice coming out weaker than I'd like.

"No." He leans in closer, eyes flitting to my mouth again, breaths converging in the space between. "Not until you're reasonable," he says.

I try to pull away, but he stops me with a hand on the crux of my neck. It tilts my head in the perfect angle for him to access my mouth.

My lips brush his when I speak. "And who determines that? You?"

"I don't see anyone else in the room." Teasing a kiss, he places his open mouth against mine, tongue wet against my bottom lip.

I squeeze my eyes shut, hoping the lack of senses will dull the desire muddling my brain, but it doesn't work. If anything, it narrows my focus to the heat of his mouth, the taste of his tongue as I meet it with my own, the groan that vibrates into me when he dips it inside.

While the kissing from last night was nice and lace with heat, all of those combined pale in comparison to the desire of this one. I realize he was holding back as he devours my mouth with his own.

I take the opening, sinking my teeth down and nipping the tip of his tongue before he can fully retreat. He jerks back. Touching a finger to his tongue, he inspects the blood on the pad of his finger, eyes snapping to me.

"Oh, did I hurt you?" Condescension drips from my voice, my tone dry as I smile. "You should just get over it so we don't ruin the night."

He stares at me for a long beat then turns away, shaking his head. A humorless laugh escapes him as he stares at the ground, contemplating, maybe actually acknowledging his hypocrisy.

He waves a hand toward my bound wrists and ankles. "I should have learned my lesson the first time." The filigree unwinds itself like a snake, slithering across the wooden frame and nestling back into place. "Listen," he says, face serious when he looks up. "A friend is supposed to meet us in the city."

I'm seething, but...his sudden shift in demeanor has me wavering. Frustration still lingers behind his eyes, but whatever plans he's made are important, crucial enough to table the conversation. Moreover, I can't turn down the chance to venture into the city.

I slide from the edge of the bed and retrieve the cloak Beau brought me from the wardrobe. "You owe me," I warn, throwing the garment over my shoulders.

I attempt to move around him and toward the door, but he steps into my path, stopping and forcing me to look at him.

"For what it's worth, I apologize for not telling you as soon as I found out." His throat bobs as he swallows, guard seemingly falling.

Then I'm staring at the Acker I've grown to care for after all our time together, the one I've spent countless hours doing nothing yet everything with before I knew he was my match or knew our futures would forever be intertwined. The man I call my friend stands before me.

His movements are careful, slow as he reaches behind me to pull the hood over my hair, tucking my braid behind my shoulder. "I didn't think it was a big deal."

"How could you not?"

A smile quirks at the corner of his mouth like he finds me cute. "I didn't think you'd care," he says, running a curved finger along my jaw. "But jealousy looks good on you."

I know my colored skin gives away more than I'd like, but there's no avoiding it. "We don't want to keep your friend waiting."

His smile comes out in full force as he moves away and to the door. He opens it, eyes locked on me as I walk toward him, and he leans in to whisper in my ear. "We'll finish this conversation later."

My face reddens at the heated insinuation, fighting the smile wanting to pull at the corners of my mouth. But all of those thoughts come to a screaming halt at the pointed gaze I feel coming from the soldier stationed to the right of my door.

Acker acknowledges them with a nod, and he hides his wandering eyes from his prince's view. As we begin our departure down the hall, I try to convince myself to ignore it, but Beau's insistence that I tell Acker niggles in the back of my mind.

"I don't like the way the one on the right looks at me," I say, voice low.

Acker slows, eyes becoming sharp despite the smile on his face. "Yeah?" He doesn't wait for a response as he pivots in place. He looks at the soldier in question. "You're dismissed."

A moment of shock makes the soldier's jaw drop, but it doesn't take long for righteous indignation to redden his features. His fellow comrade keeps his eyes averted, not wanting to be caught in the crossfire.

We're turning to resume our walk when the muttered insult hits our ears. "*Fucking brat.*"

Acker goes stock-still, and I know there's nothing I can do to stop whatever is about to happen.

Stalking back toward the soldier, Acker says, "Repeat that."

The man struggles to control his bluster, face losing all its color as Acker nears. He shakes his head. "I-I'm sor —"

Before he can finish his apology, Acker lifts a hand and catches a projectile from the soldier's mouth. The soldier howls, hands going to the offending orifice on his face, sticking his fingers inside. Acker drops the tooth to the polished floor, iron capped and bloody.

"Turn in your uniform and weapons to the infirmary first thing in the morning." Then Acker looks at the remaining soldier and says, "Find a replacement of your choosing before we get back. I suggest you choose wisely."

The soldier nods with terrified enthusiasm, vacating his position and hurrying down the hall.

I lift a brow at Acker but don't speak. The palace is quiet. The few people we pass are maidservants. They react differently with Acker at my side, less afraid, more open. I think one girl even smiles at me.

A carriage awaits beyond the steps of the front entrance. It's nondescript and black, as are the horses. The coachman greets us with a nod, holding a hand out to help me into the vehicle, but Acker waves him away, ushering me in instead.

"To the blacksmith, Harold," he says. "Thank you."

The man gives him a small bow. "My pleasure, your highness."

The inside of the carriage is sleek, wood polished to a shine, seat velvety smooth. There's just enough room for Acker to fold his height into the opposite seat, bracketing my legs with his own.

"Brace yourself, princess," the coachman yells as he urges the horses forward and we start with a jerk.

I take hold of a handle carved into the side of the door. "They're much nicer when you're around," I say.

Acker scoffs, leaning against the bench in an effort to get comfortable. "Have you already forgotten the incident in the hallway?"

"Other than him," I clarify. "His problem was he was a little too brave."

"I had a lieutenant tell me being brave and being stupid are the same." He tilts his head in thought. "But that's another reason I want you to come to training in the morning."

"To see us together?"

"No," he says, body swaying with the jumpy movements of the carriage. "To remind them of who you are: the lost princess of Maile. Being a light wielder doesn't change that."

"Why would your people care about who I am?"

"Our betrothal was considered the last and final step of putting the war to rest between our territories." He continues to shuffle to get comfortable in the small space. "We were celebrated as a promise of peace."

"But that all ended with my abduction," I say.

He nods. "Your mother became increasingly hostile, to the point she began accusing the conclave of conspiring together to abduct you. Said my father was keeping you locked in the dungeons." He smiles to himself. It's obvious there's a fondness for my mother in his words, a sort of wonder in his eyes after all this time. "Almost had me convinced too. I went and checked to see for myself."

"The conclave?"

"The leaders of the five territories. They meet once a year in a bid to uphold an accord across the land. Well, everyone but Chryse and your mother. She closed the border to Maile after killing Osiris, and no one has seen her since." He holds my stare, eyes dark and seductive in the darkness of the carriage. "Your return is a reminder of a time of peace and prosperity, Jovie, and my people need it."

# CHAPTER 48

Rust and metal fill my nose as soon as we step out of the carriage. It appears we're in the middle of the city, the cobblestone shining in the low light of the lamp posts lining the street. Although it's late and there's not a person in sight, Acker keeps close as he escorts me to the stoop of a brick building, slamming the iron knocker against the wooden door. A sign hanging from the eave reads *BLACKSMITH*.

The door opens, revealing a man with dark hair and light eyes. His dark skin makes his features all the more prominent. The collar around his neck glows in the dull light.

He smiles with all his teeth. "All hail the prince," he says, bowing his head to Acker.

Acker shoves him in the shoulder. "Fuck off, you bastard, and let us in."

The man laughs and swings the door wide, pulling Acker into an embrace. "The food is fresh out of the oven," he says, eyes curious and on me.

"Wells," Acker says, taking me by the hand. "This is Jovie. Jovie, Wells."

Wells dips his head in greeting. "It's a pleasure to meet you." He pats Acker on the back. "Olivia is excited to see you. The both of you," he clarifies.

Acker leads me through the door and into an open workshop. A giant brick fireplace is in the center of the courtyard, and soot covers the dirt ground and tables and weapons in varying stages of composition. Across the yard, we come to a second entrance, and Acker instructs me to remove my shoes. I follow Wells' lead and place my shoes next to his by the door.

"My wife would skin my hide if I tracked muck on her floor."

It's strange to enter another person's home in bare feet. It feels intimate, but I get what he means. The stone floor of the small entryway is dull but cleaned to perfection. I slide my hood back and take in the stairway and brass chandelier. The smells of food and spices fill the air.

"They're here," Wells yells upon entry, shutting the door behind us.

Acker keeps his hand locked in mine, guiding me forward with a tug. We round the corner and emerge into a dining area. A table fills the space with a total of twelve place settings, and a window against the far wall gives a view of the kitchen and the small, blonde woman behind it.

She erupts into a squeal when she sees us, shaking the mittens from her hands and disappearing, only to reappear on the other side of the kitchen entryway. "I wasn't sure what she likes, so I made a little of everything."

Acker is forced to let go of me to hug her. "As long as it's not fish."

I shoot him a scathing glare before pasting on a smile when Olivia looks at me. "I'm sure I'll love whatever it is."

"No worries," she says, hands balled into tight fists. "There are no hurt feelings in this house."

I can tell she's struggling to hold herself back from bombarding me, but I kind of want to put her out of her misery, so I make the decision to initiate a hug. She's several inches shorter than me and I have to hunch for her to reach, but she's practically vibrating when I put my arms around her narrow shoulders.

"I'm so happy to see you," she says, squeezing me.

I glance at Acker over her shoulder, and he's all but laughing at my discomfort.

Wells rescues me by pulling her away with an arm around her waist. "Liv, babe, do you need help in the kitchen?"

"Oh, that'd be great."

Wells shares a knowing glance with Acker then winks at me as he follows his wife into the other room. Their hushed voices carry through the open window.

"...not to overwhelm her."

"*She* hugged *me*."

Acker smiles, pulling out a chair for me at the end of the table. "She'll grow on you," he whispers in my ears when I sit.

Only visible from the shoulders up, she flits around the kitchen as she gets everything ready, instructing her husband on which dishes need to be served first.

"I like her," I say, meeting Acker's stare as he takes the seat next to me. "She's nice." Which is more than I can say for the majority of the people I've come across since being on land.

"Okay," Wells says, placing dishes on serving plates in the middle of the table. "We have roasted duck and cabbage, garlic potatoes, and green beans."

Olivia holds up two bottles of wine. "And your choice of red or white."

Acker stands and takes the bottles from her hands. "You always spoil me, Liv. Thank you."

He pours himself a helping of the red then fills my glass as well. I pick it up and take a drink, realizing too late that it's terrible and there's no way I'm going to be able to swallow it. I look around at their expectant faces and deposit the liquid back into the glass. They all laugh at my expense.

"That's terrible," I say, wiping the liquid from my chin. "Maybe worse than mead."

"Nah," Wells says, sitting across from Acker. "You're just used to mead. Same goes for wine. It's an acquired taste."

Olivia retrieves another glass and pours an extra helping of the white. "I prefer my drinks a little cleaner," she says, handing me the spare glass. "Try this."

I hum my agreement after I take a sip, a very conservative one. "Still not great, but better," I agree.

Olivia smiles at my honesty. "I'm not much of a drinker myself."

"That's because you can't handle more than a glass before you start taking your clothes off," Wells says.

She smacks him with the back of her hand and waves a hand over the table. "Let's eat."

My mouth waters at the steaming food as I wait to dish out my servings. Acker cuts and places a portion of duck on my plate, and I can't deny that it chips away at the lingering frustration I'm struggling to hold on to toward him.

We're all consumed by digging into our meal, the sound of silverware meeting the porcelain plates filling the space.

"Everything is delicious," I say, holding my fork laden

with beans. "Do they grow this green?"

She smiles at my question. "Usually. Why?"

I shove them in my mouth, savoring the flavor with a shake of my head. "Fresh fruit and vegetables are hard to come by in Alaha," I explain. "They're often dehydrated for preservation."

There's an awkward moment where Olivia and Wells send looks at Acker, but it's quickly forgotten as the conversation moves on to other topics, like the commissions Wells has been working on and Olivia's herb garden. They ask about Acker's travels before he had set off to find me after the Market. I never thought to inquire, but his answer is short.

"I spent the spring in Strou."

It's enough to settle their curiosity, and they move to a more interesting subject: the uncommonly high level of summer storms they've been experiencing. I watch the way they interact, the ease they have with each other, and it makes me miss the comfort of my friends. Kai, or hell, Messer as a freaking bird would be pleasant enough.

I wait for a lull in the conversation to speak. "How do you all know each other?"

Acker and Wells share a subdued look, but it's Acker who answers. "Wells was one of the five I left training with."

Understanding dawns as I look back at Wells.

He seems mildly surprised by Acker's candid answer but does a good job of covering it with a pleasant grin. "I saved his life."

"Bullshit," Acker snarks. "I saved your life."

They go back and forth over their differing opinions, and Olivia shoots me a look that sums up their bickering: *Men.* It's not until after dinner when all the plates have been cleared that the focus of conversation shifts in my direction.

"So, Jovie," Wells says, throwing an arm over the back of his wife's chair. "How've things been since you arrived at the palace?"

I thumb the stem of the wine glass. "Well," I say, glancing at Acker as he leans with an ankle relaxed over a knee. "It's...*different*, as many things are on land."

"I imagine it's a bit of a culture shock," Olivia says, leaning against Wells' side.

I tilt my head. "If we're putting it politely."

"The 'welcome' home didn't help," Acker says.

Wells waves a dismissive hand. "Your father has hunted down every last one of the inciters. They're hanging on the wall as we speak, so I doubt you'll have any more issues with naysayers."

Acker shifts in his seat, eyes sliding to me.

"What is it?" Wells asks, sensing the tension.

"I didn't want to say anything until I spoke to my father, but his whereabouts are unknown at the moment." Leaning forward, Acker deposits his glass on the table then turns his head to look at me. There's something unspoken in the gaze before he looks back at them. "Jovie and I are matched."

Olivia's gasp drowns out Wells' curse, but they're both out of their chairs in the next second. Tears are welling in Olivia's eyes, and Wells looks...

Wells looks terrified. Elated, but terrified.

Olivia storms around the table and throws herself around Acker's shoulders, tears escaping down her face. "I told you."

Acker rubs small, reassuring circles on her back. "I

know you did," he says, voice tight. "You were right all along."

"Right about what?" I asks.

She pulls out of Acker's arms and dabs at her eyes. "About you being his match."

"She told me when we were children," Acker says.

I stumble over my words. "I—wait, you knew me when we were children?"

"I did, yes," she says, mellowing some. "My family used to be nobility, so we spent many summers together when your family came to visit."

"That explains your request for an impromptu dinner date," Wells says, finally coming to after the shock of it all. He slides back into his chair, eyes jumping between me and Acker.

"I didn't want to risk the news getting out before I'm able to call off my betrothal to Irina, but it's only a matter of time before she hears about my nights spent in Jovie's bed."

I stare at Acker in irritation, already knowing there's no stopping the heat from coloring my complexion.

Olivia tries and fails to hide her grin. "It's the one and only thing I don't miss about court."

"You said your family used to be nobility?"

Her eyes slide to her husband's. Wells holds out a hand to her, and she walks into his embrace, sitting on his thigh.

"Wells is from a merchant family, so our marriage was frowned upon."

Wells glances at Acker, and there's a noticeable unease in the look. Acker releases the tension in his jaw and gives me his undivided attention, dark eyes all the more mesmerizing in the soft light of candles flickering from above.

"Wells' lack of inheritance could have been overlooked if Olivia had awakened. Breeding between Heirs and commoners is considered blasphemous to most within the royal court."

I shake my head. "That's absurd."

"It is," Acker agrees. "I've been working with my father's council to advocate for more acceptance of marriages between the gifted and giftless."

"How's that been working out for you?" Olivia asks, tone dry.

Acker's silence is answer enough.

"Anyway, here we are, happy and married regardless of those bigots," Wells says, kissing Olivia's cheek with a flourish. "Mother Nature knew what she was doing when she matched us."

I start. "You're matched?"

Olivia beams as if she's revealing it for the very first time. "We are."

Looking toward Acker, I debate revealing the book I hid under my mattress but decide against it. "I thought bonds only happened between Heirs."

"It's what is taught," Wells says. "And it's why Liv and I keep our bond under wraps. No one knows about it besides Acker and Hallis—and, I suppose, now you."

The implication is clear: I need to keep this secret as well.

"I was hoping you could share your insight," Acker says. "There's a lot we don't know about matching bonds."

Olivia and Wells share a look, and it's a full conversation without words, I'm convinced of it. There's a knowing, teasing glint in their eyes that makes me feel like I'm invading their privacy by witnessing it. I look at Acker, thinking he's as uncomfortable as I am, but he's staring at me, unaware of the conversation we're not privy to.

"Well," Olivia says, moving to her own seat once again. "What stage of the bond are you in?"

Acker and I are equally stumped by the question.

"You've at least reached a point in the match where you've both become aware of it, yes?"

I nod.

"Yes," Acker voices.

"Okay, so there's always going to be one who accepts the bond before the other."

Neither one of us needs to speak because the answer is written in the space between the two of us. Physically and emotionally, there's a clear disconnect. Olivia and Wells have both seen it since our arrival, but it's even more pronounced with Acker's blithe announcement.

"In our case," Olivia says, placing a gentle hand on her husband's thigh. "Wells refused to acknowledge the bond for months and months. It was truly the epitome of stubbornness."

"I was a stupid, adolescent boy, Liv. You're going to have to forgive me sometime in our lifetime," he says.

"In his defense," Acker says, "you were pretty terrifying."

Olivia is outraged by the accusation, eyes swinging to me. "Does anything about me scream scary to you?"

I smile, because while the answer is no…it is also yes. But I'm obviously going to take her side. "Not in the slightest."

Olivia looks at them as if to say, *See.*

"Not everyone was born with your assuredness, Liv,"

Acker says. "You've got to cut teenage Wells some slack. I once watched him forget how to tie his shoes."

Wells points at Acker. "I was hungover and you know it."

Acker raises his hands in defense. "I'm just saying, I've never had that problem."

"Anyway," Olivia says, getting everyone back on track. "With a one-sided acceptance, the bond will force you together."

"Like the dreams," I say.

"Oh, so you're at the beginning," Wells says.

"The beginning?" Acker asks.

"Dreams are only the start," he says. "It's as if the bond refuses to take no for an answer. The dreams will eventually trap you inside of them to keep you together, if they haven't tried to already."

I shake my head. A new sensation begins taking root in my chest—fear, I realize.

"They will if you're not careful. It's impossible to wake you, and it leaves your body vulnerable. Then it was on day three without sleep when my mind left me while I was totally conscious."

"Hit the ground like a sack of potatoes in the middle of training," Acker says.

Wells smirks, but it's filled with warning. "I couldn't find my way back for an entire day."

"Will the same happen with the mind jumps?" I ask.

Wells' eyebrows pull together in confusion. "Mind jumps?"

"She means melding, kind of like an oracle," Acker clarifies. "She can see from my perspective, and sometimes I can see hers."

"I don't think that's a matching bond thing," Wells

says.

Olivia lifts a shoulder. "Hard to say. We've only met one other match before, and their experience was similar in a lot of ways, but also different. I think the fact that Wells and I were teenagers played a huge part in it."

"No impulse control," Wells says, making a face.

Olivia smiles. "Also, we had limited contact with each other due to living apart and my parents disapproving of our friendship."

"You never told them?"

Her smile turns sad. "They disowned me when they realized I wasn't going to awaken."

Wells rubs a hand along the length of her back as support, but he doesn't offer any platitudes.

"I'm sorry," I say, feeling inadequate.

"It's not your fault," she says. "Plus, Acker's made their stay at the palace as minimally palatable as possible."

Acker reaches for his wine and takes a drink. "I'll be happier when my father strips them of their titles."

"Hate to break it to you, but I don't think it'll happen until you're the one sitting on the throne," Wells says.

I lift my brows at the implication, looking at Acker to gauge his reaction, but he maintains a mask of passiveness at the prospect.

Olivia breaks the moment of disquiet by announcing dessert and returns from the kitchen with a chocolate cake. Wells cuts and serves the slices, declaring it a celebration cake for the happy couple—me and Acker. It's said in jest, but the lack of enthusiasm on my part can't be missed.

Still, the cake is delicious, and the conversation shifts

to easier topics, like what it's like living on the water and what training is like for the guard. They listen and ask questions when I run out of words.

"Thank you for accepting me into your home," I say when Acker announces our departure. "The meal, the company, everything was amazing."

"We've loved having you," Olivia says, pulling me into another hug. "You're welcome any time." She holds me at arm's length and looks me in the eyes when she repeats the sentiment. "Any time."

I dip my head in a nod. "Thank you."

"I'll walk you out," Wells says, reaching for his shoes.

Acker stops him with a hand on his shoulder. "Stay. Keep the floors clean."

Harold is waiting for us at the carriage when we return. The ride back to the palace is silent aside from the wheels against the cobblestone and the horse's hooves. Acker leans against the far seat, elbow propped against the window, running the back of his knuckles across the seam of his mouth. His face is blank, but I see the worry underneath.

"What are you thinking?"

He doesn't move, eyes heavy on me as they slide my way. "You already don't want this."

My heart skips a beat. "I never said I—"

"You don't have to. I can see it. Beau can see it." He drops his elbow and stares at me. "And I never wanted to rush you to accept it, but now I'm faced with the reality that I might not be able to keep you safe if you don't."

I can practically feel his turmoil humming through the cabin. "I've never felt pressure from you, Acker, and that means more to me than you know. But...I can't

409

accept a match who doesn't trust me enough to be honest with me."

A crease forms between his brows.

"You hid the bond from me, your betrothal, and you knew how your people would react to me yet you let me go in blind. Then I find out Irina is at court." It's my turn to look out the window, not wanting to see the truth in his eyes when I say, "You would never have done those things if you didn't have doubts."

The city is cast in shadow, empty aside from the critters taking advantage of the abandoned streets. I hear him shift in his seat before I feel a featherlight touch at my knee. Looking down, I watch as he slides his fingers forward until they link with mine, pulling my hand into his. I look up and am met with Acker's soft gaze, softer than I've ever seen before.

"Know this, Jovie: I have zero doubts when it comes to you. You heard Olivia—I've always known you were it for me. I may have thought I lost you for a while, but I knew no one would ever take your place." Bracing his elbows on his knees, he brings my hands to his lips, eyes closing as he holds them there. "I'm sorry I made you doubt *me*," he says, eyes staring up at me.

I can feel my heartbeat in my throat, and I swallow in an effort to force it down before speaking. "Promise me you won't keep things from me."

"I promise," he says, voice low.

My chest nearly caves in with my next exhale, and I lean forward to kiss him. He meets my lips with a sweet, melodic pull, his hands holding my face to savor the kiss. It's all-consuming and dizzying in the best way.

There's a loud bang on the front of the carriage that breaks us apart. "We're here, my highness."

Acker licks his lips and slides back into his seat, hand still intertwined with mine in my lap. "Thank you, Harold."

I look at the window and see the arching gates to the palace up ahead. It's easier to take in since we're not barging through at breakneck speeds like before, and I'm able to get a clearer view of the cages hanging along the palace walls. I realize what I thought were animals are not animals at all.

They're people.

# CHAPTER 49

We're standing in the middle of the courtyard, waiting for Acker to finish speaking with the commanding officer of the battalion. The group of soldiers I stretched with are now gathered under the arch leading to the palace yard. Hallis hands me a sword sheathed in leather.

I motion to the men with a tilt of my head. "What are they doing?"

"They're starting their morning conditioning."

"Am I not training with them?"

Hallis squints down at me, the sunshine in full force this morning. "Acker wants to see your swordsmanship, and there's no way you'll be able to spar in the shape you're in if you run first."

He's not wrong. I'm under my normal weight, and my strength is significantly depleted. While Fia healed me through the awakening, my muscle never fully returned, and the stretching alone has my joints feeling a little too loose and sore.

Even so, I hand the sword back to Hallis. "I'll be back," I tell him, then I hurry to catch up to the soldiers as they begin their run.

Their initial pace is brutal, and I'm on the tail of the group. The path is along the interior wall of the grounds. A few of the soldiers catch a glimpse of me over their shoulders in the first turn, and I'm convinced it ignites into an all-out race to leave me behind. What I thought was brutal becomes downright agonizing.

Each breath feels like knives in my chest, each step harder than the last. I fall behind, but so do others. It's a small consolation to know they've been doing this run for weeks, if not months, and are struggling with it as much as I am. All the time I spent competing with Aurora through adolescence feels so trivial now. We should have been competing against the boys just as hard.

We've made the first pass around the palace grounds when Hallis catches up. The two of us run side by side, strides matched despite his ability to surpass me by a long shot.

"Who are they?" I ask on our third lap, looking toward the palace gates.

Two women stand before the iron bars. A young boy stands in front of one of them, her hands tight on his shoulders. He's crying. They all are, but his tears are the hardest to take in.

"His father was sentenced to the wall for not disclosing his abilities," Hallis says. "He's been sentenced to death by public execution."

Disgust sits heavy on my tongue as I look up at the man crying, hand stretched between the bars of his cage, reaching for his family. A family he'll never embrace again.

"It's cruel," I say.

Hallis's mouth thins. "I hate the practice, but King Edmond thinks it holds the Heirs accountable, and it's difficult to deny its effectiveness."

"As long as he didn't harm anyone, why does the king care if people hide their gifts or not?"

"There are good people in the world, the same as there are bad, except the bad people with magical abilities are exceptionally dangerous when left unchecked."

"Couldn't the same be said about the people inside these walls?"

"To be honest," he says, lowering his voice, "I'm not sure anyone deserves magic. If Mother Nature is real, she fucked us all when she gave it to us."

By the time the commanding officer blows a whistle to cease running, I've lost count of the number of laps we've done. The commander summons the soldiers into a line. His eyes stutter on me at the end but continue on without a word.

He orders us to do a set of strengthening exercises, and then another after that. And another, and more. The morning goes on like this for what feels like an eternity until my eyesight begins to bleed into a haze and bile coats my throat.

"Water break," he yells, sending the men scattering to the water stations.

My butt hits the gravel and stone of the courtyard, and I tuck my head between my knees to stop myself from passing out. Sweat drips down the bridge of my nose and drops to the ground.

Acker's voice pierces through the throb of my heartbeat in my head. "You're pushing too hard too fast, Jovie."

*I don't recall asking your opinion.*

There's a nudge against my leg, and I open my eyes to clearer vision, accepting the waterskin he pushes into my hand. I don't think I've ever tasted better water.

"Two minutes," the commander yells.

I need to get my legs under me before my muscles lock

up.

"Jovie, no," Acker says, reaching for my elbow.

I jerk out of his reach, and I'm impressed by my ability to stay upright on shaky legs. Acker growls my name as a warning, but I don't have energy to waste arguing with him. I find myself back in line, this time landing somewhere in the middle.

"We'll do three minutes of sparring," the commander says, eyes lingering on me a smidge longer this time. "Pairings will be my choice."

The commander picks pairs on a whim, and I don't look away or back down when he glazes over me. I observe the matches, some more entertaining than others. There are a few I would be nervous to face, and I make note of them by name for future possible jaunts in the ring. Not until after the second sparring session do I feel as if I've gotten my breathing back under control. My legs still feel like jelly and my arms are dead weight, but I can at least hear and see with ease again.

It's down to the last two pairings when it becomes blatantly obvious I won't be picked. I look at Hallis and Acker, who are watching from the sidelines of the circle carved into the center of the courtyard. My wounded pride has me sneering at them when I'm left standing at the end of training having never gotten my chance.

The commander doesn't bother to look at me when he dismisses the battalion. I'm on a rampage as I march across the yard, temper flaring as Acker laughs at something Hallis says. It falls away quickly when he sees me. He widens his stance, arms crossed over his chest as he prepares for my approach.

I swipe the sword from his waist.

"Jovie," he chastises, indignation tightening his

features. "What are you doing?"

"You wanted to see me with a sword in my hand," I declare, walking backward to the center of the ring. "Well here I am. All I need is a competitor."

The remaining soldiers slow their departure to watch the unhinged spectacle of me defying their prince.

"Not after you punished yourself this morning," Acker says, unmoving. "Maybe after a few days' time, your body will be rested enough to try again."

Seething, I turn to the open courtyard, conscious of the onlookers congregating on the veranda. "Anyone willing to go against an out-of-shape princess?" I ask in jest. "Any takers?"

The soldiers share looks between them, some grinning, others concerned. One brave soldier steps forward, head turning to Acker. I recognize him as one of the more proficient swordsmen; Talon is his name. "I'm willing, your highness."

Acker is less than pleased. "No." He turns toward Hallis.

I'm debating which insult to launch at him when he turns back around with Hallis's sword in hand.

"You want to spar," he says, stalking into the ring, swinging the sword in his hand into a readying hold. "Fine."

His relaxed stance and calm demeanor are insulting. It gives me the fuel I need to energize my overworked muscles. One last hurrah before my body gives out to prove I'm not as weak as I look.

I don't waste time. I advance, turning and throwing a backswing as the first strike. Acker throws his sword up in defense, and our blades meet with a loud clang of metal against metal. It's all too easy for him to throw me off with a push of his weapon.

"Yeah?" he says, a hint of a smile peeking through his disapproving demeanor. "Alright."

Then he advances, swinging his blade to the right. I move to block, but it's a misdirection, and I stumble from my lack of balance. He lets me regain my footing before advancing again. This time I wait until he's close before I counter his forward strike with one of my own, which he sidesteps.

I know there's no way I walk away from this match a winner, but I refuse to go down without a fight. I'll push until my sword falls or my arms give out, whichever comes first.

I give it my all. Swing, block, strike, miss.

Miss.

Miss.

Miss.

I'm gasping for breath. Acker looks as if he's enjoying a bout of child's play. He shakes his head at me, scolding me without words. He's taller and stronger. If fighting with Messer taught me anything, it's that men are weakest when you're inside their arm reach. I spin left and attack then shift left in defense before spinning again, closer and closer. I strike until he's backed to the circle's line where the only way out is through me.

"Good, Jovie," he praises. "Just like that."

I wouldn't have thought it possible, but I'm sure my cheeks somehow redden further despite my state of exhaustion. We're less than arm's length apart when he decides to strike. It's exactly what I've been waiting for.

I counter-cut his strike and am rewarded with the sight of blood as it seeps through the paper-thin cut on the back of his forearm.

Acker stares at me with a heat I can't feel because everything hurts and I think I might be on the brink of death. My arm shakes as I lift the sword to return it to him. He at least has the wits to ignore it.

"Find an elemental to chill her bathwater," he says to a servant stationed under the veranda. Then he gives me one last, lingering look before turning away.

I hear Hallis's whispered words over the wind. "Was it the oath or you holding yourself back?"

They walk too far out of range for me to hear Acker's reply, but I don't care. Surviving is good enough for me. For today, at least.

# CHAPTER 50

It's my least favorite bath I've ever had. It's not simply cool, it's *freezing*. I'm positive it's at a temperature I've never felt before when Beau makes me get in. My body convulses throughout the five minutes I'm able to withstand it before I flounder out, and I'm very grateful for the food waiting at the desk.

Beau lounges on my bed, munching on grapes and flipping through another book. "Your jaunt around the castle this morning is the main topic of conversation around here," she says.

I pull out the desk chair and drop into it. "I have many regrets in this life, and I have to say running those laps are up there."

"Don't decide yet. It made a really good impression on the commander and his men."

*Hmm.*

The plate of roasted chicken and peas holds all my attention. Forgoing the utensils, I tear apart the chicken breast with my fingers, heaving a sigh of pleasure at the perfect flavors and spices.

"Remind me to kiss Henry the next time I see him."

Laughing, Beau flips onto her stomach and props her chin in her hand. "Commander Imen told my father you'd fare better than most of his men in battle."

I pause midchew. "Your father is back?"

"He is," she says, kicking her feet behind her. "He

called a council of his advisors to a meeting this afternoon."

"No one knows where he was?" I ask.

She shakes her head. "He does this a couple times a year, disappearing without a word. There's speculation, of course, that he spends his time with hired women at the cottage on the southern beaches, but it would be odd for him to take such a frivolous trip during a time like this."

"Time like this...?"

"Your return. Possible retaliation from Roison. Then there's the fact that Irina's family is at court with concern about the state of their alliance." She shrugs like these are of no consequence to her. "And I know your mother has sent a message by now, so there's added pressure of her breathing down his neck."

"That reminds me," I say, wiping off my hands on the napkin. "I need to call my dagger."

Closing my eyes, I pretend it's on a table in front of me. It's like digging through stalks of algae. I concentrate hard to make sense of the colors and shapes in my mind, looking for something tangible to hold on to, but this retrieval is proving to be the hardest yet, even harder than finding it on the ocean floor.

Then, like someone opens a door, I see a room. It's empty except for a single round table at its center. I'm cautious as I walk toward it, spotting the black blade on the surface. I stop before it.

This is a trap. It's so obvious I'm tempted to leave it, but I promised...

What will my mother assume if I don't try? It's possible someone commandeered the dagger during transit, or maybe General Samasu isn't as loyal as he appeared. Nevertheless, it must be done. I try to be quick with it, try to snatch the dagger and disappear, but a hand clamps down on mine.

The voice is heavy with emotion and excitement. "Jo."

I look up and lay eyes on the woman who has me cornered in my own mind. There's no doubt or question of her identity because her face is my own, but stronger. Age and life have chiseled away the softer lines, replacing them with renewed strength. Copper hair, lighter than my own, hangs in waves over one shoulder. She smiles at me, eyes brimming with tears.

"Mother," I murmur as I exhale.

Then I'm back in my body, dagger clutched tight in my fist. I look at Beau in shock.

"What happened?" she says, sitting up with wide eyes.

"I..." I shake my head to stop the emotion from leaking out in my voice. "I saw my mother."

Beau leans forward, eyes alight. "Did she say anything?"

I shake my head again. "No," I say, running my hand over the now familiar weapon. "Just my name. Just...Jo."

A soft smile pulls at Beau's lips. I fight the tears threatening to overflow.

Standing from the bed, Beau envelopes me in a hug. "If she's anything like my mother, she's planning and plotting how to break you out of here," she says.

I smile. "I'm here of my own accord, remember?"

"Oh, yeah." She sneaks a bite of my chicken. "All in the name of love." She winks at me and returns to her position of leisure.

I place my dagger on the edge of my desk. The exhaustion I felt getting out of the bath is long gone after seeing my mother.

I've spent the majority of my life wondering if she wanted me. I knew what I was told, but doubt always lingered, making me wonder if she abandoned me. Seeing her heals a wound I worked hard to convince myself didn't exist.

I finish my meal and retrieve the book from under my mattress. Beau pretends to not notice, and we spend the rest of our day reading, me at the desk as I pore over the jumbled mess of text, Beau switching from the bed to one of the cushioned chairs and back again. She never truly settles.

Apparently there are many kinds of bonds, some born, others created, physical as well as mental. There's a tale of two Heirs who were gifted the ability to become one body during battles. Two heads, four arms and legs, and the ability to see all around them at the same time.

Then there are mind bonds. Similar to the gifts of an oracle, except it's only a meld between two people. There's less known about them, however.

Elemental bonds. Cursed bonds created by witches. Contractual bonds, like in the case of blood oaths.

The next bond sends a chill down my spine when I come across it.

A blood bond. While similar to a blood oath, it requires blood from two or more people and is considered the most abhorrent of all bonds. Used as a truth revealer, anyone who creates a blood oath with another while telling a lie will kill them both instantly —

I gasp out loud.

Beau doesn't take her eyes off the book in her hands. "I've been waiting for you to get to that part," she says, smug.

"Why didn't you tell me?" Better question— "Why didn't you stop it?"

"One thing you'll learn when it comes to Acker is that nothing can stop him once he's set his mind on something." She closes the book and sits up in her chair. "And you didn't ask."

I stare at the text, dumbfounded. "I thought you and Hallis were angry about the blood oath, not the…" … nearly killing us bit.

"Again," she says, throwing her hands up, book in one hand, "we are all merely at the mercy of Acker's will."

I stand and begin to pace as I read. It was commonplace for kings and queens to demand blind fealty. They'd make their subordinates swear blood oaths, and any time they felt their liege was straying, they'd test their loyalty by forcing them to commit blood bonds…and they often failed.

Too often they were eventually branded unreliable. They were banned. Anyone caught committing the crime of a blood bond would be hung on the wall. Or worse, if a lie was told, their families would be hung on the wall in their place.

"When was this book written?" I ask Beau.

"That's a question for my mother," she says. "Some time before my father took the throne centuries ago."

I scour the book for any indication of long-term effects but come up empty. The entire book seems more like a warning about any kind of bond and less of a testament to any goodwill coming from them.

Beau leaves to find us dinner, and I'm slightly panicked as I prepare another bath. This one is the opposite of my one from earlier, and I ease into the steaming water and lavender oil on an exhale. My thoughts are racing and scrambling to make sense of everything. I close my eyes and concentrate on clearing my mind. Everything feels like too much, but the steady words he spoke as he held my hand with blood seeping through our fingers replay in my head.

*And I love her.*

At the time, I thought it was nothing more than a manipulation tactic, an added caveat to convince General Samasu he was safe with me, to leave me in Kenta's hands. He spoke the words as if he was stating the color of the sky or his favorite breakfast dish, not professing his love for his match like he's always claimed is important.

Just a simple *I love her.*

A laugh escapes me, a bubble of exhilaration I can't contain before it's a full cacophony of laughter reverberating off the bathroom walls. It shouldn't matter, but I'm glad there are no witnesses to the scorching flush of my cheeks or my giddy smile as I relish the truth.

*Acker* loves me.

Acker loves *me.*

Acker *loves* me.

# CHAPTER 51

*No.*

No. No. No.

No.

A maidservant hands Acker a glass of amber liquid. He thanks her, taking a sip, face placid when his gaze catches on me. Then he freezes, body stilling, breath unmoving in his chest as his eyes stop on my face before flicking down to my bare body.

I know no one but him can see me, but I can't fight the desire to cover my breasts in the company of strange men, squeezing my thighs tight together. Water sluices down my skin from my hair, down my body and legs until soaking into the fibers of the woolen rug beneath my feet.

He blinks and looks away, jaw ticking as he clenches his teeth. Calling the servant back over, he says, "Please send someone to check on Princess Jovinnia."

The servant dips her head and disappears out a hidden door in the paneled wall, sealing me in with the party of seven men. We're in a sitting room with tufted chairs and low-lying tables laden with crystal decanters of different alcohols.

"Have we received any reports of movement?" asks the man seated to Acker's right. It's the commander from training, I realize.

Acker shakes his head, but there's noticeable tension

in the gesture.

A man I don't recognize sits across the table from him. "You alright? You look as if someone kicked your dog."

The men laugh in jest, and Acker manages to loosen a smile at their teasing. They move on to discuss the troops they plan on sending to the border, remarking on the need for fresh blood if discord is to break out between Roison and Kenta again.

Acker glances over at me then curls his fingers in a gesture that indicates I should go to him. I tiptoe around the high-sided chairs, careful not to bump the table or the glasses on it. He doesn't look at me as he widens his knees for me to step between his legs. Then he braces his elbows on the arms of the chair, drink balanced in his hand, an invitation for me to sit.

I'm shivering, the cool air amplified against my damp skin as I debate the consequences of folding myself into the confines of his lap. It doesn't matter how much I reiterate to myself that no one is able to see me, no one but Acker; the feeling of exposure doesn't dissipate.

"Don't you agree, Acker?"

"Yes," he says, voice clipped as he keeps up with the conversation. "I think a celebratory dinner would be nice."

He dares a look at me, eyes conveying everything in the split second they meet mine.

*Sit.*

It's an order. Slow and measured, I angle my body to rest on the expanse of his thigh. He doesn't move or so much as blink as I get situated. Goose bumps erupt across my skin in response to the warmth radiating from him. I balance a hand on the back of the chair behind him, careful to not put too much pressure against the material as I lift one foot, then the other, and tuck them on the other side of him. It's a tight fit, but I'm comforted by the high walls of the chair. It gives the illusion of privacy.

Acker adjusts his body lower in the seat, causing me to lean against the front of his chest, placing my head against the cut of his shoulder. He takes a drink of his liquor, voice so low I nearly can't hear him over the chatter in the room.

"Are you sleeping?" he says, eyes remaining on the men conversing around him.

Again, I know no one should be able to hear me, but I whisper back, "I don't know."

I can't remember. I'm in the bath, that much is obvious, but I can't recall being tired enough to doze off. If anything, I was still buzzed after the connection to my mother, as well as my realization of Acker's feelings.

"I think I might be awake."

He seems less than pleased by my answer. This time when he drinks, it's a healthy swallow.

"You're angry with me," I point out.

He doesn't reply—can't—but the sharpness in his eyes, the stony way he turns his head away is answer enough.

I run my fingers over the strap of daggers he always wears across his chest. "I think it's because the bond can sense how close I am to giving in," I say, letting the truth run free with my tongue.

His inhale presses against the hand I have braced on his chest. I smile, pleased with the fact that he's not totally unaffected despite his cold exterior.

"...the goods are fine...they don't have a clue..."

Words flow in one ear and out the other as I slide my fingers through the open buttons at the collar of his shirt.

"I was thinking about you." I watch as he swallows, noticing the thrumming pulse in his neck. "While I was taking a bath."

His breaths deepen, muscles taut as he remains unmoving. I lean forward, knowing there's nothing he can do to stop me, and whisper into his ear.

"Touching myself."

The muscle of his thigh tenses underneath me. "The cache is plenty stocked."

I'm impressed but also displeased by his ability to remain invested in the conversation. I place my lips on that thundering spot in his neck, tasting the skin with the flat of my tongue.

He moves then. Bringing his drink closer to his body, he shoves his elbow between my thighs. It opens me up to him, to the air as he pretends to inspect his drink. But he's not looking at his beverage. I suck in a breath, nerves and anticipation coursing through my veins.

"Have you spoken with your father?"

Looking up, Acker presses the glass against my inner thigh, using it to pull my leg toward his taut stomach, opening me up even further. "I haven't."

I dig my fingertips into the hard plane of his chest. A smirk emerges on his face as he plays with his drink, running the glass along the inside of my thigh.

"You know he lives by his own time," he says, sending a conspiratorial look around the room. It glazes me in a sweeping pass. "He'll be here when he gets here."

He drags the glass until it's almost kissing my exposed center.

"Acker," I warn, ripping my free hand from beneath his shirt, not caring about the ripple effect it causes as I brace my hand over his between my legs to stop him.

He doesn't listen. Instead, he traps my fingers under his against the glass and presses it firmly to the apex of my thighs. The glass is warm from being in his hand, and it instantly causes a fiery sensation to ignite in my lower stomach. I squirm in his lap in a bid to get away, but there's nowhere to go, not without spilling his drink or giving away that something's amiss.

A round of raucous laughter breaks out, and Acker uses it to his advantage. "Touching where?" he whispers.

Then he spreads his legs even wider, sinking me into the crux of his lap where his erection is at full length and hot against my bottom. A choked gasp leaves my lips as he angles his hips and presses, presses, presses the glass against the sensitive bundle of nerves between my legs. My breath stutters in my chest as I fight his hold.

To anyone else in the room, it looks as though he's contemplative, lost to the thoughts in his head, but his eyes are affixed to the space where our fingers are intertwined, where the glass slides between my wetness.

The only giveaway is the quickened breaths he can't hide, nostrils flaring. He bends his other elbow, bracing his temple against a fist, and it's effective in putting pressure on my upper back to keep me in place with the bracket of his arm. There's no stopping the building pulse in my body or the hum deep in my throat. He's relentless, fingers punishing over mine as he undulates the pressure, to the point I fear for the integrity of the glass in our hands.

My integrity? On the floor in shambles, because I can't fight the pleasure any longer. I'm chasing it, angling my hips, rubbing against his hard length. I close my other hand over his wrist, urging him to get it over with, and for him to put me out of my misery by urging him to press harder.

Harder.

More.

Almost...

The king walks in, drawing everyone's attention to his arrival across the room when I come, letting the moan I can't contain sink into the crick of Acker's neck. I undulate in his lap, soaking in the last few moments of bliss.

His teeth seem to crack from his restraint, but then he's quick to remove the glass. My heart is thundering in my chest as he holds it up to his father in greeting. "Come have a seat," he says.

Then he does the unthinkable and places the glass against his lips, tongue dipping to the rim when he tilts his head back and swallows the remainder of the liquid. I reposition myself on his thigh, grateful for his dark pants and their ability to hide any proof of my arousal. He sits up, hiding his own evidence by placing the empty glass on the table. He licks his lips, eyes cutting to mine briefly.

The king removes his cape and sits in the chair opposite Acker's, eyeing the assortment of liquors. "Where's the maidservant?"

As if summoned, she emerges from the disguised door, head down as she walks toward Acker. "There seems to be an issue," she says, voice timid.

Acker's voice comes out hurried. "What is it?"

"The princess," she says, eyes struggling to remain on Acker's. "Beau told me to fetch you."

That's all Acker needs to hear, and I all but fall onto my feet when he stands.

The king sits forward. "I'm sure it's nothing Beau can't handle," he says, pointed stare on his son. "We need to discuss business." If I'm not mistaken, his eyes cut to a man standing behind the servant, a man in finery with light blonde hair and striking features.

The maidservant speaks up, though her voice is still hardly audible. "I think—something's wrong," she says, hands fidgeting before her. "It seems urgent."

"You'll have to fill me in later," Acker says, walking around the servant toward the door.

The king's call to his son goes unanswered as Acker stalks out of the room. I race after him, eager to get away and also to find out what's happening to me that has the maidservant so alarmed.

People freeze in place as Acker picks up his pace, feet pounding on the marble floor as he races to my room.

"Slow down," I yell after him. "I'm sure it's fine."

He doesn't even spare me a glance, taking the stairs two at a time. "Wells said it would trap you."

A passing servant looks at Acker in confusion. "Excuse me, your highness?"

He ignores her as he turns down the hall. I feel obscene, rushing after him completely naked, but all I can do is follow him to my room. He barges in, eyes swinging around the empty space.

"In here," Beau calls.

Nothing could prepare me for the sight before me. Beau leans over the tub, now empty of water, hand propping my head at an angle to prevent my chin from meeting my chest. My eyes are wide open and unfocused as I stare into thin air. Acker climbs into the tub, hands bracketing my face.

"She's alive, but her aura—" Beau's words cut off as she looks at me. Not the physical me, but whatever she sees standing beside the tub. "Woah."

Acker looks up at me then to Beau. "What do you see?"

"It's like…" She shakes her head in awe. "Like I've never seen a whole aura until now. There are so many colors. It's unlike anything I've ever seen."

That does nothing to appease Acker, whose focus goes back to my physical body. He smacks my cheek.

"I did that," she says. "Threw cold water on her, yanked her hair. Nothing."

"Thanks so much guys." I retrieve a towel and wrap it around me.

Beau's mouth falls open in shock. "What the fuck."

"Get out," Acker orders his sister.

She looks at him as he sinks to his knees on either side of my legs. "I know you're matched, but it feels wrong to leave an unconscious woman in the hands of a man."

Acker snaps. "She's right fucking there, Beau. Get out."

Beau looks at me, and I wave the towel to let her know I'm at least a coherent participant.

"Okay," she drawls as she gets to her feet. "I claim no part in this."

"It would be weird if you did."

He cradles my face in his hands, the worry straining the crease between his brows.

Then it hits me. "The bond wants us together," I explain. "As long as I'm near you, it will keep me here."

Realization dawns on Acker's face and he stands, stepping out of the tub. "I'll come back in fifteen minutes."

"I might need more time," I tell him. "I feel *fulfilled* right now."

He understands what I'm insinuating. The physical connection we shared created an anchor of sorts. Dipping his head in a nod, he doesn't bid me any goodbyes, gaze averted and tense as he moves around me to leave.

A moment later, Beau returns, leaning against the door jamb. "He's pissed."

Sighing, I sit on the edge of the tub, offput by the sight of myself.

This is a disaster.

# CHAPTER 52

It takes hours.

Hours before I snap back into my body, nearing midnight. It's unsettling to look at myself. Naked. Exposed. Vulnerable.

When I come to, I'm quick to take another bath and get dressed. I find Beau dozing in the bed and wake her with instructions to take me to Acker's living quarters. She doesn't ask questions or inquire as to why. We walk down the main hall, stopping at an inlet with a bust on display. I look at Beau in confusion, but she shoves her fingers in the statue's nose and pulls. The wall behind it pops open.

"Every castle has its secrets," she says.

She pushes the door closed behind us, and I focus on the sound of her feet in the dark. It's a hidden passageway. It appears to stretch the length of the castle. We take a sharp turn and walk a while before Beau comes to a stop.

I don't know how she knows where we are, but she presses against the stone wall until it gives way. Then we're in another one of the main hallways. Directly across the hall is a door made of iron, and I don't need her to tell me who it belongs to.

I open my mouth to thank her, but she stops me with a raised hand. "Don't speak."

Then she stalks away, and I think I hear her gag.

Looking back at the heavy door, I raise my fist to the knocker but stop myself. I test the handle, surprised when the lock gives. The door opens to a sitting room. Dark paneled walls curve inward, and the skin of a large animal is spread across the floor.

Past the leather chairs and chess table, an archway leads to the room beyond. Bed centered against a wall laden with weapons. Swords and knives of every kind, spiked maces and helmets and other tools I don't have a name for. Acker stands in the door leading to the bathroom, arms folded with a towel draped around his waist.

Neither one of us moves.

"I don't understand why you're angry with me," I tell him.

He tilts his head, eyes stark in the lantern-lined room. "I'm not angry at you, Jovie. I'm angry at the situation."

"What situation, exactly? The fact that I appeared bare or that I appeared at all? It's not as if I get to decide."

His voice comes out quick and harsh. "The fact that I was robbed of the first time I get to lay eyes on you," he says.

A sense of relief eases through my chest at his answer. "You saw me when Fia healed me."

"It's different. I was scared for your life." He shakes his head. "Tonight, I was forced to look away, to pretend I was unaffected by the sight of my match bare before me." He grits his teeth to appease the anger he's contending with before continuing. "I couldn't touch you. Could almost taste you on the edge of the glass, but I couldn't have you."

My heart aches for him as I walk toward him. He watches me with sharp eyes, gripping the doorway as if to keep himself in place. Standing before him, I'm no longer scared to hold his gaze like I was when we first met, when he seemed all-encompassing and overwhelming. Now, I realize, I want to dive into those feelings. I want all of him, all around me.

"I didn't hate it," I remind him.

He's not swayed. "I felt out of control. I pushed you—"

"No, Acker." I step forward, our chests mere inches apart as I stare up at him. "I pushed you and you pushed back. Fair is fair."

"Not when the bond is forcing you."

I keep my smile in check as I reach for the hand at his side. He lets me take it, and I turn it palm side up. The scar cutting across it is a match to my own.

"I think I knew the night we swam with the stars," I tell him, returning my eyes to his. "If you need a blood bond to prove it, I'll do it."

He sucks in a sharp breath, eyes igniting with renewed anger. Moving too quickly for me to react, he grips my hair tight at the nape of my neck. "Never offer anyone that. Not even me."

I brace my hands against his chest. "You did."

"Because I know," he says, eyes jumping between mine. "I've always known."

"You're not listening." I tilt my head back even further, making my offer clear. "I love you."

His next breath leaves him, chest caving when he closes his mouth on mine. The anger and frustration are still there, just underneath the surface of the longing crush of his mouth, tongue eager to taste every part of me. He lifts me and I wrap my legs around his waist as he walks us to the bed. He waves a hand to the door beyond the sitting room, and there's a metallic sound of the lock sliding into place. Laying me down, he moves to my neck, but I push him away with sure hands.

"Wait."

Standing, I reach across my stomach and pull the soft material of my shirt over my head, taking my brassiere with it. I tuck my thumbs into the waistband of my pants, but Acker stops me.

"Let me," he says, sinking to a knee.

He peels the material down my legs, helping me out of the pants one leg at a time before coming back up for my panties. He places a kiss on the skin he slowly exposes below my navel. Then another, lower, lower, lower, until he lavishes an open-mouthed kiss on the bundle of nerves as he lets the panties fall to my ankles. When my body shudders, he grabs my hips to keep me still.

"Acker," I plead, threading my hands in his hair. "Please."

*Don't tease me. Don't make me wait. Just...please.*

He drags his tongue from my center, and I nearly come from the sight alone, his dark eyes shining with mirth before me.

"Patience is not your virtue, princess," he says, standing. He removes his towel, but before I can fully appreciate him, he picks me up and lays me on my back, devouring me in another kiss. I open my legs, and he sinks into the space. Hard and creating the perfect friction, he thrusts forward, and I break from his mouth to catch my breath.

He looks down at my body. "Fuck, you're gorgeous."

He maintains the push of his hips as he grabs me by the jaw and forces his tongue into my mouth. Then he relinquishes me, trailing his hand over my throat, down my chest.

"That's what I wanted to tell you the moment I saw you," he says, smoothing a palm over one of my breasts then the other.

I arch my back in encouragement, the harsh callouses of his hands creating the best kind of sensation against my skin and nipples as he traces them with his fingertips.

"I wanted to have you right there, in front of all of them, consequences be damned."

I moan when he sucks one breast into his mouth, giving it the same decadent kiss as he did my cunt, though this time it's more biting, more urgent.

"I think I would have let you," I tell him, keeping a fierce grip on his hair.

He groans from my confession, and then he's covering me again, mouth over mine. I suck on his tongue, and a quake shoots through his body. Slipping his hand between my legs, he feels the wetness, spreading it, dipping his middle finger in. I gasp.

He stops completely. "Jovie."

I open my eyes, not having realized I'd shut them.

He's looking at me with a newfound wonder. "You've never?"

I want to lie, but I don't. I shake my head.

His breath leaves him in a shudder, fanning across my chest as he looks down at his hand. "Tell me to stop and I will."

"If you stop, I might actually kill you," I say.

He doesn't laugh. "I'll let you," he says, eyes meeting mine at the same time he pushes a little deeper inside me. "If you asked me for my life, I'm pretty sure I'd hand it over on a gold platter."

It's hard for me to focus on his words when he presses the hilt of his hand against me. I angle my hips to get better traction when he grinds it in time with the thrusts of his fingers, two now as he manages to get another in.

I say his name, drawing his attention to my eyes. "Kiss me."

So he does. He doesn't stop until I'm a writhing mess beneath him. I'm desperate for the climax as I cling to him, his shoulders and hair and chest, anywhere I can find purchase.

"I want to watch you come," he says, eyes traveling the length of me once more. "I didn't get to see you when you were in my lap."

He observes the flush as it coats my neck and chest. It feels more revealing than being naked in the room of strangers, but in the best way, like I want to give him every part of me—at least every part of me I can part with. It hits me like a tidal wave and I come apart on his hand, my grip on his hair undoubtedly severe. He doesn't seem the least bit fazed as he removes his hand and looks at the evidence of my arousal, tasting the digits with his mouth.

I'm too unwound and satiated to be shocked, but I can't deny that I like the sight of the carnal act. There's nothing but pure desire and gratification as he pulls them out. His hand is wet against my hip as he positions me.

"I'll go slow," he says, swallowing as he lines himself up with my opening. "Again, you say stop and I will."

I bring his mouth down to mine, but he doesn't let me get lost in it.

"I mean it, Jovie. Tell me if it's too much."

"Okay," I promise.

Then he's pushing in. It leaves me breathless, the sensation of him taking up so much space inside me. He pauses and releases the breath he's been holding. I push the hair from his face when he looks at me, sweat creating a layer of moisture across his skin.

Then he kisses me, pushing all the way in.

It's a lot to take in. More than enough. Possibly too much.

"Jovie, look at me."

I comply, meeting his gaze, unable to stop the drop of water from escaping the corner of my eye. He sees it, eyes tracking its path, and he brushes it away with his thumb.

"I'm sorry," he says. "I almost wish you'd been with someone else, just so you could enjoy our first time together."

I shake my head, a broken laugh leaving me. "No you don't."

He shakes his head with a soft smile. "I don't."

Pulling back the slightest bit only to push forward again, he begins a gentle pace and kisses me. It takes time, but the pain subsides enough that I start to gather the low pulse of desire. Acker's breath becomes heavier, his pleasure no longer his goal, rather striving to just get through it with as little casualty to me as possible. I both admire and hate it.

I raise my hips to meet his thrusts, and he falters.

"Jovie," he warns. "Easy."

*Oh*, I hate that more.

I yank him by the hair, pulling his mouth to mine in a punishing kiss. He growls, in annoyance or acceptance,

I don't know. His thrusts become harder, deeper as I drown in his kiss. It's all-encompassing, all-consuming, and I moan with each punctuation of his hips.

He loses a grip on his restraint. A sound I've never heard before leaves his lips, something between a growl and moan as he stills inside me, pulsing. He thrusts once more before letting his weight cover me.

I'm not sure I've ever experienced true peace in my life until right now. Then, like two magnets meeting, the tether below my breasts snaps into place, an unbreakable bond stretching between us. Acker braces his weight to look at me, and if I'm not mistaken, there's a sheen of glassiness in his eyes.

I kiss him, knowing nothing lasts forever.

# CHAPTER 53

I peruse the shelves, eyes jumping over the spines as I search. It's dark in the hidden library below Greta's desk, so I carry a lantern from stack to stack, and the exhaustion in my arms from training this morning is starting to catch up with me. That said, recovery isn't as arduous as it was in Alaha. A gift from awakening, thank the gods.

I retrieve a book I find interesting and place it in the small pile I've accumulated on the floor. *Hearthstones and Talismans*, *Dark Magic*, and now *Weaponry*.

An enthusiastic voice comes from behind me. "I did it!"

Yelping, I spin around and find Acker standing on the study table. "Are you trying to kill me?" I say, hand over my pounding heart.

"Landing could use some work," he says, stepping off the table and bouncing on his feet. "But not a bad start." He leans in to kiss me.

"How are you here?" I say, setting the lantern on the table.

"The bond," he says, placing his hand over his heart. "It goes both ways now."

I push him in the chest. "Why would you do it? Where are you?"

"Relax. I'm alone in my room and I still have complete control of myself." He blinks out of existence, only to emerge on top of the table again. "See?" He leaps from the table and kisses me again like he can't help himself then scans our surroundings. "Where are we anyway?"

"Oh, you don't know?"

He peers around. "Not that I can remember. Is it part of the hidden passageway in the walls?"

I lift my brows at him. "If you don't know, then I'm not telling you."

He grins at my teasing, hands caging me in among the stacks. "I can take an educated guess and say it has something to do with Greta."

"Don't drag sweet Greta into this," I say, tugging on the buttons of his shirt.

"These books are old." He wipes the dust from a title, reading it aloud. "*Hunting Dragons*." He snorts. "What are you looking for?"

"I came to find a text on hearthstone, but anything that catches my interest, really." I undo the top button of his shirt.

He sidles up closer. "Did you find anything?"

I undo another button. "It's the oddest thing, but someone *interesting* found *me*."

Reaching for his belt, he unhooks it, lips grazing mine. "Do you think Greta would mind us defiling her hidden library?"

I smile when I reach his pants and undo the tab. "We should be quiet just in case."

He lifts me with one arm around my waist, pinning me to the shelves. "That's a you problem."

As I reach a hand inside his underwear, he sucks in a sharp hiss of air, eyes falling closed as he pushes his cock into my palm.

"You were saying?"

We've been together three times since our first, and I'm convinced it gets better every time, this one included. He drives into me with intention, each push of his hips a mission to break my vow of silence, hand wrapped around my shoulder to hold me in place. The other braced on the shelf beside my head.

It works.

He pinches my chin after we're dressed, kissing me through short breaths. "Let's place a wager on it next time, yeah?"

Then he disappears right before I reach for a book to launch at his head, his laugh echoing off the walls. Greta has the grace to pretend she knows nothing of my transgressions when I place my books on the counter.

"I know you know," I say, cheeks scarlet as I look at her. "And it won't happen again."

She adjusts the spectacles on her nose, smiling. "Don't speak on things you know nothing of," she says, returning to repairing the spine of the book before her. "I can see the future, remember?"

That only serves to deepen my blush.

She laughs. "I am the king's consort, my darling— there's nothing that could scandalize me."

"I didn't realize you and the king were still…"

"Oh, no," she says, glancing up. "We have not been together in many years, but the label remains the same in the eyes of the court."

I check the empty library and sit on the edge of the desk as she works. "Do you mind if I ask you something?"

"Of course," she says. "I'm an open book."

I smile at her analogy. "It's just…were you in love with the king?"

Her fingers slow where they're taping down the inner lining of the inside cover when she looks up. "I was, yes."

There's a sadness in her eyes that tells me not to push. I reach for my books and thank her for allowing me inside her secret library.

"A little less secret than it was this morning, I'm afraid."

The smile returns to her face. "There's nothing to be ashamed about, Jovinnia. You can never get loving someone wrong."

I let the same words of encouragement Beau gave me sink in for a moment before departing, issuing her one last thanks in return. I'm almost to the door when she calls my name.

"The king was not always the man you know him as today," she says, giving me a pointed look over her spectacles. "Every gain of wealth and power comes at a cost. It chips away at your soul a little each time. Do you understand what I'm telling you?"

She's brazen, but I dip my head in a Kenta nod and give her a small, perceptible look.

"I do."

I take the hidden hallway to my room and spend hours poring over the text on hearthstones, comparing it to what I can find in the book on weaponry. It reiterates what Acker's already filled in for me: weapons made from hearthstone belong to the maker, they're the only weapons capable of cutting someone's magic from them, and they're rare, difficult to find and cultivate.

Uma, the light wielder Acker had spoken of, was overthrown with hearthstone. She was betrayed by her lover, who ground the material into a fine dust and laced her food with it, causing Uma to fall ill. Despite proving the queen wasn't as infallible as people believed, there's still fear of anyone who wields light. After reading about her transgressions, I almost don't blame them.

My eyes begin to cross as I navigate back and forth between the texts. Both texts were written long before King Edmond took the throne, or the recorded reigns prior. There's no way of determining their accuracy.

There's this insistent longing to draw, and I keep glancing toward the sketchbook Acker gifted me. After what feels like the hundredth glance, I reach for it. I don't know if Acker is still able to see inside my mind if I draw, but there's only one way to find out. Bending back the spine, I place the tip of my pencil to the fresh paper and close my eyes.

I was beginning to wonder if my love of drawing was tied to Alaha somehow, like my loneliness was what drove my art, not my creativity, but no. It came back in full force after the matching bond snapped into place.

Opening my eyes, I start with a drag of my pencil. Truth be told, I don't know if I loved Kai. I mean, I know I loved him—do love him—but I didn't *love* him. I can see how I got it confused. He was my best friend and closest person on an island of people who didn't want much to do with me. Of course I would cling to the one who claimed to love me, the first one to kiss me, to ask how my day was, to want me.

But it's nothing in comparison to what I feel with Acker. It was easier than it should have been to leave Alaha, to leave Kai behind. I know if there comes a point where I'm forced to leave Acker, it has the potential to ruin me.

I inspect my work thus far and hate it, but that's to be expected at this stage. I'm attempting to draw a horse from memory, but it seems obvious enough, especially with the ribbon and tiara giving away its identity—me.

I hear Acker's laugh behind me a moment before he kisses the side of my neck at the exact spot I still always catch him obsessing over.

"I love it," he says, wrapping his arms around me. "Thank you."

"You seem to have an awful lot of time on your hands today." I turn to look at him. "Why are you so sweaty?"

He lifts a brow at me. "Why don't you come find me?"

"I'm studying," I say, tapping the texts.

"Suit yourself," he says. Then he disappears.

"He's going to drive me crazy," I say out loud in the empty room.

I close my eyes. The only time I traveled to him while awake was when I was in the bath. I was thinking about him then, but that can't be the only cause, because I think about him a stupid amount on the regular. No, it has to do with the bond.

I concentrate on the tether. It no longer feels one-sided, but complete. Whole. Unchanging. I follow it like I do when I call my dagger. The floor ripples beneath me, and then I'm standing in the courtyard. Hallis and Acker are standing in the center. Three dummies are positioned at the longest length of the yard.

Acker smiles, all teeth as he looks at me, not at all surprised to see me. "Come here."

It's strange to be walking in one place and sitting at my desk in another. I concentrate on picking up my pencil, drawing a happy face on the edge of my sketchbook.

"How?" I ask, shaking my head.

He does the same. "Your guess is as good as mine, but I have a whole list of new questions for Wells."

Hallis adjusts his grip on a hatchet in his hand, tucking it under his arm. "Assuming you haven't completely lost your mind," he says to Acker, eyes roaming the space around his friend. "Hi, princess."

We both laugh, then Acker trudges across the yard to the wall with weapons and props used for training. He grabs a metal chest plate. I give him my back when he gets close, and he loops his arms over my shoulders, placing the plate to my front, securing it with leather binds around my back. Hallis taps the center of my chest with the back of his hatchet, smiling like the boy from my dreams, all deviant and teasing.

"Ready to do some actual training?"

I narrow my gaze at him. "I don't like the tone he's using."

"He's my best mate, Jovie," Acker says, turning me toward a row of dummies set up at various distances. "I can't rip out his teeth."

"Pity," I say.

Acker's chuckle rumbles through my back. "You need to exercise your gift. It's like a muscle. It needs to be worked."

"Keep in mind those near you," Hallis says. "Including your match."

I stand dumbfounded. "Can I even summon my magic in this state?"

"There's only one way to find out."

"But I don't know how to...summon my magic."

Acker stands to the side, arms folded across his chest. "Do I need to remind you of the scorch mark on the front of your armoire?"

Hallis shoots Acker a questioning look. "The what?"

"That was different," I say. "I was running off of my emotions. There's no control over it."

"That's not true. I've watched you defuse your own gift to keep it from getting out of hand many times, and it's easier to turn on a faucet than it is to stop it from running."

I sigh but try to imagine a glowing ball of light in my palm. I think of the anger and jealousy I felt at Acker, summoning the memory of Irina's beauty, focusing on my guilt about sleeping with a betrothed man.

To no one's surprise, nothing happens. Maybe the guilt was a stretch. I shrug my shoulders, giving him a look that says, *See.*

Acker chews on the inside of his cheek, eyes moving toward the targets. "Maybe you need more incentive." He calls two blades from the wall, one in each hand, tossing me the spare. "Let's have a rematch."

"Oh good gods," Hallis mutters, stepping out of the way.

"I don't think this is going to help—"

I move just in time to block his incoming jab. He doesn't give me time to recover before I'm needing to block the next swing. I spin away, hoping for enough breathing room to assess a game plan, but he follows me.

I'm not limber, I didn't stretch, and my hair keeps falling into my line of sight—yet I'm able to get the upper hand and nick him in the side, the material of his shirt gaping open and exposing his skin.

"It's the oath," Acker says, looking at Hallis. "You were right."

I roll my eyes. "Didn't think it all the way through, did you?"

Hallis takes the sword from Acker's hand, assuming a sparring stance in front of me.

"This is less than a fair fight," I say, looking at Acker.

"Give him more credit," he says, arms folded.

I twirl the blade in my hand and offer it to Hallis, a customary sign of respect before sparring matches. He knocks the sword away with a swipe of his own.

"This is my one and only warning, princess. I may have one less hand, but I won't take it easy on you."

I raise a brow he can't see. He's fighting blind. The largest part of sword work is reading the body language of your opponent. The lack of a hand is the least of my concerns.

He attacks first, and I'm gravely unprepared. I make the first few moves in a desperate bid to keep my sword and body intact. Each parry is sloppy, reflexes working overtime to keep up. I yell when his blade scores across the back of my thigh.

Only then does he allow me a moment to breathe, but it doesn't last. His arm moves like liquid, body pivoting to and fro as he unleashes an onslaught against me. There's not a chance in hell of getting a strike in when I'm operating on survival alone.

"Hallis," Acker barks in warning.

The tip of his sword grazes my cheek, and tendrils of my hair float to the floor.

"She won't learn if she isn't pushed," Hallis says, maintaining his focus on my chest plate as I move opposite of him.

He tilts his head, a predator chasing its prey, grin pulling at his lips. When he attacks, I'm cut three more times: chest, hip, and calf.

"Enough," Acker says, threatening to retrieve the blades himself.

Hallis lets the sword fall to his side, giving in. I use his downed guard as an opportunity to strike. It's short-lived as he parries, regret chasing me with each of his jabs, swings, and hits that slash against my skin. I'm eating up ground as I walk backward, using my sword more as a shield than a weapon until I feel the cool stone of the wall against my back. Still, Hallis attacks, sword swinging at me from every possible direction. Eyes glazed in the heat of the battle, he doesn't let up, sweat dripping from his temples.

Then...like in the Dark Forest and against Acker, I become frustrated at my helplessness. My magic unfurls with my growing anger and explodes from my hands, first as an attack against Hallis, sending him flying back, then igniting a flame of light down the length of my sword. Shock ripples through me and I drop my guard, the light snuffing out, leaving a faint glow emanating from around my hands.

Hallis isn't moving.

Acker reaches him first, hand on his chest as he kneels over him. "You okay?"

"Yeah," Hallis moans. "Just got the wind knocked out of me."

Acker slaps him in the chest. "You deserved it." He stands and watches me come closer, eyes flying over me, categorizing each mark on my skin.

"I'm fine," I tell him between sharp breaths.

Slow to get to his feet, Hallis retrieves his fallen sword and slaps the hilt against my abdomen, placing his hand over the space my tether to Acker pulls from. "Never give away where your magic resides," he says, voice like gravel around the edges. "You signaled it multiple times. It takes one person looking at the right time to know your greatest weakness."

I catch the sword so it doesn't hit the ground when he releases it. Acker's eyes are masked, but I have no doubt Hallis can see the heartache his friend holds for him. Hallis slaps him on the shoulder as he passes.

Acker unties the plate from my chest, sending it back to its place with a wave of his hand, along with the swords.

He kisses me, quick and soft. "My bed tonight?"

I nod my agreement. Then I'm back in my room, sitting at my desk as if I was here all along. There's a burn in my muscles, a shortness of my breath letting me know whatever happens to me as a visitant affects me physically.

With Hallis's shorn hand in my mind, I delve back into the book on hearthstones.

# CHAPTER 54

I venture to the kitchen to say hello to Henry and the line cooks. It's the central hub of the palace. The maidservants are always coming in and out on requests from the nobles with gossip and rumors: affairs, alcohol intake, disputes. Any and all information regarding court transgressions is filtered through the kitchen staff.

There is always speculation about the palace and the king and his crown. There's concern regarding the stirrings at the border, fear of another war coming. The uncertainty of the Strou alliance after Acker's stunt at the celebratory dinner has made its way to the townsfolk, who have differing opinions on the matter. Some think reuniting the old alliance with the Maile is the right choice, others quite the opposite after my mother's refusal to open her borders over the last decade.

The overarching theme is their love of the prince. They're under the impression Acker will protect them at all costs. Tales of his battles are repeated and spoken of with reverence, almost in a worshipful fashion.

Also, Henry is always eager to try out his new or favorite recipes on me, and I am plenty happy to oblige.

I'm eating a cranberry muffin when Beau finds me. "You're beginning to be impossible to track down," she says.

"Me?" I say, pushing the remaining muffins toward her. "I haven't seen you in days."

"Not all of us live a life of leisure, Jo."

I inspect the dark circles under her eyes, the dullness in her hair. "Your father's been keeping you busy?"

"You could say that." She takes two of the muffins and thanks Henry. "Come. My mom has something she wants to show you."

I'm scrambling to keep up with her as she moves out of the kitchen. The temperature in the hall drops, making me shiver after being in the overheated kitchen all afternoon.

Beau's dressed in her uniform, leather armor and metal rope included. The weapon clinks off her shoulder and hip as she stalks through the halls.

Greta's eyes light up when we walk through the library's doors. "I was starting to think you got lost."

She waves us to follow her into the alcove underneath the stairs. A desk is shoved into the corner with a lantern hanging above for light. Standing on her tiptoes, Greta slides a massive text from the top shelf, and Beau and I stretch out our arms to help lower the weighty book onto the table.

"I've been looking for these records ever since your return, and I finally found them." She huffs out a breath, blowing her bangs from her face, and settles into the chair.

Four times the size of normal texts, each page creates a draft of wind as she turns it. Dust floats in the air, and Beau coughs, waving it away from her face.

"Here," Greta declares, wiping the page clean before pointing. "Your mother."

I angle the lantern overhead to get a better view. The

illustrated depiction of Evelyn is uncanny. In her youth, we were damn near identical. If it didn't have her name in script below the picture and her hair was lighter, I'd swear it was me.

There's additional text under her name, and I wipe the space clean to read it.

*Elemental - Air*

"What is this?" I ask.

"These are the earliest recordings of Heirs and their gifts."

My eyes flick to Greta's. "Is my father in here?"

I see the dismay in her eyes before she answers. "No, my darling. He wasn't an Heir."

Shock rocks me back on my feet. "What?"

"I thought you knew," she says.

"How would I have known?"

"Acker never told you?" Beau asks.

I shake my head. "I suppose it's of no consequence, but I never even thought to ask."

"Their love story is quite romantic," Greta says. "The princess who fell in love with her appointed guard. It was the height of scandal for a princess to marry a commoner. Never did one ascend the throne before or since his crowning."

"Well," Beau drawls, "that's debatable."

"All thrones are held by usurpers," Greta agrees. "But he was the first and only to do it by love."

Beau rolls her eyes.

"Anyway," Greta says, "I wanted to show you a little of your mother's history."

"Thank you, Greta. Would you mind if I nosed around in the logs for a while?"

"Not at all." She stands so I can reclaim her seat. "If

you find anything interesting, please share."

Beau pulls a spare chair close. It appears to be categorized by lineage. I flip to the front of the book and wipe it clean with my palm. King Edmond is first. He looks a lot like Acker, but I'm grateful for the subtle differences in their features.

*Elemental - Fire*

I move to close the book but the image next to the king's catches my eye. Leaning closer, I clean it with my thumb, making sure I'm not imagining things as I gaze at the slightly downturned eyes and widow's peak. Acker's mother has a smile full of mischief. Actually it's kind of condescending, even through the depiction. It kind of reminds me of...

*No.*

It's not possible.

"What is it?" Beau says, eyes fluttering around my shoulders.

"I...I'm not sure. Do you know where there's a better image of the late queen?"

She stands and leads me to Greta's desk. She's nowhere to be found as we open the floor and descend into the abyss. Igniting the lamp, Beau lifts it from its place on the wall, carrying it down the stacks of books to the furthest wall. There, partially hidden by a tapestry, is a portrait of the royal family, the king on his throne with his son at his side. Acker must have been no more than five. Behind him stands a woman with curly hair and a vibrant smile, her hand resting on her husband's shoulder.

A young Grenadine stares back at me. The crabby old woman lived next to me in Alaha. I'm sure of it.

"Jo," Beau demands. "Tell me what it is you see."

*I need to tell Acker.*

I reach through the bond and find myself in Acker's room.

The king's voice sends ice through my veins. "Keep Jovinnia as a consort or send her to Maile."

Turning in place, I find them in the sitting room, Acker's back to me as he stares up at his father's pacing figure.

"In what world are either of those options? She's my *match*," he says, voice rising an octave. "Never in history has a king been denied his match."

"But you're not king," his father says, voice cold. "You're nothing but a prince under my reign, and when I give an order, I expect obedience."

"Even if you're wrong?" Acker says.

I can't see his face, but I imagine the harsh glare he has leveled on his father, similar to the one the king stares back with as he lords over his son. It's a battle of power, of wills.

"Give me an argument to justify her hand instead of the Strous' daughter," the king says. "Give me anything other than the simple fact that you want her."

"I love her," Acker says. "Is it not enough?"

"No." His father shakes his head. "Not when you are responsible for the wellbeing of your people. We need the Strou alliance more than you need her hand in marriage."

Acker stands, and I hurry to hide behind the wall. "We can negotiate a new alliance with Evelyn."

"She'll never agree to it, son. She despises the entire conclave."

"You don't know for sure," Acker argues. "Jovie is proof Wren took her as a child. She can sway Evelyn to our side. The queen will want revenge."

"*Jovie.*" The king enunciates the term of endearment like it's a joke. "The girl who trained in the Alaha guard, who was in love with Wren's son, according to you. And you expect her to lend her mother's army and resources to eradicate them?"

"She doesn't sympathize with their rebellion," Acker says.

The king throws his hands up. "You're acting like a spoiled child."

I jolt from the sound of something slamming into stone, a scattering of objects hitting the floor. "You told me you would find a solution," Acker says, emotion making his voice tremble with thin restraint. "I put up the front. I played nice to settle the Strous' nerves while you worked out a new plan. For what? For you to tell me there is no other way? *Fuck that.*"

"The Alaha are gearing up for war, and the incident at the Market was only the beginning. Now, we have Roison joining the fight since your match's little stunt at the border. If we have any chance against Wren, against Roison's forces, we need more bodies on the playing field, and Strou has them."

"Maile's army is bigger," Acker argues. "If we can convince Evelyn—"

"Enough!" The king's command does, indeed, rattle the wall at my back. "I spoke with Joss and Urich. They are fine with you keeping Jovie as a consort as long as you take Irina's hand in marriage. They ask for at least one successor. It's a generous offer, knowing you'll most likely want to bear children with your match."

"And if I refuse?" Acker threatens.

There's a long beat of silence where I begin to wonder

if I've been discovered. Then the king says, "When did you do this?"

I don't have a visual to explain the punctuated silence. My heart is in my throat, and I strain to hear the tiniest of movements in case they decide to come into the bedroom.

The king's voice is eerily calm. Too calm. "If I ever find out you've given another blood bond, I'll chain you in the dungeons, do you understand?"

I dare a peek around the wall to get a visual of what is happening and see the king's hand braced on the back of his son's neck.

"As for your original threat, if you defy me again, I have a multitude of ways to ensure you'll never lay eyes on your match again."

The sound of the door unlocking reverberates in the stillness in the air.

"If I were you," the king says, "I'd find a way to convince Jovinnia to agree to the arrangement. Speaking from experience, it never ends well when you try to hide the truth from another. And as for our future conversations, you'll be collared."

I flinch when the door slams shut—then I'm in the hidden library with Beau's eyes on me. My vision blurs as I do my best to keep my panicked heart from beating out of my chest. I concentrate on breathing, deep, long pulls of air as I brace my hands on the ledge of a bookshelf.

In.

Out.

In.

Out.

Just because he ran out of fight against his father

doesn't mean he agrees. I need to give him the chance to fix it, to confide in me what his father has obviously been pushing on him. He doesn't want this.

I look up at Beau. Her eyes are full of remorse, as if she saw the same conversation I was privy to. Then I realize it's my aura. She knows whatever I saw is wreaking havoc on my heart and nothing she can say will stop it from fracturing.

# CHAPTER 55

I don't recognize myself.

Hair in waves over one shoulder, eyes smoked with charcoal, lips stained red. The green dress compliments my hair and eyes, its bodice draping over one shoulder, skirt falling like ribbon to my ankles. My shoes peek out from under the hem, silver like my earrings, adding additional height to my frame.

"Perfection," Beau says, smiling behind me.

Sassia holds a silver chain around my waist. "What do you think?"

It's Beau's dress, the silver belt custom to match her metal rope.

I shake my head. "I think it's fine without it."

The maidservant makes a face in agreement, having come a long way from the time she first escorted me to my room. "I think so too." She speaks a half step above a whisper now.

I turn to Beau, taking in her normal garb as she swings her legs where they're draped over the side of the chair. Although she doesn't appear to be missing out, I'm disappointed. It'd be nice to have someone to talk to, to ease my nerves some, but illegitimate children are not permitted to attend royal dinners.

Sitting up, she braces her chin on her hand on the arm of the chair, smiling at my insolence. "Remember what I told you. It is not your job to make anyone comfortable."

Easier said than done. While the kitchen and waitstaff have grown accustomed to me, the parishioners have not. They don't shy away from me, but there are also no polite smiles or courtesies. To the courtiers, I'm nothing more than a mouse in the halls.

It's why this dinner is a farce. It's supposed to be a celebration of my return, of Acker's quest to save me from the Alaha and Wren's hands, but there's not a person besides Acker, Beau, and Hallis who's acknowledged my existence in this godsforsaken palace.

Every now and then a soldier will help me during morning training, offering corrections when needed, or the even-more-rare compliment. But their interactions are kept to a bare minimum under the watch of the veranda, especially since the king has come to observe. His eyes feel like the heat of a thousand suns on our backs.

There's a knock at the door, and the maidservant opens it, announcing Hallis's presence. I tell her to let him in.

Dressed in the blackest finery, he looks dashing when he enters, hair slicked into place, black lapels of his suit accentuating his fit figure underneath. I sense more than see Beau's intake of breath, and I'm pretty sure he grins in response.

"Stand and let me see," he says, motioning for me to rise with the box in his hand.

Standing, I tug on the material of my skirt so it falls without creasing. I know it's Hallis, but the scan of his eyes over me makes me self-conscious, and my blush gives me away.

Hallis is a gentleman and doesn't poke fun. "You look

beautiful, Jovie."

"Thanks," I say, looking at myself in the full-length mirror of the vanity once more. It feels like a lifetime since I envied the women at the Market. Now, here I am, dressed in their finery, my heart tender around the edges.

"Acker was called into council with his father, so he sent me to deliver this." He opens the box and holds up a string of silver and pearls. "May I?"

I hold my hair aside so he can drape the jewelry around my neck, inspecting the necklace against my skin.

"Cadence's threaded pearls," Beau says, standing to look over my shoulder. The awe in her voice catches me by surprise.

"Who's Cadence?" I ask.

"Acker's mother," Hallis answers.

I run my fingers over the pearls, heart squeezing in my chest. It somehow gives me the boost of morale I need to walk into a room full of unwelcome stares and judgment.

Hallis offers his elbow, and I slide my hand into the crook of his arm. "Ready?" he asks.

I take a deep breath. "As I'll ever be."

Beau smiles. "You're yellow," she says, running a hand over my exposed shoulder in a comforting gesture. "Try to enjoy yourself." Then her gaze slides to Hallis. "And you too, looking as gray as ever."

Hallis actually smiles at her. "Good night, Beau."

We watch her back as she retreats down the hall, disappearing around the corner. "Does she know?" I ask him.

"Know what?" he says, sparing me a glance as we turn

in the opposite direction.

"That you're in love with her."

He doesn't miss a step or so much as blink at my bold statement. "Beau thinks everyone is in love with her, so probably."

We walk in easy silence, passing a couple of maidservants who dip their heads in respectful nods, gestures we return in kind. We run into Henry on his way to the kitchen, dressed in his finest apron, and he stops us to rave about how handsome we look. He's excited for me to taste his balsam-glazed sprouts.

Bidding him farewell, we stop in one of the chambers that branch off from the dining hall. Hallis gives me a readying look. I nod but stop short at the sound of footsteps coming up behind us.

Turning, we see Acker emerge from the shadows, legs eating the distance between us in quick strides. Dressed in a green a few shades darker than my own, he takes in my dress, my face, the silver string of pearls at my collarbone.

"Jovie." His hand snakes around my waist, pulling me to him for a kiss. "You are..." He shakes his head, eyes fluttering over my features, my neck. "Indescribable."

"What are you doing here?" Hallis says, unthreading his arm from my hand. "Your father said—"

Acker cuts him off. "I know what he said." He dips his head to the pulse of my neck, inhaling before placing a kiss to the tender spot. "And I've decided I don't care," he says, eyes clear when he looks at me. "Shall we?"

He presents his arm, and a huge part of me relaxes in his presence, smiling as I settle my hand in the crease of his elbow.

"Acker," Hallis says in warning.

Acker snaps, head whipping to his friend. "I said, *I don't care.*"

Hallis is as shocked as I am. Maybe even more so, eyes wide as he looks at his closest friend.

Clenching his teeth, Acker releases a breath through his nose. "Jovie is my match, and nothing is going to stand in the way of that," he says, straightening the cuffs of his finery. "Not you. Not some bullshit alliance. And not my father."

Sensing he's on the losing end, Hallis releases a breath, eyes turning toward the entrance to the dining hall. "I'll go first. At least I'll get a good view of the show." He dips his head in farewell, eyes lingering on Acker before sliding to me. "Princess," he says, then walks around the bend in the hall.

"I'm getting the sense your father isn't willing to break the alliance with Strou."

Acker places his spare hand over the one I have tucked in his arm. "Once we walk in there, he won't have a choice."

With me on his arm, he means.

In my heels, I'm closer to his height, creating a false sense of equality. "A more honorable woman would attempt to change your mind," I say, meeting his gaze.

His grin is nothing less than lascivious. "Honor is for the pious," he says, leaning in to kiss me.

It's all heat and promise, and I'm sad when it's so short-lived. Some of the stain of my lips transfers to his mouth, so I reach to wipe it with the pad of my thumb, but he pulls away.

"Leave it." With a dangerous look in his eyes, he ushers me to the end of the hall. "Walk to the dais. I'll be right behind you."

"You're not going to lead me," I say, stopping in my tracks.

"I'll be right behind you," he assures me, hand on the small of my back. "You'll feel me the entire time."

I don't like it, but he places a soft kiss on my lips, as if there's not enough time or space for him to ever resist placing his mouth on mine. I'm going to have to trust him.

I turn and face the draped opening to the hall lit beyond the veil...and step through. Any hope I had of going unnoticed is quickly dashed by the heads swiveling in my direction. Acker keeps his promise, fingertips pressed against the dip of my spine as we walk down the center aisle of tables, our steps echoing off the golden ceiling. Even the heads of the helmeted soldiers lining the room turn and watch.

I maintain my sight on the dais, on the king as he laughs with a nobleman before he takes notice of the dimming noise of the party. His eyes lock on mine as he turns, then his son's, face reddening in anger at the sight of his offspring's insubordination.

Slowing at the foot of the platform, I dip my head in servitude, bowing as much as I can in my skirt and heels. "Your highness," I greet him.

Acker doesn't do anything of the sort. Stepping before me, he looks his father in the eye, an unspoken challenge as he offers me a guiding hand up the stairs. Acker leads me around the table facing the congregation. We pass the filled chairs where a man and woman with blonde hair and light eyes sit. Acker pulls out the nearest seat, and I sit with as much grace as I can muster.

Then, in his most daring move yet, Acker places his

hands on the bare skin of my shoulders, leaning down to kiss my cheek in front of the entire assembly. I'm impressed by my ability to keep my blush at bay.

Acker takes the goblet on the table and lifts it to the congregation. "To the lost princess of Maile," he announces. "And to her safe return."

Murmurs of stunned reverence travel across the room as the people lift their drinks in respect of their prince. Acker drinks from his cup, eyes sharp as he takes in his acolytes, daring someone to appear less than pleased. His gaze is heavy, assessing, dangerous.

I was wrong to be scared of Acker when he sat on the throne upon our arrival, when I'm on his side of the equation. I look up at him and lift my goblet. In adoration and appreciation, I speak the words without fanfare. They're nothing more than an observation.

"All hail the prince of Kenta."

A louder, more pronounced round of agreement rings out. *All hail the prince of Kenta!* The prince who killed on the battlefield for his people, who risked life and limb to bring hope back to his land by returning a symbol of peace from its past.

*All hail the prince of Kenta!*

I look at the king, red-faced and indignant, and a smirk tugs at the corner of my lips. It seems the people have spoken.

The riotous cheers fizzle as a woman steps through the veiled opening, drawing the attention of the room. Irina steps forward, blonde hair piled high on her head, red dress dripping from her shoulders. Strou's color, I realize, matching the garments her parents wear, seated to my right.

She begins her waltz down the center of the room,

heels clacking against the marble floor, neck empty of jewels. Her beauty is almost ethereal, and although I'm the one sitting to Acker's right, I can't help but feel inadequate to be his match. Her assured steps falter as she gets closer to the stage, eyes quickly surveying the lack of remaining seats, her fuming parents...

Me in her seat.

Acker drapes a wrist over the back of my chair and winks at me, completely unfazed by the silent humiliation of the girl lost at the foot of dais. He finishes his wine and slams the goblet down on the table.

"Where's the food?" he says, looking around in question. "I thought we were here to eat, so let's eat."

A maidservant appears with a decanter to refill his cup, then another enters as the dining hall is flooded with servants delivering dish upon dish of food to the tables, ours filling up fast.

Bracing his elbow against the table, he sips from his refilled goblet. "I ran into Henry in the hall," he says, leaping into conversation.

I pretend to pay close attention to Acker's tale, smiling at the identical interaction Hallis and I had with the cook, but I am aware of when Irina takes the hint and ambles off, heels clicking in her hasty retreat.

Not long after, her parents abandon their spots as well.

Henry wasn't wrong. His sprouts are incredible.

# CHAPTER 56

*The morning after the storm in Alaha*

"What do you mean you broke the Kenta soldier out of the brig?" Kai says, eyes wide.

I shush him and pull him further behind the tanner's shop. "He was going to die."

"Yeah, Brynn, that was sort of the plan," he says, body hunched as he whisper-yells at me. "Then we were going to put his body in a boat and send him back to sea, so it looked like an accident."

"Listen," I say, urging him to calm down with a hand against his chest. "Your father made him give a blood oath to not reveal my true identity when we went in to speak to him. He's totally convinced I'm in the dark about everything, convinced I've been sheltered from the truth of magic and my bloodline." I step in close, the wind left behind from the storm creating a frenzy within the trees, capable of carrying voices with it. "I think...if I can convince him I'm naive, he'll take me back to land with him."

"Brynn, no," he says, eyes unyielding. "You have no idea what he's capable of. He's known for being ruthless on the battlefield. He could very well get a wild notion and kill you in your sleep."

"He's the prince," I stress. "He can take me to the palace. Maybe if I can get close enough to the king—"

"You can what?" he snaps, voice firm. "Kill him? Edmond, the king of Kenta, the most powerful leader in history?"

"I haven't awakened yet. I could be as powerful as you and not know it."

He's already shaking his head, pacing away from me with his hands on his hips. "He's only here to enact revenge for the Market. The explosion was supposed to look like an accident, but he must know you had something to do with it."

"I'm telling you, Kai, he's so sure of my innocence. He thinks I've been manipulated by your father all my life. I can use it to our advantage."

More head shaking. "And how is it you plan on getting to Kenta?"

"We'll take one of the fishing vessels."

He scoffs. "No one's made it across the open sea in a boat that small. You'd never make it."

"You don't know for sure."

"We know anything over an average-sized swell will shatter the hull. It happens all the time."

"Kai," I say, allowing the stubbornness in my tone to hang between us. "I'm not asking your permission."

He turns to look at me, a barrage of emotions filtering behind his eyes. Anger. Disbelief. But most of all...hurt.

"My parents would make me marry."

I look down before finding the courage to meet his eyes again. "I know."

My answer settles over him in one fell swoop before he hides it, turning away on an exhale.

"You can't deny this is the best chance we have for the rebellion," I say, softening my voice, placating. "We're going to run out of food, being barred from the Market, and it'll be even sooner since your father has stopped the fishing excursions."

He wants to argue but knows I'm right. "If the people think the prince took you," he says, almost reluctant to finish his thought, "it would send them into a panic to think one of them can come in and take anyone they like. It might put pressure on my father to consider working with the Roison after their repeated attempts to recruit us into joining their cause."

I don't want to voice my doubts, because I need Kai to think this can work. I won't point out that people won't be as concerned about an urchin as he believes they'll be. They've never seen me as one of their own.

"Dupre would have to be dealt with," I say.

Kai's eyes turn from uncertain to strategic, the leader of the rebellion peeking through. "We'd need to put his death in the prince's hands." He meets my gaze again. "All of this assuming he doesn't suspect you're orchestrating anything."

"I think…if he were to see you use your power on me, he'd never doubt it."

He nods. "It'd have to be convincing," he says. "Something beyond reproach. Something even the metal slinger of Kenta would believe to be merciless."

I think about his weird fixation on my attachment to Kai. "He believes you've influenced me to fall in love with you."

His brows come down in a hard slant, righteous indignation flaming behind his eyes. "It's as insulting as it is disgusting."

"I know, but reaffirming his judgment would solidify his suspicions."

He continues his pacing, and I wait as Kai sorts

through everything I've laid at his feet. It's a huge deviation from our plans, but it's the best option we've been given. It'd be dumb not to take it. He knows that.

"When it's discovered he's missing, they'll search the grove. I'll make sure to be the one to do it, and I'll use my influence on you."

"Okay," I say, agreeing.

He stops and looks at me. "My father gives me favoritism, but I don't know how far it'll go if he finds out I'm leading the rebellion. There's not a lot of room for error. You'll have to let your guard down."

I nod, knowing he means the shield he's taught me to keep erected when around his father.

Stepping closer, he angles my face up to his. "I don't want to do this," he says.

"I know," I tell him, hating the pain in his eyes. "I trust you."

He touches his forehead to mine, eyes pinched. "I could be sending you to your death, Brynn."

"It's a risk I'm willing to take."

He rocks his head from side to side. "If he so much as looks at you wrong—"

"I'll kill him myself."

He kisses me then lets me go. "Don't tell Messer."

"Why?"

He makes a curious face then says, "'Cause he'll lose his shit."

# CHAPTER 57

Acker twirls me, and my skirts flare, whipping around my legs when he hauls me into his body. His eyes are illuminated, cheeks flushed from the wine as he stares down at me, kissing me. The arm banded around my back keeps me anchored to him as we move across the dance floor.

He's warm and smells divine, like the sweetness of fresh rain and pine. I savor it, wishing we had more time. I'm regretting not seeking him out earlier in the day, but I think it would have made it worse, made the betrayal all the more sharp. More bitter, biting.

The music is mesmerizing. The notes from the string quartet float along the floor and up the walls to the mirrored golden ceiling, cascading from above, encompassing the entire room. It creates an emotion I can't name, but it might simply be because I'm full of too many of them to count.

It's late into the dinner celebration. The children have been sent to bed. Hallis followed not long after, just as Beau said he would. He tolerates these dinners at best. The wine has endlessly been flowing into cups, the drink's potency evidenced by the cheery and reddened faces of the leftover courtiers.

But Acker? He's happy. There's an easy smile on his face I haven't seen as often since being at court. It hurts to look at, but I can't find it in me to look away knowing

I may never get to see this side of him again. I may never lay eyes on him after this night. If I even make it out alive...

The king has spent the night on the dais, watching his congregation with a man at his side. Every time I dare a look in his direction, he seems to grow more and more agitated by the cheery atmosphere and laughs of his people.

The song ends on a flourish and cheers erupt. Signaling for a break, the band disbands with bows and promises to return. Maidservants flood in with decanters of more wine, refilling every glass available.

Acker shares a laugh with one of the other men on the dance floor, a self-deprecating comment about his drunken footwork, then leads me by the hand to the dais. The king, like the petulant child he accused Acker of being, sits sullen at the table. I watch as he holds his goblet while the maidservant fills it. He never so much as looks at her, just gulps down his replenished wine.

Acker pays him no mind as he falls into his chair, dragging me into his lap with him. "I love you," he says, placing a kiss on my exposed shoulder. It's chaste but somehow heated with promise.

It's difficult to not be infected by his splendor. "You're drunk."

The maidservant who was making her way down the table stops before us, filling Acker's cup.

He picks up his drink. "Am I not allowed to celebrate with my future wife?"

I take the drink from his hand before it reaches his mouth. "Okay, I think you've had enough," I say, smiling.

"Jovie," he says, suddenly appearing sober, eyes

clearing of their haze. "I'm not drunk."

I'm stunned into silence, heart pounding in my chest as I search his earnest gaze. "Acker," I say, mentally searching for how to respond, shaking my head with an unsteady smile. "You haven't even asked me."

He runs his thumb in the crook of my elbow, sending goose bumps across my skin. "I'm asking. Will you marry me?"

I couldn't think of a worse question at a worse time. There's no containing the tears welling in my eyes. He thinks they're from overwhelming emotions as he looks at me with so much adoration and love that I'm convinced I'm going to be sick.

I'm not crying with joy. My heart is breaking, just as Beau told me it would.

"Acker," I say, voice shaking. "I never thanked you for everything you've done for me. I would still be in my tiny shiel in the furthest reaches of Alaha if you hadn't come to save me."

His eyes remain steady as I fumble through my thoughts.

"I love you," I tell him, steadier this time. "And I always will."

He tilts his head, eyes tightening at the corners. "Jovie," he says, gaze questioning, tone edged with suspicion. "What is it you're not telling me?"

As if on cue, one of the nobles stumbles from his chair, words slurring as he fights to get them out. "Poi...son." He takes two more steps before hitting the ground on one knee, eyes fuzzy as he spits out the word. "*Poison.*" Then he loses the fight, hitting the marble floor face first with a sickening crack.

Acker looks at me in alarm, but he's swift to put the

pieces together, eyes landing on the cup I wouldn't let him drink out of. Standing, I move until my thighs hit the table.

The congregation is alarmed but sluggish as they all fight the inevitable battle. Plates hit the ground, the food splattering. Red wine coats the white floors, so stark against the white, like a preamble for the blood that will flow.

Acker sits forward, but it's too late. The mangi collar I retrieve from the folds of my dress and snap around his neck isn't enough to stop him, though. That's why Beau is there to whip the metal rope around his ankles, anchoring him to the chair. He growls as she snaps the other half around one wrist then the other, but the damage has been done. The spurs of the rope dig into his flesh, blood welling around the indentions.

He looks to his father, who's unconscious and slumped in his chair, then to the expanse of the now quiet room. Everyone is collapsed and motionless. The sound of shuffling feet and metal is loud in the otherwise silent room as the soldiers make a move toward the dais. I don't move from my spot in front of Acker, more afraid of him than twelve men.

I hold Acker's stare.

His eyes are blazing mad, neck and muscles straining against his binds, against the stones around his throat. I wait as the footfalls come closer, closer, closer. The helmeted soldiers encroach on my position, feet pounding as they reach the bottom step of the stage.

The second.

The third.

Then, when they're a single step away, Acker speaks. "Yield," he demands, and the men freeze in their tracks.

A grin tugs at the corner of my mouth. Whether it's of his own accord or the oath's, it makes no difference. I'm slow to turn my head, but I look over my shoulder, eyes zeroing in on the one man I recognize underneath the palace's uniform, his familiar shoulders and frame near the back of the group of men waiting for the killing orders from their prince.

"Messer," I call.

I can see his smile underneath the slit of the helmet a split second before he moves. He slices through the neck of the man in front of him, and the soldier falls to his knees with a howl, hands straining to stop the flow of blood squirting from his jugular.

The rest of the soldiers turn to handle the threat coming their way, but it's no use. Messer cuts them down one after another. The swing of his blade is a practiced work of art, smooth and precise. Bodies hit the marble with loud clattering of metal. They're all dead within minutes.

Messer places his blood-soaked sword on the table and removes his helmet, pushing his sweaty hair out of his face, and breathes out with a smile. "B," he says. "Finery suits you."

I roll my eyes at his teasing and turn my attention back to Acker. Nostrils flaring with every breath, he doesn't speak. Doesn't need to. The revulsion and loathing as he stares back at me are loud enough.

Swallowing, I push the leftover plates and cutlery out of the way then sit on the tabletop. "Acker."

He jerks in his chair, sending rivers of blood sliding down his wrists, but his eyes never falter. They're weapons of their own.

My eyes shoot to Messer and Beau. I need to gather

myself before I continue. The pain lancing through my lungs intensifies with every breath. The only way I'm going to get through this is if I trap it within myself.

Beau nods at me in encouragement.

Ignoring the wound inside my chest, I return my gaze to Acker. "I have an offer for you."

There's a coldness creeping into his features I never wanted to be on the receiving end of, but I continue as if I'm unaffected.

"Seize your father's crown, and we'll leave your council untouched."

He doesn't so much as blink in the face of my proposal. "Why would I care to usurp my own father?" he asks with a chilling calmness.

I shrug like the answer is obvious. "To prevent the war looming over your people."

A smirk graces his face, replacing the coldness with something even more sinister—callousness. "Mighty big promise from a lowly girl who lived in squalor in Alaha."

His words are meant to hurt, but I return his smirk with one of my own. "You were so dead set on Wren being evil, on Kai manipulating me, that you never considered the real truth," I say, bracing my hands on the table, leaning forward for him to see the guile in my eyes. "*I* am the bad guy."

His eyes shutter, but he recovers quickly. "Is that what you tell yourself?" he smarts back. "That you're the real leader of the Alaha rebellion?"

"I'm here, aren't I?"

I jerk my dress above my knees, crossing my legs to reach the straps of my heel to unbuckle the shoe, letting it fall to the floor. Looking up, I'm unhurried as I do the same to the other shoe, knowing I'm giving him an indecent view. He clenches his teeth but doesn't look any lower than my neckline.

"Contrary to your belief, Acker, your father is the one calling for war." Sliding from the table, I call my dagger, inspecting the black blade in my hand. "He wants to finish what he started centuries ago, to gain rule over all of the territories."

Eyes shifting to the weapon, he tightens his hands into fists. The blood falls from the arms of the chair in steady drips.

"Surely you see it," Beau says from over his shoulder. "Our father's need to control the gifted, his desire to return the land to the dark ages when Heirs were worshiped like gods."

He huffs a humorless breath of laughter. "Like how I saw my sister and match betraying me while they were right under my nose?" he says, voice dry. "Can't say that I have."

Beau and I share a look. This is going to be as difficult as we expected. Revealing the truth about his mother may hurt us in the end if he doesn't concede.

"Here's the deal, Acker," I say, twirling the dagger, mimicking the movements I've witnessed him perform countless times. "Your father is withholding the Market with the intention of forcing Alaha to return to land. I suspect he's been picking off our fishing boats for years, chipping away at our food supply, and we gave him the perfect excuse to cut us off without blame from the conclave. Wren denied Roison's bid to join their cause out of preference for peace, but he'll soon be out of options. It's either join the fight or let his people starve."

"If you sympathize with their plight so much, why

don't you let them into Maile territory?" he says.

"Oh, we will," Messer chimes in with a placid smile. "The young and old and whoever doesn't want to fight."

This unsettles Acker, his already strained muscles beginning to tremble with his barely contained rage. He's fighting the bonds along with the collar. It's not a matter of if he'll break free of Beau's hold, but when.

"But you can prevent it," I say, drawing his attention. "Take the throne. Agree to coexist with Roison, with my mother, and no war needs to be had."

He narrows his eyes at me, confusion marring his handsome features for a moment before it's gone. "You could have accomplished all of that and more by ruling by my side."

A painful lump forms in my throat, and I swallow to speak past it. "Not while your father holds the throne, and you know it."

Shaking his head, he says, "You should have played the long game."

"As your whore?"

The realization flashes across his face.

I nod. "You know as well as I do he'll never agree to you taking my hand. He wants me to play the same role Greta has, and I refuse to be a prisoner to the matching bond, to be forced to wear a collar and never allowed to leave."

He looks at me with unfiltered disgust. "You'll always assume the worst of me."

"You're wrong," I say, shaking my head, hating the emotion peeking through. "I'm offering you the throne because I know your heart. You deserve the crown."

Tilting his head, he stares at me for a moment before abject horror fills his face. "Jovie. No."

I don't have the heart to answer him, knowing he'll never be able to forgive me either way. Acker, sensing what's coming, yanks on the rivets. The metal rattles in Beau's grip, and I know he's on the verge of escaping.

"After all your talk of Wren wanting ultimate power and women sitting at his feet," I say under my breath, desolate, "it's a shame you can't see your father for who he is."

Messer speaks from behind me. "You would think his father was the one who held the power of influence and not Wren."

It's meant as an offhand comment, but Beau and I share a wide-eyed look.

"*Black*," she whispers.

My face goes slack with the realization.

"We don't have a lot of time," Messer warns.

I brace my hands on either side of Acker. "The day I arrived at the palace," I say, "when I was kneeling, I couldn't stand. At the time I chalked it up to nerves, but I think I was wrong. I think your father influenced me to remain on my knees before the congregation."

"You're reaching," he says. "My father's gift is the same as mine."

"Except the oldest record Greta found states it's not," I say, hoping he sees the truth in my eyes. "It's fire."

He's taken aback, eyes flaring in surprise before he conceals it.

A woman's yell peals through the hall. The maidservant takes one look at us on the dais, the prince captured and the king indisposed, and runs back out of the room.

Time's up.

Pushing from Acker's chair, I stand. The weight of my

dagger feels heavy in my hand as I look at the king.

Messer holds out his hand. "Let me do it, B."

I shake my head. "Do you decline my offer to seize your father's throne?" I ask Acker, already knowing the answer.

He doesn't respond, eyes glacial, not a hint of the man I fell in love with. Beautiful and deadly, I mourn him already, and he's right in front of me.

I look at Messer. "Give the order."

He nods and sticks two fingers in his mouth to signal the waiting Maile soldiers with a piercing whistle. The three men emerge from the shadows with one goal in mind: find the fifteen nobles and eradicate them.

I leave Acker, focusing on my singular task at hand: kill the king. Drool falls from Edmond's mouth, pooling onto the table. All that authority, but at the end of the day, he is nothing but a man. Grabbing his hair, I tilt his head back to expose his throat, bringing the sharp end of my dagger to his throat. I press—

Acker's voice stops me. "*Wait.*"

I don't move, only shifting my eyes to look at Acker through my lashes.

"You owe me a life debt," he says through clenched teeth.

It takes me a moment, but I figure out what he means. Kai.

He didn't kill Kai despite having every right to do so...because I begged him not to. Commotion sounds as Kenta soldiers flood the room, but I hold Acker's gaze. I came here with one goal in mind, but if I fulfill it, it might make me as evil as the man I've always hated.

I switch my attention to Beau. She's struggling to maintain her hold on Acker, teeth bared in concentration. As difficult as this has been for me, I can only imagine her plight in betraying her own flesh and blood.

"Where's the king's magic? Can you see it?"

She pants between breaths. "The right side of his chest. Near his shoulder."

I don't think as I lift my arm and bring the dagger down in the assumed area.

"Again," Beau yells.

I do it again but harder, shoving the blade to the hilt. And I feel it, the hum of magic dying against the dark blade before going still inside the king's chest. It could possibly be a fatal wound if they don't get a healer to him fast enough.

I dare a look at the Maile soldiers fighting off the onslaught of Kenta men. They continue to file in, and it's only a matter of time before they overwhelm the three fighters. No, four—Messer is within the fray.

Stalking toward Beau, I hold out my hands. "Give me the rope."

She shakes her head. "He's going to kill us as soon as he's free."

"He can't harm me," I remind her.

She looks at her brother, the barbs buried so far into his skin the metal isn't visible past the torn flesh and blood. But none of that stops him from creating more and more slack in the binds.

"Go," I tell her. "Get Messer and get out. I'll meet you when I can."

She's reluctant but hands me the rope, sparing her brother one last glance before descending the dais and into the madness. I don't bother maintaining the tension on the rope necessary to keep Acker contained.

The best thing I can do for my friends is to get Acker as far away from this as possible, and there's not a doubt in my mind who he's going to come after first—me.

Like a monster unleashed from his cage, Acker stands with a wicked stillness. Blood spills to the ground, splattering across my skirt and bare feet. Although I know he can't hurt me, I'm terrified.

I turn and run. I'm equally relieved and frightened by the sound of his shoes hitting the floor behind me. I escape through the inlet the maidservants take from the kitchen. The hall is narrow as I turn the corner and take the staircase down two steps at a time. He's faster than I am, and his footfalls echo too close for my liking. Too close, too soon.

I've just entered the kitchen when I'm swept off my feet. I scream. I can't help it. Fighting with all my might, I throw my elbow back, angling my body to shift his hold. None of it works. He grabs me by the back of my hair and throws me into the wall, catching me by the throat before I can get my feet steady underneath me. His hand is wet against my jaw, but it doesn't help to dislodge the punishing grip of his fingers.

Out of the corner of my eye, I see a panther appear at the top of the stairs. Messer releases a snarling yowl as he pounces forward. I lift my hand at my side, signaling him to refrain from attacking, and he skids to a stop before reaching the bottom step, paws slipping on the bloody stone floors.

*Acker can't hurt me.*

But no matter how many times I repeat it to myself, my heart pounds tenfold inside my chest. For the first time since he realized my intentions, Acker's true emotions peak through. Heartbreak and disappointment and disbelief shadow his features, eyes shattered as he looks into my eyes.

Messer paces the stairwell, claws digging into each side of the wall as he waits.

"Acker," I murmur, desperate for him to see the sorrow mirrored inside of me.

Then he kisses me.

I open to him instantly, hungry for his connection. The bond between us is smothered by the mangi stones around his neck, and it creates a hollow feeling where the tether resides. His kiss isn't anything but a painful goodbye, but I take what he's willing to offer me. I submit, letting him have his way as he devours me whole in one kiss.

Then it's gone, and when I open my eyes to look at him, the hate has returned with a vengeance. He slaps me across the face. I'm stunned.

Covering my face with my hand, I look up at Acker as I right myself, and he's bracing his head in his hands, face contorted in pain. He grunts through clenched teeth as blood begins to drip from his nose.

The oath is returning the favor.

"Leave," he orders, spittle flying from his mouth.

Hallis appears at the opposite end of the hall, but he doesn't come closer. I sidestep around Acker, the shock of his strike still hot on my skin. I keep my eyes on him, and Messer does the same with feline grace, lifting his upper lip and showing Acker his elongated teeth as he passes.

Acker shouts. "Go! Before I kill us both."

My chest caves as my heart finishes cleaving in two.

I leave him and don't look back.

# ACKNOWLEDGEMENT

As always, Alicia, thank you for being the first to read all of my worst drafts. I've sent you a lot of half-finished thoughts over the years, and you're always willing to dissect them with me. Thank you for your patience and love.

Dani, thank you for being my voice of reason when I need it most. You know when I need a gentle hand or when I need to be shouted at with all capitals. I value both equally.

Marlon, thank you for being so supportive this past year. You gave me the time and love to pursue something that may never have a real return, just because you know it makes me happy. I love you. (And for helping me with that one word I was struggling with.)

Caitlin, thank you for your ability to take my messiness and make it beautiful...even if it is borderline torture. And also, for your patience.

Murphy, thank you for making art that fits my vision and love for this book perfectly. I'm so excited to put this book on my shelf.

It's been seven years since I published a book. I've had endless amounts of support even since leaving on hiatus, and I'm forever grateful for the friends who've remained. Your encouragement means more to me than

I can ever articulate. During times of doubt, I'd lean on your kind words to power through. Thank you will never be enough.

# ABOUT THE AUTHOR

**Rachel Schneider**

Rachel Schneider lives in South Louisiana with her husband and daughter. She loves curse words, crawfish, and all things romance.

Goodreads: Rachel Schneider
Facebook: facebook.com/rachelschneider
Email: rachelschneider.author@gmail.com
Instagram: rachelschneiderauthor
TikTok: RachelBeeps